Arisen

by

S.E. Lucas

With illustrations by Kathryn Briggs

Arisen

Copyright © 2014 S.E. Lucas

**ISBN-13:
978-1502799999**

Cover Design and interior illustrations by Kathryn Briggs © 2014

All rights reserved. No part of this book may be reproduced, duplicated, copied, or transmitted in any form or by any means without the express written consent and permission of the author.

This is a work of fiction. The names, characters, places, and incidents are fictitious or are used in a fictitious manner. Any resemblance to any person or persons, living or dead, as well as place or places is wholly coincidental.

This book is printed using the Ryman Eco font. For more information on the 'World's Most Sustainable Font', please visit: http://www.rymaneco.co.uk/

For more information about the Author and Illustrator, please visit:
www.selucas.com
www.kathrynbriggs.com

Printed in the United States of America

From S.E. Lucas -
To my wife and my son

From Kathryn Briggs -
To Dave, who is alright.

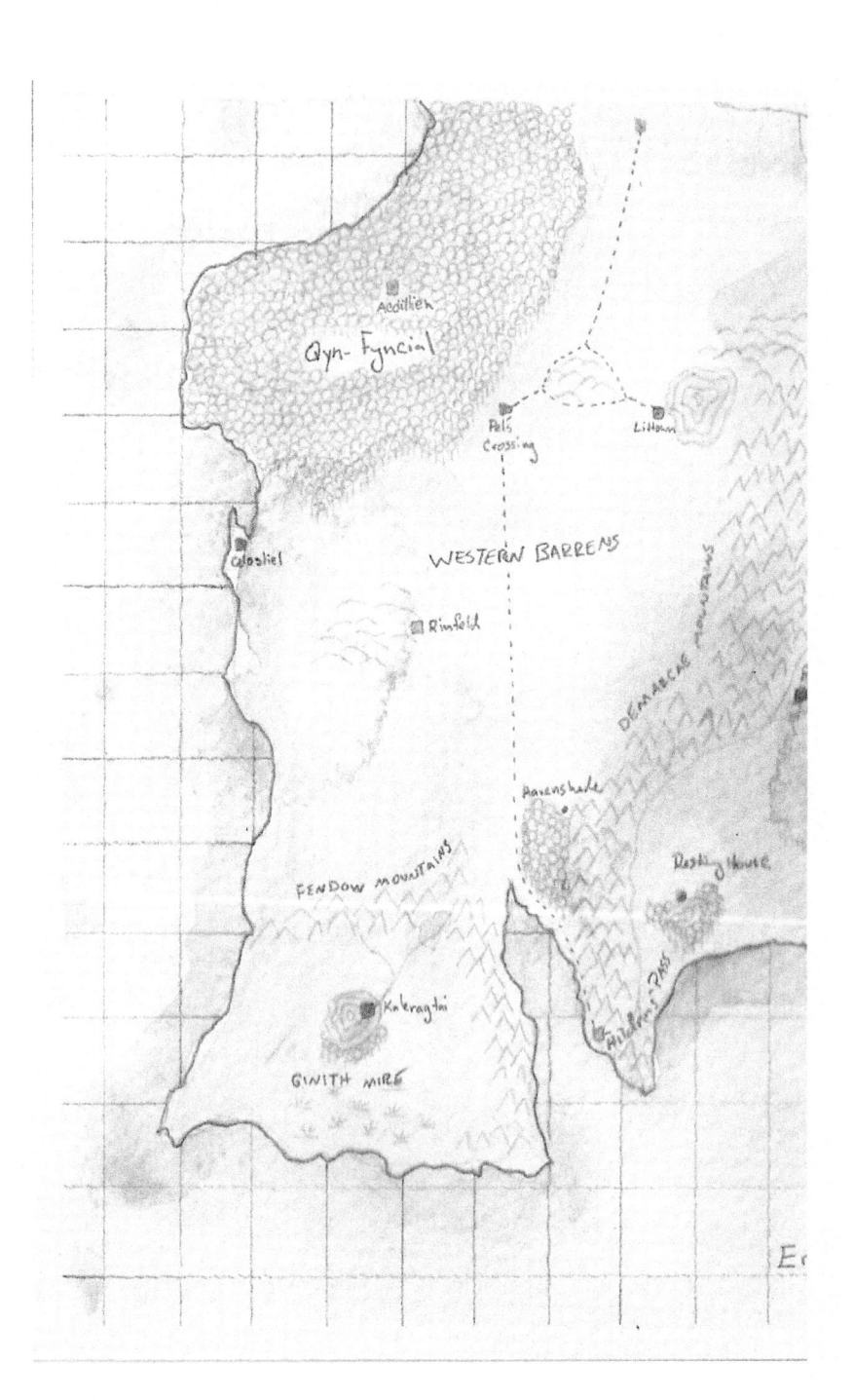

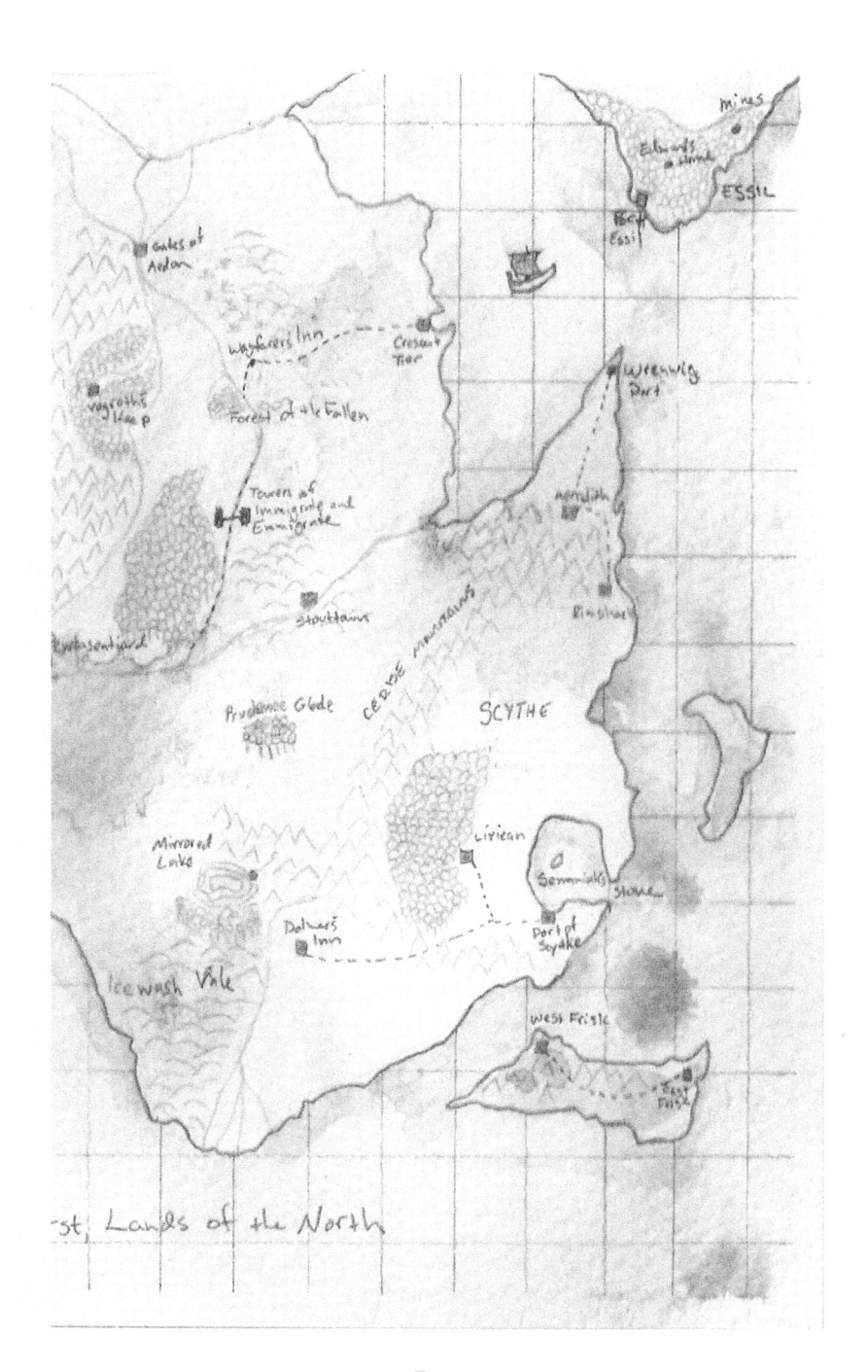
mines
ESSIL
Gates of Aedon
Wayfarers Inn
Crescent Tier
Wrenwig Port
Forest of the Fallen
Stouttown
Prudence Glade
SCYTHE
Mirrored Lake
Port of Scythe
Icewash Vale
West Frisk
East Frisk
st, Lands of the North

Contents

The Girl at The Lighthouse

Of Fish, Forests, and Fire

The Tall and Short of It

The First Cards Are Set

Winds of Change

The Weary Wayfarers

The Standard Is Set

Secrets and Gifts

Fallen Spirits

The Second Stack Sets and Falls

The Response and The Reproach

A Bleak Day for Bleke

An Airing of Differences

The Passover of Haze-

In The Keeping of Lazdrazil

What Witched Dreams May Come

The Fates of The Families

The Remembrance

The Crux

Standpoints

Smoke and Mirrors

A Flame Is Snuffed Out

Havenshade

"And so, when the latter days of Her dominion wither into transgression,
The children of the old way shall be born for and from the earth,
That they shall mature among each of the highborn races of women and men,
That the torments will effervesce and spread across all of the nations,
That their endowments will afflict the world with war, deprivation, and death,
And through their sufferings, all people shall recognize the descents arisen."
From, *the Songs of Semmiah*

The Girl at The Lighthouse

When you are lost in the cold, unrelenting seas of darkness and despair,
She shall come unto you as a beacon, a light, the truth, and the way.
From, *the Songs of Semmiah*

    They called her a witch, a breach, a soul-less child. She lived a solitarily unusual life, yet comforted with her doting father, Harald, and her over-protective mother, Joane. All-together, they cared for and lived at The Light of Crescent Tier. 'The Light' symbolized the massive lighthouse spiraling sixty feet above the entire city of Crescent Tier. The coast line naturally curved inward from the sea, providing its 'crescent' shape, while fourteen levels, or 'tiers', cascaded more than two hundred feet from the cliff's ledge downward to the water's edge. Occasionally, if one peered meticulously enough, she materialized, staring out at sea like a listless apparition atop the Lantern Room surrounded by the iron-girded Widow's Walk. The young woman's name was Hazel.

She was born on the floor in the humble cottage attached to the daunting lighthouse. The miniature size and artless aspect of the cottage made the dwelling an obvious after-thought in respect to The Light. A great windmill creaked and moaned as the sea breeze spun the fins turning intricate gears within. These operated the massive milling wheels below, while they primarily turned the mirror and flame within the Lantern House above. She was born in the shadow of The Light; born without notice or care; born without scorn; yet born a Child of the Old Way.

And so, Hazel was a sorceress. A great, painstaking plan had been arranged so that Hazel would be born that particular way. Her prowess and gifts were no mere accident or no act of fate, but rather the exhaustive efforts of Ivindfor helped along by a few others. The process of how and why Hazel became a sorceress rested with Ivindfor and those few others. What predominantly mattered to Hazel was her long, straight, aquamarine hair; her large, round namesake eyes; her light lavender lips, pale skin, and waif-like structure. How her very appearance branded her a pariah. How her isolated life at The Light insinuated some malice toward those of Crescent Tier. How she had been blamed for numerous tragedies the people had incurred. Unfortunately, no one cared to understand the true stories. Believing in the superstitions and applying blame was uncomplicated for the citizens of Crescent Tier; consequently, Hazel was very much alone.

When younger, the cruelty of others was not solely limited with other children; criticism was often harsher from the adults. Hazel sometimes accompanied her mother to Market Street for groceries and supplies. As an infant, her body was hidden in the shade of a basket that Joane carried her in. Then, as she grew, her body learned to walk and run. The sunlight radiated off of her body as she glided like a ghost among the living. Without any wrongdoing of her own, the natural stages of growth allowed the world to see Hazel as different; as a threat.

By the age of seven, Hazel had grasped the disdain of her own oddities. She barely smiled and was often ridiculed to tears by many other children at the Academy. Each morning, she pleaded with her parents to stay at home, yet Hazel was sent away with the hope she would someday be accepted. After months of verbal abuse, the girl came home bruised, cut, dirty, and her clothes disheveled. Harald and Joane no longer pretended things would get better, and never sent Hazel to the academy again.

Even though her early years of life were sad and hurtful, there were moments that mimicked happiness. One of these fleeting instances occurred at the most horrible of remembered places: Top Tier Academy.

Top Tier Academy was an educational complex constructed on the top tier of the city. The building housed the wealthiest and most affluent children in the city. As the city descended to the harbor below, the highest level seated those with most wealth, and then as the levels dropped lower, so did family incomes and lineage. Although Harald and Joane were not wealthy, they did live highest. So, they were privileged to have Hazel attend Top Tier School. However, this did not mean she belonged.

During that one lunch hour, in that first week, of her first and only year, Hazel had a pleasant experience for which she cherished throughout her childhood. The girl gathered just enough courage to start a conversation with a couple of other children. Curiosity motivated her more than the hope of friendship. There on a bench under a gray willow tree sat a boy and girl who seemed altogether too familiar to the sorceress.

The wind swirled in the tiny leaves of the tree as Hazel approached and quietly asked them, "We've met before, I am quite sure-", her sentence waned in the breeze as if floating away, waiting to be caught and responded to.

The boy scowled and only shrugged his shoulders as if not really hearing, or caring. The other girl, however, retorted quite clearly and boldly, "I know who *you* are. Everyone knows who *you* are."

Hazel tipped her head to the right and stared uncomfortably at them both for a long time. The girl who snapped at her was quite tall for their age. In fact, she towered over the other girls and boys by a head and a half. Her hair was wavy, and black except for the inch thick streak of white that ran with the front edge of her part. The color of her eyes reminded Hazel of the farthest shade of blue in the sea, which complimented the smooth, bronzed pigment of her perfectly complexioned skin. Her round face offered a sense of softness, yet the sternness set into her mouth and eyebrows revealed tension and nervousness. Hazel knew her from before they had attended school. Her name was Ava.

The boy sitting next to Ava was somewhat opposite. He was hardly average in height and weight for a seven year old. He was paler than Hazel, and appeared sickly due to his mop of dull, coal-black hair, thick eyebrows, and nearly solid black eyes. His face was a sharp triangle accentuated by his narrow nose. Hazel even thought his teeth were oddly shaped and jagged. Hazel found him cold and unattractive. His name was Morclyf.

"Make her stop staring at us like that," the boy muttered to Ava.

Ava peered down at Hazel and brashly sneered. "Listen, we do not want you near us. Understand!"

Hazel repositioned her head and looked upward at the tall girl. Unsmiling and unaffected by Ava's rant, she softly replied, "You are like me. Pretend all you want. Blend in with the rest of them. In the end, you both know what you are." She paused for a moment as Ava's lips pierced and contorted with anxiety, then continued: "Our parents were once friends. I remember playing with both of you when we were very young. Of course, now we keep ourselves separate. I suppose I would embarrass your families." After several moments of silence, Hazel finished with, "We hear the voices that are not our own. We understand the language, the meaning, and we speak it back."

Morclyf sat more poised and interested than he had a few moments before. Open-mouthed, Ava was aghast and bewildered at what to do. Hazel gazed at and out beyond them. Ava's breath began to steam and roll like fog from her mouth. Hazel lifted her hand and the fog settled silently onto her palm. The cloud of moisture turned to water as it ran down and around to the back of her hand, then dripped onto small stones on the ground. With each drip, the stones popped and bounced slightly in the air.

Ava threw her large hands on Hazel's shoulders and shook her several times until the transformation finished. She leaned close to Hazel's ear and whispered hoarsely, "Never do that again!

Never! People will harm you if speak about voices and make this happen out in the open. Our families have protected and raised us as normal as possible. Do you think you can insult them, us, and everything Ivindfor has been working for?" Hazel shivered a little, but stood firm in her place. Ava panted, trying to regain moisture in her mouth and her composure. "Do us all a favor and act as normally as *you* can. Ivindfor will come for us one day, but until then keep your mouth shut and leave us alone!"

Ava shoved Hazel aside and stormed off through the yard and inside the academy. Morclyf sat smiling at the stones he had made dance, while not noticing that Ava had left. He lifted his head the smile turned to an ugly frown, as he approached Hazel he uttered, "Yes, we were friends once, but things have changed. It is obvious that your parents never taught you the manners you ought to have. There are rules. There are disciplines and courtesies one must have to be at Top Tier. You might believe we are the same, but I am better, much better, than you will ever be."

Morclyf thudded her shoulder as he followed Ava into the Academy. Hazel stood with tears in her eyes. The tears, however, were not from sorrow. A small smirk formed in the corner of her otherwise down-turned mouth. She was happy not feeling alone. Ava's breath had thickened, Hazel drew out the moisture over her hand, and Morclyf popped the stones as each droplet of water fell. As they used their powers collectively, Hazel felt (and later, Ava and Morclyf admittedly felt) normal.

Isolated at The Light with her family, Hazel slowly found her smile again. She spent much of her time sitting at the cliff's edge listening to the wind and waves, while she threw scraps of food to the seagulls who hovered just above her. Ten years had passed since that day in the schoolyard with Ava and Morclyf. In that time, she learned what she needed from her parents and from the feelings and voices she communed with. The Light and little attached cottage became her sanctuary. The grassy fields sprawled like an ocean that kept the cruelty of people far away. She wished neither to see anyone, nor be seen.

Yet, Harald and Joane continually worried about their daughter. As she grew older, the more distant Hazel became. The young woman gladly helped with any chore and responsibility. She never misbehaved or complained about the life they led and yet, to her parents, Hazel always looked sad and far away. Joane wished for her daughter to share whatever thoughts and feelings she might have, just so they could stop wondering themselves. For Hazel, silence was not defense to keep others away. Rather, she was silent so she could listen and take everything in.

She would sit for an hour without having a significant, meaningful thought. Hazel would stare off into nothing but be affected by the wind on every hair of her body, head, and in her ears. The language she heard was not altogether audible, yet a sensation that produced meaning and purpose. The transcendent exchange within Hazel and the air was effortless, comforting, and frightening all at once. When she spoke back, she learned that she could question, command, or simply converse with the air itself, more-so through movements that involved her arms and body. As she seemingly often danced, the winds would tell of far off places, peoples, cities, monsters, and fables. Then, one day, the winds whispered, "Ivindfor has come".

The man's shadowy image strolled deliberately up a road that slowly wound through the wheat fields to The Light. From a distance, he was just a blur in the sun as the warm summer dust swirled up around him with each shamble. At times, he would pause, look up at the destination ahead of him, and then continue gently, as if measuring each step. Hazel observed him curiously from the widow's walk atop the lantern house. She was neither anxious, nor apprehensive. She just waited.

Ivindfor treaded through the dry, sandy soil with a head bent. The wind shifted slowly around and then away from him. During each one of his breaks, he gazed at the lighthouse with a distinct memory. There were so many years, so many in between his visits, so many hiding within his mind that the memories would take a few minutes to find and visualize. Ivindfor remembered when the first off-white stones were carved from the cliff face and lifted into place. He recalled how the great windmill facing the sea was set, and how it first spun the gears and wheels inside. He saw the brilliance of the light as it first shimmered into the night sea

"They called her a witch, a breach, a soul-less child."

giving hope and safety to sailors. He thought of the fire that ravaged it and the friends and family who had rebuilt and lived there.

How many years? How many people had cared for The Light? He could not remember time as a number anymore, only as movements carrying him from place to place.

As Ivindfor approached the humble cottage, Harald and Joane emerged through the solid, sun-bleached door. They both squinted through the brightness of the afternoon sun as he gazed back at them. Harald was a tall, thin man yet his arms, legs, and shoulders were chiseled from years of labor. Joane was petite yet carried just enough weight to accentuate the natural curves of her body. Both had skin that had been tightened and tanned by the wind and sun. They also had dark, thinning hair with several streaks of gray forming from the temples back. To Ivindfor, his friends appeared so much older since the last time they met. He disliked how the effects of aging reminded him that someday they would pass on, while he possibly lived on.

"I know it's been a while, but we don't look *that* horrible, do we?" Joane reacted to Ivindfor's slightly grimaced face.

Ivindfor grinned sheepishly and was embarrassed by his expression. He then gave each a long, hard embrace. Looking down at Joane he replied, "I never had much luck hiding my thoughts from you." Joane smiled up at Ivindfor and patted the dust off of his plainly woven brown and gray shirt and pants. To her, his clothes seemed too common and ordinary for a man of his importance.

Once settled into the simple chairs that skirted a low, large round table, Joane offered cool tea along with cheese and dried wheat bread. "So, I suppose you're here to take Hazel, then," she nervously asked.

"Joane, for goodness sake, the man just sat down! How do we know...?" Harald commented.

"Well, excuse me! But we haven't heard a word from him for two years now," Joane replied sharply. "I think we deserve to know what's going on. Where have you been and what has been so important that you couldn't send a message?" She directed the last part to Ivindfor who sat unmoved, but understood her agitation. She sniffled, cleared her throat and continued, "The least you could have done is given me some warning so that I could have done something with this house, or prepared a special meal." Joane sat with her arms crossed and waited for an answer, but the twitching of her right foot signaled her anxious irritation with his arrival.

She was upset that he was there to take Hazel away to Havenshade. With the utmost caution Ivindfor replied, "Joane, you know I am an insincere man, when it comes to manners, but you also know that this day would eventually come." Joane eyes filled with tears that began to roll down her cheeks. Ivindfor put his hand on his bowed head and both Harald and Joane looked at each other, as he continued. "The past two years have been extremely difficult. Soon after we last met, my sister, Lazdrazil, finally discovered the children after all these years. Honestly, I'm surprised she didn't find them sooner. As the children grew older and a bit more powerful, she noticed someone in particular - Hazel." He paused and gazed at Harald and Joane, who appeared wide-eyed and very disturbed.

"What do you mean?" Harald questioned.

"I mean, Hazel's power was interfering with Lazdrazils'." Ivindfor uttered quickly. "And so, Lazdrazil asked questions, then demanded answers, then searched for her and the others on her own. My father has helped me conceal them as well as possible, but the time has come for them to leave."

"I don't understand. Are the children in danger of her? Is she after them?" Harald continued to ask. "We could have helped you."

"No. And no, you couldn't help. If you would have tried, then Hazel would have been exposed immediately." Ivindfor replied. "It was best to keep everyone living as normally as possible. Lazdrazil doesn't mean any real harm. She's just jealous and angry with me for not including her."

"She's a crazy witch, if you ask me," Joane muttered through her clenched teeth. "That woman is evil. She came from the Fendow, and regardless of your father's intentions...no one can take that kind of evil out of someone."

"Lazdrazil isn't..." Ivindfor did not feel like making excuses for his sister's behaviors. "I know, I know. That's one reason we didn't include her. But, because Hazel has such incredible talents and gifts, Lazdrazil has learned just about everything now. Everything except, Havenshade. She doesn't have the knowledge, or power to enter my home. So, I think the children will be safest there. Besides, they have changed into young men and women. Their powers have grown and changed with them. Aelen cannot hide what them much longer. It's time for them to follow me there."

"And what if we don't *want* to follow you," echoed a sharp voice from the shadows of the staircase. The adults turned and saw the faint glow of Hazel in the darkness. Joane strolled over and stretched out her hand, welcoming her into the room.

"Hazel. This...this is Ivindfor," Joane stated. "This is the man who we've been telling you about for so long. It's alright."

Hazel never met Ivindfor before. Her parents told her stories of him, and how her was responsible for how she was... Yet, she never laid eyes on him before. She apprehensively walked down the stairs and was troubled with the knowledge that he had visited her mother and father. Hazel had wondered for years why he had not visited her, over and over in her mind. Why he did not comfort her, or give her some confidence in who she was? Now, as the great Ivindfor sat in her home, Hazel felt indifferent.

Hazel stared at the scruffy, unkempt man sitting in their home. He seemed less noble than the stories she had heard. She imagined a man whose presence would define the moment. The Ivindfor who sat before her had dirty, brown, wavy hair that fell to his shoulders; stubble across his face; and the clothes he wore were the tattered rags of a beggar. This reality shattered all of her dreams of how she imagined this day would be, as well as, the hope of what was supposed to be a better life. She guardedly sat opposite of Ivindfor never gazing away from him. He sat across from her in a lump of dusty clothes. He did not look at her, but focused on the teacup cradled in both of his hands.

"Disappointed?" Ivindfor directed at Hazel. Without a reply, he continued. "I don't blame you. Your mother and father are exceptional storytellers. They have always made me more than what I am. And, don't blame them for anything else, especially the school and city issues. I asked them to send you, and to keep you there for as long as possible."

Hazel sat motionless, heavier than her parents had ever seen her. Ivindfor continued to gaze into the teacup. The tea inside had started to ripple and swirl. "I've heard all about your problems with the people, your school mates, and your sadness." Ivindfor singed, almost mockingly. "I stayed away and didn't interfere because – you've deserved this life. However difficult this life has been for you, it is yours and yours alone. Did you honestly think you were special?"

The air within the cottage changed. The pressure fell from everyone and everything else and clung around Hazel. The tea in Ivindfor's cup swirled so fast that it began to spill over the lip, and he grinned out of the corner of his mouth. Then, all at once, Hazel lifted herself from the chair, stretched out her right arm, with a livid sense of strength and power lifted Ivindfor's head. His eyes met hers and he witnessed the anger that made her body shake. Hazel drew a long breath and voiced: "How dare you. How dare you say I deserved scorn and ridicule! You knew all this time! You knew my depression, my loneliness, my hopelessness! And now you want me to go away with you? You can go, but leave me ALONE!

With a hard emphasis on the last word, Hazel stormed out of cottage and ran to the cliff's edge. Ivindfor motioned with raised hands to Harald and Joane to stay as he quickly went after her. Once outside, he turned the corner and moved toward the eastern side of the cottage and the yard between the cliff's edges. Hazel caught a glimpse of him and extended out her arm. A gust of wind blew up over the bluff so hard that Ivindfor was knocked solidly against the back wall of the cottage. "STAY AWAY FROM ME", she shrieked over the sound of the air rushing around them. He crawled, clawing into the ground trying to reach her. Hazel stood tall, still, and unaffected by the wind and dust whirling around her. She gazed without pity at the man desperately fighting against the rushing force against him. Finally, as he reached her feet, Ivindfor peered up to her with a great smile on his face and yelled joyfully:

"That's it! That's the way! Can't you see how much strength you have? No one else is more powerful than you. No one else is braver! It's all because of what you've had to endure! Please understand. Please forgive me, Hazel."

Within a few moments, the wind and sound subsided. Ivindfor kneeled on the ground waiting for her answer, but instead she offered silence, stillness, and only her hand. For Ivindfor, that was enough. He stood close to her while she gazed at him with tears in her eyes. She was confused and drained with his arrival. This was not the way she had imagined it would be so many times before. She had always wanted him to save her.

As they walked back to the cottage, Ivindfor dusted himself off and said. "Before we leave for Havenshade, I'd like you to come with me across the sea, to Essil. I have some friends I would like you to meet there. We'll talk about everything inside with your folks." Hazel sighed heavily as if surrendering the last remnants of tension within her. Ivindfor put his arm around her shoulder and offered, "You are going to be just fine. We just need time to talk and trust each other a bit more. You have been through enough in your life."

Hazel shifted her eyes at him a little as Ivindfor declared: "I think it's time that you see the world, and it's time that the world sees you!"

Of Fish, Forests, and Fire

May you be counseled against the evil of your own arrogance,
like a spark, if untamed shall burn from within
and then consume you.
From, *the Songs of Semmiah*

    Deep in the cold, northern forests of Essil, a young man dreamily gazed from the small, frosted window of his lofted bedroom. The sun crept over the treetops to expose the frozen mists roll gently over the snow banks and slither from the dark trees surrounding the cabin. Each morning, the boy would watch the sun's rays sparkle and fade as the wind pushed the fog from within and out of the forest. Often, the young man sensed that the forest was breathing out the mists, as if the trees were alive in that way. The contrast and constant change amazed him, and he never took for granted the beauty enveloping the start of each day.

"Edmund!" Called his father from below. "Come on. The morning's slipping away. You know I need to ride over to Bridgeport, and you've got your chores to do!"

Edmund scooted across the heavily blanketed bed and scrambled to get dressed. He knew his father, Bryght, was in a hurry this morning. The journey to Bridgeport and back would take most of the day and Bryght was uneasy about leaving Edmund alone. Rooth, Edmund's mother and Bryght's wife, had traveled to Crescent Tier. Rooth's sister was expecting to give birth soon and she traveled to help their mother and celebrate the delivery. So, her two 'boys', as she called them, were left on their own.

The cabin they lived in was small but comfortable. Since Rooth had left, the tidiness of their home had gone astray. Dust, dirt, small articles of garbage, crumbs of food, dishes, and clothes could be seen littered nearly everywhere. There was an obvious absence of order and cleanliness. Also, the air hung heavy with the smell of stagnant, sweaty clothes and food beginning to spoil. If she were to have walked through the door, her two 'boys' would be given the 'glare', then silenced and shunned for a week. Rooth was a compassionate woman, but when it came to her home, she was particular and very business-like.

Bryght stoked the fire, and ashes overflowed onto the floor. As Edmund stepped down the ladder to his loft, he heard his father say, "Ah, for goodness sake! Boy, we have got to get this place cleaned before your mother gets back." Edmund snickered a little as Bryght made fun of them. They moved aside several tools, plates, and pans laying on the table. Then, Bryght plopped some oatmeal in what appeared to be clean bowls, then tossed a warm piece of toast into Edmund's waiting hands. They sat across from each other and began eating their breakfast, which tasted as unsavory as it was presented.

"Once we're done with breakfast, I'll need your help packing up the wagon," Bryght commented. "Then, I'll be off and you can meet up with Waddle at the river. Just make sure you stick to the path."

"I always do," Edmund replied. "Don't worry, I've gone to the river by myself before."

"I know you have, but either me or your mom have been around before. I don't like you being alone out here in the woods," Bryght said worriedly.

"Well, Waddle will be there. So I won't be," Edmund comforted.

Waddle had been a good friend and neighbor for nearly thirty-two years, since his birth. His true name was Kasper, but everyone called him Waddle. This nickname originated from the way he walked. Waddle's legs ceased growing in length when he was seven, but his torso and arms continued to develop normally. So, the shortness of his thick legs made him shuffle and sway awkwardly. Waddle never minded his nickname. Those who used the word never said it in a harsh, derogative manner. Waddle was a respected, generous, and tough man. The kind of man other women wished their husbands could be more like.

Waddle was an industrious, intelligent gentleman who lived alone. His parents had both died fifteen years earlier. His father was lost in a mining accident at Divis Irn; his body was never recovered. His mother, determined to find him, died from an illness on the journey to the mines. And so, Waddle continued his life by being the surrogate older brother to Edmund, who was almost half his age. They spent most of their days together fishing, exploring, or inventing new tools for everyday use. They enjoyed a brotherly relationship without having to compete for space and time within their own homes. For both Edmund and Waddle, their relationship could not have been a better one.

Outside the cabin, Bryght and Edmund finished packing and securing the supplies in the wagon. As Bryght lashed and knotted the final rope he lectured, "Now, make sure to pack all the gear you need. That way you won't have to come back for anything. Make sure to pack a lunch. Don't forget those candle-bobbers that Waddle came up with, either. Lastly, follow the stinkin' trail! The ground is way too soft and I don't want you sinking out there alone. Alright?"

"Just go already, or you won't make it back by dinner. I'm seventeen! I'll be fine on my own for few hours. You worry far too much." Edmund answered.

Bryght frowned, gave his son a strong hug, and Edmund patted him on the back. Bryght hurriedly hoisted himself in the wagon. As he shifted in the seat, he turned looking down at his son and said, "One last thing," Edmund rolled his eyes. "Take your pen and paper and practice writing while you're fishing. Ivindfor said he'd be back soon and I don't want him blaming me if you haven't improved. I know you don't want me to worry, but that's part of being a father," he paused looking out past the team of horses as if contemplating, then turned back and stated: "You know what? I'm not bothered by letting you go out alone, I am more bothered by the fact that with each day you don't seem to need me as much. But, I suppose that's just a part of growing older, on both ends of the stick."

Edmund looked a bit confused at his father's sudden burst of insight. He grinned and kicked the ground a little. He gazed at the balding, large man with a clean, pleasant, and round face. Edmund realized that within the man (who he believed was invincible) had just exposed a small insecurity. For an instant, Edmund saw a flaw in the perfect picture he had of his father. Or, was it that Edmund noticed an adults' perspective and realization? Still confused, Edmund listened to one last thing before Bryght rode away into the darkness of the forest:

"Be good, have fun, and be careful. See you tonight – I love you."

As soon as Bryght rode out of sight, the temptation to mess around was enormous. Edmund had free reign of the house, grounds, and could do whatever dangerous, impractical activity he wanted. He had always wanted to pile snow up to the roof, drag his sled to the peak and ride all the way into the tree line. Or, he could crawl back into bed and doze the morning away with dreams. However, Edmund knew Waddle would certainly inform his father if he didn't show up at the river. So, he gathered his fishing equipment, packed a few slices of bread and dried meat for lunch, scooped together paper, ink, and a pen, but left behind the dirty dishes from breakfast.

Once in the forest, Edmund stayed near the white painted rope tied to very particular painted trees, which marked the safe path to reach the river. As he walked further into the forest, Edmund noticed that the ground became softer and considerably more saturated with water. Moisture leaked through his boots and his socks were soon soaked. Trudging through the muck proved difficult and slow. Several times, Edmund almost lost a boot into the suction ground.

The mists were denser, as well. Edmund's visibility was less than ten feet all around him. Occasionally, he would finger the rope as a precaution not lose his bearings. The dew dripped from the needles of the tall pine trees, which blocked nearly any sunlight from reaching the ground. Sporadically, beautiful white mushrooms glowed very lightly from the base of the trees. These would sometimes catch Edmund's eyes in the rolling fog and cause him to lose focus. During these moments, he would stop himself short, grab the rope, and secure his bearings.

If a person were to stray from the path Bryght had found, marked, and partially developed, then the outcome for survival was bleak and gruesome. The ground, especially closer to the river, was so malleable a person could sink and remain trapped. The marshy landscape divulged stories of animals and people who attempted to travel through unharmed. Sometimes, Edmund heard the screams of an ensnared animal off in the distance. He would listen with sadness, as the animal struggled until engulfed, and then went silent. The sound haunted him and made him cautious and anxious of entering the forest.

Finally, the sound of water lapping over rocks reached Edmund's ears. He knew that the slope down the riverbank was directly in front of him. "Waddle, are you out here?" he shouted out into the mist. Edmund listened carefully and peered through the rolling haze. Then, a flicker of light bounced in the air and floated lazily on the quiet water. Edmund knew that was Waddle's answer. The bobber was topped with a globe and candle. This was Waddle's invention, and worked extremely well in the constant fog. A fish would take the bait underneath the water, the bobber would sink, and the water would extinguish the candle. This allowed the fisher to see that he had a bite, rather than relying solely on the feel of their line and pole.

As Edmund meandered down the riverbank, he noticed the candlelight disappear then heard the splash of oars. Waddle was rowing across to him. "About time you showed up," Waddle yelled over the creaking noise of the boat. "I was just about ready to search for you."

"I'm not alone, I'm with my babysitter, aren't I?" Edmund mocked.

Waddle beached the boat hard into the soft sand. "Listen, I'm not your babysitter. Although, considering how immature and absent minded you normally are, it's not a wonder that your folks worry so much. There's going to come a day that you have to just grow up, Edmund."

Edmund watched as Waddle muscled the boat into place by himself. Waddle was a foot-and-a-half shorter than Edmund, but proved himself ten times stronger. Edmund admired, and imitated most of what Waddle did. Waddle gained a sense of pride in knowing that Edmund looked up to him. At times, he also enjoyed the responsibility of teaching, talking, and caring for Edmund. While at other times, he enjoyed being at home away from the noise of another being. Today, however, Waddle knew his duty was to make sure Edmund stayed out of trouble, which meant Edmund needed to quit joking around.

"Well, get set and get fishing already," Waddle ordered. "I've already caught three this morning." They situated their poles and rested for a while in stillness. Edmund lit a small lamp, took out his book, pen and ink. Waddle broke the silence, "I can't believe you're going write and fish at the same time. You'll never catch anything. Besides what does writing have to do with anything out here?"

"I have to practice," Edmund retorted. "It's just like any other chore. Besides, my father said Ivindfor could be back any day now and I need to show improvement."

"Well, reading and writing is waste of time, if you ask me," Waddle remarked. "Just a bunch of words that can be read, repeated, and twisted into what anyone else wants them to mean."

"Maybe," Edmund paused, thought about what Waddle said, then with a sigh wanted to change the topic. "I've never seen Port Essil, or the sea. You've gone there with my father, haven't you?"

"A few years ago. There's nothing there but a lot more people and water for as far as you can see," Waddle gazed out into the mist focusing on the candlelight. He appeared to be mulling over something as his faced clenched and twisted over conflicting thoughts. "You know what," he began. "I've never really thought about how different we are. You dream about traveling the world, seeing different places, and the people who live there. I'm happy out here not dealing with any of them. You write stories about the good and bad, the real and pretend in life. I would rather deal with infallible numbers and measurements. My dreams are of machines to make life practical and better. You seem more interested in finding the answer to the meaning of life, or at least asking the questions about it."

"At least we both have dreams, even if they are opposite," Edmund replied. "Maybe we can appreciate them both, even if we don't understand them."

"Nothing you say never makes sense." Waddle sneered and shook his head.

They both laughed and picked on each other while they continued to fish throughout the morning. At lunchtime, Waddle commented, "We haven't had a bite in a long time and the only fish we have are the three I caught before you showed up. Not that I'm blaming you, or anything. But something's not right. Seems like all the fish have just, disappeared."

"Maybe the hot springs toward the glacier is cooler and they went upstream," Edmund added.

"Nah, if that was the case, then there'd still be fish swimming by us. This is different. And the mist has been getting thicker every hour. There's a perfectly logical reason, I just need more time. I'll figure it out, just wait and see."

Soon after, they cast out their lines and tried their luck again. Edmund casually peered over his book now and then, while Waddle stared attentively at the flickering lights. Several times,

Waddle would grab hold of a pole; even Edmund's and yank furiously back as if crazed with determination.

"I don't know exactly what's going on. The bobbers are moving around like someone's sliding them across the water, but they're not going down!" Waddle and Edmund looked out and saw the candles move and sway, but never sank. Then, Waddle's eyes opened wide and his mouth dropped. "Oh, no. We have to get out of here! NOW!"

"Why, what's going on?" Edmund naively asked.

"The ice is breaking up at the spring. The fish are gone because the water is getting warmer, a lot warmer." Waddle breathed heavily. Edmund had never seen Waddle remotely afraid before, but the look in Waddle's face made Edmund realize they were in severe trouble.

Waddle grabbed Edmund's arm tightly and looked intensely into his eyes. "Get your things, get up the riverbank, and get on the path, and run home. There's no time, just go!"

He pushed the young man's shoulders hard, but Edmund turned and shouted, "What about you? Aren't you coming with me?"

"Just go before the river rushes and rises. I've got to get my boat pulled up, or it'll get broken up in the ice flows. Don't worry; I've been through this before. I'll be right behind you. Now, get going Edmund and DON'T LOOK BACK!" As Waddle finished stressing the last part, they both heard a distant deep moan, a bone-crushing crack, and the smacking splash as large pieces of ice fell into the immense basin of the springs.

From within the green waters of the lagoon, fire pushed molten earth upward. The flow of red-hot rock broke the surface of water and spat lava, which sizzled harshly as it cooled. The cycle of fire pushing earth, the heat melting water into vapor, and the cold air solidifying stone continued, forming a primeval elemental column. The ice that filled the pond split apart, melted, and floated down river with the raging waters. Water flooded the riverbank as the ice ripped apart trees and gouged the soil. The explosion of unbridled energy caused such a momentum of destruction that the noise sounded like a monster bellowing. The energy of all the elements at war with each other washed down the river toward Edmund and Waddle.

Edmund clawed and scurried up the slippery riverbank. His heart pounded so loudly in his head that he could barely feel, or hear anything else. Grasping ahead of him, he fortunately clutched a painted tree. He felt the rope as he trudged through the icy muck. The river water crept up through the already saturated ground. The muck was slowing him down too much. Every step was awkward and unbalanced. He tried to focus but kept dropping things, and while trying to recover lost his balance and direction. He looked back for Waddle but he was not there. Edmund heard the sound of the monster rushing toward them. Waddle yelled out as the flood reached them. Edmund faintly perceived his voice over volume of noise. Edmund spun around calling and peering through the grayness for his friend. Nothing but the violent river responded.

In the confusing minutes of spinning and back peddling to find Waddle, Edmund noticed that he could not see the painted trees. He could not feel the white rope. He stood absolutely still as if time stopped. Gradually, the cold ground crept up the side of his boots. Edmund could feel the grimy soil underneath swallow him up. Nothing solid was stopping his descent, rather the earth gently shifted to accommodate his body with the ground itself.

Panicked and desperate, Edmund twisted his head to find any sign of a branch. He strained not to move his legs. He knew any motion could make him sink even faster. Then, to his left, a bare branch stretched out as if pointing a bony finger at his head. Edmund grasped the thin branch and pulled it down toward him. He begged that it would not break. Gingerly, he inched his way up out of the muck and closer to the trunk of the tree. In the attempt to free himself, Edmund lost his left boot. The icy mud made the muscles and bones throb with pain. There he stood, with a solitary foothold, somewhere on a solitary tree.

He grasped and dug his finger-tips into the slippery bark of the tree. Sweat poured down from his forehead and into his eyes, stinging them. Tears mixed along with the sweat as he held on to the tree, gasping in fear. He tried to pull himself out of the cold earth. Edmund's body shook with exhaustion. He lost the path. He lost his friend. He lost the courage to even move. At that moment, all Edmund wanted was his father to be there, to take him home. He cried out for help. But his voice was consumed by the mists and raging river.

Back at the cabin, Edmund's screams sounded like an animal fighting the pull of the forests' empty floor.

The Tall and Short of It

Unless blinded by shrewd conceit and harsh contempt,
Neither a person's difference in height, weight, color of skin, eyes, or hair;
Nor even their name and nation should matter.
So only then, may your heart notice the nature of another's true character.
From, *The Deeds of Sophina and Petrik*

"I can't believe you were only fourteen feet, if that, from the path," snickered Bryght. Edmund hung his head in embarrassment and sunk deeper into the blanket surrounding him. Several laughs resounded in the cabin, as new guests and strangers filled every corner. "Don't get me wrong, I'm glad you're safe – it could have been a lot worse."

"Yeah, he could have been fifteen feet away," chuckled a very short man of only three-and-a-half feet tall, who was cleaning plates and cups in the kitchen. Everyone in the house laughed again, with the exception of Hazel and Edmund. Edmund replayed the moment that the Stout, named Isor, sprang onto the tree Edmund clung: Isor had hung upside down on a branch, had snickered, and then remarked, "Hullo there! You must be Edmund. You're right where he said you'd be. My name's Isor, a friend of Ivindfor's. You're going to be all right, but by the looks of all the bark you've scraped off this tree, I think, it might be a goner." And so, Isor whistled out to Ivindfor who carefully slogged over with a line and they helped Edmund up from the mud and back onto the path.

Outside the cabin, Edmund heard Waddle chopping wood furiously. Ivindfor informed Edmund that they spotted Waddle pinned with the ice flows in his boat. They dragged him out of the boat kicking and screaming just as the craft broke apart and floated away. Waddle decided to take out the anger of losing his boat on some much-needed firewood. Edmund knew better than to bother Waddle when he was in a bad mood (especially if he had a sharp object) and settled in the cabin happy to know his best friend was safe.

Looking around the cabin, Edmund noticed his father, a peculiar looking girl, and a massive man all busy cleaning and creating dinner. Earlier, Bryght had rushed over and hurried Edmund into his bedroom to change out his wet, dirty clothes before introductions could be made. Once alone, Bryght gave his son an overpowering hug. Bryght wiped a few tears from his eyes as he told Edmund how he had met Ivindfor about halfway to Bridgeport. Ivindfor and the girl persuaded him to turn around and stated that they felt something powerful was about to happen. Luckily, they made it back in time to save Waddle and somehow Ivindfor knew that you were safe on that tree. Edmund seemed confused as to how they knew where he was, but disregarded everything except for the contentment of being home again.

"Stop pestering the young lad, Isor! That's an order!" the massive man's voice boomed over the laughter and everyone became quieter. The great man was a Vald named Captain Vekt and the Stout, Isor, was his Best Mate. They sailed on the ship known as the Vagabond, which had brought Ivindfor and Hazel. Ivindfor insisted that they travel along, even though both men hated traveling by land and fell ill several times along the way.

Seafarers become accustomed with motions of the seas, but apparently the jostling of a wagon on land confused their equilibrium, just as a land-man might get seasick. Edmund relaxed and for the first time focused on the physical appearances of the guests in his home.

Captain Vekt seemed to be at least ten feet tall and stooped occasionally in the vaulted living room of the cabin. He had red, bristly hair, eyebrows and beard; a deeply tanned, ruddy face, and wild wide brown eyes behind a thick nose. The Captain wore a weathered blue suit that loosely hung over a stained off-white shirt. A wide black leather belt with a heavy, silver buckle wrapped around his midsection, while a hefty, oversized scimitar settled tightly through and near his right side. Edmund observed this and concluded that the Captain had the rare trait of being left handed. This was proven as he saw the Captain lift a tankard of ale with his sizeable left arm. Overall, Artemis Vekt gave the impression of being gentle yet intimidating because of his size. He helped with any chore without touting his rank, except to Isor, of course.

Isor, Vekt's Best Mate, was an attractive middle-aged man, although extremely short. Isor was about three-and-a-half feet tall, thin, and extremely muscular. The black curly hair on Isor's head was neatly trimmed and he was clean-shaven. The triangular face was symmetrical and proportionately perfect with his body. The Stout had the stereotypically long hands and fingers of his people. Unlike the Stout tradition of walking with their thick square bare feet, Isor wore calf-high black suede boots. His twinset was black, fitted, and his shirt, unlike Captain Vekt's, was pressed vibrantly white. The two men made a very odd couple, yet the girl that they had brought along seemed even stranger.

Hazel glided about the cabin as if weightless. Edmund saw how her delicate movements were fluid and free. However, she carried herself with a confidence prevailing over every task. She was lovely, in an unusual, intriguing way that Edmund could not quit grasp. At times, he would catch himself staring and flinch embarrassingly away just before being caught by her returned glance. Hazel did not dwell on Edmund, for her cares were with Ivindfor and what he had told and taught her while on the voyage to Essil.

By the fire with Edmund sat Ivindfor, who appeared the same as he always had. However, Ivindfor's face appeared withdrawn and tired. Edmund recalled the same look four months earlier when Ivindfor stopped for a night. While Bryght and Rooth spoke with him late into the night, Edmund fell asleep listening to the rhythm of their quiet voices. When he awoke the next morning, Ivindfor had already left. The only remark Ivindfor made to Edmund was "practice writing every day. I'll return very soon. Be kind to your parents, and also for yourself."

"Edmund," Ivindfor began, which woke Edmund from his daydreams. "You're a brave young man. You managed to pull yourself together and remain calm in a situation that could have killed you. As long as you get out of any scrape, narrow or wide, then you've just dodged death by another day. Not everyone gets the chance to say that."

Edmund peeked through the drawn blanket and smirked at him. Then, Ivindfor continued, "What happened today was no accident. Hazel and I could sense the pressure building underneath the Intean Springs. The earth was sending a message." Within a heartbeat, Edmund was startled as he heard a noise slowly whisper one word: "redress". The sound was not heard in the cabin, nor was it audible through his ears, but resounded within his whole body. As if Edmund was a tuning fork, and the sound vibrated within himself. At the same moment, Hazel dropped a pan she was drying. Everyone turned toward Hazel wide-eyed, paler (if possible), and terrified.

Ivindfor shot from his seat and ran over to her. "Did you hear it?"

"I-I-I h-heard the sound – from the fire," she stuttered.

"What did it say? Was it a man or woman's voice?" Ivindfor glared directly into her eyes anxiously.

"It was neither and both at the same time," Edmund said to Ivindfor. "And the word was 'redress'"

Hazel nodded. Ivindfor snapped around, leapt over furniture, and grabbed Edmund roughly around his shoulders.

The blanket fell away from Edmund, who was more afraid of Ivindfor than of the voice he had just heard with Hazel. "How did you hear that? You aren't one of the children. You shouldn't be able to....." Ivindfor panted and shook his head like a madman. "Not right. Maybe because we're so close. Doesn't make sense."

Bryght strode over and took Ivindfor by his shoulders and guided him away from Edmund. Hazel was still in shock, as everyone looked over at Edmund who seemed perfectly fine. Ivindfor twitched when the fire popped and spit cinders up the chimney. Obviously, something about the voice and word that Hazel and Edmund heard disturbed him greatly. Bryght offered Ivindfor a glass of brandy. Isor escorted Hazel to a padded stool away from the fire and motioned for Edmund to scoot over to her. The cabin fell hushed and stilled.

Even Waddle's constant hacking of wood stopped. Then, he burst through the door with a pile of wood stacked in both arms, which shattered the silent awkwardness in the cabin. "I could have saved my boat, but nooo – you just had to drag me away!" He yelled out. Everyone jumped in surprise. Waddle walked through the room as if nothing just happened at all, and the others slowly returned back to what they had previously been doing. No one mentioned the incident, the sound, or the fire again.

The group ate dinner and made the best of what room was available. Captain Vekt sat uncomfortably in a corner. Isor perched himself on a stool. Edmund and Hazel sat together on a rug far from the fire, while Bryght, Ivindfor, and Waddle took the remaining chairs. The company relaxed and listened to the fire steam as the wind rattled the windows. Finally, Ivindfor asked, "Captain Vekt, do you mind telling us a good story?"

The Captain took in a deep, throaty sigh and replied, "That's a grand idea! And I've got just the story, too!" Isor rolled his eyes knowingly expecting the only story Captain Vekt ever told. Regardless, he and the others nestled into their positions and waited for Captain Vekt to begin.

"This is an old story, and it is well known to both the Vald and the Stouts," Captain Vekt's voice rolled in a low singing way. "This is the tale of Petrik, the Vald and Sophina, the Stout. Long ago, the races of this world deeply mistrusted each other. They lived strictly within their own borders, and did not even trade among one another. During this time, a wealthy Vald named Kern had three sons: Jern, Lark, and Petrik. The two eldest sons were honorable, hard-working, and respectful of their lineage. Petrik, however, wandered their lands and dreamed of venturing out beyond their borders to see what the world could offer.

"Well, one day Petrik began walking and walking, further and further until he became lost and alone. The harder he tried to find his way back home, the more astray he became. For three days he roamed through unknown woods, landscapes, and met many new dangerous animals. He feared to sleep and had very little to eat. Petrik's ideas about seeing the world were overcome with hunger and fear. He started to believe that he would die alone in that wilderness. The forest never seemed to end, and there were no signs of his people anywhere.

"Then, just as Petrik had about lost all hope, he approached the edge of the forest. At first, he thought that he had returned home. Then, looking out over the grasses, he understood that he had traveled to the other side of the great forest. Cautiously, he stepped out of the darkness of the trees and into the sunlight. Just as he felt the warmth of the sun on his face, a whizzing sound whirled at him as a bola spun around his head. The two smoothly sanded rocks struck against the sides of his head and Petrik fell to the ground unconscious.

"Sophina, a renowned Stout warrior, ran to her prey wielding the famous magical sword named Endingknell. When she reached Petrik, she gazed in awe at the size of him. He was almost three times taller than she was, and yet with one blow she had the giant at her mercy. Petrik moaned reaching for his head as he woke from the bashes against his skull. Sophina quickly raised Endingknell with the intent to end Petrik's life, but then unnaturally paused. Her instincts encouraged her to strike, but the magnificence in Petrik's face and countenance held her back. It is said that Sophina's mercy for Petrik resonates Our Lady Semmiah's instruction that people should pause and listen with their hearts rather than immediately react with their might.

"As Petrik awoke with the smallest woman he'd ever seen, he wondered if he was still dreaming. They introduced each other, and spoke at length about who they were, where they came from, and from there on began a legendary relationship. Together, they were able to navigate Petrik back home. They kept their friendship secret and met in the forest as often as they could. For many weeks, months, and over a year they met secretly in the solace of the trees. One day, however, they were followed by people of Petrik's Vald clans and Sophina's Stouts. There in the forest, as the two lovers sat, warriors from both races converged and rushed towards each other with weapons drawn.

"Sophina unsheathed Endingknell and struck the sword into a great outcropped stone that Petrik and she had been sitting on. The sound deafened the oncoming warriors and they were stunned to the ground. As their warriors and family members recuperated from the powerful shockwave, Sophina and Petrik proclaimed their love for each other, and explained how much both races had in common. Bewildered, the warriors on both sides listened to their story, and were inspired to share their friendship with one another.

"And so, that is the legend of how the Vald and the Stouts first became allies and then kinsmen. In fact, Joiner Road in the Rifted Forest is said to be the same path that Petrik and Sophina used. The way is still used today as a trade and traveling route between the two races. On Joiners Road, a statue was built of them, which celebrates the meeting of our two peoples. It remains a symbol of peace between the two nations, and always will. People say that Endingknell is somewhere in a stone in the forest, but for as much as people have sought it, no one has ever found it. But, thanks to the ambition of Petrik to strive out beyond his own borders, and to Sophina who showed compassion above impulse, our people have shared a communion, a harmony, and a wealth with each other ever since and shall, ever after!

Applause echoed throughout the cabin, which startled the dozing Isor as he fell with a thud to the floor. Everyone laughed and felt relieved from the prior events of the day. Ivindfor stood and congratulated Captain Vekt on a well-told story. The others stretched and gathered themselves for sleep, as night had fallen over the forest.

"We need to set off early in the morning, if we plan to get to Port Essil by nightfall," Captain Vekt remarked, trying to get comfortable on the floor. "The Vagabond should be ready to make way as soon as we get there. And with Hazel aboard, we should make Crescent Tier by the next morning. It's a shame she won't always be with us. The trip sometimes takes a day-and-a-half, but with Hazel it only took half as long. You're a wonderful young lady, Haze'."

"Thank you for the kind words, Captain Vekt," Hazel blushed and glanced appreciatively when Vekt used the shortened "Haze". She had not said much the entire time at the cabin, and Edmund listened to every syllable trying to get a glimpse of who she really was. "It has been an honor and pleasure to have been a part of this voyage. I hope we will have others as well."

"And she speaks with the manners of a princess," Isor remarked, gleaming with awe and appreciation.

Hazel blushed again and headed for Edmund's lofted bedroom. Edmund glanced to his father with a questioning eye. "Oh, right," Bryght started. "Hazel's going to sleep in your bed, and you'll sleep on the floor tonight. Don't worry, I'll be joining you – Ivindfor's got my bed. Waddle, you'll have to curl up somewhere in the kitchen since Isor's claimed the dining table. This definitely isn't an inn, and to be honest a stable would probably be more comfortable."

"At least the place is clean again," Ivindfor retorted. "Otherwise, Rooth would have the two of you out in the stable – permanently!" They all guffawed, and one by one faded into a noisy, snoring sleep. Hazel laid in Edmund's bed dreaming of Petrik and Sophina as she watched the moonlight dance through the trees outside the small window. She thought how serene the view was and while in his bed felt a connection with Edmund that sent a small shiver up her spine. She drifted asleep dreaming of how wonderful love can form from even the greatest opposite of people. Down on the hard cold floor, Edmund dreamed of how awesome Sophina's sword Endingknell must have been.

Port Essil was definitely not what Edmund had envisioned at all. The sun had set so he could not take in the beauty of the blue sea. Even the lapping of the waves was drowned out by the town filled with obnoxious people who had been drinking too much. He was also unaccustomed of traveling so far, so his body ached from not moving much in the wagon. They passed houses, stores, inns, and headed straight for the docks. Captain Vekt intended on making good time and was very excited to get back on the water. Again, both Vekt and Isor became nauseous from the bumpy wagon they were in, and they cursed traveling on land the whole way. Their attitudes changed, however, as soon as they heard the seagulls and the scent of sea air wafted through the air. For them, they were home once more.

Twelve Stouts scurried on board The Vagabond. They were quick and ready to assist the company on board. Ivindfor had spoken to Bryght, Waddle and Edmund concerning the voyage and what would occur once they reach Crescent Tier. Edmund knew that it was time to be the scribe Ivindfor always intended him to be. Ivindfor required someone to write the story of the children of the old way. Bryght had been on enough adventures with Ivindfor to know that Edmund would be safe. Bryght also knew that this journey was not meant for him, and that Bryght should stay behind.

Ivindfor pleaded with both Bryght and Waddle to at least travel as far as Crescent Tier. Ivindfor encouraged Bryght by pointing out that he could be with his wife again, and also visit his estranged brother, Bleke. After they mumbled and argued over the subject, Ivindfor finally won them over. Waddle only agreed because he might acquire an excellent deal on a small boat at the docks there.

As soon as they were off the wagon, the company rushed up onto the ship. The Vagabond was a sleek yet wide vessel. The ship had two sails and a tall cabin built in the middle. Captain Vekt happily patted every plank and laughed so hard his whole body shook. Waddle and Edmund, however, trembled from nerves, as they had never sailed on the sea before.

Ivindfor gave those who were not used to sailing a few herbs along with a flask of fresh water, which would help with motion sickness. "I suggest that you try to fall asleep as you can. The trip will go easier on your stomachs that way. And, when you wake up, we should be there!" He left Bryght, Waddle, and Edmund to themselves, and escorted Hazel to the bow of the ship. Edmund watched them as he wrote some notes, but he did not want to intrude on their conversation. They appeared deeply involved and whispered words Edmund did not understand. Edmund felt out of place and less than necessary to Ivindfor.

Edmund laid restlessly down below in the ship's central structure. He had dozed off and on during the journey to Port Essil, and found it difficult to sleep. He was thankful that he did not feel sick from the constant bobbing of the ship. He smirked at the thought of being like a candle bobber out on the water. "How different a day can make in a person's life", he mused. One moment, he was clinging to a tree for dear life, while the next, he felt like he was inside of a log. Agitated from the snoring and motion, he ventured outside to get some fresher air.

On deck, there were several Stouts manning the ship. Isor wheeled the vessel at the stern, while Captain Vekt napped on a wooden chair closely behind him. The other Stouts busily checked navigation maps and ropes. At the bow, Ivindfor was curled up in blankets, as Hazel gazed out into the night. Edmund shivered as the cold night air rushed against his back. He heard the large; square sail above him fill and tighten with the wind. Quietly, Edmund walked toward Hazel. The rhythm of water splashing against the ship matched each of his footsteps.

"Oh! Edmund!" Hazel exclaimed as she turned to see him right behind her. Ivindfor grumbled and resettled himself at the sound of her soft voice.

"I'm sorry. I didn't mean to scare you." Edmund shyly replied.

"That's fine. I take it you couldn't sleep. The company would be nice, if you don't mind. We really haven't had a chance to talk, have we?"

"Not really. Things were kind of hectic back at home. Seems like so long ago."

"Well, the journey has just begun, and there's a lot to see and do."

"What *do you do*?" Edmund asked bluntly and then quickly reeled in shock of his own forwardness.

Hazel just grinned and tipped her head wonderingly and replied, "Don't you know who I am, or who all the children are that Ivindfor's gathering?"

"Bits and pieces. I really haven't understood all that's going on."

Ivindfor's voice grumbled as both Hazel and Edmund startled at the unsuspecting voice. "Well then, I had better fill you in on some of the details. Especially if I want you to write a decent story. Right?"

"Sorry, I didn't mean to wake you," Edmund quickly apologized.

"That's quite alright. I should be the one keeping Hazel company. Thank you." Ivindfor struggled getting to his feet as though he were an old man creaking out of a chair. Edmund gave him a hand as Ivindfor said, "Thank you again, Edmund. Sometimes my age sneaks up on me."

"How old are you, exactly," Edmund blurted out and again reeled from his own forwardness.

"You are a blunt one, aren't you?" Ivindfor smirked. "Just like your dad was at your age. Never thought much before he spoke, and always spoke before he gave a thought about who might hear it," he paused and stretched and Ivindfor's back cracked down his spine. As his arms lowered to his side, Ivindfor slowly exhaled, "I am seventeen hundred and something-*ish*. I prefer to use hundreds instead of thousand. Makes me feel a little younger."

Edmund and Hazel gasped in unison. "That's impossible," Hazel remarked. "My mother and father mentioned your age a couple of times, but I never believed them. I always thought they were just fooling around with me."

"Oh, that's nothing. My brother Beohlor, my sister Lazdrazil, and my father Aelen are much older than me," Ivindfor stated. "I am the youngest, and some would say most foolish."

"How can that be? Are you immortal? How did you become so old?" Edmund ran off at the mouth, shocked and a little concerned.

"No, I am not immortal. I can be killed and die just like anyone else. Yet, like Hazel," Ivindfor shifted his gaze toward her, "I was born with another spirit along with my own."

Edmund glanced at Hazel and she returned to him. "What he says is true," she remarked softly, then continued carefully, "How old was Semmiah?"

Ivindfor continued to gaze at Hazel, but his eyes became weary with remembrance. Then, he spoke in a throaty whisper, "She was three hundred and fifty-seven when..."

"We know," Hazel finished and rested her hand on Ivindfor's.

Ivindfor smiled slightly and added, "Everyone knows what happened to my sister, Semmiah. Don't they?"

"So the myths and stories are true," Edmund said out loud to himself as he leaned back in astonishment.

"Yes, for the most part," Ivindfor replied and changed focus. "I have known your family for generations, Edmund. I have so many stories and histories to tell you. Both of you. But I want to wait until we are with the others. There was a reason that I wanted you two to meet before the others assembled," Ivindfor paused and gazed hard into both of their faces and took a deep breath. "There is one story that I will share with only you, and I hope you will keep it secret until the time is right."

Hazel and Edmund glanced at each other and nodded with anticipation. Seeing their agreement Ivindfor continued. "This story will give you a better understanding of what is happening, and what will inevitably occur. You may not comprehend everything I relate to you, but please just listen and do not interrupt." Edmund and Hazel lowered themselves on the damp floor of the ship and waited for Ivindfor to begin.

"Recently, I visited Edmund and his family. I was in Essil investigating rumors of a creature in the Divis Irn Mines. Men often died in the mines because of air quality and collapses. Working there is a perilous profession, but the money they make for themselves and their families sometimes outweighs the risks.

For a long time, I dismissed the information about a creature, in part, because I was busy keeping an eye on all the children and the stories seemed a bit too far-fetched – even for me. Finally, Maggie, an old friend of mine and the owner of the Bridgeport Inn, summoned me to Essil. Her son, Elo, had returned from the mines with horror stories about people missing. She said Elo couldn't bear to step even one foot past the entrance. So, I journeyed to the mine Divis Irn. What I found reinforced my belief that all I have done has been worth the effort.

"I went there disguised as a miner myself. Old Grudgener, who owns the place, would never have let me in unless he thought I'd actually do some work. So, down into the darkness I went, and in the darkness I found the creature. It was not wholly a man, or beast; but more machine than flesh. He, as it referred to itself, called himself Oostlin. He had pale green eyes, a metallic body gears and legs like a spider, and a framed metallic torso of a man grew from where the spider's head would be. The skin on his arms had been sewed on and was gray and shriveled. Plates of metal were bolted in places, especially his head and hands. This thing was truly like a monster. Within the body of the mechanical spider a small furnace fueled the gears, as smoke and steam poured from small stacks on top. Oostlin was one of the last surviving Syndustrians. They were a race of men once. In order to survive, they molded themselves with machinery. Not only in body, but with their minds, as well. I still don't know how he could have survived all these thousands of years.

"Oostlin was not alone. There were others that he had made in his likeness. Many of them were accident victims that he dragged off and 'saved'. I saw at least twenty, men, women, and a few children who had been reconstructed by his methods. When I told him who I was, the son of Aelen, he recoiled in fear and memory of my father's name. He knew the power my father had and did not wish to cross it again. So, you might ask, 'why didn't I kill the creatures'? I suppose, like Sophina, I chose mercy and besides, I had no power over these things. And also, I saw that Waddle's father was among them.

"Now, Edmund, you cannot say a single word to Waddle about his father. He is no longer the man he once was, and he should be considered dead. I left them in the dark of the mines. But before I left, Oostlin pledged not to capture, or 'save' – as he considered it - any more people. Although he promised, I know more will be taken. I didn't tell anyone what I witnessed. Grudgener wouldn't have believed me, and the workers would still take the risk for the coins regardless of what I said. So, I left, visited Edmund's family, sailed the seas for a while, and then visited Hazel. I have not said a word of it, until now.

"Now, the story has been spoken. The words are ours to share and ours to keep private. Words and language create the connection and meaning between all things. Whether spoken aloud, thought, or felt, our expressions send a signal. Hazel, through language and communion is where our power comes from. We channel the earth's power through the spiritual language we share with it. Yes, the world has a language of its own. All worlds do. The earth is a living being, and we are each a part of its whole. Although he considers himself a cursed man, my father's long life allowed him to learn the language of the world. From him, I was made, and from me: the children of the old way.

"There are others who also study the language of the world. These people are called wizards, witches, and even priests. They often work within the rules of their rulers, and practice their arts in secret, or in hidden sanctuary. Hazel and I, as well as the other children, are sorcerers of the world. We are bound with a spirit of the world, and we are given the ability of communion with it. Wizards and the others must ask the forces and spirit of the world to do their will. If a wizard is intimate, or has a familiar with the spirit, or perhaps is just old enough, then sometimes the world obeys him. That is very rare and that person is usually very dangerous.

Ivindfor paused for a moment and let all that he said settle within Edmund and Hazel, and then continued. "I will end by saying this: A long time ago, all of the races once lived together with my father, and spoke as one with the world. After the last battle with the Syndustrians, they divided and left the Valley of Aeden. Now, they expand, take resources from one another, and wage war for it. Even the Vald and Stouts are showing signs of distress. Captain Vekt has been away from his homeland so long that he does not know the truth; only the pleasure of his fairy tale. The purpose the children have is to bring the people back together again. To show that we have more in common with each other and the world than we have separately from it. If we fail, then the wars that follow may ruin us all.

Hazel and Edmund witnessed Ivindfor's appearance change as that of an old man. As he spoke the words, his features aged along with them. The story seemed to take the very life out of him and caused him a great sadness. With a gigantic sigh, his body improved to its familiar state. Hazel and Edmund sat unmoving and awed at the man before them. "Edmund, do not write any of this down until after we leave Crescent Tier," Ivindfor instructed. He glanced compassionately toward Hazel, "Keep the boat going swiftly. I think we've lagged a bit. I am going for some rest now. Please, keep this to yourselves. I will talk more and answer questions later. Hazel, make sure to wake Edmund up so that he can see Crescent Tier at sunrise. Trust me, it's something you will not want to miss!"

With that, Ivindfor disappeared below the deck, leaving the boy and girl speechless. Edmund took Ivindfor's blanket and curled in the warm spot he once lay, and surprisingly fell fast asleep. Hazel gazed into the night. Her mind raced with all that Ivindfor had said, and she felt privileged to know Ivindfor's secrets. She commanded the wind to blow harder into the sail, the waves carried the boat faster. Far off in the distance, a flickering caught her sight. The Light was calling her back home.

The First Cards Are Set

The worthiness of one's spirit will be reflected through the purity of body and circumstance.
And those born of physical and mental deficit, rape, incest, or lesser breed,
They shall bear the deeper depravity given, and will be offered to judgment, shunning, or death.
Only through the purity of one's subjugation to Her, shall their souls profit.
From, *the Songs of Semmiah*

Morclyf's black eyeball peered through a polished brass telescope. As the barrel swiveled from left to right, his sight caught the glimpse of a familiar aquamarine haired girl. She was far below on the docks of the harbor of Crescent Tier. She had just stepped off a ship, and was surrounded by two men and what appeared two boys. Morclyf studied the group amid other Stouts, Captain Vekt, and Crescent Tieriens scurrying against the weathered dock planks. He saw Hazel smile and speak to them all as if she were royalty returning home. Morclyf wondered for a few moments exactly who accompanied her. Then, with a scowl of realization, he knew exactly who was with the 'witch' of Crescent Tier. The lines in his forehead deepened, then the brass telescope Morclyf gingerly held crinkled, like a wadded piece of paper.

The neatly groomed, dark-haired young man turned away from the deformed telescope and saw his father, Ketteric, supportively leaning on the doorway, observing him. "I assume you saw the girl," Morclyf's father solemnly gurgled. "And of course, Ivindfor. I'm not sure who the others are, though."

"I don't care about them. They're nothing more than lower level scum," Morclyf stammered furiously. After a pause, he glared to his father, "Why did he take *her* before *me*? You said that you were close friends with Ivindfor? I guess you're not as close to him as those public servants from The Light. Are you?"

"Harald and Joane Phlude have been friends of mine for a very long time, and I will not let you disrespect them, or their daughter," Ketteric motioned with his outstretched hand for his son to remain silent, then continued. "Just because your mother, and everyone else in this forsaken city, speaks awful of them, it does not give you the authority to do the same. You would be wise to choose your words and your tones wisely. Ivindfor will not tolerate your spoiled upbringing for very long," Ketteric paused bringing his hand back to rest near him. "I fear for you. He can be a patient and gentle man, but he can also torment your life. I should know. He gave me you."

Morclyf sneered at him boringly, then chuckled. "I'm not afraid of him. Besides, when Mother hears he didn't visit me first, Ivindfor will be worse off than anyone."

"Even your mother knows better than to irritate Ivindfor. She will blame me." Ketteric noted. "Once you leave here, Morclyf, the protections and excuses I have provided for will not be tolerated. You must understand your place, rank, and order within Ivindfor's following."

"My place is where I choose," Morclyf sneered. "If Ivindfor thinks I'm going to do whatever he says, then he's in for a disappointment."

Ketteric gazed at his son for just a moment and quickly turned away in years of tired disgust. He wondered and blamed himself for Morclyf's outcome. In the back of his mind, he had hoped that Ivindfor would be able to help his son in a way that he failed to do. As he left the room and walked down the expansive, marbled hallway, Ketteric heard his son expound, "By the way, send one of the Help to get me A NEW TELESCOPE!"

Ketteric paused, bowed his head, and realized that Morclyf would always hate him, while down the hallway he heard his wife, Vessa, scream about how poorly a servant had washed the dishes. Ketteric shook his balding head, as the weight of his shame showed in his humped back and crooked shoulders. The once proud and fit man was now a crumpled and stressed mass, hobbling through the misery of his own halls.

Far below on the bustling docks and boardwalks of Crescent Tier, Edmund was dizzied by the motion and people surging around him. Never had he been around so many people, or so much commotion. Hundreds, if not thousands, of different sized women and men moved and murmured like a choreographed dance and chant. Bryght grasped his shoulders as they meandered with Waddle, Ivindfor and Hazel to a side street where they could yield and talk for a few moments. Just before they turned, Edmund glimpsed once more at The Vagabond and the very jovial Captain Vekt. The Captain shot a quick wave as Edmund did the same before disappearing into the alley.

"Now, we have much to do and not much time to do it in," Ivindfor commented. "I've sent a messenger ahead to Morclyf and Ava. They should be ready when we arrive. I've told them to meet us near the Statue of Semmiah on the thirteenth bell. That should give us enough time. I think. They won't be glad I'm not stopping by, but we'll have ample time to chat once we leave Crescent Tier."

"What do we need to do while we're here?" Edmund questioned.

"Well, the first errand you and your father have is seeing your grandmother, mother, and aunt," Ivindfor smiled and shifted his hands onto his hips. "I've rented a room near Midway Court where Hazel's parents are meeting us. There, they can spend some uninterrupted time together. I have council with the new Priestess of Semmiah in the Temple. Waddle, I wonder if you would come with me. I think you might enjoy seeing the Temple, and Dannihlia may have a few words of wisdom for both of us." Waddle wanted to ask Ivindfor why he thought either of those things, but shrugged his shoulders in a half-hearted acceptance. "So, like I said," Ivindfor continued. "We'll gather together at the thirteenth bell. And enjoy yourselves – we're in a great city! Take in each little feature! Sometimes the most important aspects are those that seem the most different. Bryght, give my love to your family, tell Ravina I'm terribly sorry. See you both very soon!"

Ivindfor hurriedly entered the busy thoroughfare, grasping Hazel's hand and Waddle's shoulder as the others waved goodbye. For the first time, Edmund noticed the ugly expressions other people made as the three of them passed by. Not only were their expressions objectionable, the citizens made a noticeable effort to sidestep away from them. Although Hazel and Waddle did not seem affected, Edmund felt angry and helpless because of how other people treated his friends. As they blended out of sight within the crowds, his father spun him around by his shoulders and shook him a little out his thoughts.

"We're going this way," Bryght pointed beyond the narrow alley they were in. "Your grandmother's house is down a few blocks. I know you don't remember, but you've been here before." Edmund looked confused at his father as he continued. "You were two-and-a-half years old. We sailed over and stayed for a month. That way your grandmother and aunt could see you. *That* was a long month. Let me tell you. You see, your grandmother has never liked me much for moving your mom so far away. So, don't be surprised if she's a little short with me. But, maybe I deserve it."

Edmund grinned as his father winked at him. They walked briskly through the shadowed, calm alley. The two story houses were crammed together, while the street was so narrow the morning sun could not reach the ground. Edmund noticed that the once constant winds were gone and the stillness offered a dank, musty smell. The houses were haphazardly built with roughly cut sandstone rock that had been stacked as well as possible. The shuttered windows and roofs were made of grayed driftwood. The cobblestone street had worn unevenly from traffic and time. The quiet eeriness reminded Edmund of the forests from home, yet this place, the lowest of levels, made him feel unpleasantly stifled and depressed.

"This is it, number 45," Bryght announced as they stopped in front of a shabby looking, skinny two-story house that resembled almost all the others. "It's not much, but this is the house your mom grew up in. Well, go ahead knock on the door." Edmund timidly walked up to the door, and wrapped his knuckles against the weatherworn wood several times.

The door creaked open into the house and an older woman emerged from the darkness of the house. She scowled at Edmund, then shifted her squinted eyes to Bryght. After several moments, she realized who they were. Her scowl widened into a bright smile toward Edmund. "For Semmiah's Sake, you mustn't be Edmund! You're a young man now!" Her strong voice echoed down the street. Edmund nodded as she lunged, giving him an unexpected, hearty hug. "And I see you've dragged along some garbage with you," she said eyeing Bryght squarely.

"Pleasure to see you too, Ruda," Bryght offered.

"Come on in, Come on in," squawked Ruda as she motioned them inside. "Ravina's water broke this morning, and we've been busy helping her along. She's a week-and-more early! It's going slow, and it'll probably take us through the night. It's that Ivindorf's fault! Whenever he comes around, any woman who is close to having their baby suddenly goes into labor. Never liked that man! Never will! He's been trouble for this family ever since Rooth met you, Bryght. So, actually it's really your fault, Ha, ha!" Ruda slapped her hands against each other, then playfully tapped Bryght against his cheeks.

Bryght rolled his eyes and said, "His name is Ivind-FOR, not IvinDORF! He's helped us out more times than you can imagine."

"Well, whatever his name, I still don't like him and that's that!"

Bryght sighed in response as he took a seat, then wondered aloud, "By the way, is Drex still at sea?"

Ruda shuffled to his side and whispered throatily, "Don't mention his name! We haven't heard a word from him in three months. Rumor is that he's been captured or killed off the coast of Scythe. So, do something right and shut your yap about him. Got it?" Her scowl had returned as she pointed directly at Bryght's nose. He nodded, then she seemed to relax. Suddenly, behind a curtained doorway, Rooth glided into the sitting room and swooped Edmund into her arms.

"I thought I heard your voices!" she exclaimed, crushing Edmund with a long embrace. She stood up and gave Bryght a long kiss before squeezing him just as hard. "So good to see you. I've missed you two so much. Edmund you look thin. Has your father been feeding you?" Edmund smiled, overcome and awed at the refreshing sight of his mother.

"He ate enough even though the meals weren't nearly as good as yours," Bryght remarked as he leaned back in the chair, arms crossed. Edmund gazed at his mother as she stood with her arm around his father. They stared at each other, their eyes twinkling a little. Rooth tucked back some strands of her dark, yet graying hair behind her right ear. Edmund noticed how refreshed and revived her face appeared. Her dress, gait, and posture were different as well. Being with women instead of her boys had brought back a femininity in Rooth that Edmund had rarely, if ever, noticed before.

They settled in to conversations that lasted through the morning hours and into the early afternoon. Ruda and Rooth took turns watching over Ravina, but the chatter never paused. Stories unfolded about their travels and time spent apart. Edmund commented and answered occasionally, but mainly listened. He enjoyed the time with his grandmother, and the accounts she gave of his mother's side of the family.

While throughout the day, Drex's name was never mentioned again.

By the time the fourth bell had tolled, Ivindfor had escorted Hazel to her parents, exchanged pleasantries, and had climbed the steps to the Temple of Semmiah with Waddle. Their morning had been full of glares, rude comments, and even shoving matches as they pushed along to reach Midway Court. Waddle was completely exhausted and frustrated. Hazel, however, was unaffected. She was ecstatic to embrace and speak with her parents again. Waddle was aloof toward Harold and Joane, even though they showed sincere kindness. After meeting with Hazel's parents, Ivindfor convinced Waddle to continue with him, even though he knew Waddle was in a foul mood.

The Temple of Semmiah centered Crescent Tier, rising fifty feet from the Upper-Midlevel to the cliff's ridge. Ivindfor and Waddle squinted at the massive, square, stone structure. Waddle enjoyed that the exterior was designed more like a fortress than a religious icon. Scattered in the architecture, small rectangular slits for windows were chiseled. No decorations, symbols, or grandeur graced the exterior. This was not a place of celebration, but only lamentation, learning, and repentance. Semmiah was regarded as the savior from death to the Crescent Tieriens, and by living by her lessons and believing in her sacrifice could one's spirit live on.

As Ivindfor and Waddle approached the entrance, they were greeted by a pair of guards armed with long spears, while also wearing polished decorative armor. Ivindfor knew that these guards were for ceremony than for protection, yet from the expression on Waddle's face, the muscular guards gave the impression of security and seriousness. After verifying the meeting Ivindfor had arranged with Priestess Dannihlia, the guards reluctantly allowed them into the Temple. A 'Maiden of Semmiah' ushered them through a maze of dimly lit hallways and levels until finally reaching the Inner Atrium.

The Inner Atrium of the Temple was brilliantly illuminated with natural light, as dozens of mirrors reflected light throughout the structure. At the center, the Atrium rose at least forty feet. Near the ceiling, water cascaded and resonated from the natural cliff wall, spilling into a wide, shallow circular pool in the exact center of the floor. Exotic, colorful flowers filled the air with sweet fragrances, as song birds and doves flew freely through the air. Waddle eyed every detail as he awed at the images. The contrast between the stark exterior and the beauty within took even

Waddle's breath away. Ivindfor, however, marched purposefully while gazing at one thing: the illustrious, white robed woman, who sat delicately upon one of the several benches surrounding the pool of water.

The Maiden leaned toward Dannihlia whispering into her ear, then departed the Atrium in silence and without acknowledgment. The Priestess' white robes glowed against her deeply brown skin and black hair. The young woman motioned for the two men. Waddle nervously shuffled not sure whether he should bow, kneel, or how to act. So, he followed Ivindfor's movements as perfectly as he possibly could. They took their place across from the Priestess and Waddle witnessed that Dannihlia must have been fifteen years old, perfectly symmetrical, and unflawed. The Priestess of Semmiah embodied a positioned regality and royalty. Her full lips, nose, and wide brown eyes complimented the balanced cheekbones and exposed collar bones. All at once, he became considerably humiliated and ashamed of his own appearance. Ivindfor, however, was completely calm and casual, and not at the least affected by the adolescent woman viewing them.

"Welcome, Ivindfor and Kasper, to the house of your sister, our savior Semmiah," the Priestess sung. Waddle's mouth hung open in shock that Dannihlia knew his true name. "You have not visited the Temple for a long time Ivindfor, but Lazdrazil did mention that you have been very, very, busy."

Ivindfor gently tapped Waddle's chin, allowing him to close his gaping wide mouth. "Lazdrazil never liked this place, nor my sister," Ivindfor returned. "You're young. You don't understand our history. Dannihlia, please be wise and very cautious when dealing with Lazdrazil."

"She said something similar about you, and please do not say my name," she stated as she gazed at Waddle. "It is disrespectful for the lowly to know my name, especially one of your fledglings. By the look of his deformities, he should have been cast off a cliff long ago. I heard rumors you kept with poor company."

Waddle's adoration for the Priestess suddenly turned into agitation. Ivindfor quickly wrapped his arm around him and whispered, "Whatever you do, shut up and let me speak for you.

No matter what I say. This is not the place, nor the person to lose your temper on." Ivindfor shifted to Dannihlia and remarked, "I have always tried to respect the women who have led the people of Crescent Tier, regardless how far they lead them from the truth. I am here to speak with you as an ambassador, and as an ally. Please do not insult us."

After a deep breath and a moment of meditation, the Priestess continued the conversation, "You are correct, Ivindfor. This is an official visit and my casual candor was improper. You have taught me an important lesson today. Thank you. May we begin again?"

Ivindfor nodded and patiently waited for her to speak, which was always customary when in a formal meeting with the Priestess. "In your letters, you stated that the children of the Old Way are familiar with their individual powers, and you are allowing sanctuary and study at Havenshade. You noted they will play a pivotal role in the outcome of future events, yet you only entreat me with vague information. What do you want from Semmiah's house and the City of Crescent Tier, Ivindfor? Are we supposed to be afraid and prepare for war? Or, should we embrace you as a friend who will help us against some unknown enemy? My predecessor, Priestess Ingris, spoke a mainly of your 'greatness' and little of your purpose, yet there are rumors that give me great concern."

Ivindfor rubbed his hands together near his chest, while debating heavily on how specifically to respond. "I've aided and protected the people of this city before they even washed up on these shores. I am here to warn you now of the dangers coming to you and your people. Please listen with an open mind, and consider all of the things I speak of with some sense of rationality."

The Priestess gazed at him dispassionately, then responded, "I consider all threats serious, but we do not fear death. We live to desire death. We have our doctrines that ensure the purity of one's death. The only dangers we fear are those that flaw our purity into the afterlife. But you are know all this. What evil conspires against our beliefs, Ivindfor? What dangers us? The Scythians? The City of Pentasentinal? The Valds and Stouts? We have been a country at peace for decades upon decades! Please, I implore you to reveal the monster who threatens us!"

Ivindfor leaned toward her as he spoke, "You know of my brother, Beohlor. He helps keep watch over of the Fendow still held in Ginith Mire. He has reported that they have developed machines to cut through and even fly over the mountains Aelen rose so many years ago. When the Fendow escape Ginith Mire, they will wage war against every nation in this world. They will not take prisoners. They will not take wealth. They will take away every life, every belief. Scythe has his eyes upon the City of Crescent Tier also. King Horithyn is jealous of the cities wealth, and Lazdrazil will gladly side with him to see your downfall. If Scythe attacks, then they will take your people away as slaves. The King will turn this Temple into a brothel and this city will be left in ruins. The children who follow me will one day unite the nations as front against the evil that may destroy us all. Please, do not forsake the opportunity, especially when the time comes. Even though you do not agree, or even want to believe in them, please accept and ask for their help."

After Ivindfor finished, the Priestess gently stood from the bench and strode elegantly around the pool of water. She thought deeply about what Ivindfor spoke. Dannihlia was not rushed to react without being open and considerate, as Ivindfor had asked. At first, she felt anxious, but then her thoughts became defensive and contradictory. Still, she focused through her immature emotions and prayed for clarity. With her eyes closed as she knelt by the water, she listened to the splashing of falling water. Dannihlia dipped her hands into the water and let the substance trickle and drip off her fingers. As she lifted her arms over her head, the coolness ran down her arms, into her neck, and then down through her spine. In what appeared divine epiphany, Dannihlia rose and returned to her seat across from Ivindfor and Waddle.

Perfectly poised, the Priestess of Semmiah chantingly replied, "The Fendow are a forgotten myth. No one has seen one in ten lifetimes. Even if I admit they do exist as a threat, no one would believe me. The fact that you warn me of those people makes me question your intentions. Even more, I am appalled you believe

King Horithyn of Scythe would dare wage a war with us! Those ignorant heathens lack the ability to follow any kind of order, and they could hardly unify their clans to wage an attack. I do not see the justification of your warning. However, I am certain I should be cautious of *you*, Ivindfor. I have been told that you plan to overthrow each nation with your precious prodigies. Perhaps you are the deceiver I should be concerned with. The House of Semmiah has granted you its graces in the past, but now you must leave here as an unwelcome guest. You shall not be admitted into this house while I rule it, nor do I further ensure your safety, or those who serve you within Crescent Tier. Our alliance, for what it was, is over."

"I regret your decision, Priestess of Semmiah," Ivindfor spoke coldly and methodically. "And in time, I believe you shall regret it as well. Nevertheless, if there is any cause or need you may have, contact me - as Semmiah's House always has."

Ivindfor stood and lightly tugged at Waddle to follow. They both bowed their heads slightly and walked toward the entrance of the Temple. Bells chimed from somewhere high above. Children of varying ages entered silently and climbed flights of exposed stairs and hallways around the Inner Atrium. They were met by Maidens and drifted away into various rooms for their daily lessons. Waddle had not noticed that aspect before, but took one last glance at the scenery, which had altered him from when he was first amazed by it. Now, he felt the beauty of the Inner Atrium was a façade that hid the ugliness of its prejudices and discriminations. The people and the Priestess of Crescent Tier made Waddle feel ashamed of himself, as if he were not worthy of his life, because of his legs, because of his differences. All Kasper wanted was to return home.

Several more guards arrived and eyed them heavily as Ivindfor and Waddle emerged from the Temple. The cool sea breeze swirled with the warm sun as seagulls circled above the water, docks and ships in the distance. Waddle paused for a moment and gazed across the sea wishing to catch a glimpse of Essil. A guard commanded him to "Move along, or be thrown out!" Waddle quickly pivoted toward Ivindfor who was nearly thirty feet ahead. Waddle tried to catch up with him, but a mass of children entering the Temple surrounded him, making it awkward to maneuver. At times, he had difficulty-seeing Ivindfor ahead of him, yet he persisted on.

Ivindfor rushed forward, frustrated and upset at the outcome of his meeting with the Priestess. He stopped suddenly and remembered that he had forgotten Waddle. Ivindfor turned seeing the short, young man fighting the oncoming flow of children, like a fish attempting to swim upstream. He waited and watched Waddle weave in and out, sometimes bumping and stumbling through them. Ivindfor realized the mistake he had made by bringing Waddle to Crescent Tier. Ivindfor had hoped an outsider's point-of-view might give him good advice, but now Ivindfor understood Waddle's mind was clouded by Dannihlia's demeaning remarks.

As Waddle breathlessly reached him, Ivindfor grabbed his shoulders and said, "I apologize for bringing you here, Waddle. I didn't intend for this to happen. They believe differently about people who...."

"....are disfigured and 'impure'. Yeah, I understand perfectly, Iv'. I'm not suitable with the perfect picture they've created around here; the smudge on the canvas, so to speak. Don't worry, it takes more than stupidity to hurt my feelings," Waddle grimaced as he finished Ivindfor's sentence, and the two men set forth up the steep stairs to the top. Although Waddle joked about his experience at Crescent Tier, Ivindfor wondered if this irritation would someday manifest into a real fury, or if it would just be a whimsically forgotten dream. Ivindfor knew for certain that Waddle was changed somewhere deep within. How that would affect him, Ivindfor could not see.

Waddle questioned Ivindfor about Semmiah, Scythe, and the Fendow as they traversed toward the top of the city. Ivindfor pointed out the architectural differences between the wealthy and poorer tiers. The sorcerer tried to generalize the long histories that went along with each of Waddle's curiosities. Moreover, Ivindfor was reluctant to provide Waddle with too much information about how discriminatory and demanding Crescent Tier life was. So, Ivindfor tried to tell exciting and adventurous tales which would help relieve the tension of the day. As the thirteen bells finished tolling, they finally reached the Statue of Semmiah, and waiting for them were the others, just as Ivindfor had planned.

At the top level of Crescent Tier, all of the buildings' rooftops (including the Temple) met flush with the landscape. If someone were looking from a distance away, all they would perceive was the Statue of Semmiah and The Light, and sea water beyond. An unknown secret laid beneath the ground fifty yards from the Statue and city. In the event of an attack from the south or west, a three foot thick and fifteen foot tall stone and iron wall could be raised around the city within minutes. As the wall raised, a dry moat ten feet wide opened in front of the wall. The design had been manufactured by Beohlor, as a gift to the third Priestess. The wall was a well-guarded secret, which allowed for an element of surprise and defense.

The Statue of Semmiah stood thirty feet tall behind the Temple. The image was of Semmiah hung and nailed to a great oak tree, which portrayed how she was initially put to death by the Scythians. The story reported that Semmiah had been judged and sentenced to death by being hung, nailed to a tree, and burned alive. And so, the image of Semmiah being hung and nailed to the tree became the banner and inspiration for their faith. The Statue of Semmiah celebrated and reminded people of Semmiah's sacrifice for their wickedness. There was a beauty in the curvature of Semmiah's body along the natural curves of the tree, but also a scene of excruciating pain, torture, and victimization.

On the south side of the Statue, Hazel sat on the ground with her mother and father. Next to them, Bryght, Edmund, and Edmund's uncle Bleke also lounged. Ava stood alone further from the others, while north and right of the monument, Morclyf slouched near his father. His mother, Vessa, stomped back and forth nervously kicking up dust. When she caught a glimpse of Ivindfor, she marched over to him with stern glaring green eyes. "How dare you visit that aberration of a girl and castaways before us? Do you really think that they are so much better? I'm not sure I even want Morclyf go with you, especially if you cannot see a greatness when it's right in front of you!"

"So good to see you again, Vessa," Ivindfor smiled and said sarcastically. "I see you haven't lost your flare for being blunt."

"I'm not afraid of you, Ivindfor, and from now on Morclyf had better get treated the way he deserves." Vessa sneered pointing a finger straight into Ivindfor's face.

"I'm sure Morclyf will receive all he deserves," Ivindfor retorted.

Vessa turned still holding out her finger, yet now she directed it at Ketteric's sideways smirk, "Oh shut up and wipe that look off your face! You should be the one standing up for Morclyf, not me."

Waddle stared and shook his head at the raving woman as he walked over to Bryght and Edmund with Ivindfor. Bleke, Bryght's brother, stood nearby and prepared to introduce himself when Ivindfor interjected, "Waddle, this is Bleke, Bryght's brother and obviously Edmund's uncle. Bleke this is our *friend* Kasper, or better known as Waddle," Ivindfor stressed the word *friend*, as a warning not to stare or make a condescending remark. Over fifteen years had passed since he last saw Bleke, and Ivindfor was not sure whether his personality would make this trip worse for Waddle, or not.

Bleke was a tall, dark, and handsomely dressed man, yet his face was deeply scarred. He reached out his hand to shake Waddle's and said, "I am pleased to meet you Waddle. Bryght and Edmund speak very highly of you, and I'm grateful they have you as a friend." Waddle took his hand, a little taken aback, nodded silently, then without much to say, settled near Bryght and Edmund on the ground. Bleke looked at Ivindfor's curious expression and continued with a grin, "Time can change people, Ivindfor. In fact, I just recently arrived from studying with Jarred Jacobi at Qyn-Fyncial. He sends his regards, and wishes you would visit soon. I'm surprised you didn't notice the change in me. But, Jacobi did say you've had a lot on your mind."

Ivindfor's face dropped. When he had last seen Bleke, he was joining the Temple of Semmiah as a Steward, but now he stood in front of him as a Wizard of the Old Way. As they grasped hands, Ivindfor felt Bleke's energy pass between them. Their spirits and power connected to one another, and the two men embraced and understood the gifts each possessed.

"I would never have believed you, a wizard," Ivindfor began. "Seems you've done well. Although the journey has been rough, I see. I wish we had more time, together. I have so many questions."

"We have time, if you allow me to accompany you for a while. I would love to get to know Edmund better, and help in any way I can. I am yours for as long as you will have me."

"Excellent!" Ivindfor threw his hands in the air. "I need all the help I can get with this lot." He laughed and looked down at Bryght and Edmund. "Where's Rooth? I hope everything's alright."

Bryght answered back, "Ravina went into labor. Rooth said goodbye earlier, but really needed to stay and help. It's fine with me, the house was a little crowded anyway. And Ruda told me to tell you to 'get outta town'. She's blamed you for Ravina having her baby early."

"I asked you earlier to say that 'I was sorry'. It's not like I can turn my magic off, it just runs through my veins!" Ivindfor scoffed and snickered, as did Bryght and Edmund. Waddle frowned, feeling a little left out, and Edmund noticed that he appeared more sullen and distant than usual. Ivindfor left them for a moment and spoke to Hazel, Harald, and Joane. Joane's eyes filled with tears as Ivindfor wiped them away. He only spoke with them for a few moments before turning toward the lonely Ava. He motioned for her to join them, as well as Morclyf and his parents.

"Ava, where is your mother?" Ivindfor asked softly.

"She sends her regards, but felt it was more necessary to be at the Temple this evening." Ava politely replied. Her sad, almost frightened face reminded Ivindfor of Ava's mother, Therese. Ava's body, however, had developed into a vibrantly strong. Unlike most women of Crescent Tier who did not wear fitted clothes, paint their eyes, or wear jewelry, Ava wore pants that fit into knee high boots and a leather corset over a dark blue blouse. Even a small section of cleavage showed, which had caught the attention of the men earlier on. Ava dressed with empowerment, yet her eyes reflected sorrow. Ivindfor did not press the matter, nor did he make Ava feel any more uncomfortable than she already was.

Ivindfor gently handed Hazel, Morclyf and Ava a blank, worn, oversized card. As the children looked at them inquisitively, Ivindfor simply took several steps away. He tilted his head as the group awkwardly gazed back at him. Then, after a moment, Ivindfor smirked and began a little lecture:

"I have often wondered why we behave in the manners that we do. Throughout my life, I have met so many different people, from different upbringings, and different points-of-view. Most people have the ability to define what they deem good or bad; what is acceptable or inadequate. People can follow what is defined for them, or follow how they define themselves.

He continued: "One struggle we have is whether we become consumed by other's judgments of us. Whether we ignore other point-of-views that clash with our own. Whether we force others to obey our ideals. Or, whether we forgive and accept the criticisms, so that in our humility we may admit our own flaws and develop a better understanding of who we are. Our differences create our own individualities, yet we have to be careful how we discriminate those around us. Even though we have our own uniqueness, we also share base commonalities. Hopefully, in time, you will learn what the meaning of all this is and pursue justice with every movement you make.

"So, I gave out blank cards. These are not ordinary cards. As our journey begins, the cards will fill with an image, or images that reflect who you are. Hopefully, they will offer insight on the personality you display to those around you. They are uniquely yours and will not work for anyone else.

"To the parents, thank you for all of this. Without you, your children would not be who they are today. If for any reason they choose to return home, or if you choose to come to Havenshade, then they are free to go and you are welcome to stay. I have given you all papers laying out the roads and stops that we will be making before we reach Havenshade. Thank you so much for being my friends, and for being a part of something so much larger and so much more important than any of us.

"Lastly, please behave and be kind! We have a very long journey ahead of us. I'd rather not smack one, or all of you for making trouble. There! Enough said." Everyone queried at Ivindfor's sudden quirkiness, as he bellowed at himself. Then, he strolled passed them to the cart which was full of their belongings and cried out: "Well, come on! We're running late! Hug up, say goodbye, and let's HEAD OUT!"

Winds of Change

*Just when you're satisfied with who you are,
some one, or thing will come along your way,
changing all that you'll ever become.
From, the notes of Edmund*

    The sun waned against the western sky, as the two men and four children of the old way marched along the westward road known as 'Wayfarer's Way'. The grasses and crops of the surrounding fields lilted and weaved with the movements of the wind. Grasshoppers swirled, bounced around them, and scurried away as if they knew what they were. The clattering noise of the city slowly faded and was replaced by the low hum of swooshing grasses, chattering birdcalls, the low croaks of prairie frogs, while the chirps of serenading crickets welcomed the twilight. On their right lay the high Dorman Mountains, which sloped into the Silverleaf Hills and their first stop – The Wayfarer's Inn.

Earlier, Ivindfor and Bleke harnessed themselves around the rough leather straps attached to the wide, wooden cart, as the four children strolled on either side. Morclyf sarcastically questioned aloud why they did not have horses to pull the load. The others wondered internally why the two men did not simply use their powers to command the cart to move on its own. How could these men of authority subject themselves to such degeneracy? What they saw was the sorcerer and wizard as asses in front of a cart.

　　Once they were far enough away from Crescent Tier – far enough from the traffic of farmers, and other travelers; Ivindfor and Bleke released themselves from their burden. With sweaty lips, they whispered a few words to one another, and then Bleke nodded several times to Ivindfor. Edmund's uncle walked around the right side of the cart where Morclyf and Ava had been strolling, and Ivindfor stepped towards Hazel and Edmund.

　　Ivindfor wiped the sweat from his forehead on to his dusty shirt, drank long gulps of cool water from their barrel on the cart, and remarked, "We didn't want to bring anything along we didn't necessarily need." He panted a bit as Hazel's and Edmund's eyes watched intently. "So, until we could get far enough from the city, neither Bleke nor I felt comfortable 'changing' with the possibility of being seen," Ivindfor looked over his shoulder and the cart. "Transforming, as we can, tends to...*upset* people. You're welcome to watch, but the first time you see this happen may be – let's say - *unsettling*." Suddenly, from the opposite side of the cart, Morclyf and Ava rushed from around it panting, as panic set into their faces. Ivindfor opened his arms and offered, "Oh. I see Bleke didn't give you any warning. Come here! Don't worry, I'll try to explain...."

　　Edmund curiously peeked around the edge of the cart to see Bleke transforming before his eyes. His 'uncle' was no longer a man, but had shifted into some sort of animal. Bleke grunted as his body rapidly grew, thrust, and stretched outside of himself. The whole awful contortion took less than a minute, and when finished a full bred oxen stood in front of Edmund, huffing long, deep breaths of air. On the tip of his horn was a polished ring that Edmund had not observed before. The oxen, now Bleke, noticed

Edmund staring and politely nodded his head, snorted, then moseyed to his place in front of the wagon.

"You see. Bleke and I have learned to alter ourselves into other living creatures and then back again. Of course, we can't transform on just a whim. So, we generally use a string of hair, drop of blood, or some other piece of the creature we want to emulate," Ivindfor paused as the children caught his attention from Bleke. "In order to change back, it helps if we have something of ourselves. Bleke has his ring that he was wearing on the horn, so he can still be connected to his true form. Without it, if Bleke lasted long enough as an oxen, he could lose sense of who he really is. Then, he would become the oxen."

"But how can you become something with just a hair?" Morclyf breathed heavily, still wheezing and disgusted.

"The theory is complicated, and I'll explain it when the others have gathered at Havenshade. Right now, in short, we are all bound by all of the same materials. Bleke and I capable of taking the material of another living being, melding it with ourselves, and then we can shift it for our purpose...For a while."

"How long can Bleke stay like that?" Ava questioned timidly, not sure of the situation as safe.

"Well, that depends on the will of the wizard," Ivindfor replied. "The longer he stays in that form, the greater his spirit becomes the form. It's dangerous if we are not fully prepared of the consequences."

They walked over to Bleke, the oxen, and hitched their cart to the massive animal. Edmund reached out and stroked the animals' side, still trying to believe that this was truly his uncle. The course hair and skin heaved under his calloused hands.

"Can he understand us, and does he know who we are?" Edmund asked.

"Well, of course, he knows who we are!" Ivindfor smacked the backside of Bleke. "He can see, hear, and remember everything around him. His senses, however, are those the oxen and so his perspective will be different than our own. That's all."

Ivindfor and others began walking down the road, as sun had quickly caught up with the horizon. The sky above was darkening, while the brilliant oranges, yellows, and reds floated in the western sky.

"I watched over all of you in different forms through the years," Ivindfor commented, as the children looked at him. "Oh yes! I've been watching over you since the day you were all born. Whether as a seagull, or cricket, or cat, or whatever...I always took time to see how you were all doing. In fact, I remember being in a jar for almost a week before a flea came by and I was finally able to change into it. It was very difficult to turn into something else when not in your true form."

"I had a cricket for a week, once," Morclyf interjected. His pale, triangular head twisted and eyes shifted adding: "But it disappeared. Was that you? I thought my mom, or a servant threw you out. And to think, I was going to feed you to the crows."

"That's the danger of trying to be something you're not," Ivindfor swiftly responded. "Always follow the way you are, unless you're prepared for the long term consequences." Ivindfor retorted. "By the way, Morclyf, tell the others about your uniquely feathered cloak you're wearing."

A sudden upward chill from the soil replaced the warmth of the setting sun as Morclyf strutted along with a cloak completely created from black, iridescent feathers. As Ivindfor watched and walked ahead guiding Bleke, Morclyf proudly detailed the origins of the strange looking garment to the others:

"Well, there had always been these pesky ravens that would fly and tap at the windows. They made a racket all the time and left a horrible mess, if you know what I mean. So, one day I made a tall, clay bowl, like a vase really, and filled it with seeds. I opened a window, left the bowl on the ledge, and waited for the stupid things to fly in. One by one, they would land and stick their heads in the bowl. It took practice. But if I timed it just right, I learned to move the clay quick and strong enough to crush their heads as they went for a seed, without breaking the vase! And, as a prize, I took the feathers and made this."

Hazel, Ava, and Edmund's eyes were gaping wide with horror at the thought of Morclyf crushing the skulls of the poor birds, even Bleke snorted through his large oxen nose. Morclyf, however, smiled proudly as he trotted and paraded the cloak fashionably. For him, the pride came from the ability to deceive and conquer, while he improved his power. Rock, earth, and minerals always called to him, and he always understood their deep, dark, and rough meanings. Morclyf valued the density, weight, and longevity the earth revealed to him. The cold, unwillingness for change intrigued and inspired Morclyf.

"Well, if we're in the mood for roasted raven to eat, you'll come in handy, Morclyf," Ivindfor mocked, hoping to lighten the mood. The others grimaced, as Morclyf sneered at the joke; he was lost prancing about in his own world.

"By the way," Ivindfor continued. "Now that it's darker, you can see the faint firelight glow from Stouttown to the south. The light from the northern glacier is from the Dorman guard tower of Divis Krolvim. Both nations are allies of Crescent Tier, and some of the people believe in Semmiah. But I fear, there may be trouble between them. Tonight, however, we have each other."

After several hours, Ivindfor asked Hazel to walk along with Bleke. In a whisper, he persuaded her to lift the burden of Bleke's own weight and the cart with a simple gesture of air. Morclyf, Ava, and Edmund had gotten weary of walking and had hopped onto the tailgate of the cart. Ivindfor slipped backward, keeping the children company, while watching Morclyf pulverize small pieces of gravel to dust in his open hand.

"You have a knack for ravaging things. Don't you Morclyf?" Ivindfor snidely pointed out. Morclyf never quite caught on that Ivindfor generally made fun of him, and yet they were both proud of his abilities.

"How are you, Ava?" Ivindfor asked. "You've been so quiet, I thought we lost you at some point."

Ava's sad, round face lifted briefly - startled by the attention toward her. She generally appeared bothered if people noticed her, always aloof, and remained in the background. She was as tall, if not a little taller, than Bleke, but managed to keep herself distant, almost camouflaged. She had a skill for altering the humidity touching her to the colors that surrounded her. Sometimes, without even trying, she would appear to vanish completely. As Ivindfor looked at her, she blended heavily into the background and shadowy shapes of the cart, like a chameleon trying to hide from a predator.

"Why don't you tell the boys a little about yourself," Ivindfor prodded. "You are an interesting person, even if you don't believe it yourself."

Edmund and Morclyf shifted their eyes toward the odd appearance of Ava, then at each other and shrugged. By now, they were both getting used to the odd things popping up out of nowhere. Ava shivered and shook of the disguise which clung to the night air. She then directed her sultry voice out to Ivindfor, more than the seemingly uninterested boys.

"Well, I'm partly Vald and partly Median," she awkwardly started as if representing herself. "I live with my mother Therese, and older half-sister Camilla. My mother was married to wealthy Shipholder, named Durik and together they had Camilla. Durik died while on a trading mission to the Arch Isle, near Scythe. Our family has always been deeply religious and deeply involved with the Temple. Even after I came along."

"I heard you were a surprise to your family," Morclyf smirked and nudged Edmund sneeringly.

Although embarrassed and hurt, Ava stutteringly continued on, "My mother, a Half-Vald herself, had an affair with another lower class Vald after Durik had passed, and in her 'weakness' she conceived me. The prior Priestess before Dannihlia devised a plan with Ivindfor to incorporate the whole incident, while not ruining the reputation of Durik's family and Camilla with the Temple. So, I was born as a sorceress of water, but announced to others as an adopted child found and brought in from the wild. My mother became an example of charity, my half-sister became even more popular for having to endure me. I became an example."

"Do you know who your father is?" Edmund questioned, insensitively.

"Her mother never disclosed that information to her Edmund," Ivindfor stated for Ava. "And her father has never been told he had a daughter." Ava's face was amazed that Ivindfor knew information she was never privy to.

"Let me know, I've been wondering for years," Ava strongly stated, as she readied herself for the answer. She was energized with the anticipation of finally knowing the rest of her story. She bit her lips nervously as she waited for his reply.

Ivindfor tilted his head, shoulders slumped, and his eyes lifted toward the Vald sorceress. "Now isn't the time, Ava. I'm sorry."

"Why not?" she shot back.

"All you need to know is who you are...and *what* you are. I have a feeling you have gifts even I couldn't give you..." Ivindfor's lips curled into a smile, as his eyes twinkled with insight.

Ava actually grinned and leapt off the cart embracing Ivindfor. He, in turn, wrapped his arms around the small of her back. The two boys watched as they kept moving further away in the cart.

"Think they'll catch up, or should we stop," Morclyf pondered.

"Hey, Hazel. Stop!" Edmund yelled and jumped from the cart. He ran up to where Hazel stood, puzzled.

"What's going on back there?" Hazel queried, as she leaned seeing Ivindfor and Ava in an embrace.

Edmund shot over his shoulder then responded, "They're having a moment, I guess."

"More than a moment," Hazel mumbled to herself.

"What?" Edmund asked.

"Nothing..." Hazel's eyes squinted as her lips pursed. Ivindfor lifted his eyes and felt Hazel's jealousy against the tip of hairs on his fingers. Ivindfor knew that Hazel could snatch Ava out of his hands with a mere flick of her wrist, yet grasped Ava closer in defiance.

After several minutes, Ivindfor and Ava rejoined the others. Ava wiped off her remaining tears, and settled in closely to Morclyf. He squirmed a little from the invasion of his personal space, but refused to make a fuss about it. Ivindfor took the reins from Hazel and commented that, "She'll be alright". Hazel rolled her eyes and moved aside, without a word. Ivindfor saw Edmund scratching words in the lamplight a little ways off and yelled a strong, "Come on, Edmund! Let's get going". Edmund furiously finished scribbling and Hazel reluctantly started for rear of the cart.

In mid-stride, Hazel froze completely still, then turned toward Ivindfor as if possessed. "The winds have changed," she whispered eerily. Ivindfor turned to the westward sky, noticing what Hazel heard. Ava darted to Hazel's side and exclaimed, "Aelen is in the rain..."

Very nearby and rolling quickly, ominous clouds gathered and swallowed stars in the dark night sky. Ivindfor cursed himself for not noticing. He leaned over, whispered into Bleke's ear, and Bleke stomped his feet anxiously. The wind began to blow more forcefully and erratically from both the south and west.

"Now what's going on?" Morclyf said as he joined the girls.

Hazel yelled out, "I hear Lazdrazil!"

"and Aelen!" Ava finished.

"It's Lazdrazil and my father," Ivindfor shouted over the wind. "They're having one of their arguments, and I don't think we want to be out here in the middle of it!" He turned back and spoke to Bleke again. Flashes of light began to fill the air above, and thunder rolled over the Silverleaf Hills. Heavy raindrops began to spit sporadically around them. Then, as Ivindfor turned to the children, he noticed Edmund aside, writing by himself.

Edmund huddled cross-legged on the ground against the wind and thudding, sporadic drops of rain. A few wet drops spat on his page, smearing the words and creating watermark. Edmund scratched into the paper even as he felt the wave of the world come within him.

The purple flash of lightning erupted above him, through him, and below him into the soils. All at once, Edmund's breath was taken away and brought back again by the spirit of the world. In a moment, Edmund died and the world created what Ivindfor feared to make. From flash, flame, wind, rain, and grounded earth the world made Edmund a sorcerer of Fire.

After regaining himself, Ivindfor crawled along the soggy ground and clutched Edmund's body. His wet hands steamed from the heat emanating off of Edmund. Ivindfor frantically tore pieces of his clothes and wrapped them around his hands. He scooped Edmund's heavy and limp body over toward the cart. Lightning and thunder continually flashed above them, yet Ivindfor focused entirely on the boy in his arms.

Still staring at Edmund's steaming, burned body, Ivindfor frustratingly ordered:

"Morclyf, grab Edmund's things out there -
You're coming with me!
Hazel, Ava, stay with Bleke.
He'll take you to the Wayfarer's Inn!
We'll be there waiting for you.
I can't take you all.
Stay covered in the wagon, and don't get out!
Bleke knows the way!
I know you're scared, but trust me.
It's not far. I'll see both you very soon!"

Ivindfor gently set Edmund down on the saturated ground, as the raindrops hissed from each heated drip on him. Hazel took her rain soaked cloak and laid it over Edmund and his heat forced steam to flume upward. Ava fearfully faded into the raindrops and also the waters Edmund rested. Hazel panicked against the forces she could not control. She backed away sodden, shaken, and afraid.

Morclyf scurried on his heels, crashing into the side of the cart. Ivindfor rushed to his side saying:

"Once I turn, climb onto my back and hold on tight with your thighs. You need to hold on to Edmund. Take these rocks and shift them over your hands so Edmund doesn't burn you. Hurry! We don't have much time!" Ivindfor took a long, white hair from the bracelet he wore around his wrist and shoved it into his mouth. Within a few moments, Ivindfor painfully transformed into a gigantic albino stallion. Morclyf paused holding the rocks in his hands unsure of whether to obey the order Ivindfor had given him.

"Do it, Morclyf!" Hazel screamed as tears streamed down her face.

"I'm not sure I can," Morclyf said, shaking his head.

"Do it, or Edmund will die!" Hazel begged. "Please, Morclyf!"

Then, from out of the shadows Ava reappeared and grabbed Morclyf by his shoulders crying out over the wind and rain, "FOR ONCE IN YOUR SORRY, SELFISH LIFE - DO SOMETHING FOR SOMEONE ELSE'S SAKE!"

Morclyf's black eyes narrowed as he tore away from Ava's grip.

"FINE!"

He cried out and throttled the stones from his hands straight into the air. He watched them spiral and return as lightning flashed from above. Morclyf stretched out his hands, and as the rocks touched his fingertips they molded perfectly around his hands, like gloves. He snarled at the stiff discomfort, turned toward Ivindfor, gritted his teeth, and then lifted the earth near the white horse in the shape of a stairs.

The white steed stood perfectly still as Morclyf with seemingly inhuman strength grabbed Edmund's scalding body, marched up the slippery steps, and tossed him onto Ivindfor's back. With a heaving jerk, Morclyf pulled himself behind Edmund.

Tears of pain and frustration filled Morclyf's eyes as he pointed with a shaking, stone finger to Ava and Hazel, as they scurried under the canvas of the cart. As the girls looked upward, they heard Morclyf scream:

"Keep each other safe! No matter what, bring yourselves back to me!"

In a flash, Ivindfor raced out into the tormented night towards The Wayfarer's Inn. Hazel and Ava peered through the rain as they vanished away into the night. Bleke's oxen nose snorted and began pulling the wagon through the muddy ground. As Ava and Hazel scurried and secured the canvas around them, two silken raven feathers from Morclyf's cloak haphazardly blew in and settled haphazardly onto one another's hand.

The Weary Wayfarers

You've all been forced into this life.
Your own survival relies on whether
to accept, change, or kill another.
From, *The Lectures of Ivindfor at Havenshade.*

    With bloodied hooves, Ivindfor reached the Wayfarer's Inn within an hour after Edmund had been struck by lightning. The rain that had beaten down on them had finally softened to foggy drizzle. Several times, Ivindfor believed they would pass by the Inn, or lose their direction entirely. His senses, however, proved accurate enough to guide them to dimly lit haven on the edge of the quieted Silverleaf Hills.
    The Wayfarer's Inn was the endpoint destination for the few people who traveled the road between Kehl's Crossing and Crescent Tier. The Wayfarer's Inn was owned by Khan 'Breaver' Korgennson, his wife Karell, their daughter's Knelli, Katrin, and their son Kalevel. Their family lived, slept, and worked the Inn like

a farm. No one had a holiday, or day off. Each family member found their niche, while Karell managed each person's responsibilities, like clockwork. For her, time was measured not by hours but by visitors. Each visitor required an allotted amount of time, no matter how rich, or how poor. Their service was a product, and everyone who entered through the front door of The Wayfarer's Inn received the same treatment and billed the same rate. The Wayfarer's Inn was known for its equity, relaxed atmosphere, but adhered to respect for all those who entered their massively reinforced wooden front doors (high enough for the tallest of Valds, with a smaller door fitted for the smallest of Stouts!).

This night, however, Ivindfor was not going through those legendary front doors.

Exhausted and cold, Morclyf limply slid off the white stallion's back, thudding into the wet mud. Edmund trembled uncontrollably and then fell alongside Morclyf, moaning. Ivindfor steamed from the heat within him, as well as, from the burns across his backside. In the dim light of the Inn, Morclyf caught a glimmer of a beautiful necklace braided within Ivindfor's mane. Within moments, he became ill as witnessed Ivindfor's body mutate to his natural form. Ivindfor heaved and panted, while blood trickled from his hands and feet into the thick, wet mud.

Morclyf viewed his own hands, seeing the stone gloves charred black from holding on to Edmund. 'How can he still be alive?' he wondered internally, and grimaced at the heap of ragged, burned cloaks heaped on the ground. He concentrated back on his hands and clapped them together. The black stone cracked like ice and crumbled to dust on the ground. The raven cloaked young man stretched and clenched his aching fists as he crawled toward Ivindfor.

"Let me help you," Morclyf offered and reached around Ivindfor, raising him up.

Ivindfor screamed with agony, pushed Morclyf away, and staggered forcefully against the wall of the Inn. Morclyf saw Ivindfor bash his head against the wall, over and over, as if a madman. After what seemed days, a small door slid open at eye level, and a pair of eyes peered out of the light.

"Who's there?" A woman's voice whispered out.

Ivindfor lifted his face into the window and responded, "Karell, there's been an accident, we need the room."

"Ivindfor! What's happened to you?" The woman quickly uttered.

"Just please, let us in. There are two boys with me." Ivindfor stuttered and spit blood on the ground. The woman tried to gaze out around Ivindfor to see them, unbolted the secret door and Ivindfor crashed down at her feet. He spurted through bloody lips, "The boys' names are Morclyf and Edmund. Wear gloves to carry Edmund inside – he's the one on the ground...in a heap...burnt." Ivindfor's eyes fluttered and closed.

"Breaver! Kalevel! Get out here! Now!" A large, bearded, bald man, and a young, full blond-headed boy emerged into the pantry where Ivindfor laid. "Pull him out of the way, there's a couple more outside." Karell commanded as she stepped over the unconscious man and inspected the scene near their stables. Morclyf sat in the spot Ivindfor had shoved him down. He wheezed, as the wind had been knocked out of him. Edmund moaned in the heap of trembling rags.

Karell rushed to Morclyf and asked, "Are you Edmund?"

"N-no, I'm Morclyf," he mumbled back, then pointed and redirected her to Edmund.

"Up you go, boy." Karell guided Morclyf through the pantry, the kitchen, the back storeroom, and then through a small door. Everything swirled in Morclyf's mind, as two other people swished by in a blur. Morclyf heard something about gloves, As Morclyf was gently laid down, he saw Edmund also set unresponsively on a dirt floor. As Karell situated Morclyf, she opened a small stove to start a fire. "No fires. No fires at ALL!" Ivindfor sputtered from the pantry. Karell peered through the small door, but did not question him. She shut the stove and tended Morclyf again. Knelli brought a half-dozen blankets and piled them near Morclyf. "Three more are coming soon. Right behind us. Two girls and a man," gasped Ivindfor and collapsed in the tiny, secret alcove.

Quickly, Karell assembled the family and given instructions for each to follow. Katrin ran outside and collected several pale-blue glowing solar-mushrooms for light. Ivindfor demanded no fires lit within the room. Knelli gathered clean water, bandages, and a basket of bread and fruit. Kalevel mopped away the mud and blood that had been tracked into the kitchen through the pantry. Breaver went back to the bar, casually restoring the semblance of normalcy. Karell gathered and mixed herbs, potions, and salves she had hidden in the storage room that would help heal Ivindfor, Morclyf, and Edmund.

Once her children were finished with their duties, she directed them to concentrate on the responsibilities of 'Inn' work. Karell made several trips in and out of the secret room that was once a bear cave in the hillside that butted to the back of The Wayfarer's Inn. Water dripped occasionally from the recent rain, and the floor was musty and stiflingly damp. She wanted to move them to a drier, healthier room but she knew that would cause more trouble for her and Ivindfor than it was worth. Lastly, she took a deep breath and prepared herself for the labor of healing the wounded 'boys'.

She stood straight in the low room. Karell always felt taller in the small cave. Her chest heaved from the prior work, as sweat glistened on her round cheeks and smooth neck. Her curly blond hair was pulled back and wrapped in red handkerchief. Karell's blue eyes glowed from the faint light of the solar-mushrooms scattered around the floor and in small alcoves where candles once sat. She took one last moment, her hands trembling against each other, before attending to the wounded. She noticed Ivindfor sat next to Edmund and Morclyf stood by his side. The glowing solar-mushrooms created enough light to identify their features. Karell quietly stepped along the floor and placed the blankets on floor next to Ivindfor and Morclyf. "What are you two doing up?" she whispered. "I'll tend to him. You need to rest. Both of you, now."

"Morclyf and I are fine, Karell. Thank you, though," Ivindfor replied and raised his healed hands as if nothing had just occurred at all. "Morclyf's thighs are little burned but he'll put some salve on after he gets changed out of those wet clothes."

"I'm feeling much better, actually," Morclyf bowed his head in perfect politeness and courtesy. Then, he gazed back down and stated, "Edmund's the one we need to worry about."

Ivindfor stood and revealed the burned form of the boy to Karell. The smell of his flesh began to fill the room and she gasped at the sight of him wheezing and trembling. She wanted to ask a hundred questions about how the accident happened, but instead she straightened up, gathered her remedies, and began her work.

"I'm going to wait in the pantry for the others," Ivindfor said as he walked to the door. "Karell, may Morclyf borrow a set of clothes from Kalevel?"

"Of course. But the boy needs his rest," she confronted him.

"Morclyf still has work to do. We all do, if we're going to save Edmund's life." Ivindfor hurriedly disappeared for several minutes. Then, he stepped into the doorway, threw some clothes at Morclyf and told him to "meet me in the pantry when you're done."

Morclyf walked gingerly through the kitchen and into the pantry as Ivindfor told him. "I know I've been crass and stern, but I'm proud of you for what you did tonight. You have no idea how grateful I am that you are here," Ivindfor softly spoke to Morclyf. "Now, what am going to ask is even harder than what we just went through, but trust me." Morclyf's eyes widened with suspicion, as Ivindfor continued. "Please go outside and bring in a dozen or so rocks about the size of your fists. Quietly take them into the back room. Hopefully by the time you're done, Bleke and girls will be here. We'll need their help as well."

Morclyf looked up at Ivindfor and asked, "Is Edmund going to die?"

Ivindfor hesitated, then replied, "When Edmund was struck by the lightning, the world made him a sorcerer of fire, just like you're primarily a sorcerer of the earth. I could feel the spirit in him, as you may have. How else he is changed – time will only tell. I don't think the transformation will be easy for Edmund. But, we need to help him heal as quickly and as well as we can. I should have seen this coming. I failed him and possibly all of us."

"We're all in it together, now," Morclyf sympathized. "My father always says, 'Don't bother worrying about what you can't change, only worry about dealing with what you have'. I never quite understood what he meant by that, but I guess I'm starting to learn. I suppose that's the way with most things. You really don't know what something means until it crosses your path."

Ivindfor shook his head and snickered a little, "Morclyf, I never would have considered you the philosopher. Perhaps there's hope for us all. In the meantime, there's work for us to do."

Morclyf slid through the secret pantry door and searched for the rocks in the darkness. Ivindfor watched through the peep hole, waiting for Bleke to arrive. His mind raced with thoughts of what had occurred earlier that night, and Ivindfor's his head pounded with ideas of what to do next. He wondered what Edmund would become, and if his powers could be controlled. When Ivindfor began to make the children, he did not implement the world's request to children of fire. Fire was too unpredictable and savage. Ivindfor feared children with that spirit would never learn to restrain that power of their union with it. Now, the world forced Ivindfor to try.

After a half-an-hour, Morclyf finished his assignment. Ivindfor sent him back into the room with Edmund and Karell. Soon after, a tired and jostled ox dragged up to the door. Ivindfor leaped out and helped Bleke out of the harness. Before Ivindfor was finished, Bleke had already transformed back into his true form. Ivindfor snagged the ladle from the water barrel several times and Bleke gurgled the liquid sloppily each time. Ava and Hazel sleepily slipped out of the cart, each girl stood wearily, clinging on to each other and a shiny black feather.

"Is every one alright?" Hazel questioned.

"As well as can be," Ivindfor replied and motioned with his finger to his lips for them to be quieter.

Ivindfor situated the cart next to the nearby stable wall, and then helped Bleke to his feet. He propped Bleke against the wall while he opened the door, met by Katrin.

"Sir, my mother told me to escort the girls into the room and suggested you and your friend enter through the main door. Perhaps then, the patrons won't suspect anything unusual. My father will see to your needs at the bar, and I have prepared the guest room with the bell, if the children need you. Mother says to get rest. You know well enough not to argue with her." The strawberry blond young woman flashed a smirk and wink.

"Wait! Tell Morclyf to come here. Please," Ivindfor pleaded. Within a moment, Morclyf appeared before him in the doorway. Both Ava and Hazel gave him a smile, but he did not return the favor. Ivindfor put his hand on Morclyf's shoulder, staring straight into his black eyes. "Now, Morclyf, this is very important. I have one last request. Put the rocks you collected close and around Edmund's body. Watch over him with the girls. If you need anything, there's a string that will ring a bell for me. I won't be with you tonight. You all need to just focus on Edmund and speak to him. Even if you fall asleep, your spirits will stay connected with him through your dreams," Ivindfor paused for moment as he shifted glances between the girls and the boy, then with a deep sigh he squeezed Morclyf's shoulder and whispered throatily: "Those rocks you'll put down...If Edmund wakes up and tries to hurt you, or the girls – *Crush him!*"

The last part echoed in Morclyf's mind and he shuddered. All Morclyf could do was blink. That was enough for Ivindfor to know the boy understood. Bleke sorely stumbled along with Ivindfor as they disappeared around to the main entrance of The Wayfarer's Inn. Katrin guided the children to the small, secret room. Morclyf waited in the storage room for a few moments while Ava and Hazel changed. His stomach ached from the idea of killing Edmund. Birds were one thing, but a person was on a completely different level. Morclyf paced and debated with himself whether he would follow Ivindfor's order, if the situation arose. Then, Katrin motioned for Morclyf into the room, and he grudgingly entered afraid of the burden he carried with him.

The young women sat wrapped in blankets on a bench far across from Edmund. They both appeared to be in shock at the sight of the poor boy. Karell and Katrin finished applying the ointments, salves, and bandages left the room without a sound. Morclyf stood alone near the doorway, looking at the pile of rocks on the floor. With deep sigh, he stepped firmly toward them and placed each one evenly and gently next to Edmund's body.

"Morclyf, what are you doing?" asked Hazel, in a low but forceful whisper.

Morclyf peered over his shoulder as he laid the last rock and replied, "Ivindfor told me to surround Edmund with these stupid stones. I'm doing it because *I* decided, not because I was told. And if Edmund wakes up and tries to hurt us, then I'll do what needs to be done. I won't let him hurt you," Morclyf looked intently at Hazel and realized Ava sitting next to her and quickly added, "Or any of us."

"What gives you the right to know if he's dangerous," Ava added. "We're all tired, scared, and now we're supposed to be in charge of him? I don't know what's going on anymore. I'm not sure Ivindfor knows either."

"Well, Edmund's changed, like one of us," Morclyf replied as he sat on the floor near Edmund's head. "He's been fused with the spirits of fire. The way Ivindfor acted, seems like Edmund will live, but that he'll be a danger to us," after a brief pause Morclyf continued. "What I don't understand is why Ivindfor doesn't heal Edmund, himself. You two should have seen the mess he and I were in when we got here. Covered in blood and his back was burned so bad he screamed when I tried to help him up. Then, after only laying down a few minutes right where you two are, he stood up perfectly fine – as if nothing happened to him at all. There's something not right about Ivindfor. I don't trust him. I know my mother doesn't."

"Well, your mother is a nutcase! Ivindfor's has a lot more power than we do," Hazel furiously defended. "Who knows what Ivindfor can do, but I'm sure that he has his reasons for leaving us with Edmund. He's worried. Ivindfor never meant for any of this to happen. He most likely doesn't want to interfere with something he's not sure of and probably blames himself."

"Interfere? He's interfered with our whole lives! I think he's scared out of his wits," Morclyf sneered. "Why isn't Ivindfor here now? If Edmund's so dangerous, why did he leave him with the bunch of us? I know, that way *he* can stay safe, away from the harm, and see if Edmund burns us all to bits."

"Ivindfor would never do that!" Hazel clenched her hands and shuffled her feet. The stagnant air in the tiny cave tried to move with her emotions, but she could only make it radiate just off her skin. "Ivindfor has only had the best intentions for us. Sure, he may be a little *off,* at times, but I trust him. Our parents trust him. And I swear, Morclyf, if you say another horrible thing, I'll, I'll..."

"What? Make my hair gently blow in the breeze!" Morclyf mocked.

Hazel stomped in front of him, reached her right hand close to his throat and snarled. "No, Morclyf. I'll take away your squeaky, annoying, little voice." Suddenly, all the moisture and air left Morclyf's mouth. For as hard as he tried, he could only filter enough air through his throat to keep from fainting. Then, from across the room, Ava knelt down from the bench, swayed her long arms forward, then to her chest. As she performed the spell, what air was in the room swirled and twisted Hazel around until she landed hard on the bench.

"That's enough!" Ava cried as she pointed at both of them. "I've had it with both of you. We're supposed to be here for Edmund. We're supposed to be here for each other. I don't care how rational or irrational Ivindfor might seem. All I know is that we are stuck with who we are, and where we are! So is Edmund. Don't you see? Ivindfor is probably trying to test us, wondering if we can even work together! So, quit fighting about who knows more about something that none of us knows anything about!"

Hazel and Morclyf stared amazed at Ava's raving remarks. She had spoken so fast and in such an inclined pitch that neither of them knew how to respond. Once Ava settled down, agitated but controlled, they slyly shifted their eyes at each other and giggled a little.

"I suppose we're all a little crazy," Hazel remarked.

"Speak for yourself, blue-bonnet. But, sometimes, I feel like there's someone else inside. You know?" Morclyf admitted after the tease.

"Exactly. Like having another voice and body acting out things out for you," Ava agreed.

"If you ask me, there's enough voices in here to wake the dead," Edmund wheezed without opening his eyes, or moving.

The other children froze and glanced horrifically at one another, then they slowly turned their eyes on Edmund. Morclyf inched his fingers towards a couple of the stones, ready to strike

Edmund down, then bolted back alarmed by Edmund's sudden coughing fit:
"For Semmiah's Sake! Ring the stupid bell!"

The Standard Is Set

> In the dark, a frayed flag flapped
> Against the stain, smoke, and stench
> Of the wounded, of the dead,
> And of the spirits rising.
> From, *The Seeds of the Fallen*

"Wait!" Edmund gurgled. "Don't call for anyone. I-I won't hurt you. I-I'm too weak. I can barely breathe. I just need some water, please."

Hazel cautiously glided toward Edmund and tilted her head at the bandaged boy. Edmund was wrapped so tightly he appeared mummified before them. She lifted a pitcher of water from the floor, and poured a small amount into a clay cup. Ava and Morclyf shook their heads and mouthed the words "no". She ignored the shaking of their heads, and held the cup just above Edmund's lips. She noticed her hand shaking terribly. With a little rise from her left hand, the water crawled out of the cup, down the curved side, and dripped onto to Edmund's lips. Edmund flinched at the cool liquid that moistened his mouth, and he felt the water run through his throat and into his abdomen. Hazel desperately tried to stay still until the water emptied from the cup.

"Thank you," Edmund sputtered. From his mouth, steam rolled out as if the water had put out a small fire within him. Hazel peered at the others and slowly backed away.

"I-I can't see anything," Edmund spoke stronger.

"There are bandages on your eyes, Edmund," Hazel replied. Ava moved closer to Hazel, while Morclyf remained focused on the rocks around Edmund.

"Am I hurt badly? I don't remember. I hear someone else. Who's there?" Edmund mumbled.

"Get Ivindfor," Morclyf muttered through his teeth.

"Let me take the patches off your eyes for a bit," Ava ignored Morclyf and felt miserable for Edmund as he struggled to understand what had happened to him. She reached from a distance and slowly peeled away the two patches that covered his eyes. Both eyes were swollen, black and blue. Ava stepped away and allowed Edmund a moment to himself. They witnessed him trying to lift his eyelids several times. Finally, they fell back exposing a milky whiteness that washed out any eye color Edmund once had. The three other children gasped and Edmund let out a small moan of his own.

"I still can't see, but in a way, I *can* see," Edmund tilted his head slowly and painfully as he gazed straight at Hazel, Ava, and then Morclyf. "I don't see your bodies but somehow I can see *you*. I can see two different colors swirling together. You're each different. But the same. I don't understand..." Then, Edmund fell unconscious, and the children turned to one another in disbelief.

Morclyf walked over to the string hanging by the door and gave it several hard jerks. "I was going to do this earlier, but I was too busy focusing on those stupid rocks! Thanks a lot! I almost wet my pants because of you two! So, excuse me, I am going to the toilet!"

At the moment Morclyf was leaving the room, Bleke forced the door and they bumped forcefully into one another. Morclyf shuffled around Bleke and pointed to the girls and said, "Go talk to them, I've got to go!" Then, he awkwardly stammered off, obviously trying to hold his bladder.

"What's wrong? Did Edmund wake up?" Bleke questioned quickly, as he still trembled wearily.

"For a moment," Hazel replied. "Edmund said he couldn't see."

"So, I took off the bandages on his eyes," admitted Ava sheepishly. "He said he could only see our spirits."

At the sound of his uncle's voice, Edmund cracked his eyes just barely enough to see the smoky shape of a wolf swirling within the other of Bleke's spirits. Bleke gazed heavily at Edmund. "Put the bandages back on so the swelling goes down. I'll let Ivindfor know later; he's entertaining the other guests with stories and keeping our disguise alive, you might say."

Morclyf wandered back into the room and flung his arms in the air, "You know what Ivindfor's doing out there?" he bluntly commented. "I saw him through the kitchen window drinking and singing with some bard with a horribly tuned mandolin! What kind of idiot did our parents get involved with anyway?"

"One of the best men you'll ever meet," Bleke sternly retorted. "And you'd be wise to learn some respect. That man is keeping us all safe from what would other-wise be a drunken, spooked mob."

Morclyf was taken aback at Bleke's powerful response and quickly took a seat on the floor. Ava jumped at Bleke's demeanor and gently replaced the patches on Edmund's eyes. Then, in a completely calm tone Bleke announced, "You all need to get some sleep. I'll stay here and watch over Edmund. We'll take shifts. Ava, I'll wake you first, then Hazel, and then," Bleke paused and peered narrowly at Morclyf.

The children tried to get as comfortable as they could and soon drifted off to sleep. Bleke folded his legs and sat on the damp floor against Edmund's rocks. In the glow of the solar-mushrooms,

Bleke's mind raced with anticipation, fear, sadness, and guilt for what happened to his nephew. After gazing at him for a long time and feeling the energy within him, he softly whispered, "You are the pendulum, the keeper, and the seer of all within us. We will fear you. Because you, my dear boy, have the power to destroy us all."

Two days passed.

Edmund woke, spoke of spirited bodies briefly, and fell back to sleep. The ensemble at The Wayfarer's Inn had created a comfortable method of watching over and taking care of him. Ivindfor would enter the room for only a few minutes at a time to get a progress report. Otherwise, the children focused their thoughts and feelings toward the recovery of their newly formed peer. Then, on the third day, Edmund rose with a bent head and situated himself in a sitting position. He loosened the bandages around his hands, reached to his eyes, and pulled the patches away. Edmund looked around the room with clouded, eerie eyes.

Bleke silently sat next to Edmund and quietly whispered, "Good morning nephew, you seem better today."

"I feel as though I am in a dream. But every time I wake up, the more real it all becomes," Edmund answered sadly – tears falling from his eyes. "I remember my life before all this happened, and I have tried to go back, fought the change in my mind. But now. Now, I feel everything. I can start to let go of what I used to see. I can start to let go of what I used to be."

"The change is different for all of us. Trust me, I understand," Bleke sympathized and lightly held his nephew's hand. "In time, the 'normal' life you once had will seem strange; even more useless than the one you have now."

"Do mother and father know?" Edmund asked.

"No. Ivindfor wanted to wait until we knew more."

"Good, I'd rather they know after we get to Havenshade," Edmund directed. "I don't want them to worry. Do you think that's alright?"

"You're the best judge of that, although I know they'll be really upset."

"We're all upset. Might as well not add more mud to the mixture," Edmund grinned. "So, have you and Ivindfor talked about what's going to happen. I've heard bits..."

"Well, Iv' and I have had several, 'disagreements', about what to do next. He plans to leave in three days whether you're ready or not. He's sent messages out to the parents of the twelve other children to meet them at designated places and at designated times," Bleke was silent for a moment as he looked over at Ava, Hazel, and Morclyf, who were still sleeping. "They've watched over you. Talked about you. Talked to you. And they've even grown to like each other a little, I think."

"I know they have," Edmund replied and stretched out his arm as if caressing them from a distance. "I've seen their spirits connect when they open up to each other, and I've seen their spirits withdraw when they argue. It's peaceful sometimes, but also frightening, too."

Edmund sat silently with his uncle and then brought up a totally different subject. "Does Ivindfor still want me to write?"

"Well, Iv' has been working on getting someone else for that job," Bleke expressed. "Kalevel, the Innkeeper's son, wants to go, but the family isn't too keen on the idea. So, we'll see when we leave, if he's coming along with us."

"I hope so. He's told me some great stories while the rest of you slept," Edmund mentioned. "He seems like someone itching to get away from here and have a life of his own."

"Well, if he does come along, he's in for one bumpy ride."

"Tell me about it!" Edmund laughed a little, then coughed. The other children stirred and gazed at Edmund sitting upright for the first time since the incident. Bleke smiled and waved at them to come over. Edmund stared at them as if he could see them as plainly as before. They each said good morning, and in surprise, Edmund suggested that they all partake in some of Karell's minted mouthwash before continuing their conversations. They were all taken aback, but laughed at the truth of Edmund's newly heightened sense of smell, and sense of jovial humanity. They realized, for the first time, he was just as they were.

Now that Edmund was recovering, Ivindfor made more efforts to visit him. Ava, Hazel, and Morclyf had moved into another room and even ventured outside from time to time with Bleke. Edmund also noticed his energy and how it reacted to others. He saw how others would connect with him. Yet, whenever he tried to reach out, they would retreat away. Even Ivindfor, who flowed within everyone all the time, would not come near Edmund. As troubling as this was, Edmund knew why and began to accept their hesitance. He began to understand the meaning of isolation, prudence, and choice.

Kalevel became Edmund's most prominent guest as the next days passed by. They often sat and talked about Essil, sharing different stories they knew, and wondered about the plans Ivindfor had for helping keep peace among the nations. For some reason, Kalevel's spirit did not fear Edmund, but rather gravitated toward him. Perhaps this was because Kalevel was a singular; a free spirit and did not comprehend what Edmund truly was. Or, perhaps the love of stories, writing, and simple things related them together. Whatever this bond was, Edmund was thankful for it. He showed nothing but kindness, respect and appreciation for the friendship that had formed.

On the sixth morning, Karell entered the dark room and found Edmund sitting upright in a wooden chair. When no one was in the dark small room, Edmund felt his blindness most and would often lose track of time. Sometimes, he would wake up in the middle of the night thinking morning had come. Relief came as the alchemistress crept in with a breakfast that filled Edmund's nose with wonderful smells.

"Good morning, Karell," Edmund said softly and pleasantly. "I can only suppose that it's morning by the smell of the eggs, sausage, and – are those raspberries?"

"Why yes, there are raspberries this morning. You're sense of smell is already heightened. That's good," Karell said as she positioned the tray on the table next to him. "Although, you forgot the..."

"Fresh milk," added Edmund smirking.

"Know it all," she giggled. "Anyway, how did you know it was me? Do I smell over the breakfast I prepared?"

"No, not at all," Edmund thought of a way to explain to Karell the image he saw of her. He thought he might just refer to the way she always smelled of lavender, but instead replied, "Well, everyone has a different spirit. Mostly, the shape is different, or the color, but yours is like a rainbow. I don't understand quite why, but that's how I know you."

Karell noticed Edmund stare at her, as she felt a little violated knowing that he could see her in a way she could not. Then, she pulled a chair next to him and looked over the wounds on his arm, legs, and across his chest. "You know. I've been told the day I was born, a rainbow blossomed after a terrible storm. All my life I have had good luck with the things I practice. You, however, are the first person I have not been able to fully restore."

Karell continued to inspect the areas that would not heal as she groaned and muttered under her breath at the sight of them. Edmund could tell she was more displeased in herself than the actual condition of his body. "Maybe I need more time," Edmund suggested, as he carefully lifted some sausage to his mouth.

"No. I am afraid all the tricks I have in my cabinet would have worked by now," she remarked absolutely. "These wounds are from a deeper magic than I can fix. Much deeper."

"I vaguely remember Morclyf saying something about Ivindfor healing himself. Why can't he help me? And why doesn't he visit me?"

Karell hesitated and sat motionless for several long moments, then asked Edmund in return, "How much do know about Ivindfor, Edmund? I refer precisely about his powers and his own spirit. Not the man himself."

"Not much, I guess. Although, he only has one strong spirit. The other spirit is fragmented. The rest of us have two strong spirits intertwined. Ivindfor always retreats from me – as if afraid."

"I think I need a word with the old man myself," she said lightly. "The questions you ask oughtn't to be answered by me, but by him. Besides, you need to eat and perhaps take a nap. I'll send Ivindfor around in a while. In the meantime, relax, enjoy the food.

I'll check on you again very soon." Edmund listened to her gentle and kind voice, wishing he could physically see her face.

As Karell left, Edmund felt the dark void close in around him again. He neatly managed his breakfast, and thought about Ivindfor. The image of the man was still in his mind, just like his family, friends, and many others he had met on his recent travels. Now, though, the pictures he created were more like dreams, not at all like an actual memory. Sometimes, he did not trust the recollections as authentic. Only as illusions he still desperately clung on to.

With a full stomach, Edmund wobbled to the floor, and once comfortable, found himself very tired. Now blind, drifting to sleep was a very conscious experience. The sensation of his body letting go, allowed his intertwined spirit to flourish like a wave of vibrant warmth, consuming everything that troubled him. For a split second before falling into dreams, Edmund smiled at the incredible love that lived and burned within him.

Karell nudged Edmund awake a few hours later. As Edmund opened his eyes, he noticed Ivindfor was in the room with her. "Oh, hello. How long did I sleep?"

"Not long, but long enough I suppose," Karell tenderly whispered.

"How are you feeling, Edmund?" Ivindfor plainly asked.

"As well as can be expected, I suppose," Edmund replied, hoping to soften their seemingly stoic moods.

"Karell mentioned that you had spoken of me and had some questions," Ivindfor spoke quite seriously and almost sternly, as if Edmund had crossed a line. "I can give you some of the answers now, but more importantly, I have an idea on how to return your sight, as well as, possibly getting rid of your other spirit."

"Well, I just wanted to wake you up Edmund, which I've done," Karell interjected and began to leave the room. "I have a laundry list of things to do, and that reminds me, I have laundry to do! Besides, this is no concern of mine nor do I want any of it" Then, Edmund saw her small rainbow fade away as he returned his gaze toward Ivindfor.

"I know I haven't been available. Nor, have I been very helpful," Ivindfor began. "But I've been busy sending messages to people, keeping our profile low, and trying to decide what to do."

"I don't blame you," Edmund spoke intimidated by Ivindfor's brutish tones that he had never seen before. "I'm still the same Edmund as before, just a little less but also a little more."

Ivindfor stood and stomped on the floor. His voice echoed against the walls of the small room. "You are not merely a boy anymore, Edmund! Within you is the power to inflict uncontrollable destruction, pain, and fear! Do you understand the consequences of me even keeping you alive?"

Edmund shimmied closer to the wall, very afraid and worried Ivindfor might actually hurt him. He could feel the spirit inside of him swell and search for the element that it commanded. Ivindfor's spirit swirled wildly within his body, and Edmund noticed for the first time how a spirit could lose control of itself - if its host lost their connection with it.

"I have been torn between my love for you and the desire I have for the future of many people. So much is at stake. It's been hard for me to risk the better good of so many people over the welfare of just one boy," Ivindfor continued. "But, I have been counseled by most of my friends and family. I believe, as they do, that you had been chosen by the world for a long time. Maybe since the beginning. I lied to the great spirits and did not help create the incarnate spirit of fire. My fear was that I would not be able to teach someone to control something so unstable. Now, I don't have the choice."

"I-I'm sorry if I've done something, Ivindfor," Edmund was crying now and horribly upset that he had somehow caused all Ivindfor's hardship.

"No, Edmund," Ivindfor paused realizing that he had blamed all this on Edmund. He bowed his head and shamefully accepted his own failure as he saw the wounded, innocent young boy in front of him. For the first time, Ivindfor reached out to Edmund. For the first time since the lightning struck, Ivindfor took responsibility for the actions of his past that had now determined the future.

"You are not to blame. I should be the one wounded and burned. It's so much easier to blame so other people for the mistakes you make. Sometimes, you lose sight of what's really the truth. I'm sorry and I don't expect you to understand, or ever forgive me."

After sensing Ivindfor's sincerity, Edmund cautiously asked, "So, you didn't want to heal me because you wanted me to die?"

"As bad as it sounds, a part of me did want you die," Ivindfor shamefully admitted. "I didn't want you to suffer, and I didn't want to suffer your powers. But I want you know, Edmund, that although I can heal myself, I cannot pass that on to others. That is something all our spirits can do with the help of our minds. But the art of healing ourselves, like I did, takes many years to develop. The gift does require a price, unfortunately. But that can wait for another day."

"You said before there may be a way to restore my sight and my old self, though?" Edmund began to relax and speak less hesitantly.

"Well, that brings me to another very hard and disturbing aspect of this whole mess," Ivindfor began and gritted his teeth a little. "As I said before, I corresponded with friends and family. They all agreed that..." Ivindfor lingered to say the next words, as if they would slice apart his throat if he tried. "The only one who might be able to help you is my sister, Lazdrazil."

"But, haven't you been hiding the others from her all these years?" Edmund shockingly asked. "How can she help? And even if she could...Would she? From what you've said, Lazdrazil has a grudge against us and would rather see us dead."

"Well, the grudge is more against me than any of you," Ivindfor answered. "And although she has her faults, I don't believe she would ever hurt any of you. Honestly, I think she would rather see you hurt me. It would be more poetic for her that way."

"So, do you think you can travel?" Ivindfor asked.

Edmund's mouth opened in desperation to comprehend why Ivindfor would risk everything in going to Lazdrazil for him. "I can't believe you would take that kind of chance, just to make me better."

"Edmund, I don't expect you, or any of the others to understand my motives as to why I do things the way I do. For me, if there is a way to cure you, then I will do what it takes to undo the terrible wrongs I've committed. Even if it means I must go to Lazdrazil. We'll leave when you're ready. If at all."

Ivindfor walked toward the door, and Edmund saw his spirit trailing behind. Edmund felt an enormous swelling of energy within as his spirit moved toward Ivindfor's. Without any doubt, Edmund raised himself to his feet and answered Ivindfor confidently:

"I don't need time to think anything over, Ivindfor! I trust you! I always have! I'm not the boy I once was. I see so much more now than I ever would have in my entire other life. I think it's time your sister met us all, Ivindfor. It's time you stopped hiding and protecting us. This is what you've been waiting for, isn't it? I believe in everything you've ever told me. I believe in Bleke, Hazel, Ava, Morclyf, and myself. Let Lazdrazil know the power she may have to contend with. Let us bring her into the light of the fire!"

Ivindfor spun around smiling, as if pleased to hear Edmund's orders. He was pleased with Edmund's reaction and he was pleased to finally have a sense of direction again. Even if that direction meant the spirit of fire would also be among the other children of the old way. At times, Fate interjected Ivindfor's reasoning and intentions. He accepted this as one of those times.

So, with wildly excited eyes, Ivindfor saluted Edmund and announced, "We'll leave for Lazdrazil in the morning! And soon, all the children of the old way will be at the shores of Mirrored Lake!"

Secrets and Gifts

> Our eyes are portals of souls,
> Our ears are reservoirs of songs,
> Our noses are filters of scents,
> Our tongues are twisters of tastes
> Our touches are tremors of tenderness.
> From, *The Poetry of Kalevel*

    Ava found Edmund sitting on his bed in the silence of the secret, dark room. "Hello, Ava," Edmund whispered.

    "How long have you been awake?" she asked quietly, stunned by his recognition.

    "I'm not really sure. I don't have any sense of time anymore. I sleep when I'm tired. Sit around when I'm not." Edmund remarked, melancholy.

    "Are you excited about leaving? I know I am," Ava said before Edmund could answer. "The Innkeepers and everyone here have been so nice to us, but now that you're coming around, it'll be good to move on."

"I suppose," Edmund replied, as if not really interested.

"What's wrong? I hope you know that you can talk to me. I know *I* don't talk much, but if there's something that I can do to help..."

Edmund lifted himself from the bed and walked the few steps, stopping directly in front of her. He did not speak. He did not move. Ava suddenly felt nervous for the first time in several days. She glanced over to the string and wondered if she should bolt and pull for help. She waited for a moment longer, her chest breathing heavily, and her heart pounding hard.

"You can see the spirits, can't you?" Edmund asked sternly.

"I-I don't know what you mean, Edmund," Ava replied and took a small step back toward the string.

"What I mean is, you can see spirits. Like I can see them. Like I've told you," Edmund followed Ava's step. "Why haven't you told anyone, or at least me? Don't you think I'd understand?"

"I don't see spirits. At least, not like you do," answered Ava truthfully. "I only see, rather feel, the spirits of the dead. They speak to me to. How and why, I don't know. I never mentioned it you because I don't quite understand it myself."

Ava's eyes began to tear and her face became hot with emotion. Edmund spoke softly and reached out for her hand. "You have a second spirit with you, Ava. Who is it?"

"My grandfather, my mother's father, died last year," she began. "I was really close to him and he loved me a lot, even though he knew I was different. I was with him when he took his last breath, and somehow his death became a part of me. As I said before, I don't know how it happened. Please, don't tell anyone, alright?"

"You need to let Ivindfor know, if he doesn't know already..." Edmund paused while still clasping Ava's hand. "Maybe he can give you some insight. Then again, Ivindfor's not one for giving any definitive answers. Just remember, you can always talk to me. I promise not to tell anyone."

Ava became aware that they had been holding hands a long time. They both felt the heavy awkward silence, and then let go. "I think we should get going. The others are probably ready to go," Ava remarked. She picked up Edmund's bag that was on the floor and began walking toward the door. "Can you follow me well enough? Or do you need me to guide you?"

"Thanks, but I'll try to manage on my own."

"Oh, for Semmiah's Sake!" Ava exclaimed so suddenly that Edmund stumbled into her side. "I forgot that I came was to give you this package."

"A package for me?" Edmund asked in surprise. "What is it? Who is it from?"

"Bleke flew in late last night with it. He said his master, Jacobi, created something that might help you. Do you want help opening it?"

"Sure," Edmund shrugged and excitedly shuffled back to the bench. Ava sat close with her hips brushing his, which made Edmund feel strangely uncomfortable and yet soothed at the same time. She clasped his hands, and they untied the plain paper wrapped around an equally plain box. Edmund felt the box on every side as Ava also inspected a way to open it. "I don't see a way of opening the box at all," commented Ava.

"I do," replied Edmund, as he smirked slightly. "Jacobi has a horrible sense of humor, but I like it. And I know why you were sent in here to give it to me." Ava leaned back wondering what Edmund was talking about when he lifted the box to her. "Take it," Edmund said. Ava held the rectangular box in front of her. She could see no lock, seam, lid, or hinge. To her, the box appeared to be just a block of wood. Edmund continued: "The top edges of the box are slightly rounded. Can you feel?"

"Yes. Barely," she answered.

"Now, hold the box flat in your hands. In the center of the top is a tiny hole."

"I don't see a hole."

"Trust me, there is one. I think if you concentrate hard enough and push enough air through the hole, the box will open up."

"Really? But won't I break whatever is inside, too?"

"No, I think the box will open pretty easy. There aren't any nails, or anything holding it together. Don't ask me how he did it, but the design is genius!"

"All right, if you say so," Ava sighed, and then focused on the box. She could not see the hole Edmund had pointed out, but trusted his instruction. As Ava concentrated, she saw a miniature dust devil swivel above and then into the box. Within a matter of seconds, the sides of box fell back, and the top popped into the air and bounced on the stone floor.

"Oh!" Ava cried. "That was amazing! I didn't expect *that*! I didn't even try!"

Edmund laughed at her excitement, as she unwrapped a pair of goggles with ruby red lenses. The goggles had been wrapped in a note 'For Edmund'. Ava unrolled the paper, but there were not any words inside.

"That's odd, a note with nothing more on it?" she mused.

After a moment, Edmund realized what kind of note it was. "Here, let me hold on to it," he said. "It's probably written in wizard's words, and I'm the only one who can make words show up. Watch..." Ava leaned so closely into Edmund that he could feel the warmth of her breath tingle the hairs on his neck. Then, as if his fingers bled the ink, brown words appeared, which Ava fragrantly repeated in Edmund's ear:

Dear Edmund,

Bleke and Ivindfor informed me of your unfortunate, and yet blessed incident. I hope you are recovering well. After careful consideration about the effects of your transformation, I have developed these lenses. You might wonder why a blind boy would need these. Well, my young man, you will see more than ever before! The goggles are filters. I assume your eyes, although unseeing the physical world, will now see the spectral world, entirely. The goggles will allow you to see animate life. Animals, insects, plants, and people will be dimensional. Unfortunately, the earth, air, and water will remain black to you. I am curiously jealous of your gifts, Edmund. I await to meet you, and some day to discuss all the glories (and miseries) you witness!

Yours Truly,

Jacobi
P.S. *NEVER, NEVER, let anyone else wear the lenses! Burning, itching, blindness and even DEATH may occur. - Cheers!*

"Well, that's a little odd," Ava commented. "What did he mean by 'the spectral world'?"

"I think he's referring to the spirits of all living things," Ivindfor's voice echoed from the doorway toward Ava. "That's why Edmund's been stuck in this room for so long. We've been afraid to expose too much of the world to him. The solar mushrooms are safe because they only glow after they've been cut down. Everything alive has an 'essence', and if you can see ours, then you'll see every plant, insect, and animal that make up this world. So, Bleke asked Jacobi to make those lenses, and they've arrived just in time!"

"Are you sure they're safe?" asked Edmund, as he fumbled with the goggles.

"I've never doubted Jacobi's work, or his word," Ivindfor replied assuredly. "Besides, what else can go wrong?"

"Well, hopefully not 'Death'" Ava retorted rolling her eyes.

"Good one, Av'! All right then, let's get your things. Everyone else is saying their goodbye's to Breaver and his family," Ivindfor informed and waited for Ava and Edmund to follow.

Edmund left the small secretive room. He closely shuffled behind Ava's spirit, as it glided along in front of him like a ghost. He became aware of several voices speaking to each other. The air instantly smelled fresh and Edmund's attitude began to lighten. As they entered the tavern section of The Wayfarer's Inn, Edmund heard the interesting speech of a man he had heard before. He thought for a moment to place the voice, and then realized he had not met Breaver, the Inn Keeper, yet.

"Wrell, Redmrund," the Innkeeper haphazardly began. "Grood tra sree yar brack orn yer freet argrain! Ire reckon yar train't hreard mere vrice brefore, brut trey crall mere Breaver. 'Cruz Ire grot ar problerm wirt mere 'r's', dorn't yar knor. Sor, rone trime Ire wars groing orff about breaver's arn' tar nrame struck! Ire kinder gort rused tar irt arn' tar orther's t'irs reasy tar rerember!

Jurst knor thart yar arlways wrelcorme art tar Wrayfarer's Irnn! 'Cerpt breaver sreason. Were rawful frull dart trime or'yrear!"

Edmund tried to comprehend all the words the Innkeeper sputtered, then politely said, "Thank you sir, for all that you and your family have done for me and my friends. Without your help, I'm sure things would have turned worse."

"Nrah! Nrot writ R'Ivrindfror writ yar! Stray tra crourse! Writ R'Iv, yrou'll bre rust frine!"

Edmund nodded his head hoping to conceal a small giggle that was forming from the man's speech. He knew it was wrong to think of his speech impediment funny, but for some reason happiness flowed through him at the sound of it. All through their conversation Edmund watched, as Breaver's spirit washed over him, as if warm water over his skin. Then, Ava grasped his tenderly bandaged hand and led Edmund, at last, outside. Before exiting the safely secluded Wayfarers Inn, Ava carefully slipped Jacobi's glasses onto the bridge of his nose and around his ears. Edmund situated them a little, and slicked back his now white hair. Then she lightly flirted, "You look stylishly smart, with a twist of creepy! Now, you definitely *are* one of us!"

Edmund laughed. "Feels funny to have something on my nose. I'm going to hold my eyes closed until we're totally out in the open. Tell me when we're out there."

They passed Hazel, Morclyf, Kalevel, Karell, Katrin, Knelli, Bleke, and Ivindfor as if in a royal procession of some kind. They all stared at the young man, as Ava stopped at the Inn's threshold, and moved to Edmund's side, still holding his hand. She bent down and whispered huskily into his ear, "All right, Edmund. You can open your eyes now."

Trembling slightly from nerves, Edmund slowly lifted his eye lids behind the ruby red lenses. His mouth dropped. He squeezed Ava's hand harder, and she held his. His breath quickened, tears swelled, and he felt the heat of his spirit swell within.

As Edmund peered through the blackened earth and sky of the prairie, he saw and sensed every auburn-ivory colored spectral blade of grass waving, grasshoppers flitting, mosquitos hovering, birds zigging, ground squirrels scurrying, rabbits hopping, foxes dodging, dogs yielding, horses standing, cattle grazing, and people walking. In that void, the goggles gave Edmund a strangely accurate sense of distance and size. After several deep breaths, Edmund averred, "I never thought I could see something so beautiful, and yet everything fearing me."

Fallen Spirits

> The roads that we go,
> The paths which we choose,
> Whether difficult,
> Or easy going,
> Are ours to wander.
> Yet, those routes are not,
> Ways traveled alone.
> From, *The River Less Voyaged by Kalevel*

    Sullen, Edmund lagged behind with his uncle as the rest of the group walked along the path toward the Aeden River, also known as Inte Aeden. The river was only a mile, or so, from The Wayfarer's Inn, and Ivindfor secured a raft from Breaver. The spot was once popular for people venturing southward, before the odd stories by other travelers. The Inte Aeden was a generally quiet and easy river to maneuver. For years, trappers and hunters took the river to the Towers of Emigrate and Immigrate, where they traded their goods with the Valds and Stouts. Now, the Inte Aeden was quietly hushed with a murky, brown coldness that moved people to the roads through Stouttown.

"I'm sorry you're disappointed, Edmund," Bleke apologized. "I was sure that the glasses would make you happy, but obviously, I made an incredible error."

"No. No, it's not the glasses, or what I've seen that upsets me," Edmund replied and took hold of his uncle's hand. "You wouldn't believe the things I can see. Jacobi was right about the intensity surrounding us. The lenses help keep things separated and contained. I know it sounds crazy, but there's so much happening all at once! I never expected this. I'm glad you thought of these though. It's going to take time to get used to them, that's all."

"I understand....When Jacobi helped me become the wizard, there were a lot of changes I did not expect. Over the past ten years, I've grown accustomed and comfortable with them, as I'm sure you will. Unless, Lazdrazil can change you back, of course."

"I don't want to be changed back to what I was," Edmund bolted and replied. Bleke nodded in approval, knowing what Ivindfor had already revealed the day before. Bleke wanted to hear it from Edmund, as a confirmation, of sorts. They walked along for a while without saying a word, listening to the wind, the birds, and the insects hum and sing around them. Then, Edmund posed a question to his uncle that Ivindfor had failed to answer, "Why does Ivindfor only have little wisps of his other soul?"

Bleke slowed his pace to a halt, and thought carefully about how to answer. He rubbed his hands together, then answered softly back, "When we use the language of the world to perform spells that disrupt the natural state of time, space, or ourselves, we sacrifice a piece of souls. This does not mean every time that we use our talents to ask, command, or transfigure the world we pass along a part of our souls. However, to rapidly heal, teleport, speed or slow time, or create things requires a great deal from us. These must be used with caution."

"Did Ivindfor use his soul to help create the Hazel, Ava, Morclyf, and the others?" Edmund inquired.

"Yes. Much of his own spirit was spent to make the children who they are today. So, you can see why he's so worried about them."

"What happens if he uses the rest of his power? He hasn't much left?"

"Well, the only one us who ever used all their power like that was Ivindfor's twin - Semmiah."

"So, Semmiah used all her power when she died?"

"Yes. She gave up her gifts as she was hung and nailed to the tree in Scythe. Ivindfor was made from the spirits of the living, while Semmiah was created from the spirits of the dead. They were made by their father, Aelen Everlast. He's had a hand in making all things as they are today. Semmiah sacrificed herself to change the world for the better. But martyrs only leave a legacy that tend to be twisted and fitted to the needs of what people want, not what was truly been intended. Although, we have a way of stealing..."

Edmund felt sadness for his friend and master Ivindfor, while not hearing Bleke's ending comments. He realized just how much Ivindfor had invested into the future of all people and all of nature. "Do the others know about this?"

"Not to the extent you see. But, Ivindfor will explain everything once we get to Havenshade," Bleke ended their conversation as they caught up with everyone else, waiting at the boat landing. The sound of the river reminded Edmund of home, although refreshing, depressed him. He missed his mother and father. Less than two weeks ago, he was at home - safe in the solitude of the forests. Now, Edmund's life was intertwined with the world, the others, Ivindfor, and his future seemed more ominous by the day.

"If you look carefully, you can barely see the blackened top of the Gates of Aeden," Ivindfor pointed north across a grassy plain on the other side of Inte Aeden. "To the south, we will pass the Maedril's Mount and the Forest of the Fallen. Then, we'll stop at the Towers and pick up a few of the others. If things go smoothly, we'll move on and camp somewhere east of Pentasentinel. Hazel, if you don't mind, please help our passage along as you did from Essil."

"No problem," Hazel smiled and excitedly obliged. Edmund saw the air spirit within her grow and swell against the small sail attached to their raft.

They floated comfortably down the river and everyone relaxed with the gently rocking current of water. The raft was square and thick with a small lean-to in the middle for shade. There, Morclyf and Edmund lay silent and dreamily watched the small white clouds drift by in the ocean of blue sky.

"Would you really have crushed me, back at The Inn?" Edmund mused to Morclyf.

"Depends," Morclyf shrugged.

"On what?"

"Whether, or not, you tried to hurt us."

"But, were you really ready to kill me, if you had to?"

"I wasn't ready for anything. None of us were. I just knew I had to protect the girls...and the mission," After an awkward, reflective pause Morclyf continued. "It's strange. One minute, I was burning and helping save you, then Ivindfor told me to hurt you. I don't want to have to be in that spot ever again. But, I would bash your skull in if you tried anything on us. The three of us have been together long before you. That won't change. Never will. Just because you've become one of us, doesn't mean you are one of us. Got it?"

"So, this means I don't get one of your feathers?" Edmund teased. Morclyf rolled his eyes and turned away.

Edmund crawled from beneath the small lean-to on the boat, and maneuvered to where Kalevel sat. They shared a few stories together, and they laughed over some gross jokes they both knew. Morclyf lay back like a large raven wrapped in a shadow. He heard their muffled voices and cringed at their laughter. Morclyf debated why he hated Edmund, or rather why everyone else did not hate him. To Morclyf, Edmund was the onset of pain and without reward. The black haired and black eyed boy gritted his gnarly teeth in the frustration of not being favored.

From inside his cloak, Morclyf pulled out the card that Ivindfor had given him. He hadn't bothered looking at it until now.

The dirty, brown card was blank. Then, black watermarks swirled around from nowhere. To Morclyf, the card developed depth and dimension, as more ink bubbled together. A picture emerged, faded, and then resurfaced again. The card was alive within his pale hands. Morclyf scowled at the image of a lone raven tied to a single tree branch. Other birds, white and free, flitted on the opposite side of that same tree. Morclyf understood that he was the one tied off alone. He tucked the card away, gritting his teeth even more.

After an hour, Ivindfor announced they were at The Tower of Maedril. There, the Inte Aeden forked to the right and left in between a one hundred foot pillar of stone. Trees grew from the crevasses and leaned as if they were going to fall into the river at any second. They noticed that the rock formation had a rusty hew and the trees had black bark with black needles and leaves. No birds flew or sung around the trees. Nor did they see any animals scurrying around on the forest floor. There was only the silence. Not even the wind blew. Nor could Hazel make it move.

Hazel no longer commanded the air and water as she did upriver. Bleke worked hard to guide the boat toward the left fork. Kalevel noticed his struggle and began helping with an idle oar. Quickly, Ivindfor assisted with another oar. Morclyf lay underneath the shelter unaware and uninterested in the situation. Ava took Kalevel's place near Edmund as Hazel stood frustrated at the front of the bobbing craft.

"What's going on Ivindfor?" she yelled over the splashing water. The river had gotten wilder and the rushing water drowned out the silence. "Why won't the air or water speak or listen to me?"

Looking over his shoulder while working an oar with the current, Ivindfor shouted, "We are traveling through cursed waters now. Older magic than me runs through this land! None of our powers will work here! It's actually an exciting story, I'll tell it to you when things calm down!" Water sprayed up at him and he laughed as if on an amusing childish ride. Bleke and Kalevel, however, were not amused, and their frustration showed plainly on their scowling faces. "Just hold tight everyone! We'll be through this in just a few minutes! Ha, Ha!"

Ivindfor was right. Within three minutes, the raft lifted less and the water splashed less aggressively. The current was still swift, but the river smoothed and reflected the high banks. To the right, The Forest of the Fallen raised, as sheer rock faces lingered from where the Tower of Maedril had formed. Rust and black colored pine needles covered the ground. Still, there were no animal sounds or sightings seen by the travelers. And still, no breeze bustled the leaves into song.

"Ah, well, here we are at The Forest of the Fallen!" exclaimed Ivindfor. "Hazel, relax, don't bother with the water.' Hazel frowned and sat on the raft with her knees pulled to her chest. "So, who wants to know what this place is all about, eh?"

Every hand shot up, except Morclyf's. Kalevel was so excited he snatched his writing equipment and situated himself directly in front of Ivindfor. He brushed his wavy, red hair out of his face and gazed up anxiously with wide green eyes. Bleke grinned at Ivindfor's stage presence and now easily steered the boat by himself. Ava, looking frightened, nuzzled close to Hazel and Edmund as they joined Kalevel to hear Ivindfor's tale.

"Long ago, before I was even made," Ivindfor gestured grandly and spoke lower and louder. "There was a great and terrible battle. The last battle between the Syndustrians and the Nations of the Old Way. Here, my father Aelen and my brother Beohlor with hundreds of sorcerers and wizards and thousands of soldiers fought against the Syndustrian's revenge. As the battle raged day and night, the Nations of the Old Way began to see victory; until the Fendow, the First-Fell, marched to the Syndustrians' aid. Their betrayal marked almost certain defeat. Many people from the Nations lost their lives. Great magic and machines were wielded by both sides. All seemed lost for those of the Old Way. Then, Aelen came forth with all the fury and power of ice he could muster. With a glacier, Aelen cut against the ground and drove the Fendow away. He pushed them back all the way to Ginith Mire. And Beohlor, with his newly forged war hammer named Tremor, pounded and lifted the earth, entombing the remaining Syndustrians. At the top of the carnage and waste, Beohlor clashed with the Syndustrian Warlord; and there, after a hard battle, struck Maedril down into ground - forever."

"But before the fatal blow, Maedril cursed the land and all the souls who died on it. And so, it is said the trees growing here hold all those souls captive. The fruit and nuts are poison. The running waters are tainted by their blood. No creatures dwell here. And the voice of the world is mute. Only death lingers where death was wrought. This is their legacy which eventually divided the Nations and declined the Old Ways."

Ava trembled with her eyes squeezed shut. Edmund could see the spirit of death vibrating and reaching out toward the forest. Beads of sweat formed on her forehead, but when Edmund grasped her hand she was cold as ice. "They call to me and moan as if still dying. They want me to set them free," she whispered to Edmund. Hazel noticed Ava's condition and tried to connect with her. Death, however, denied her entrance into Ava's essence. Hazel jumped up and yelled, "Ivindfor, something's definitely wrong with Ava! Look!"

Ivindfor snapped out his performance and saw Ava slouched and shaking. He bent down and wrapped his cloak around her. "What's wrong child? Did my story frighten you?"

Ava tilted her head to him with tears running down her face, "I'm so, so sorry. I didn't try to...it just happened when grandpa died." Her fumbled words were enough to let Ivindfor understand that she had some power of the dead. He backed away with a concerned and cautious look on his face. The memory of his sister, Semmiah, filled his heart with sadness and he pitied Ava for procuring this curse.

"Why didn't you tell me, Edmund?" Ivindfor questioned monotonously.

"She asked me not to," Edmund replied flatly.

"I would have chosen another way, if I had known," Ivindfor stated and paced back and forth gazing at Bleke who shrugged. "If you want me to do what's best for you, then all of you need to be open with me. From now on, our journey will become more difficult, so tell me what the hell is going on!" His voice grew sharp as he spoke until yelling out the final part and slamming his foot against the raft. Everyone felt ashamed and embarrassed, especially Ava. Edmund, however, got to his feet and stared directly at Ivindfor.

"That's easy for you to say, when half the time we don't know what you're doing!" Everyone gazed in amazement at Edmund's outburst. Even Morclyf peeked around the lean-to in surprise. "I understand the price you paid for all of us to be here, but for Semmiah's Sake...!"

"Don't say her name," Ivindfor had his back to Edmund but slowly turned, only his head rotating at first. Edmund realized what he had just done and felt a panic fill inside. As soon as Ivindfor faced Edmund squarely, his voice sounded restrained and controlled, as if he tried desperately not to totally lose his temper. "Edmund, forgive me. How could I be so inconsiderate," then Ivindfor's nostrils flared, took a deep breath, and yelled. "I'm sorry for trying to keep all of you in check, and keeping you all alive! Yes, you're still children, but how many children do you know who can wreak havoc against the world by merely thinking it? It's not easy keeping you all from destroying the world. Ungrateful brats!"

Ivindfor spun around and sat away from them all brooding and angry. Ava trembled harder as Hazel held and comforted her. Morclyf shrugged his shoulders and relaxed back under the shade. Bleke gazed away unresponsive and unsupportive to Edmund. The raft was as silent as The Forest of the Fallen. Kalevel crouched alone with tears in his eyes. Every member of the crew seemed isolated, irritated, and depressed. Perhaps the foulness of the Forest itself affected them and their attitudes. None of them could feel happiness. Nor could they connect and bond as they did before. Nothing seemed truthful, honest, or secure. Ivindfor rubbed his face hard and contemplated whether his little following was already falling apart.

They traveled together in a cold awkwardness. No one moved, except Ava who shook as if she had a fever. After an hour-and-a-half, the rugged, shadowy forest gave way to soft, golden grasses that whispered in the wind. Hazel and Ava lifted their faces and breathed deep sighs of relief. Bleke smiled as his dark hair tossed in the breeze. Ivindfor clapped his hands and leapt to his feet enthusiastically and announced, "Well, thank goodness *that's* over! I forgot how heavily the Forest plays with your emotions. Powerful stuff! And you, Ava, I am truly sorry. And

Edmund," Ivindfor paused for moment as Edmund looked up at him, "don't swear at me. It doesn't suit you."

"I should have realized the power of the Fallen, as well," Bleke added. "We should have taken another way. This was a good lesson for us all, though. We all have emotions that play into how we interact with one another. Sometimes we offer compassion, while at other times we commit offenses. Either way we act, we present a part of ourselves. As the saying goes, sometimes the truth hurts. But in being true, we are also being genuine to who we are."

Bleke's words lifted smiles to everyone on board. Morclyf's eyes twinkled a little as he, too, felt a sense of consideration within him. Edmund could see the spirits of everyone swirl and flit again, while off in the darkness the muted wisps of the grassy spirits and flying insects danced as well. Bleke pointed down river and announced, "The bridge and towers are in view."

In the distance, stone towers on either side of the river raised over the horizon. Kalevel quickly scribble a drawing and captioned a few notes as the others gazed on curiously. "Before we meet the Stouts and Valds, let me inform you of a few things *not* to say to them," Ivindfor instructed, stressing the word 'not'. "Never stoop or crouch to a Stout, nor jump or step up on something to meet a Vald eye to eye. Also, don't ask how the weather is 'up' or 'down' there to either of them. They really hate that. Oh, and most importantly, make sure to spit on your hand before shaking hands with them. Otherwise, they'll take it as an insult and either step on your foot, or smack you over the head!"

Everyone looked at each other with curious amazement at the mannerisms of the people they were about to meet. Then Ivindfor continued in a more serious tone. "I chose you four first for personal reasons. I'll admit, I am closest with your families than any of the others. And so, I feel closer to the four of you. Being first has its advantages, satisfactions, and rewards. But, always be aware that there will be someone out there to take that place. Rank is an abstract that rises and falls through circumstance. Do not let your pride get in the way of also being humbled by the experiences we've just had together. Do not use them as trophies to hold over the people you will meet. Rather share your experiences with them and offer insight so we all may grow.

After a few moments as Ivindfor graced each of them with a look, he smiled widely, "Well, that's that. Freshen up and get some good spit going. We've got good impressions to make!"

The Second Stack Sets and Falls

A Vald, a Stout, and a Sylfaen walk into a bar....
Wait - The Sylfaen couldn't have walked into the bar because the
Vald and Stout would've thrown the pretentious snob to the
tearoom across the street!
From, *Birch the Bard at Wayfarer's Inn*

Two square towers rose on either side of a bridge that crossed the Inte Aeden. They were known as the Towers of Immigrate and Extradite. Both Towers had the dual purpose of allowing people in, or excluding trespassers out of the Stout and Vald nations. Hundreds of people herded like animals through the system, which comprised tattooing symbols that meant 'exodus', or 'advent'. To leave the nations of the Vald and Stout was relatively easy, but for someone to return required admission by the Approval Court within the Tower of Immigrate. Where the symbols on a person's body were marked identified the status you belonged, the date, and previous convictions (if any).

Those who were leaving, could wait with family members on the bridge before being escorted either to the docks along the river below, or through the gates to the country they were going. The bridge was not made for traveling across but for allowing those leaving to spend a few last moments with those that may be staying behind. It is said that more tears had fallen upon the planks of that bridge than drops of rain. The bridge was neutral territory. Of course, there were guards patrolling to keep the peace, but everyone treated the bridge with respect. Very rarely, if ever, had a serious crime been committed. There was an unwritten code that everyone seemed to understand and obey. Those who left did not go in fear, but with hope and purpose. Those who wished to return, did so from failure or loss.

Among those crowded together waiting to leave was a tall, thin, and pale boy who clutched his left shoulder. Moments before, his older brothers had taken turns digging their knuckles where he had just been marked. Behind this rusty haired boy were his parents severely pointing and yelling at the grimacing brothers, Hrillin and Hrent. They sauntered off to the railing and snickered behind their parent's backs. The boy just held his head bowed in humiliation as his two younger sisters looked at him with embarrassment.

"Shake it off, Weslo," bellowed Westril, the boy's father, so the brothers could hear. "Your brothers are dolts, anyway. It took both their brains just to come up with the idea to smack you there. One of these days they'll both be taken out by a falling tree for lack of sense to step out of the way."

Weslo's lips almost turned into a smile at the thought of his brothers being driven into the ground by a timbered tree. Even Weslo's sisters, Wini and Willow laughed a little. However, their mother, Myr, scowled bitterly at the thought of any harm coming to any of her five children. "Don't you dare wish harm to those boys!" she reprimanded Westril, as she struck his head with her large bag. "They may have the manners of trolls, but they are still your sons! Our sons! And we should be just as proud of them as we are of the rest."

Weslo could hardly stand it when his mother defended his brother's or sister's actions toward him. All his life, he had been humiliated for being different, not because of his powers, but because of his small stature. He was almost 35 (seventeen by non-Vald/Stout calendars) and stood less than six feet tall. He was the shortest Vald any one could recall. While his bony features, and odd hair and matching freckles made Weslo stand out even more. He was an easy target for others ridicule and never understood why it made so many others feel better about themselves.

Westril's hand sunk into his own thick curly black hair, as he rubbed the spot where Myr's bag had landed. "What've you got in there? Bricks?" Then, he walked in front of Weslo, still flinching a little, and said to him, "No matter what, people are going to say things that are going to hurt. And, at times, people will *do* things that hurt," he said peering back at Myr. "But at some point, you need to ignore who or what you've been called, and be content with who and what you are. I know it sounds easier than it may seems. It's not. I love you Weslo for who you are. I can only hope you can love and find peace for yourself, too."

"Oh, encrusted pinecones!" Myr shrilled. "Weslo, I love you only as mother can, which is more than a father can – I'll let you know," she sneered back at Westril. "And happiness is fool's hope. Succeed in something and be proud of it! Have a goal and reach it! Manage or supervise something and lead it with strength! The rest is just for hobbyists, if you ask me!"

Weslo stood silent and then reached up giving his mother a hug. He knew she meant well, even though he did not totally agree with her. He raised and rolled his eyes to his father, who nodded back. Weslo thought his father was over dramatic and made too many excuses for him. Weslo understood both of their views, but was always stuck in the middle of every argument, issue, or downright brawl. He stepped back and gazed lowly and awkwardly around looking for something to change the subject. Then, he noticed familiar Vald and Stout faces approach them through the crowd.

"I th-think the r-rest of our g-group is here," Weslo stuttered, as he always did. This speech impediment made Weslo terrified to speak, so more often than not, he just kept silent. The fear of hearing himself stumble through a simple sentence was worse than any verbal insult anyone could shout at him. As odd and strange as everything else was about him, Weslo felt frustrated most about his inability to control the simplest spoken words with his mouth. He preferred thinking. Where within his own mind, the sounds were perfect and unblemished. As the rest of his family saw the Valds and Stouts come toward them, Weslo shifted behind as if hoping not to be seen at all.

"Good to see you again, Gringritch family," Westril announced as he spit in his hand and shook their spitted hands.

"Enjoying the day off, I suppose," smiled a fat bellied, casually well-dressed Vald known as Hrin, the father of Vigil. He swiveled his head groaning, as his neck popped and cracked. "Rough journey when you're not used to it. I don't like to travel, especially if it means leaving my family for any length of time. A man's got to make his family first, you know."

"Well, this a great day for all our families, especially the children," said a lyrical voice from below the two Vald's. Her name was Thaenia, who was dressed in layered colors of green silk, and her son Yhan, clad the same (except in blue) stood closely next to her. They all spat in their hands and shook with smiles and courtesy. Myr nudged and pried Weslo to join the group. He sheepishly greeted himself, yet somehow in the commotion found himself clumsily spinning around trying to keep up with everyone's 'hello's'.

"Ouch, you dolt! You stepped on my foot," screamed a rough voice from behind Weslo. A girl scowled up at him as she clutched her foot. Her name was Terrese. She was a tough looking, broad shouldered girl with dry, dusty hair, brown eyes, and leathery skin. She stuck her thumb between her index and middle finger and made a fist in the air. Her father, Delmor, and her mother, Cerrin, grabbed at her hand and apologized for the rude gesture. So far, the gathering of the future leader's world seemed more like an awkward and ill-advised family reunion. They stumbled over each other, tried to make conversations, but were always distracted by someone from their own family or someone else's actions. Then, just as they all began to settle down and relax, they all saw Sytheria marching forcefully toward them.

"Well, isn't this just the most laughable thing anyone could imagine," Sytheria's voice rose higher with every syllable, until it cackled at the end. She was the last Vald to arrive, and did so with and entourage of assistants and her father, Aegil Mallister. He was a jolly, fit, clean-cut looking Vald and the Lead Mark of the Alting. He held the highest rank in the lands and his family was royalty. Sytheria's blue eyes pierced sharply at the rest of those gathered. She brushed her black hair from her face, and then placed her hands on her curvy hips indignantly.

"We *are* still in the Valdic-Stout Lands, aren't we?" Sytheria snarled through her black lips. The others knew exactly what she meant, and on queue they all bowed before her and Aegil.

"Sytheria, that will be quite enough," Aegil ordered. "For goodness sakes, we are all friends on this bridge, and we are all equal in our own ways." Sytheria rolled her eyes and turned toward the assistants to check over the luggage and contents. "Now, let me be polite and shake all your hands." The commotion once again commenced as they all tried to shake hands with the most important man in their countries. Several guards watched over the affair, making sure that Aegil was safe at all times.

"There, that's better!" he exclaimed. "Well, has any one seen or heard from Ivindfor?"

"No, we all just arrived a few minutes ago," Westril spoke trying to sound as dignified as he could.

"He and others should be here shortly," added Cerrin. "It worries me, though, that they were coming down the river."

"Ah, The Forest of the Fallen," replied Hrin. "Nasty place, I hear. Not the sort of way I would have chosen, that's for sure."

"Especially for the children," chimed Thaenia. "They've had such a difficult journey. I've seen darkness for many days now. And darkness ahead under the pale moon light."

Many of those gathered looked uncomfortably at each other at the fortuneteller's proclamation. Then, Sytheria rebounded back into the group and stated, "It is absolutely insulting that Ivindfor would pick up those snots from Crescent Tier before me! And now, there's a new one! Some blind, fire-brat named Edmund and his converted uncle. Does Ivindfor even know what he's doing? Do any of you know what we're doing?"

"We all trust Ivindfor's ways, Sytheria," Vigil pointed out. "I believe we need to build bridges that will connect our cultures together. Like the one we stand on now. Without them, our journeys will be longer and more difficult."

"Oh, you and your stupid bridges!" Sytheria snapped back. "I'd like to burn them all to the ground!"

"For a pretty girl, you got one ugly tongue," replied Terrese coarsely. "I guess make-up and fancy clothes can't cover everything up."

Sytheria opened her shaking hand and a large nail lifted from the floorboards of the bridge. She spun toward Terrese and with a long arm stroke, motioned the nail toward her. Terrese stuck out her small, strong hand upright and as the nail approached, pieces of metal broke away until dust splashed against Terrese's palm.

"Sytheria!" Aegil screamed furiously into her face, grabbing her shoulders. "What do you think you are doing? Especially in public of all places! You had no right..."

"I have all the rights entitled to me, father!" Sytheria yelled back. "She's just lucky she's learned to shift forged metal, that's all."

"This is outrageous!" yelled Westril and Myr in unison. Soon, the other parents and children were yelling, shoving, and stepping over and under each other. Bridge Guards marched in from either side and began to argue with Aegil's royal guards, who had rushed first into the tussle. Innocent bystanders and families soon found themselves also caught within the fray and the whole bridge became one motion of pushing and shoving bodies, both giant and small.

Weslo, however, had managed to slip through to the staircase that lead down to the river platforms and docks. He gazed up at the multitude of bodies that stepped and climbed over each other. He tried to find his parents, but only noticed his brothers wildly smiling while knocking around anyone they could. Then, quite startled, he noticed an extremely strong Vald man and an equally built Stoutess standing right behind him.

"'Scuse me," the Vald said politely but loudly over the noise. "I twas wonderin' per chance if yeh're named Wezlo? Me name be

Hrowllind, 'Hrowl' for short, and tiss be me pertner, Atana. We be friends of Ivindfer, ya see."

Weslo turned paler than usual. He was not accustomed of being approached, other than to be bullied. So, when these two strangers stood in front of him, his first instinct was to flee. But, seeing that he had nowhere to run (and he definitely was not going up into the mob above him), he only stuttered a small, "Y-yes".

"Goodt, ten. Atana twas right!" Hrowl continued. "'Spose it'd be best we stay down here out o' ta way. 'Sides, once Atana and I git goin' there t'ain't much dat'll stop us. Ya see, Ivindfer hir'd Atana an' me as guides, or protectors, or such."

"What my good friend is trying to say is; we're mercenaries hired to protect your sorry butts," Atana blurted out without even glancing upward. "We know enough about what Ivindfor's doing to be a part of it, but that doesn't mean we're going to be friends, alright? The way I see it, Hrowl, we're going to have to raise our rate with ol' Iv."

"Oh, I tink we'll be fine. Dey're jus' kids, ain't dey. All dis is jus' a friendly misunderstandin'. Tat's all," Hrowl laughed, but Atana stared seriously at the commotion above.

"D-do you th-think w-we should w-wait down below, f-for Iv-I-indf-for?" Weslo offered.

"Would be best," Hrowl agreed.

"Yeah, I don't want to find any of our stuff missing either," Atana replied. "Thieves and pickpockets are going to start up any time now."

Weslo jumped a little and scurried down the stairs. He found his belongings that had been taken down earlier by customs and sat silently and safely as if he were on an island, alone. He sat sullenly with his head bowed down and wondered how and why he was ever born to the fate he was in. He never believed that this day would come. He never believed he could be one of Ivindfor's followers. All Weslo really wanted was to disappear from everyone and everything. He hated worrying about everything all the time, while waiting for the next bad thing to happen.

Almost with instinct, Weslo looked up river and noticed a small raft approach the bridge. He squinted and saw two men and several children gazing, mouths agape, up at the rabble of people above them. He turned toward Hrowl and Atana and his eyes widened at the multitude of weapons and armor they were fitting themselves on their body. With a small, careful wave of his hand, he caught their attention and pointed up river. "I-I think th-they're f-f-f-inally h-h-here!"

The Response and The Reproach

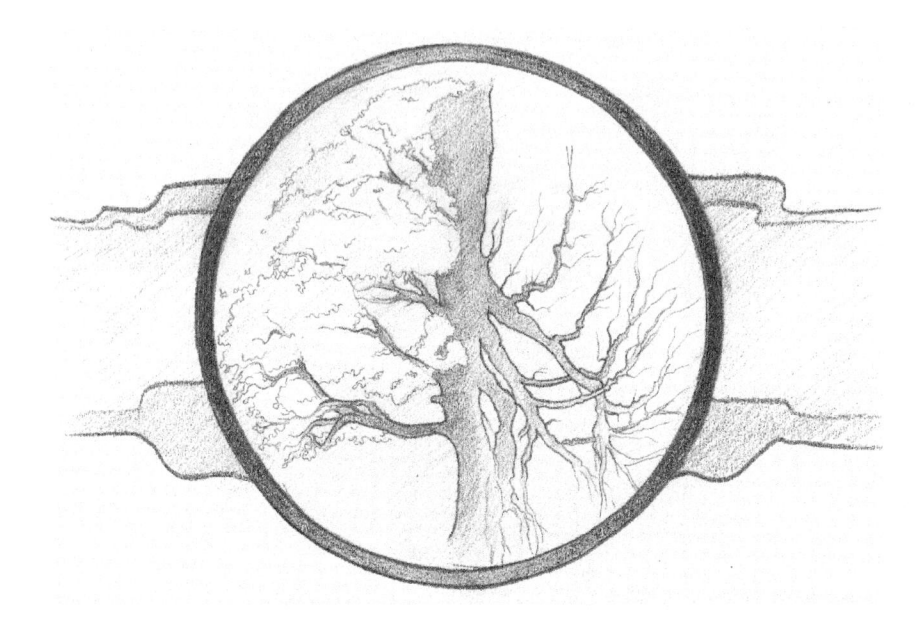

What happens when we die?
Only the dead know.
From, *The Lectures of Ivindfor at Havenshade*

As Ivindfor stepped onto the dock, Atana, Hrowl, and Weslo noticed the reddened color of his blazing face, while the veins popped from his neck and head. If it were raining, his rage would surely have steamed right off of him. With pierced lips and bulging eyes, he stomped his way toward the trio, who winced and feared what might happen next.

"I see only one of my company present," Ivindfor sneered emphatically. "According to my recollection there should be a total of five children I hired you to have ready and safe when I arrived. Obviously, I should have hired people THAT COULD COUNT!" As Ivindfor regained his composure, the sorcerer rustled Weslo's hair as he passed saying, "By the way, it's good to see you again, Red."

Without waiting for a response, Ivindfor swirled away from them flourishing his cloak. He tapped his fingers at the railing of the stairs and wondered just how to quell the conflict that ragged on above. "Have either of you at least secured another raft for us?" He asked with his back still turned away from them.

"Yes, sir," Atana responded.

"Well, then. Why don't you load what you can and give some of the supplies to Bleke? I have a feeling we'll need to leave very quickly once we have the children."

Atana and Hrowl scurried the supplies, crates, and sacks together as Ivindfor had ordered. There was an eerie silence by the water, while the noise from above washed down onto them. Still, Ivindfor tapped his fingers and clenched his jaw, as if chewing on his own thoughts. Ava found herself amazed at the bridge itself and entirely ignored the people on it. Hazel, Morclyf, and Bleke watched her as she twirled around and inspected each beam with great admiration. Then, she casually walked backward toward Ivindfor and spun with an unusual smile on her mouth.

"Ava, I'm a little busy at the moment," Ivindfor commented, not looking at her.

"I have an idea," Ava flirted.

Ivindfor turned and rested his arm against the railing as if trying to decide if he should take her seriously. Ava, almost seductively, leaned in and whispered her thoughts to him. As she stepped back, Ivindfor tilted his head for a moment and a small smile curled on his still firm face.

"You'll have to give up some of your spirit," Ivindfor said. "It's not worth it, Ava."

"Do not suffer the living, for the dead yearn for release," she sung in reply.

Ivindfor squinted his eyes not sure he believed her. "I suppose. But make sure you put it back the way it was. I need to talk to Bleke for moment."

Ava spun gleefully and noticed the confused expressions on everyone else's face. She shrugged her shoulders and skipped over to the bridges massive beams and supports. Ivindfor motioned for Bleke. Once together, Ivindfor informed him of what the plan was and how to proceed.

"Ava, Hazel, and I will try to clean this mess up. We'll keep Atana along, as well," Ivindfor stated. "You, Hrowl, Edmund, Morclyf, and Weslo can start on without us. We won't be too far behind. Hazel can help us make up for some lost time with the current. Once you get to Wil's Landing, go by land around east of Pentasentinal and meet the others near Prudence Glade. The trip will last through the night, so try and get some rest this afternoon. Besides, it will be better to slip by the city at night."

"Are you sure about splitting everyone up? And leaving me in charge of Edmund with the others?" Bleke uncertainly asked. "I'm not as skilled as you think I am."

"Well, maybe this is your way to prove yourself," Ivindfor responded. "Besides, I need you to scout ahead and make sure the other children are safe. I believe in you and we won't be far behind. I'll send messages to the children that you will meet. Be kind and open with them. Hopefully they'll act a little more civilized than these. Good Luck!"

Ivindfor spun around and ran up the stairs, surveying the commotion of bodies fighting and pushing against each other. "Ava, give me few moments to clear the area. I'll yell down when it's alright for you to begin." Ava gazed up and around the bridge studying the posts, beams, and boards that crossed and connected like a puzzle.

Bleke looked up at Ivindfor and saw that he was waving at him to go. As he waved back acceptingly, several men shrieked as they fell from far above into the river. They had been pushed by the onlookers (Weslo's brothers) who were laughing from above. Bleke gazed at Ivindfor again, who was waving even more frantically now. Bleke turned to each in turn as he yelled, "Alright, Hazel, Kalevel get your things and yourselves on the dock, now! Hrowl, Weslo let's go, you're with me. Hrowl, take the rudder. I know I'm going to need a nap. Atana, watch over the others. We'll see you on the far east side of Pentasentinal at Prudence Glade."

Within moments, everyone and everything had shifted into the places Bleke had ordered, and within those few moments several more people had splashed into the river and were being carried past them with the current. With long, heavy poles, Hrowl and Bleke pushed the raft also into the current, floating away from the dock. Everyone gazed back at the expansive bridge as they drifted away. Bleke, however, had already slipped into the shade of the lean-to, preparing to fall asleep.

"Well," Morclyf started sarcastically. "It was fun while it lasted."

"What is that supposed to mean?" Edmund asked.

"By the time they catch up to us, Hazel and Ava will have made new, probably better friends and won't give us the time of day."

"Don't be ridiculous," Edmund responded. "Besides, I think Ava likes me."

"She's always been that way, you dolt. I thought the same thing once, too. But they're all the same. Give them something new and exciting and they gloss right over you like leftovers from the day before."

"What? That doesn't even make sense," Edmund added. "If they are really our friends, then they'll be there for us when it really counts later on. If not, then we'll know that, too."

Morclyf sat for a moment and added one last remark, "Edmund, some day you're really going to get your feelings ripped apart and you'll wish you were dead. After that, you won't be so ready to give others a second chance. And hopefully, I'll be there to say 'I told you so'."

"Maybe, Morclyf. But until then, I think I'll just enjoy the ride."

They both sat quietly as their friends disappeared when they turned with the curve of the current. Weslo sat at the front of the raft alone, looking into the river and where they were heading. He never once looked back. As the commotion and noise faded away, he relaxed in the comfort of the solitude. His smile grew wider and wider as they traveled further on. For Weslo, leaving home that day was one of the happiest moments he had ever known.

Back on the staircase, Ivindfor surveyed the mob before him. He stretched and raised his arms together toward the middle of the bridge. Slowly, he separated his hands. His arms trembled into his shoulders, as if there was a great pressure willing them from movement. But as his arms moved, the people, who were still fighting and unaware, meandered to either side of the bridge. Their bodies closed in on each other, and they were unaware that Ivindfor was in control. The only people unaffected were the parents and children of Ivindfor's following. Suddenly, they realized that they were alone in the middle of the bridge and witnessed Ivindfor below with open arms and a scowled face.

"Ava! Now! I'm not sure how long I'll be able to hold them all back," Ivindfor shouted as his arms shook violently against the pressure and movement of the crowds.

Ava stood next to one of the massive posts that went deep underneath the river. With her eyes closed, she gently slid her hands along the smooth, wooden surface. Then, with a heavy gasp, her eyes shot open as she felt the spirit of death release from her and fuse into the posts and beams of the bridge. The dead pieces of wood shuddered and heaved Ava away. She caught her balance kneeling and staring up as the posts and beams began to move and snap from the ropes, stakes, and nails that held it in place. Ava quickly moved her hands back onto the post, while focusing all her energy and thoughts on what she wanted done. All at once, Ava was a part of and channeling everything, yet completely isolated and focused by her power.

What happened next was one of the most extraordinary scenes any one on that bridge would ever see in their lives. With sudden shattering cracks and moans, the high wooden bridge snapped away from itself and transformed into a being of its own accord. Two large posts lifted and splintered off attached wooden braces for knees, while arms formed from some of the trusses spanning the bridge's length. The arms rumbled and glided under the area where the children stood. Then lastly, the railings shifted vertically upward like antennas still clinging on with guardrails loosely attached. The railing turned until two knotholes focused in on the group of children and adults who looked just as shocked and horrified as everyone else.

With a single, fluid motion the wooden giant lifted the cluster of families from what remained of the bridge. They all shifted and wobbled for balance on the remaining planks. Wood snapped deafeningly and the construct fell away from the middle outwards. By now, the personal guards of Aegil Mallister were trying desperately to rescue their stolen leader. Yet, for all their might, they could not take a step forward. The fighting had stopped and most people were desperately trying to flee through the towers. Yet, all anyone could do was walk and spin in place, as if they weren't in control of their own actions. They witnessed the bridge collapse towards into the river below. They also witnessed the great wooden giant turn and gently set the families down onto the docks where Ava stood, as if stretching out a serving tray.

As if on cue, the families scurried and leapt off of the platform of broken floorboards. The giant gazed at Ava, who beamed with adoration, and he actually winked at her with one of his knot-holed eyes. Ivindfor rushed down of what was left of the staircase and joined the shaken children huddled together. The giant raised itself straight again. The floorboards had created hands and fingers from which nails and rope dangled. The wooden giant stood still as if waiting for instructions. Then, from either side of the river, arrows began pelting and sticking into him. With each dull thud, the giant flinched as if being pricked by little needles.

Ava gasped at his agony as the arrows flew harder, and rushed over to one of the giant's legs, murmured softly, then carefully backed away. The wooden giant lifted a leg from the river, splashing mud and water onto the docks. Ava had tears running down her face now, and the giant stretched out a huge, wooden finger and brushed her cheek. She flinched as a few splinters pricked her skin, but Ava smiled at the giant's offer of tenderness. Then, the great wooden giant slowly pivoted and stepped clumsily up river.

"I promise, I'll come visit you as soon as I can!" Ava yelled and the giant twisted his eyes and waved back, flinching occasionally at the pierce of an arrow.

"Ava! I told you to put the bridge back!" Ivindfor yelled and rushed to her side.

The tall girl with the white striped black hair simply smiled widely and stated, "I can't put something back that's not mine anymore. He needs to go and be what he is now."

"Ava had tears running down her face now..."

"Where did you tell him to go?" Ivindfor replied.

"I told him to go to the Forest of the Fallen. No one will bother him there."

Aegil stomped toward Ava and Ivindfor. "What in the world have you two done? You've destroyed the bridge! This is a catastrophe for our people!"

As the other angry parents gathered around Aegil, Ivindfor turned toward them with a serious glare and looked up at the fuming Vald. "Oh, it's just a bunch of wood anyway! It's been broken before and you people have always seemed to rebuild it just fine. A more important issue is why all of you were fighting on it in the first place!"

"But, we don't have the time to discuss that right now. And if I were you," Ivindfor directed to all of the parents and siblings," I would try to find a way out of here now, before the archers run out of range and start shooting at us! Say a quick good-bye to your children. Westril, Weslo is fine. I'll send letters about our progress, until then – 'Live well and die better'!"

The last part of Ivindfor's statement was a customary farewell between the Valds and Stouts. They knew he was serious and they knew he was also serious about the archers. More and more people had shifted their attention toward them. Most of the parents hugged their children and helped load whatever belongings they could still find in the wreckage of the bridge. Hazel, Atana, and Kalevel helped as much as they could and quickly helped everyone onto the raft. Everyone except Sytheria.

"I am not going with this lunatic!" she screamed in protest.

Aegil came to her side and defended her, "Ivindfor, I cannot allow you to take her. This is all too much. She has a right to stay and her place is here with us."

Ivindfor shook his head in disgust, simply lifted his arm, and said, "Sytheria walk onto the raft. Now."

With a jolt, the girl stepped forward against her own will and continued toward the raft. "Father, help me! Make him stop! I don't want to go!"

Before Aegil Mallister could respond, Ivindfor interjected, "We do not have time for this! I paid a great price to give these children what they have and you promised to help me a long time ago. She isn't just your daughter, she is also my apprentice. For now, she is mine!" Ivindfor turned one last time to the families and stressed with urgency, "Ava's pet is out of range. We have go, and you have to go. Now! Stay near Aegil, you'll be safest with him. Once again, 'Live well and die better'." With a flurry he spun and jumped onto the raft. "Atana take the rudder. Vigil help me push off. Hazel get the current moving and the rest of you grab a paddle. We've got time to make up!"

Unable to resist his commands, everyone obeyed like a finely disciplined ship crew. As they entered the current, the raft gained exceptional speed. Behind them, Aegil's personal guard had managed to make their way down to the river. Devout and courageous, they protected everyone with their gigantic shields as shots from slings and arrows pelted down on them. Their only escape appeared to be on a raft, as well. Then, the Towers of Immigrate and Extradite thundered as pieces stone and wood collapsed down. Some structural parts of the Towers were collapsing around the crowds below. The civilians and guards scattered in the dust, forgetting about the families below. From then on, however, the Valds and Stouts would always solemnly observe that day as 'Disbridgement Day'. For most, the event marked an end of peace and prosperity, symbolizing an era of uncertainty and unrest.

Ivindfor trembled and clutched himself. He lost his hold on those aboard the raft and everyone looked back to see the dust cloud rise above the horizon. Stunned, they sat motionless. Then, tears began to fill all of their eyes as they tried to grasp the magnitude of what had happened.

Ava couldn't breathe and began choking. "It's all my fault. I can't believe what I just did." She began to fade like a chameleon, but out of control. Hazel wrapped herself around her, trying to help calm her down.

"Do you think anyone is hurt? Should we go back to help?" Yhan asked helplessly.

"Yes, there are people hurt, possibly dead," Ivindfor replied gruffly. "But no, we are not going back."

"What about our families? Our friends? Our people? We have powers that could help them?" Vigil stood intense and poised for action.

"Well, let this be a lesson for all of you," said a composed Ivindfor. "No one here is without blame for what's occurred. All that's happened has led us to this moment and from here the future is made. We all had our part to play, whether we like it, or not. Because of me, you were born as you are. Because of your parents you behave as you do. Because of your peers, you act and react the way you do. Because of you, a struggle arose on that bridge. Because of that, I reacted out of anger and allowed Ava to do something I should have handled myself. Because of her, everything fell apart."

"Now listen carefully," Ivindfor spoke louder and with greater clarity, controlling the actions of those on board once again. "Never suppose you do not matter, even in the smallest of events. You all can think and believe whatever you want. When you speak and act, everything becomes affected by it. Just see what has happened here today. Can you all see how simple words and actions lead to more severe consequences? Can you all see how in the rashness of anger, wisdom is forgotten. Even with all my years, I still make mistakes. Sometimes, I think regret is never painful enough. Someday, maybe enough hurt will keep us all from making mistakes."

After about a half-an-hour, Ivindfor crumbled to the floor, exhausted. The warm breeze washed over them all as they silently and sadly flowed with the river.

"I have much to do. I also need some rest, as I'm sure all of you do." Ivindfor softly said and let go of his will upon them. He grasped for some paper from Kalevel and pricked his finger allowing blood to drop onto a dozen pages or more. In between each drop, Ivindfor would mutter something under his breath. Then, once completed, he rolled, tied, and threw each piece of paper into the air. Seemingly, out of nowhere, birds swooped down, snatched each note, and then flew off in separate directions. With heavy eyelids, Ivindfor raised his head with effort and spoke, "Atana, wake me when we get to Wil's Landing, or if any of our passengers give you trouble. And if anyone does make trouble for

Atana, I'll do more than just control your body, I'll make you suffer a little within it." He fell back completely unconscious and snoring.

Atana glanced around at the children who were now looking toward her with frightened, yet drowsy, reddened eyes. Wondering what she had gotten herself and Hrowl into, she merely looked ahead and steered the raft confidently. One by one, the children fell asleep with the rocking of the boat. Kalevel sat writing, sometimes pausing and weeping, as he tried to find the right words to describe what he had seen that day. Hazel focused on the current moving beneath them, gazing lazily at the afternoon sunlight reflecting off the water and sparkling like candles into her eyes. For some reason, she thought of her new friendship with Edmund, Morclyf, Ava and also Bleke. "Perhaps," she thought, "there is more hope in the future than you believe, Ivindfor. Perhaps, what lies ahead is the remedy that will make us all whole."

A Bleak Day for Bleke

"Most of the common creatures are rarely prepared when the old way is released against them with rage and wraith. Although, as the final moment of their life arrives, that last petrified and bewildered expression on their face always amuses me."
From, *Aereste, Sovereign of Pentasentinal*

    Hrowl sat high on 'Gauntlet', an auburn, gigantic, Valdic steed, which he acquired at Wil's landing. Hrowl's head constantly rotated, as he keenly observed the landscape around them. Tall grasses grew close to the road as only an occasional, far-off tree could offer a slip of shade from the late afternoon sun. Prancing behind Hrowl, Weslo held the reigns and walked aside a pony named 'Geoff'. The small animal strode with an easy gait, even though it pulled a small wagon over-loaded with supplies, along with Edmund and Morclyf. Absent the group was Bleke, who had shifted and flown ahead as a common hawk. Concerned about rumors of "odd-folk" passing ahead of them, Bleke decided to scout their intended route for any signs of danger.

Edmund sat next to a cramped and uncomfortable Weslo. Neither boy spoke, as they felt awkward at the way they had met. Weslo enjoyed the quiet and the few passers-by they seen on the long, straight road. Edmund worried about the others and wondered how far behind they were. The situation of traveling without Ivindfor made him nervous, even though Bleke was watching out for them. Something about Bleke, especially the scars made by the Razorback Wolves, made Edmund question his uncle's fortitude. Ivindfor appeared trustworthy of Bleke, so Edmund passed his own uncertainties cautiously aside.

As he reflected on Ivindfor and Bleke, Edmund remembered a task Bleke had asked him to take care of in his absence. Fumbling through his satchel, he felt for the texture of the card he was to give Weslo. The gritty, thick paper finally found his fingers. Edmund struggled as it caught on the inner seams of the leathery bag. Thankfully the card did not rip or bend, and he held it on his lap suddenly unsure how to explain and give it to Weslo.

"Um, Weslo," Edmund squeaked clumsily and noticed the boy startle at the sound of its name. "Bleke wanted me to give you this card. Everyone, I guess, is getting one." Edmund's voice trailed off a little discouraged at the realization that Ivindfor had not presented him with one. Even though he knew his part was unexpected and even though he couldn't see quite properly, Edmund thought by now Ivindfor would have crafted something by now. Edmund shook his head from his selfish notions as he saw Weslo's arm hang listless near his own. Edmund was awed that Weslo's spirits did not recoil from his own. Maybe Weslo was unaware of Edmund's transformation, or perhaps he simply was not affected by it.

"S-so, w-what is th-this s-supposed to d-do?" Weslo stammered embarrassingly.

Edmund replied, "Well, as far as I can tell, the card is supposed to create an image of how you see yourself, or sometimes it reflects how others look at you."

Weslo, who held the card in one hand while the reigns in the other, kept shifting his gaze from the road back to the card to see if any images surfaced. After a frustrating minute or more, Weslo was about to put the card into his own shoulder bag between his legs, when his eyes caught what appeared like swirling ink taking form. He looked up at the road for a moment. When he gazed back down on the card, he witnessed an image of himself walking, then stumbling and sliding over words that came shooting out of his mouth. With a sigh of disgust and regret, Weslo stuffed it away and tried anxiously to focus on the road again.

Morclyf, meanwhile, played with some polished stones that he spotted on the riverbank at Wil's Landing. At first, he just held and felt the smooth texture of each individual rock. Then, as he overheard Edmund's mention of the cards, the memory of his own images overshadowed the connection he had made with the stones. And one by one they shattered to dust, sifting and blowing from his hand. Opening and rolling his eyes in aggravation, Morclyf turned and added, "Don't be too disappointed from what you see, Wes- I think it's just one of Ivindfor's way of playing mind games on us. That's all. Once you spend some time with him, you'll see what I mean."

"Just because you don't have the sense to understand the images doesn't mean Ivindfor's trying to trick you," Edmund shot back. "The cards are supposed to help you understand yourself better. Shed some light on who you really are, or at least how you feel."

"Well, I feel like an idiot wasting my time with you! That's for sure!"

Weslo sat silent and looked ahead as Hrowl turned his scowling head with his fingers to his lips. "I-I think w-we n-need to k-keep it d-down," Weslo whispered and motioned toward the Vald. "D-do you th-think B-bleke'll b-be back s-soon?" he quietly forced out.

"You know," Morclyf replied. "When we arrive at Lazdrazil's, maybe she can fix your dysfunctional tongue after she's done with Edmund. I mean, it's really getting on my nerves."

"Morclyf," Edmund grumbled. "Shut up before Hrowl starts using us for target practice! Just turn around and leave us alone."

"W-whatever you s-say, E-e-edmund" Morclyf muttered sarcastically under his breath. Edmund turned around and huffed a deep sigh. Both boys felt frustrated with each other. Not so much from their differences, rather from how equally pigheaded they both were. No matter how Morclyf harshly criticized, Edmund countered with a defense, and neither boy ever felt they won. Which only frustrated them even more.

"Actually, Weslo," Edmund began to answer his question about Bleke, "I believe I see him up ahead sitting in a tree." Weslo peered ahead, tilting his head, as he tried to see beyond Hrowl and the Cavaldale.

"I-I don't s-see him," Weslo commented.

"Up ahead, there is a cluster of trees. He looks like some kind of bird perched on a branch, to me. But I'm pretty sure that's him."

Curious, Morclyf turned and peered in between the two boys and noticed a hawk clumsily keeping balance on a low tree branch. Leaves were beginning to drop from the tree, as if in autumn. "Would you look at that? Why are all those leaves dropping from that branch he's perched on? And is that an arrow sticking through his wing?" he wondered aloud. Edmund, however, could see exactly why the leaves were falling and moments later the whole branch cracked dead to the ground. Bleke tumbled down along with the withered tree limb and thudded to the parched ground. Hrowl waved them to hurry on as he galloped toward the injured bird.

The Vald leapt from Gauntlet and tried to handle the hawk as carefully as he could considering his massive, thick hands. A minute later, the boys were at his side, dumbfounded on how to help. "Mirclyf, git some clotht, bowel o' witer, an' ta' medikin kit from ta vagon. It'd be all in ta big trunk. Veslo, git a fire stirted. Use ta metal pail, we don't want ta whole grassies ta rage up 'round us. Be quick, now! Mister Bleke's in bid shipe."

"What can I do to help?" Edmund asked nervously.

Before Hrowl could answer, Bleke tumbled from the Vald's enormous hands and began convulsing. The hawk's feathers began to shake away as Bleke screeched and vigorously attempted to shift back to his human form. Slowly and horribly, his body returned, the fiber of his clothes wrapped around him, and finally his voice screamed painfully into the air. Exhausted, he slumped to his side, shivering.

Edmund and Hrowl moved closer to him as he panted, dripping sweat and blood. "Uncle Bleke, can you hear me?" Edmund asked softly as he knelt beside him.

"Clear as a bell, my boy," Bleke replied with twitching smile. "Help me sit up, won't you?"

They gingerly lifted the wounded man up and Edmund knelt behind him for some support. He felt blood drip from the arrowhead and shaft that stuck through his left shoulder. Hrowl carefully slit open Bleke's shirt and inspected the wound and the arrow. His eyes narrowed and his face grimaced at both, then with a sigh he gazed into Bleke's eyes.

"Looks worse than it feels," Bleke replied to Hrowl's concern.

"Looks as if ya git nicked in ta vein. You're bleedin' like crizy. Mire if'n we pull tis slug out o' ya. A silid mital irrow. Haven't sin one o' tese in a ling time. Cin't brike em' cline enough to rin tru, or bick." Hrowl scratched his full beard and considered what do, when Morclyf arrived with the supplies from the wagon.

"Here are the..." Morclyf stopped short when he saw Bleke's wound and blood coming from it.

"Tank-ya lid. Here, tike sime o' tis cloth and wrip it on ta bickside, while I do ta front. 'ave Edmind hold it, once you've got it. Edmind, hold it firm a'right?"

"Morclyf, fetch some paper. And quick," Bleke pleaded.

Morclyf rushed back to the wagon and found some clean sheets of paper in Edmund's bag. Considering the circumstances, he was sure Edmund would not mind him rummaging through his things. Besides, Morclyf knew he personally had not packed any paper worth writing on, and frankly did not know if Weslo even knew how to write. After flinging several objects carelessly over his shoulders, Morclyf snatched a few sheets of clean paper. Within moments, he was back by the bleeding Bleke with crumpled paper in his trembling hand.

"Good. Thank you, Morclyf," Bleke said and noticed his shaking hand tightly gripping the paper. He grasped it gently. "Don't worry, everything will be alright. I'm sure none of you expected such an adventure, now did you? Well, I need to hurry and get a message off to Ivindfor."

"Here, my pen," Edmund offered.

"Won't need it. Thanks anyway, Ed'." Bleke replied and touched his wound softly until blood pooled onto his fingertip. Then, he held the finger over a piece of paper, thought for a moment, and let the droplet fall onto the page. In a flash, the stain vanished completely, and Bleke handed sheet back to Morclyf. "Roll and tie it up for me, would you?" Just as Morclyf had finished tightening a slip-knot, a bird swooped down, dropped a note from Ivindfor, circled back and snatched away the one in Morclyf's hand. Morclyf jumped and began swatting the air, as the bird flew high off into the air.

"Excellent timing!" Bleke blurted, spitting a little blood over his lips. "Let's see what news there is from old Iv." Weslo approached as he opened the letter, and they all stared at the empty page. Then, magically, letters and words began to appear and disappear in succession. To his surprise, Edmund could see the words wafting like smoke in his hazy eyesight. He excitedly followed each letter with enthusiasm. Altogether, he letter was this:

Bleke,

Unfortunately, since you left, things have fallen apart. Literally. Ava brought the bridge to life, let it go, and then the towers began to crumble. The children are stubborn, tired, but fine. I have sent messages to inquire about the parents and their condition. Hopefully, they survived and will remain safe. I suggested they seek shelter at the Wayfarer's Inn until things quiet down (which could be a long time)! We should not be too far behind. Hope all is well.

~Iv

"Well, he certainly knows how to make an exit," Bleke responded.

"Ta bridge ire gone?" Hrowl asked dumbstruck.

"I'm afraid so," Bleke replied in a more sensitive tone. "I'm sorry for you and your people."

Hrowl gazed off in remembrance and imagination of what the disaster must have been like. Edmund was smiling though and blurted out, "I could read that! How in the world do you do that?"

Bleke painfully chuckled and throatily replied, "It's wizard's writing. You throw your thoughts into a drop or two of your blood and it comes to life to the reader it's addressed to, and only he or she can unlock the words. Pretty amazing, huh?"

"I'd say! I can't wait for you to teach me how!" Edmund replied.

"Firs', we gotta figure how ta kipe 'im from dyin'," grumbled Hrowl. "You might like vizard vritin', bit ta ting in 'is shouldir be a vizard's irrow. Brickable only by ta vizard more powirfil thin ta ine who mide it. Since he ain't done 'imself yit, I rickon it's more powirfil tan Bleke. Im I rit?"

"Too right. Our friend here knows a bit about magical weapons."

"Bin 'round a fiw ta know not ta be 'round tem t'at all," Hrowl replied. "So, giss we wit for Iv' ta git hire, ten."

"I don't see that we have much choice," agreed Bleke.

"Who did this? Was it Lazdrazil?" Edmund queried.

Bleke sighed and replied, "No, I wish it were. They were Sylfaen's from Pentasentinal disguised as servants of Lazdrazil. It appears Aereste has discovered what Ivindfor is up to, as well, and sent them. And from their response, they're not pleased about what Iv' has done."

"Sylfin's? Ire yi sire 'bout t'it?" Hrowl questioned. "Thi nivir come out o' ta city. Mist be pritty piss'd 'bit ill tis."

"Language aside, I would agree with you, Hrowl. Ivindfor seems to be making more enemies every day." Bleke glared about the Vald's choice of words.

"E-excuse me," Weslo interrupted. "B-but, a-are w-we still g-going to n-need the f-fire?"

"Fire!" Bleke shouted at Hrowl. "I told you absolutely no fires!"

"I pinicked in' forgot," Hrowl gruffed. "'Sides, t'ought I'd hive ta burn ta vound."

"Put that fire out!" Bleke ordered.

Weslo stepped back and felt as though he had done something horribly wrong, but before he turned to walk away, Weslo gazed at the arrow for a long hard minute.

"Weslo, I meant now!" Bleke barked, but Weslo did not flinch or react. He was entranced in a thought that did not budge his concentration.

As Weslo began to speak, everyone noticed he did not stutter once, "Hrowl, you said that the arrow could only be broken by a wizard more powerful than the one who made it, right?" Hrowl nodded still amazed at Weslo's steady, fluid speech. "By my count, we've got four sorcerer's here. We can do it together." Weslo's speech was so strong and spirited, that everyone felt energized and positive that they could actually break the wizard's arrow, pull it through, and heal Bleke.

"Well, I'm up for not bleeding to death," Bleke responded with raised eyebrows. "Besides, who know long it may take Ivindfor to catch up with us. Although, he's going to be really mad that we let Edmund use his powers," he turned to Edmund and continued. "I trust you, Edmund. I know you haven't got a clue what to do, but that's the beauty of it. Your spirit will guide you, as long as you command it with confidence."

Edmund nodded hesitantly, then looked up at Weslo. His spirits were melding together as one, as was Morclyf's. Bleke, too, was preparing himself as the spirits fused together, interweaving their colors into something new. Although anxious, Edmund was more focused than he had ever been in his life. He felt prepared and willing to perform whatever task needed to help his uncle.

"Edmund, get some fire," Weslo ordered. "When you come back, we'll be ready to help break and pull the arrow out. Morclyf, we'll need to stand and hold the shaft behind Bleke."

As Edmund walked around the wagon to the fire, Bleke eyed and whispered to Hrowl. "Once this is done, I may pass-out. No, I know I'll pass-out. I told Ivindfor that we'd be crossing through the cover of the grasses to Prudence Glade. Make sure to scout for the Sylfaen's before going into the glade. They may very well be waiting for us there. If there's any doubt, wait for Ivindfor. Do not try to approach them."

Hrowl nodded. "Don' worry. I'll kip tem sife for ya. Jist hing in tire'. Hisn't bin one o' yir brightist diys, ih?"

"No, my friend, quite a bleak one for this Bleke. That's for sure!" Bleke responded and laughed harshly as blood spit up over his lips and down his chin. He could feel the arrow throbbing and emanating magic into his body. He was constantly trying to counter the effects, but knew he could not last long. Then, with a deep sigh, he closed his eyes and prepared to help the boys any way he could.

Edmund returned from the wagon with a ball of flickering fire dancing in the upturned palm of his right hand. He was staring at it, not in amazement, but with control. Morclyf's mouth dropped open, while Weslo signaled with his finger to his mouth as to not mutter a sound. All around them, the sounds of birds, bugs, and animals vanished. The wind was even stilled. Weslo grabbed Morclyf's hand and placed it over his own which was wrapped around the bloody arrow shaft, just below the arrowhead. Each boy inhaled deeply as they felt their powers surge and bond together against the arrow.

Hrowl retreated back, giving Edmund room in front of Bleke. The flame glowed, as the faint smell of burning flesh filled the air. Without speaking a word, without glancing at his uncle, Edmund stood entranced, as if waiting for some signal, or order. "Give us another minute, Edmund," Weslo whispered and shivered. "When I say 'now', grab the arrow. We'll try to help from up here, but...it's...not...letting...us; The arrow's being...difficult."
In the background, Geoff, the pony, and the Cavaldale beat the dirt with their hooves. Hrowl nervously watched Morclyf's and Weslo's forearms tremble, and he was about to reach out and stop their endeavor, when Weslo's eyes widened and his mouth screamed, "NOW, EDMUND!"

With lightning speed, Edmund flipped his hand over with the ball of fire and grasped around the arrow. With his other hand, he cupped the flames confined and focused. The fire danced violently around the metal bar forcing enough pressure against Edmund's hands that he could not clench his fists tight. Bright white light and sparks leapt through his fingers and his hands. The light became so intense that Hrowl could no longer gaze directly at it, as Edmund's hands vanished in the intense heat. Hrowl did notice, however, the wounds Edmund had were beginning to smoke and smolder through his clothes. He grabbed the bowl of water, ready to dowse him at any moment.

Bleke convulsed as beads of sweat ran down his face and dripped over his closed eyes. Embers from the arrow shot towards his chest and face, but the small sparks did not make him flinch. The boys tried with all their might to hold steady as the arrow fought back from being broken. Edmund's eyes were narrow and wild as he felt the spirit within him fuel the fire while protecting and regenerating his skin. Morclyf and Weslo could feel the heat transfer up the shaft through Bleke and toward their hold. They focused on breaking the metal as Edmund burned through it. Then, with a terrible, explosive crack and hiss, Edmund fell backwards as the shaft finally broke clean, while in the same moment Weslo and Morclyf yelled in unison: "PULL!"

As the arrow slid through Bleke's body, sparks shot out in front of him, then at his back until it was finally out. He shook furiously lifting his head skyward, then silently fell to his side. As Bleke hit the ground, a small puff of smoke came from his wound and floated away. The boys hurtled to the ground unconscious, and the remaining parts of the wizards arrow fell to the ground and dissolved into the dirt.

Edmund lay on the ground grunting, and yet still holding the fire in his cupped hands. Smoke swirled around him and he felt paralyzed by the force of the fire spirit. The wild, elemental energy wanted to feed on anything and everything it could, even Edmund's body if it had too. Edmund, however, used all his strength to control and fade the spirits' power, but seemed overwhelmed. Hrowl tossed the bowl of water over Edmund's head, and steam hissed immediately. The light in his hands diminished, and Edmund's body shook in the shock of the cold water. Hrowl ran back and threw more water on him, as if trying to extinguish a campfire. Finally, after a half dozen bowls had been emptied, Edmund's body stopped sizzling, and he slept, panting heavily.

Hrowl rushed over and knelt near Bleke, who was breathing hard but steadily. The wound had been seared shut on either side of his shoulder and was blackened from the burn. Then, Hrowl peered over at Weslo and Morclyf who lay unconscious. Hrowl fumbled with what salves and medicines he could find in Edmund's bag, and applied them gently on Bleke and Edmund, who sighed and moaned from his touch.

After frantically making room in the wagon, he stood scratching his head over the laying bodies and said out loud, "Yip, ol' Iv's not goin' ta bi hippy 'bout tis. In' hire's Hrowl, hivin' ta pick ip ta mess tat teese know-it-all's mike! Itini wis spot-on. Whit did wi git oursilfs in ta? Jus' one middle iftir inothir, if ya isk mi!" Then, he carefully rested each of the children and Bleke comfortably into the wagon, tied Geoff alongside his Cavaldale to help pull, and disappeared through the tall grasses and setting sun toward Prudence Glade.

The sharp, steady throbbing from Bleke's shoulder woke him out his deep sleep. He blinked and rubbed his face trying to focus his hazy eyes. The continuous creak of wagon wheels created an overwhelming head ache, as well. Wild dreams and restless visions haunted him throughout his slumber. He was glad to be awake again and away from the imaginings his mind had made. The day was cloudy and he could smell rain somewhere in the distance. Soft rumbles of thunder barely confirmed his awareness of a storm. After taking several sighs and clearing his dry mouth, Bleke managed to scoot himself up, realizing none of the children were with him.

Carefully turning his stiff neck, the wizard noticed a large man driving the wagon. At first, Bleke anticipated Hrowl, but this man was too small to be a Vald and yet larger than any median. Weakly, he squinted and shifted a little more to see who the driver was. He accidentally kicked a barrel noisily tipping it over and alerting the driver's attention. The mysterious figure stopped the wagon and turned his body toward Bleke, who could hardly move in his tired state.

"Well, it's about time you woke up," said a low, powerful voice. Bleke desperately tried to recall who the man was. "By the look on your face, you don't remember who I am. I suppose it has been a while, and your marbles might still be a little stirred up. Does the name Beohlor bring back any memories?"

Bleke calmly nodded in reassurance, and roughly asked, "Where are the children and Hrowl?"

"Oh, they're safe enough, I guess. And Ivindfor isn't upset at all about what happened a few days ago. He's just happy you're alive and told me to get you to Havenshade right away."

"A few days ago? Is that how long I've been unconscious?" Bleke shook his head in disbelief. "What's happened since then?"

"Well, after I heard that *my* Towers had been broken up a bit, I asked a friend of mine to fly me there from Divis Torgul, but then I spotted you all sneaking through the grasses. I figured something was wrong and joined up with Hrowl, who filled me in on what had happened. Long story short, the Sylfaen's had the other children and their parents held captive at Prudence Glade. They gladly expressed that Ivindfor and any of his followers were considered enemies of Pentasentinal. Those Sylfaen wizards put up a pretty good fight, but Sovereign Aereste didn't send his best. That's for sure. I hate having to kill off wizards. No matter what the reason, it just never feels right." Beohlor paused in distressed reflection, then continued, "Good group of kids, though. They even helped Hrowl and me with some of their tricks. The parents were scared to death, especially since they can't go back home to Pentasentinal, now."

"Where is everyone then?" Bleke asked.

"Well, they finally made it to Lazdrazil's. Edmund was in even worse shape, but I think he'll turn out fine. The other two boys just needed some rest. Ivindfor sent the parents from Prudence Glade to Dohlemar's place. He'll keep them safe and find them new homes, in time. I tell you, Bleke, Ivindfor's really made a mess of this whole thing. I know he's trying to bring the world together, but right now, he's ripping it apart all along the way."

"Sometimes, I wonder if I chose the right path to follow," Bleke added groggily. "Do you think Ivindfor's still got a chance? Is all of what he's doing really for the greater good, Beohlor?"

Beohlor thought for a moment, and as he was about to reply, he noticed that Bleke had already fallen asleep. And yet, he softly replied, "Ivindfor hasn't cared about good or bad for a long time. The object of his intentions is revenge."

An Airing of Differences

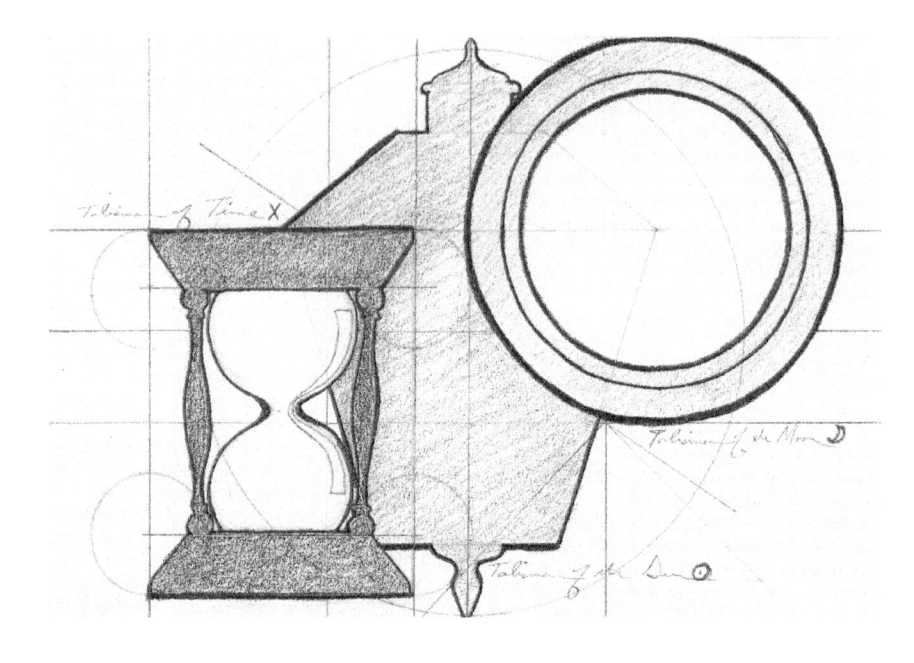

> The wind whispers truths and comforts,
> Be'ware of what you receive,
> Be'ware of what you believe,
> The wind hisses lies and deceits.
> From, *A Scythian Proverb*

"They all hate me," Ava whispered anxiously to Hazel, as they both peered through the dense fog at the Valdic and Stout children who were gathered many yards away.

"They don't hate you, Ava," replied Hazel. "They're just worried, like the rest of us. Especially the new ones."

"Oh, I'm sure they've heard all about how I destroyed the greatest landmark of order and rule in the whole world!" Ava exclaimed as she paced around Hazel. "But I'm telling you this,

Hazel," she said and stopped suddenly snapping her finger straight toward Hazel's reeling head. "I did not do anything to damage the Towers! When I felt the bridge, I knew which supports to take and which ones to leave. Besides, the Towers' foundations were firm and deep into the rock bed – I felt a deeper power there. There is no way the bridge could have made them crumble. I know it!"

"How else could they have been damaged?" asked Hazel, a little offended at Ava's finger and tone. "We were already traveling down the river. Who else could have done it? I know you didn't mean to, and maybe it was just a series of acts working together...." She shook her head trying to figure out a logical theory of the events, even if only through her imagination. "I don't know, Ava. I just can't see any other way..."

"Somebody else did it. I'm not strong enough to do damage to structures of stone, no matter how old, or new," Ava said as she looked down into Hazel's eyes. "I know there was enough support. I felt it, heard it, and I only took what I needed. You have to believe me."

"I believe you," whispered a voice that was not Hazel's at all. Both girls' eyes blinked and widened at each other for a moment, until they were alerted to the presence of another girl suddenly next to them.

"My name is Vaespril," the girl whispered again. Both Ava and Hazel took in the loveliness of her dress and charisma, with an air of jealousy. Her long hair was as black as the night sky and shimmered as if tiny, glittery stars were twinkling from within. She had long, narrow dark eyes that stretched on a face that had a round, golden complexion. She appeared neither too harsh, nor too feeble. She was the epitome of her race. Vaespril was a Sylfaen.

"Where did you come from and how much did you hear?" Ava snapped back.

"I'm sorry," Vaespril replied as she bowed her head a little. "I see you both have not been around other air-borns before. I saw how upset you were and eavesdropped. We can hear all sorts of things through the air, but you already know that. And Hazel, you're somewhat of one too, aren't you? I heard you've been blessed with controlling two elements."

"That's true," Hazel replied hesitantly. "But, how do you know so much about us? We haven't been told anything about you, or much of anyone else."

"Ivindfor has been sending messages constantly," Vaespril replied excitedly. "We've been kept informed about everything about your journey. It's as if we've been with you the whole time. I just wish that you had been with us at Prudence Glade. Thank goodness Beohlor and Hrowl showed up when they did. Otherwise, I don't think we'd be having this conversation."

"They were Sylfaen, like yourself," Ava added suspiciously.

"Yes, they were," Vaespril quickly agreed and then retorted, "but they are not like me at all. They were sent from within the Pinnacle of Pentasentinal. My family and I are just simple people who live within the outer market streets. But I don't suppose you understand what that really means."

Hazel smiled a little and remembered Crescent Tier with its own levels and classes and people. "You'd be very surprised how much we may understand what you mean."

"Wait. Why do you believe me," Ava interjected rudely. "The first thing you said is that you believed I didn't harm the Towers. Why?"

"Oh, thank you! I almost forgot," Vaespril said refocusing her reply. "When the Sylfaen wizards held us captive, they bragged about how strong they were. They boasted that they were the ones who 'tried to bring the Towers down', and that they were going to 'bring us all down', as well."

"You see, Hazel, I told you!" Ava spun and shoved her finger back into her face.

"Yes, I guess you did!" Hazel said, and swished around her. She was obviously more interested in what Vaespril had to say than celebrating Ava's innocence. "Do you know why they wanted us dead, Vaespril?"

"Well, not exactly," she replied shrugging her shoulders. "The rest of us think the Sylfaen's, who control Pentasentinal's security and courts, are afraid they'll lose their power to some of us. It seems ridiculous to be afraid of children, though. I mean, really, we hardly even know how to use our powers. Right?"

"Fear is a great motivator," Hazel commented, knowing the fear people in Crescent Tier had seen in her. "I'm sure they wanted to get rid of us early on before we really do become a threat."

"The only threat I see is a madman leading us right into the lair of our supposed arch-enemy," another girl said, as she, too, appeared from apparently nowhere.

"What the-," Ava spun around to find a tall (yet shorter than her), pale girl with brilliant, short blond hair, save for two black stripes that ran along the oval of her thin face.

"This is Slytemnestra," Vaespril announced.

"I prefer 'Slyte'," the girl corrected with a wicked grin.

"Ivindfor is not a 'madman'," Hazel advocated. "He's having just as hard of a time with all of this, just as we are, if not more. And as far as taking us to Lazdrazil's..."

"Don't say her name!" Vaespril shouted, looking terrified. "The wind carries it to her from where ever in the world! Even the slightest whisper can let know who and where you are. She even whispers back, especially in your dreams."

Hazel shifted her glance to Slyte whose expression of the same fear confirmed what Vaespril said. "Ava have you ever heard her?"

Ava shrugged and admitted, "A few times, I would wake up from the strangest dreams. Like they weren't my own."

"It was her," Slyte added. "I've heard that she keeps the Talisman of the Moon," she rolled her eyes realizing that Hazel and Ava were unaware of what she was talking about. "It's one of the three Talisman's of Time. Don't you two know anything? The Sylfaen's have the Talisman of the Sun, which can bring hidden things into the light, as well as manipulate fire and what is seen. It is also the center, the constant, the way to get back to the beginning, or the road to the end."

"What about the Moon?" Ava queried shyly and uninformed.

"The Talisman of the Moon hides and distorts the world as it can be seen, or known," Vaespril interjected. "It is a portal into dreams, into the unreal. It can manipulate the shadows of the unknown."

"What is the third Talisman?" Hazel asked frowning at not knowing the answer herself.

"The Talisman of Motion," both Slyte and Vaespril said in unison.

"Who keeps it?" Hazel prodded.

Slyte grinned again and nodded over toward Ivindfor, who was still conversing and reassuring the parents from Pentasentinal. "Nobody knows for sure, but we think *he* keeps it, probably at Havenshade. Otherwise, I'm sure he would have used it by now. He probably wishes he had brought it along."

"The Talisman of Motion is the energy and revolution of all things in the universe," Vaespril instructed. "With it, one can stop the movement of anything focused on, for as long as the user wills it. It manipulates energy at its very core."

Hazel and Ava both pondered the information about the Talismans silently, until again, the presence of a person emerging from seemingly nowhere made them both jump. Except this time two boys, Yhan and Vigil appeared, both smiling.

"You girls gaggle so much, we couldn't hear what Ivindfor was saying anymore," Yhan smirked, while Vigil smiled wider. "By the way, my name is Yhan and this Valdic lout is Vigil. Just thought we'd come crash your little party, if you don't mind."

"Well, I guess a little more hot-air won't hurt," Slyte sneered coyly.

Vigil turned to Ava and apologetically stated, "I heard what Vaespril said about the Sylfaen's and the Towers. I'm sorry if we seemed to blame you, or even hate you. I told the others, too. I'm glad it wasn't you. But, I still don't agree with what you did with the bridge. That was uncalled for, in my opinion."

"I thought it was brilliant," Yhan exclaimed and winked up at Ava, who half-grinned in response.

Hazel suddenly felt very out of place. She knew that she possessed some air-born traits, as Ivindfor and Edmund had seen, but she was not born as one. She began to step away from the group, when Vaespril grabbed her hand. "Don't go, Hazel. It's all right. Your spirit is welcome with us, even if unintended. I hear you're the same as 'her'. You know who."

"Yeah, I heard the 'Lady' controls two elemental powers, as well," Slyte added. "I've also heard that you've been defeating some of her spells toward Crescent Tier, and she's not too happy about that at all."

Hazel's cheeks tried to flush pink in embarrassment as she responded, "All I know is that Ivindfor's sister, LAZDRAZIL, is a selfish witch that has serious control issues. She keeps slaves, for Semmiah's sake! And she uses her powers for the sheer pleasure of seeing other people suffer. No wonder she's alone. I don't think anyone else could freely stand to be around her."

A strange breeze lifted through their hair as Hazel finished her sentence. Then, Vaespril spoke with nervous tone. "You know we have to go to her. All because of him."

"Exactly," Slyte agreed. "I've been wondering what is with that guy, anyway."

Hazel gazed through the mist at Edmund, as he lay motionless in a cart, while Weslo, Morclyf, and Hrowl looked after him. "His name is Edmund," she snapped back. "And he's been through more than any of us could 'deal' with."

"I know what his name is," Slyte responded uncaringly. "What I wonder, though, is why we're all risking our necks to get him healed? Why isn't Ivindfor taking him alone? Seems like a huge risk. Especially for something Ivindfor didn't want created in the first place."

"Edmund's more important than you know," Hazel commented and stepped close to Ava. "We were there when it happened, and we helped him in the darkness. I feel Edmund will be the one who will make us whole."

"Or, maybe," Vigil interjected, "Edmund will be the one who consumes us all."

"We have to believe that Ivindfor knows what he's doing," Ava announced. "I know it's hard to see how any of this makes sense, but he's all we've got."

"Well then, I think we're all in a lot of trouble," joked Yhan. "And by the look of it, the others aren't too confident, either."

Hazel peered through the denser fog at the new members of their group. "I heard their names earlier. But, who are they again?"

Slyte stepped confidently in front of Vaespril and spoke authoritatively. "Well, the two scruffy, pasty, smaller ones are Fulcrum and Orpholys. Fulcrum's an earth-born and Orpholys is like you, Hazel, water."

Vaespril stepped in, shooting a look to Slyte, and added, "They prefer to be called Dorman's. They're a very proud people and pretty tough, too."

"They live and work in mines and forges, Vae'," Slyte sneered, while Vaespril raised an eyebrow at her use of a shortened nickname. "Although, some are talented gem cutters and jewelers. If you're ever in the mood for amazing jewelry, there's no better place than in Pentasentinal."

Yhan interjected by adding his comments on a girl who shyly smiled as she watched a boy play with his dog. "That girl over there, watchin' the dog is Hythrae. Don't know much about her, but I think she's a cousin of his."

"Who, the boy with that weird dog?" Ava wondered.

"Yes. His name's Pahl, and his shaggy, pig-bear looking dog is Snarffle. He's probably the most normal-looking kid of any of us, I suppose," Vaespril replied. "He's a water-born, but really hasn't shown any skill, or desire to use his spirit in any way. In fact, he hasn't even said a word the whole time we've been together. And Hythrae has been gawking over him since we got together. I'm not really convinced their related, though," she frowned peering at Yhan, discontented that he might know more than she did.

"Maybe they'd rather just be a normal," Vigil added as if he, too, wished *just* to be normal.

"Oh, I think the idea of 'normal' escaped us all a long time ago, my friend," Yhan chuckled.

"Well, speaking of *abnormal*," Slyte lilted. "The sullen, scummy boy by himself is Driskal. He's a piece of work, let me tell you."

"Driskal's fine," Vaespril retorted sharply. "He's had a hard life. Another water- born. He ran away from his parents quite a while ago. I guess he's been living in the sewers of Pentasentinal. Don't know how Ivindfor ever found him. Or, how he even got him here."

"Oh, Ivindfor has his ways of making people do all sorts of things," Yhan interrupted. "Too bad, though, I mean, that he's been in sewers, you know."

There was a pause as they all reflected on the other children. They caught glimpses of returning eye contact and realized that they were being talked about too. Ivindfor was shaking and hugging the families from Pentasentinal and Vaespril and Slytemnestra saw their parent's wave at them to return.

"I guess the party's over," said Slyte, as she and Vaespril sauntered away from the group. Hazel watched them leave and caught the sight of Ivindfor as he walked to the cart where Edmund lay. The parents left with Atana, and disappeared into the mists toward the wizard, Dohlemar's home. There, the families would stay and possibly make new homes. Those left behind were tearful, yet consoled one another. Hazel shifted her gaze again on Ivindfor. With all her focus, she awakened her air elements to carry the conversation she anticipated he would have with Edmund to her.

Ivindfor dismissed Morclyf, Hrowl, and Weslo from their company and propped himself up into the cart next to Edmund. "How are feeling, my foolish, brave boy," he said with a grimaced smirk.

"The constant itching has stopped at least, but I'm still really sore," Edmund tiredly replied.

"You saved your uncles' life, and surprisingly enough, I'm glad you used your powers to do so. Besides, by performing the spell, everything is permanent. No powers any man or woman possess can divide your spirits now. They are entwined and inseparable. How do you feel and think your parents will feel about all this?"

Edmund scowled for a moment imagining the anger and frustration they would feel, then relaxed and replied, "They'll be upset, worried, angry, and happy that I'm still alive. I suppose they'll be a lot of everything. But hopefully they'll understand. I am still me. Aren't I?"

"Of course you are! They love you very much, Edmund. Me on the other hand; not so much after this. Your father and I have had some great adventures together, but this may cause a rift that will not be easily healed."

"I believe true friendships never really change," Edmund said hopefully.

"Ah, but they do, Edmund, just as people can change. Just look at yourself,' Ivindfor entreated. "Do you honestly think that Waddle will not treat you differently now that you're a sorcerer?"

Edmund paused for a while and thought about home, his family, and friend. For the first time, he realized how different his relationships would be with them. Even the interactions with Ava, Hazel, and Morclyf were different from when they first met. Now, with all of the new faces and diversity within their group, Edmund wondered what other changes would follow.

"We will be crossing Mirrored Lake to Laz's Keep very soon," Ivindfor pointed out. "I need you to make a decision that only you can make." Edmund scowled again, as he waited for what other new issue he would have to deal with. "Now, Edmund, I need you to choose three people with whom you want to watch over you while we're with Lazdrazil. I understand that you don't know many of the children here very well, but I'm not asking you whom you trust, or who're friends with. I want you to choose people who you will be responsible for you. Concentrate and really look at them. You've mentioned how spirits can connect, or move away from one another. Perhaps they can show you more than you realize."

Edmund continued to scowl, knowing he'd want Hazel, Weslo, and Ava with him, yet humbled Ivindfor by tenderly sitting up to view the others in his own 'sighted' way. Ivindfor added, "Being trustworthy is a belief, Edmund. Responsibility can be seen in one's confidence, or fear." By now, Edmund had identified all of the children's spirits through their color and size. Yet, as he focused his mind on who was 'responsible', Edmund noticed their intensities fade, or swell. At that moment, he also realized he had the power to see into the very nature of their personality.

"How is this possible?" Edmund asked in amazement.

Ivindfor smiled at Edmund's quick progress, 'You've gained insight to the ethereal realm."

After a moment more, Edmund mouthed aloud three names, "Fulcrum, Vaespril, and Driskal."

"So be it," was Ivindfor's only reply, and then quickly helped Edmund lay to rest again. "I have one last request," he bent and whispered in to Edmund's ear. "From now on, you will be closest to me. We must both be confidants with one another. I will need your sight to help make certain decisions. I hope to include you, and your thoughts about them."

"That sounds like a lot of responsibility," Edmund said with a sarcastic yawn.

Ivindfor chuckled and continued, "You're a lot like your father, Edmund. At times, this feels like the days when he and I were together, causing mischief of one kind or another. I am very thankful that you are here with me."

"Just get me up and on me feet again?" Edmund lightheartedly pleaded.

"Right," Ivindfor agreed and scooted himself off of the cart and walked briskly toward his following. He called over to Kalevel and asked him to sit with Edmund, as he wanted time with the other children.

Hazel stood feeling violated and betrayed. Not only did Ivindfor give her the early impression that she was his most favored, he had led her to believe that she would be an authority along with him. "Perhaps," she thought and frowned, "when people change, those who are affected change, too." She unclenched her fists and lightly glided, unenthused, toward Ivindfor and the others collected together.

Ivindfor began: "From this moment on, changes may occur that are out of my control. Well, frankly, a lot of things have happened that have been out of my control. So, if you would all take out the cards I've given you, we'll get started." They all searched around for the dirty cards given to them upon introduction. Once Ivindfor saw them revealed, he continued. "Good. Once we cross Mirrored Lake, none of you will be have the ability to use the full strength of your powers. It is one of Lazdrazil's greatest defenses. Also, there are too many of you for me to watch over all the time. Which reminds me. Fulcrum, Vigil, and Driskal. You three will have the duty of watching over Edmund once inside the Keep. Now, I need you to give your card to someone else and hold his or her hand for few moments. It doesn't matter whom. This isn't a test, just reinforcing your memory." The children awkwardly found a partner closest to them. "Alright. Look at the image on the card and take your time. It is very important you remember this. Once we cross over Mirrored Lake, your mind may play games with you, and this will be the anchor of knowing how you were before we crossed. These images will be your connection between what is real and what you believe is real." After several minutes, Ivindfor circled the area making sure his pupils were performing the requested task, and gazing periodically at the cards. Then, he instructed them to return the cards, preparing to leave. "I don't intend to frighten you, but for once I have the chance to offer you some safeguard. Not that we need it, necessarily. But one never knows." Ivindfor caught himself nervously stammering as he also saw his apprehension in the children's suspicious eyes. "We'll all be just fine, just fine." As Ivindfor turned, he mumbled to himself, "Well, most of us..."

What Ivindfor couldn't see were all the air-borns' widened eyes and reaction to his last, secretive words.

The Passover of Haze-

> From over the river, from over hill,
> Through the misty morning, through the clear night,
> The winds whisper the name of Lazdrazil
> Whose ghost will haunt us, whether dark, or light.
> From, *Finley's Fables for Young Children*

    As they followed Ivindfor closer to Mirrored Lake, the children observed how the mists grew denser, and how much damper and colder the air felt. There was no distinction between the humidity hovering with them and the water dripping off trees and onto them. Everyone was miserable and their thoughts grew as dank as their surroundings. Finally, they came out of the tree line and on to the pebbled, slippery bank of Mirrored Lake, which was, not to their surprise, just as uninviting as the forest around it.

"No one touches the liquid of this lake!" Ivindfor warned. "Pahl, make sure your wretched dog doesn't try to go for drink, or it'll be the last thing you ever see him do. The liquid is not water, nor anything quite natural. This is Lazdrazil's own making. Whoever touches the liquid will become it, and so the lake grows. Many adventurers and poor souls have perished into this place over the years. Make sure you're not one of them."

"Then how do we cross?" wondered Morclyf as he flippantly willed stones into the silvery, steady liquid.

"Cut that out," Ivindfor swatted from afar. Morclyf instantly reacted as if being throttled at close distance, dropping his will and focus. "We wait for the boats to arrive. I'm sure she's well aware we're here."

"So, we just wait then?" Morclyf sneered in response to his recent punishment.

"Yes, Morclyf, we wait."

"If the lake swallows everything it touches, then how can boats float on it?"

"Morclyf," Ivindfor spoke with a frustrated sigh, "By now, you should realize that what a sorcerer, or sorceress creates can also be manipulated by them."

"Kind of like you with us," Morclyf shot back quickly.

Ivindfor turned his head slowly and narrowed his eyes. Before he could reply, however, they both noticed Pahl attempting to hold Snarffle, as the dog barked repeatedly out over the lake. "Everyone. The boats are here!" Ivindfor cried out. "Line up and absolutely no fooling around! It's time to meet the Lady of this place, and we must push aside our fears for the sake of the path we now follow."

Through the murky air, three curvaceous, honed, grayed, driftwood boats slowly emerged into sight and scraped onto the rocky shoreline. No waves rippled, no natural motion carried them, and no pleasure was found in their approach. The still eeriness was broken only as a raven cawed in the far distance of the forest behind them. Then, as a ramp was lowered from the stern of each boat, a servant dressed in shimmering silver cloaks stepped briskly forward until they met with Ivindfor. They neither bowed nor shook Ivindfor's hand, nor did they greet him with any words. The three men merely stood and waited for Ivindfor to make the first move.

"As I am sure you know, we are here to see the Lady Lazdrazil. I am her brother, Ivindfor, and these are my followers. She has honored us a visitation upon my request, as one of mine is in need of healing."

The middle servant brushed back his hood, which exposed his thin perfectly composed face and thinning gray hair. "Greetings to Mirrored Lake. My name is Izwold, Headmaster of the Lady's Keep. The Mistress has been anxiously awaiting your arrival, second son of Aelen. She regrets your journey has been so difficult. Our Lady offers whatever comfort you and yours require."

"We appreciate all that she is," Ivindfor said with a small nod.

"You're etiquette and dialogue surpass you, sir," the servant complemented and nodded in return. "Let us lead you to Our Lady, then."

Ivindfor divided the children individually into which boats they would travel, and when he approached Hazel (who barely looked at him with a frowning countenance), he whispered. "I need you to be in the farthest boat. I have a feeling your powers won't fade as we cross, but do not show any sign of it. We may need that element of surprise later on."

Hazel shot him a look of surprise, then caution, as if questioning his motives. "Am I just a plaything for him to take notice, or ignore whenever he wants?" she thought. Yet, considering the circumstances, she obeyed his order and joined those boarding the farthest of Lazdrazil's boats.

The crafts were long and shaped like a 'u' all around. The sides were high, so that, when the children, even the Vald's, sat down, no one could see the lake outside the gray hulls. The wood was smooth driftwood, and blended in with the swirling, murky mists developing around them. Ivindfor watched as Fulcrum, Vigil, and Driskal carefully carried Edmund into the boat between Hazel and himself. The servant motioned for Ivindfor to sit as he raised the ramp into position. Ivindfor shook his head and remained standing, peering hard through the fog at the other boats. Accommodating his denial, the servant jostled to the other end, whispered a few words into the air, and the boats moved hauntingly and silently over Mirrored Lake.

Unable to comprehend time or space, the crossing felt tiresome and long for everyone except Ivindfor. He stood focused, concentrating on the other boats as they slid over the unmoving fluid beneath them. Occasionally, he would glance at the children who were with him. At first, they appeared as they did on shore. Then, gradually, each child at different intervals grew solemn and withdrawn. A few even began to whimper, as their elemental spirit disconnected from their own. No longer could they understand the language that had been part of them. No longer could they feel the energy that had given them strength. They felt average and empty for the first time in their lives.

Ivindfor, however, saw this as an opportunity for them to fully understand the differences they have with common people. He secretly hoped this would lead them to understand the marvelous abilities they enjoyed. He knew how lonely most of them had become. How frightened they were to be who they were, as if they were afraid of not having the support of their spirit to help them in the smallest of thoughts and actions. They shuddered, like they were lost in withdrawal, emptiness, and heartbreak.

The only one of the children still satisfied was Pahl. He sat in Ivindfor's boat and smiled stupidly, as he held Snarffle closely to him. Pahl had never shown interest in listening and speaking to the water spirit within him. In fact, he spent much of his life trying to stay as far away from anything liquid his whole life. As much as his water spirit tried to connect with him, the further away Pahl's spirit drifted. Ivindfor was not exactly sure why Pahl acted this way, but he could clearly see that these moments were probably a few of the happiest Pahl had ever known.

Hazel sat and tried to mimic those close to her, as she remembered their voyage through the Forest of the Fallen. And yet, all she knew now was how horrible and tortured the others appeared. In a moment of compassion, Hazel comforted the others by saying, "I know we feel alone and empty, but we have each other and that still means something." They nodded and winced as if trying to be hopeful with her, but she saw them quickly drift within their own melancholy losses.

As time elapsed, Hazel noticed the elemental powers within her grow more intense than ever before. The tuning fork vibrations reverberated so hard within her, she felt as if her skin would shudder from her body. The power swelled, as her memory recalled the night Edmund was struck by lightning. The whole might of the world channeled through then, her as it did now. Hazel could not comprehend her connection with those events, and being on Mirrored Lake. Nor could she deny the forces affecting her. Entranced with the intensity, Hazel connected with Edmund's spirit through her own, trembling with fear, pain, and pleasure.

Edmund lay half-awake, not sure of the circumstances within and around him. He dreamed about his home and family in Essil, yet there were ferocious and shadowy images frightening him about it, too. Edmund considered them thoughts related to the internal and external pains throbbing like he had never known before. Now, he understood why Ivindfor was so worried. The fire within him wanted to consume everything, and controlling that power had been Edmund's focus ever since using it to help Bleke. As he closed his eyes, Edmund suddenly knew Hazel was there with him. He was aware of her and the spirit of the world working through her. She took his breath away, gave him hers, calmed the fire, and allowed him relief.

Steadily, the mists faded and allowed a glance of the setting rising against the high sides of their boats. With gasping open mouths and a few pointed fingers, the children of the old way viewed the smooth, white cliffs soaring so high that they disappeared in the clouds above. Doves, swallows, blue jays, and cardinals fluttered freely, as their songs echoed against the rocky walls. Then, as black as the darkness of night itself, Lazdrazil's Keep materialized before them. The ethereal dark stone walls juxtaposed the white cliffs with a severity making the place difficult to view without a dull pain in the back of one's eyes.

The Keep was not a fortress. The black marble curved elegantly as the whole design rose and twisted upward like a chambered nautilus. The ornate delicacy in each aspect of the windows and walls destroyed all of their previous preconceptions. None of the children had ever seen anything this spectacularly majestic in their lives. With great anticipation, they heard the familiar scrapping of stones as the vessels stopped. Slowly, the gray wooden ramps were lowered on the opposite side the children had entered. Vividly and vibrantly, Lazdrazil, Mistress of Mirrored Lake, posed like royalty before them.

Wearing an iridescent white gown, Lazdrazil glowed like the moon as she contrasted with the black marble of her home. Two guards clad in full silver platemail armor escorted the Lady down a dozen polished steps, which ended at a marbled pathway. She elegantly glided toward the damp, dirty children who had lined themselves shoulder to shoulder along the pebbled shoreline. Lazdrazil had deep lavender skin that sparkled as if she had placed miniscule, unmoving beads of watery glitter upon her face. Her black hair was tightly curled and close to her scalp, exposing her high forehead, eyebrows, and wickedly pale blue eyes. Lazdrazil glowered over the bowed children like a general inspecting his ranks.

Her steady eyes paused on Edmund, as he lay next to Vigil, Fulcrum, and Driskal. Without a word, she moved smoothly and swiftly next to him and knelt. Edmund was hypnotized and paralyzed by her wide eyes, and immediate perception of unlimited power. As Lazdrazil's dark lips parted, she gently and melodically sung, "Edmund, I am Lazdrazil, daughter of Aelen. Through what powers I have, I promise to heal and comfort your wounds. Fear not, son of fire. Soon, your pains shall be only a memory."

Lazdrazil raised herself, still staring into the boy's eyes and returned to her previous position. Yet now, she stood with her back to everyone as they strained to see her while still bowing. With a clap of her hands, a dozen male and female servants rushed from within the dark entranceway. Izwold stepped hastily to her side, as if on cue. "Have Edmund taken gently to the Resting Room. Please, have the children escorted to their quarters and prepare them for dinner. Our guests will be in need of cleaning, dry clothes and a warm meal."

"Yes my Lady, right away," Izwold nodded, and then directed the other servants as if conducting a symphony. They all danced gracefully into place in front of the waiting children. Two men lifted the stretcher and began walking past Lazdrazil. Fulcrum, Vigil, and Driskal followed closely behind. As they passed her, Lazdrazil sternly inquired, "Now, where do you think you three are going?"

The three boys stopped abruptly and jumped at the sound of her ascendant voice. Fulcrum bravely turned to her, replying as stately as he could muster, "Our duty, given by Ivindfor, is to accompany and oversee Edmund's welfare."

Lazdrazil glared at Fulcrum indignantly. Then, with quick turn of her head, she snapped a sneer toward Ivindfor and then back again toward they boys. This was the first acknowledgement she tended toward Ivindfor, and it was so brief that no one else noticed. "Very well, Fulcrum. You, Driskal, and Vigil may follow and stay with Edmund. But, perhaps next time, before you make actions within my house, you should ask permission?"

Fulcrum stood dumbfounded the Lady knew their names. He nudged Vigil and Driskal nervously to respond with him in unison, "Yes, we apologize my Lady." They stumbled awkwardly behind the servants carrying Edmund up into the dark, cavernous Keep. Eerily, all the other children watched them disappear into the darkness. Then, quite insouciantly, a servant led them where Edmund and the three boys entered.

Ivindfor sauntered to the right of Lazdrazil who held out a listless waiting hand. He nonchalantly lifted up the palm of his own dirty hand as she delicately lowered hers onto it. "My dear little brother," she coyly began, "You have worked so hard to keep them from me. Yet, considering the state they are in, I'll be surprised to see if any them will still wish to follow you from here."

Ivindfor tilted his head, gazed at his children entering her home, and then retorted with smirk, "Laz, as always, your perception of these children is skin deep. There is so much more to them than meets your eyes. Even if I showed you, you'd never appreciate or understand them for who they truly are."

With a throaty chuckle she replied as they slowly strolled hand-in-hand, step-by-step of the marble the stairs, "You always were the brooding philosopher, Ivindfor. Come now, let us pretend that I will be the kind, generous sister, and you will be my patient, honoring brother. For the children's sake, at least."

"For the children's sake," he mocked, as they drifted from the fading haze of daylight and into the shrouded Keep of Lazdrazil.

In The Keeping of Lazdrazil

> There laid a young Fendow woman,
> Grasping onto life, dying in the dirt,
> And Aelen, the Everlast, came to her,
> Giving her life, giving her power,
> So she would develop and rise
> As a daughter of the old way,
> Forevermore known as Lazdrazil,
> The Lady, The Mistress, The Blighted One.
> From, *The Seeds of the Fallen*

Most of the children stumbled and tripped up the unending spiral staircase that spun around the outer edge of the enormous chamber. Level after level they climbed. The throne room beneath them shimmered in a silvery, crimson marble no one had ever seen before. Hundreds, if not thousands, of mirrors followed the spiral staircase circling and reflecting light into an effervescent eternity. Gasps of amazement were heard as they passed other children going in their rooms. Kalevel was one of those gaspers.

He stood alone in the middle of a comfortably sized room. The furnishings and decoration took his breath away. Never in his life had he seen furniture, linens, drapes, or clothing of such quality and care. The female servant, named Gratil, stood at the doorway, observing his awe. "There are dry, clean clothes on the bed for you, Master Kalevel. In the corner, there is a basin with which to clean yourself. I will return within the hour for dinner. The Lady has prepared a special evening for all of you," she stated pleasantly and openly.

Kalevel turned with his mouth still open, then remembered something he had noticed on their way to his room. "Gratil, may ask you something?" he wondered aloud to her. She nodded politely and he continued. "Many of the servants are wearing belts of either black, silver, crimson, or white. What do they mean, if anything, and why aren't you wearing one?"

The woman smiled and replied, "I was told you were inquisitive. The belts are symbols of rank and loyalty among us. Black is the lowest, then crimson, silver, and lastly white. I do not wear a belt because I am free, yet I have chosen to stay and serve the Lady."

"Why don't you leave?"

"Why should I leave a place as this? The Mistress of Mirrored Lake has given us all incredible and comfortable lives. She is a merciful woman. There are many who do not understand her. I hope you will write well of her, and us."

"You say this as a free woman, yet can you truly speak freely. Without fear. Without consequence?" Kalevel asked raising an eyebrow.

"Ours is a somewhat different way of life," Gratil replied. "But even the wisest people debate what is good, or what is evil. Never let your perspective interfere with what you see, Kalevel. The mind often blinds us from just simply recognizing what is now."

Kalevel gazed at the floor and tried to understand what exactly she meant. After an awkward pause, she mentioned once more that he should prepare for dinner, then exited closing the door. He ogled around the room, terribly afraid to touch or move anything out of its orderly place. Everything seemed too perfect. He searched for some flaw in the room, but could not find one. As he changed and washed himself, his heart raced with confusion concerning his own preconceptions about Lazdrazil and her Keep, and Gratil's remarks and behavior.

A few moments after getting fully dressed, a knock sounded at his door. "I haven't taken that long, have I," Kalevel thought as he opened the door. In the hallway stood a different female servant. She was shorter, older, and wore a white belt that matched her white hair. "The Lady wishes your company," the woman softly said. "She mentioned that you should bring along your writing instruments."

"Where are we going?" Kalevel hesitantly asked.

"To the Lady," the woman smartly replied.

After another awkward moment, Kalevel realized the servant was not leaving without him, nor was she going to let him procrastinate. He quickly scooped his bag into his arms and joined the woman on the landing. As he followed her, Kalevel noticed how pleasant the clothes felt against his skin. The texture and weight flowed with his body, and made him more relaxed with every downward step he took. They descended four full turns until finally reaching the bottom. The throne room was hectic with people setting tables, chairs, flowers, and banners. Kalevel's apprehensions were quickly turning to admirations as his senses became overwhelmed with the celebration around him. So much so, that Kalevel did not notice Ivindfor watching, as he sat in Lazdrazil's elevated throne.

After crossing the lively room, the servant escorted Kalevel down a narrow spiraling staircase. He noticed the air was different and the stone work much less ornate, almost crude and ugly in comparison. After several turns, they walked down a long, shallow corridor. Several passages led from the main, but Kalevel could not tell where, or to what they led. Then, at the end of the passage, a plain wooden door appeared before their lamplight.

"I can go no farther," the woman said and pulled from her robe a small glowing mushroom. "No fires are allowed past this door. Once you pass through, you will not find the same way back. Only the Lady can lead you back and she waits for you on the other side," she paused sensing Kalevel's worry. "No harm will come to you, my dear boy. Some of your friends are already there with her. Very few have seen what lies behind this door. Honor and remember it well."

With those words she returned down the hallway, and left Kalevel alone at the threshold. Surprisingly, he was relaxed and reached for the door latch without hesitation. At first he pushed, then realized the door opened toward him, as if he were the one inside, keeping something out. He shrugged off the puzzle of the door and entered into the dark. His glowing mushroom offered just enough light to see a few feet around him. As he reached out, his hands found no walls or ceiling. Just darkness.

Kalevel slowly slid his feet across the musty floor. "Hello?" his voice squeaked. After taking three small steps, he felt the floor disappear beneath his toes. A gust of air from below rushed around him and slammed shut the door behind him. Kalevel jumped, then dropped backward and onto the floor, quivering with fear. As he slowly inched forward, from seemingly nowhere she emerged, glowing like a star in the black of night.

Kalevel retreated hard against the door as she floated in front of him. "I see that Tryn forgot to mention that the floor ends," Lazdrazil said as she glided onto the landing. Her brilliance lit the area far more than Kalevel's mushroom, and he was dumbfounded at her power. Lazdrazil stretched out her hand with a slight wave, hoping to regain his attention. "Come," she said softly. "Edmund and his companions are down below. There is something I wish to show you."

Kalevel raised himself and tried not to tremble as he grasped her hand. As soon as their skin touched, he sensed an energy course through him he had never experienced before, and her hand was the softest, smoothest thing he had ever felt. "Do not be afraid and do not let go of my hand," she stated to him. He held her hand a little tighter, clenching his eyes tightly, as she led him to the edge of the landing. "Take a deep breath, Kalevel. Now."

As she said the last word she pulled him off the landing, they began a soft descent through the darkness. They did not fall fast, nor did he feel like his stomach had jumped into his throat. They just floated, like a leaf falling from a tree. Kalevel felt air rushing under and around them. He relaxed so much that he almost let go of her hand, until she recaptured him. After a long minute, they finally reached the bottom of the shaft. Through an archway surrounded by solar mushrooms, he witnessed Driskal, Fulcrum, and Vigil sitting together near a softly bubbling pool of water. Edmund was submerged in the steaming water with a breathing tube affixed across his face.

"Just as I told you," Lazdrazil noted as she lightly strolled by the boys. "I brought you here, Kalevel, so that you may witness and write of these events. There are few who know about this place. This is the Basin of Amelior. Beohlor, in his graciousness, created the earthen surround for me a long time ago, as well as, the passage and Keep above. None may enter without my permission and without my permission, none may leave. The Basin of Amelior is a blessed gift and curse of the world," she paused as Kalevel stood dumbfounded staring at the Basin and at the boys. "You may begin writing now," she commented, smiling.

He scrambled together his paper, ink and pen and scribbled what she had just mentioned. Waiting a moment, Lazdrazil continued. "The spring that flows and fills the Basin contains minerals and other properties that can heal, restore, and even bring a person back from the dead. But, the waters also can wash away the very being and soul of a person," she paused and walked near the Basin dipping in her fingertips. Kalevel paused in surprise and concern.

"For Edmund, his wounds were made from the very foundation of the world itself. I cannot break the bond he has made with the world's spirit. I can only repair some of the damage caused by it. I will not be able to bring his normal sight back, nor can I rebuke the spirit of fire. As you may be aware, he does not wish it so. The waters will mend his flesh, but his mind and spirit are his own. Yet not entirely, as you three know."

Kalevel finished his notes and asked, "What is the hourglass for?"

Lazdrazil turned as if he had spoken out of turn and with disrespect, yet answered politely, "The hourglass is to measure time, Master Kalevel." Her eyes met his and Kalevel cringed at the realization he may have been too forward. She continued, "The process takes a precise amount of time. I have diagnosed certain wounds may take more time than others. So, with the help of these young men, Edmund will be lifted and set properly for the proper amount of time. Is there anything else?"

He understood Lazdrazil's tone as a warning rather than a real question, but before he could control himself he blurted, "Why do you keep this hidden and not help the rest of the world with it?"

Lazdrazil poised her head highly and glared down at the boy. Her lips pierced as she paused for a long moment. Fulcrum, Driskal and Vigil sat wide-eyed and motionless, waiting for her wraith to finally show. Although, Lazdrazil just stared and squinted. Then, she tilted her head forward, as if she was listening to something far off in the distance. "We are going to be late," she said flatly, walking past Kalevel and through the archway. She turned and spoke to the three other boys, "After the hourglass empties, turn it three more times, then move Edmund as I instructed before. Then, turn it again five more times. I will return before those cycles end. Get rest and take turns. Remember to eat. This will be a long night for all of you," then she shifted her blue eyes at Kalevel and stated, "Hurry now, *we will be late!*"

Kalevel looked to the Driskal, Fulcrum, and Vigil who urgently motioned for him to go. So, he grudgingly gathered his things, unsatisfied his question was not answered. As he entered the shaft, he waved at the three boys and shrugged, "See you later," then took Lazdrazil's hand and floated back to the landing. As they passed through the simple wooden door, Kalevel noticed the passage was completely different. Instead of a straight hallway with other passages, the way curved and forked at different intervals. "This isn't the same way, is it?" he blurted out.

Lazdrazil sighed heavily, yet glided effortlessly through the passage. Kalevel followed closely, yet he was disgruntled by her resistance to answer his questions. He comprehended she was a powerful woman, but she was the one who summoned him. "Did she bring me only to let me see and know what *she* wanted me to?"

He thought to himself. "Or is this some kind of game she's playing with me?" He pondered and sighed as they walked up the staircase he had descended earlier.

"When you arrive at Havenshade, Egylene will teach you some better manners than your family has. You may be the son of a famous innkeeper, Kalevel, but not every place you travel is an Inn. Is it?" Lazdrazil said dryly.

Kalevel wanted to respond but understood she really was not asking him anything at all, but rather suggesting his place was much lower than she tolerated. They entered the throne room where servants were finishing the table for dinner. Near the entrance door, Kalevel spotted a dozen or more people who appeared to be entertainers. Then he noticed Lazdrazil staring at Ivindfor, who still casually sat in her throne with one leg dangling over an arm. "I certainly hope Egylene will do something with you all. Obviously, none of you will learn anything about etiquette from my brother!"

She left Kalevel and moved effortlessly toward Ivindfor as he watched the children walk down the spiral stairs. They were dressed in the most beautiful clothes most of them had ever worn, or even seen. Without a word or touch, Lazdrazil gently lifted his leg from the arm of her throne. Then, she took his hand and led him down a few steps to the long dining table. He parted and took his place on the other side of the long, ornate table.

Lazdrazil smirked as she saw how happy and vibrant the children were when they raced toward them. Lazdrazil greeted them all, like a long-lost, loving aunt. Most of the children thanked her for the clothes and were in awe of how wonderful the table was set. Morclyf, Terrese, Orpholys, and Weslo, however, moved closely to Ivindfor without saying a word to the Lady. Hazel acknowledged neither of them and walked as plainly as she could, standing silently behind a seat at the middle of the table.

Lazdrazil caught Hazel from the corner of her eye. Her gaze uncontrollably irritated Ivindfor, who scowled toward his sister, as if he caught her in an evil thought and disapproved of it. Lazdrazil winked and laughed a little at Ivindfor, as she directed the children to find their seat. Ivindfor glanced over at Kalevel, who stood exactly where Lazdrazil had left him. With a gently wave, he motioned for the boy to sit next to him. "How are the boys and Edmund?" he asked Kalevel once he arrived.

The boy shrugged his shoulders and simply noted, "All right, I guess." Ivindfor squinted his eyes and looked deeply into Kalevel's. Then, he turned toward Lazdrazil at the far end of the table and caught her staring at both of them. Kalevel sensed a tension he felt would grow into something horrible that night. He keenly noticed Hazel sensing the tension, as well. Hazel glanced and stared at Kalevel for a moment, and he felt they were all reading each other's minds.

Suddenly, the reverberating sound of a gigantic gong jolted everyone in their seats. Servants rushed around the table and stood behind each of the seated guests obediently. More servants arrived with various platters of colorfully delectable meats, fruits, and vegetables making their mouths drool from the aroma. Hazel shifted her eyes back and forth between Ivindfor and Lazdrazil. At one end, the Lady sat poised, regal, and enjoyable in the eyes of every other child. At the other, Ivindfor sat in his frumpy, dirty clothes he had been wearing, while he leaned back in his chair with his feet perched on the edge of the table. Interestingly, most of the children ignored him altogether.

As dinner progressed, another gong jolted them again. This time, performers, acrobats, and musicians paraded around and majestically flung over the table as they entertained them. Laughter and applause continually echoed in the massive room. Yet, Hazel sat still and restrained. By now Kalevel had also shifted and slunk down into his chair, as if trying not to be seen. They both noticed that Ivindfor did not eat or drink anything at the table. And so, they did not either, although their minds and stomachs argued with their decisions achingly.

Finally, after all the plates were whisked away and the performers had finished their acts, Lazdrazil raised herself and motioned for everyone to quiet down. "For all that has been said of me. For all that has been rumored. For all that I have been accused of. May tonight prove that I am a generous woman: a woman of compassion and consideration. May tonight offer you comfort and fond remembrances for your journeys ahead. I am honored to have finally met you all. May your futures be filled with goodwill and gain," as she paused, claps of applause filled the room and died away as she continued.

"Now, with my brother's help, I'd like to show you something very, very old. Long ago, before the races left The Valley of Aeden, they danced what was called 'The Rowing of the Rays". The dance was usually performed on the solstice days, allowing for openness and honesty. The idea was for people to express their troubles, transcend their spirits, and pass through themselves as the season passed with them.

Ivindfor sat unmoved and expressionless as the excitement of the others swelled around the table. "Shall we show them a little of our history, dear Ivindfor?" she shouted over the noise. With a simple nod, Ivindfor accepted, stood, and then spoke very clearly and authoritatively, "As long as Hazel is our constant."

Lazdrazil froze, remained rigidly poised; then smiled and responded, "I can think of none better!" Her eyes strained not to look at the girl, as Hazel apparently did not care and only blankly stared ahead of herself, not really focusing on anything at all.

The commotion of people moving, servants attending, and furniture leaving was a dizzying sight to behold. In a way, all of the motion itself was a dance. People moved in and spun around through each other in so many ways that there seemed to be a practiced rhythm to it all. Then, after the hall had been cleared, Ivindfor and Lazdrazil positioned the children in distant rows across from each other, and Hazel was motioned to the center of the court.

Ivindfor strolled to her and whispered, "Listen carefully to us both. When the time is right, reveal the secret from the ship. And then, when the time is right, reveal what is still within you."

Hazel gazed up at Ivindfor with an expressionless face, then winked and raised the corner of mouth. Ivindfor grinned and sauntered a little as he left her for his position farther down the aisle of spectators. Just as they had been seated at dinner, Ivindfor was at one end of the room, while Lazdrazil stood at the other. She motioned for one of the musicians, spoke to him softly, he bowed and returned to his entourage. After a few moments, a repetitious

"At one end, the Lady sat poised, regal, and enjoyable..."

melody softly filled the room, and the chatter fell into an anxious silence.

The "dance", as Lazdrazil mentioned, was more of a contest of powers and spirit than a real dance. Each person on either opposite side would, in turn, take three steps, or "spins", then vocalize a truth about the other. Also, they would invoke a harmless charm on the "constant" that stood in the center. As the partners reached the constant, they would rotate and switch sides, spin and dance backwards to where the other began. And so, Lazdrazil began.

With the rhythm of the music, the Lady lightly stepped ahead three paces. She clapped her hands. The music halted. She loudly stated, "Ivindfor has a birthmark the shape of donkey on his butt!" To everyone's surprise, Ivindfor laughed. And then, they all relaxed and laughed with him. Then, she swirled a soft wind, blowing Hazel's hair around her face. And everyone continued laughing.

Then, Ivindfor stepped forward three times with the music and clapped his hands. He tilted his head a little and with piercing eyes sternly stated, "Lazdrazil blackmails and threatens Pentasentinal so that she can have these luxuries you see before you." Then, he stretched out his hand and drew a circle in the air. Hazel responded by spinning several times before stopping. The laughter quieted at Ivindfor's sharp remark.

Everyone glanced at Lazdrazil, whose face had become stern. She continued her steps and said, "Ivindfor has been plotting your existence ever since he saw Semmiah tortured and killed by the people of Scythe! You're all his little pawns, in a very old game." Lazdrazil swung her arms and lifted Hazel a little off the ground, then dropped her down.

"She has crept into the dreams of men, women and children and tortured them with nightmares, just for the pleasure of seeing their pain." Ivindfor made Hazel's arms wrap around and pat herself on the back. As their discourse became louder and bitterer, the children lost their smiles, while their eyes filled with a cautionary sense of fear. Hazel also felt the intensity with each turn as she became pushed a little harder each time.

"Did you know that Ivindfor has killed innocent people to provide your families with what they have; he has made your lives what they are, and he will ruin you all – just like he did Edmund!"

"She helps the Fendow as they try to break free from the country our father imprisoned them to. She is a traitor of our way!"

"Ivindfor does not wish to make any of you kings or queens. As I said, you are only pawns in war that he has helped create!"

"Lazdrazil, you are not what you appear to be, and through your malice, you have polluted The Old Way with a wickedness that has rapidly torn this world apart."

"You do not care if world survives the Fendow, or each other. All you want is for these children to help you destroy Scythe. You want them to pay for killing Semmiah."

As Lazdrazil finished, she and Ivindfor were standing close to Hazel at the center. Hazel was extremely disheveled, dizzied and her dress was fraying and ripping. She breathed hard as she tried to focus and balance herself. In two turns, they would be heading back to the other's position. Hazel felt something was about to happen, and she felt Ivindfor was about to unleash it.

"There is another threat, more dangerous than the Fendow, more dangerous than any of the Multicastes, more dangerous than YOU!"

"There is nothing in this world I have not heard mutter even the slightest breath. You are the only danger in this room and I am beginning to regret my hospitality."

"You will regret every wrong, every offence, every lie you have ever told when they come to your doorstep."

Lazdrazil stepped, and then seriously spoke and *asked* something of Ivindfor, instead of insulting him. "You cannot lie in this dance, Ivindfor. Who do speak of?"

Hazel peeked at Ivindfor who winked at her quickly. She turned to Lazdrazil and shouted out strongly for Ivindfor, "Syndustrians still live!"

Lazdrazil faltered and stepped backward, overwhelmed by Hazel's words.

Deep below, the boys witnessed the water ripple as Edmund shook violently.

"This cannot be," Lazdrazil sputtered, as her composure and posture began to fail her. "They all died the day I was reborn."

Ivindfor stepped backward as if still performing the dance and stated, "They have no need of alliances, no need of luxuries, no need of country, Lazdrazil. They will come and destroy everything. Hazel speaks the truth."

"She lies. You twist her tongue out of turn!" Lazdrazil snarled.

"He does not control me," Hazel sneered in return. "You do not frighten me! And none of you deserve me!"

Lazdrazil inhaled and exhaled heavily as she narrowed her eyes on Hazel. "How dare you, child! You have no idea what forces are at my will. You will suffer for you insolence, little girl!"

Just as Lazdrazil braced herself and raised her arms to cast down her wraith, Ivindfor cried out, "NOW, HAZEL!"

A terrifyingly high pitched whistling originated from the uppermost height of the nautilus and descended toward them. Air swirled furiously down around Hazel. Dust and debris funneled around her, but she was unaffected – not even one aquamarine hair moved. Everyone, including Ivindfor, shielded themselves as the currents of air and rubbish pulled and pushed around them. Lazdrazil tried furiously to release Hazel from the wind, but could not break through Hazel's power.

As she saw Lazdrazil's eyes widen with apprehension, Hazel thrust her hands forward and forced the witch's wind back at her. The Lady of Mirrored Lake supported herself and relentlessly pushed harder. Mirrors cracked. The marble floor wobbled and lifted. Everything sucked into their whirlwinds. The pressure built within everyone else's ears and eyes. Then, something happened that was even more horrifying than the dueling sorceresses.

Lazdrazil, who concentrated so hard against Hazel, changed in appearance. With every push and force of her spirit, parts of her skin shifted into jagged, sharp peelings, as if petrified scars from burns emerged. Her skin turned from the pleasant light lavender to a deep, muddy purple. Her hair began to fall out in clumps as she metamorphosed into the visage of a true Fendow. With all her strength focused on Hazel, Lazdrazil revealed her true form for everybody to see. She played right into Ivindfor's trap. As soon as she realized what was happening, Lazdrazil, in all her vanity, tried to regain her appearance by shifting focus. But in doing so, Hazel gained control, flinging the Lady across the room and violently into her throne.

Far below, as this occurred, Edmund jolted out of the water, ripped the breathing mask from his face, and screamed, "HAZEL!"

In reply, far above, Hazel cried out, "EDMUND!"

Ivindfor spun around and dashed toward Hazel and grasped her hand. His instincts beckoned them both to Edmund's aid, but as he started for the staircase he witnessed the pale, horrified faces of the other children. Behind them, Lazdrazil's servants and guards emerged from the shadows. The musicians and performers had already rushed to the entrance, but they were unable to open the doors. Hazel pulled, urging Ivindfor down the staircase. Ivindfor's mind and heart raced, but his body was paralyzed. He stared at his unconscious sister limp on her throne.

"Come on. We've got to get Edmund," Hazel pleaded.

"We can't leave the others," Ivindfor whispered, not really sure who he was talking to.

Orpholys, Terrese, Morclyf, Weslo, and Sytheria fought the servants by kicking, hitting, and even biting them as they grabbed at them and the others. Lazdrazil awoke, reanimated her gorgeous appearance, stretched, and regained her dominating composure. Sweat ran down Ivindfor's forehead as fear clouded his mind. Hazel tried to keep the guards at bay, but Lazdrazil countered her every offense. The crushing weight of his own failure brought Ivindfor to his knees. Hazel was shocked, even angry, that he did not even try to fight back. She turned to Lazdrazil, whose face was beaming with a glorious confidence of victory.

The Lady casually sauntered toward children individually, gazed into their eyes, and ran her long fingers over their face. One-by-one, their eyes closed and their bodies went limp into the arms of a servant. Lazdrazil's smile grew wider with each passing child. When she was finished, The Lady glided in front of Hazel, who was exhausted, and sung, "They dream pleasantly and peacefully now. They have no more cares. No more worries. You, however, must make a choice, my dear Hazel. For dreams have a way of turning into dreadful and inescapable nightmares."

Hazel violently trembled with both fear and anger. She glanced at Ivindfor who had fallen to the floor in defeat. His weakness in their time of greatest need caused a smirk of satisfaction across Lazdrazil's face. "I will enjoy watching these brats polish my floors for the rest of their lives. Did you really believe I would allow your little following to leave my house, Ivindfor? The leaders of the greatest cities and nations are all against you. Most of the remaining wizards and sorcerers are against you. Even the world is disappointed with you by shifting your former scribe with sky fire. Don't you see that we're very content with the world we've created? I never understood your obsession with being friends and helping the common folk. They certainly do not need to know who controls them! But, you just had to try, didn't you? How many failures will you need before you realize to just give up?"

Ivindfor knelt submissively on the cold marble. Lazdrazil was veracious. He was a failure. He had lost them for trying repair his lie to the world and healing Edmund because of it. He felt Lazdrazil's words penetrate his soul and completely weaken him. There was no possibility of prevailing against Lazdrazil in her home alone. But as he stared at the marble beneath him contemplating surrender, Ivindfor remembered there was a power deeper than her own within the foundation and walls. "'polish my floors'. Of course. Beohlor!" Ivindfor said to himself. Then, Ivindfor lifted his eyes and scowled up at his sister. "This may be your Keep, Lazdrazil, but this place was not built by your will."

She squinted at him with a questioning smugness as Ivindfor raised his hands high above him and slapped them down onto the marble floor. As the echo of the clap resonated high into the chamber, Ivindfor cried out, "Beohlor! Beohlor! Beohlor!" Each time he said his brother's name, he fiercely slapped the floor. As his hands hit for the third time, Ivindfor's fingers curled and sunk into the stone.

Lazdrazil's eyes flashed wildly wide. She whirled around and viewed the children and screamed, "Where is that measly scribe! Where is Kalevel?"

Before she could obtain a response, the floor vibrated near Ivindfor and Hazel. Hazel jolted just enough to scurry a few feet away. His hands lifted from within the floor, and from the stone rose the large, marbled hands of a man. In just a few moments, a stone replica of Beohlor stood hand in hand with Ivindfor. "Edmund and the boys are at the Basin of Amelior. I believe Kalevel is trying to get to them. He may be with one of the servants," Ivindfor whispered to the stone figure. "They need your assistance getting out. Please, save them."

As the chiseled Beohlor nodded his head, chips of rock broke off onto the broken floor. The sound of stone rubbing together echoed through the room. With a heavy step, Beohlor plodded and pounded toward the staircase. Lazdrazil swiftly glided to an urn of liquid resting at the side of her throne. With a wave of her arm, the watery liquid rose and wrapped around her arm. She slashed her arm at Beohlor, and with each swing the liquid shot from her like a whip. Every time she struck him, gauges were made against his stony back. Beohlor flinched as if in pain, but continued until reaching the staircase. As he disappeared through the doorway, a stone slab grew from the floor, impeding any followers.

Ivindfor helped Hazel to her feet, and she leaned heavily into him. They both saw Lazdrazil slowly glide backwards and turn toward them. Ivindfor strategically moved Hazel behind him as he prepared himself for what would happen next.

"You know once Kalevel, Gratil, and Beohlor return with Edmund, this game we're playing is over," Ivindfor boldly informed. "You won't be able to overcome us all."

The Lady kept gliding toward them without saying a word. Her uncompromising glare and the liquid swirling around her arm suggested that Lazdrazil was far from relinquishing anyone. She halted several yards away from Ivindfor and with a curled lip replied, "I am tempted. Very tempted, Ivindfor, to take every precious ounce of air from every one of these little fools and finish this now."

"If you harm any of these children any more than you already have..."

"I know, I know, you'll take the life of everyone in this Keep," Lazdrazil mockingly finished.

"Then, let us go," Ivindfor stated. "There will be enough battles in the days to come, for all of us."

Lazdrazil cocked her head and pierced her lips, as if contemplating something else, "One request, little brother."

"Go on,"

She glided up to him seductively, then spun around with him until she hovered in front of Hazel. "You may think I want this girl, but you're wrong. Hazel has no loyalty. Deep down, she only wants to be the best. She could care less who she impresses. Whether you, or the children, or even myself, all Hazel wants is to know that she is better than everyone else. Don't you?"

Hazel sheepishly gazed up at her. Her face was pink with embarrassment. Not because Lazdrazil focused on a flaw she may have. Rather, Hazel was frustrated at the fact that Lazdrazil was right. She could not help her jealousy, or the desire to prove herself. Hazel had never needed to be accepted by others before, but now that she was with others like her, the competition overwhelmed her. Lazdrazil knew Hazel's desires, almost as if the Lady were looking into a younger version of herself.

"I only request one very simple thing, Ivindfor," Lazdrazil paused and gazed into the scruffy face of her brother. "I promise to deliver you all safely to the other side of the lake, if," she paused. "If you let them sleep through the night here."

Ivindfor glared back and quickly responded, "I'll meet you half-way. I'll let them sleep through the night, but *not here.*"

"Ugh. *Fine!* You're all beginning to bore me anyway," she sneered with an eye-roll of disgust apathy. Then, with a snap of her fingers and rush of wind the massive entrance doors opened inward, and knocked over the entertainers who were still trying to escape. "I am tired of these runts. Take them out of my house!" she barked at her servants who quickly obeyed. "And you," she pointed to younger male, "See that another wagon is sent to help them on their journey." She turned toward Ivindfor once more and comment sarcastically, "It is always such a pleasure having you visit. I never quite know what to expect from you, and I have never known quite what to do with you. We have had some fun, though. I am certain there will be many more days like this to come."

"Those who will be challenging us will not offer terms as easily as we may, Laz," Ivindfor said with serious sadness which made the Lady pause for a moment as she returned to her throne.

As she returned the liquid from her arm into the urn, the stone in front of the staircase grinded loudly downward into place. Edmund, who was dripping wet through a cloak, ran into the room. He saw Ivindfor and Hazel, who rushed over and grabbed him with open arms. "Are you alright, Hazel?"

"Are you?" Hazel replied.

"I suppose. Just a little muddled. Like I'm still half-asleep."

As Fulcrum, Driskal, Vigil, Kalevel, Gratil, and the stone Beohlor carefully approached, Ivindfor spoke to Beohlor, "Thank you. We'll see you soon, hopefully by morning."

Beohlor turned toward Lazdrazil and waved good-bye. She flicked her wrist and rolled her eyes back at him. He stomped to the place where he had emerged, laid himself down, and sunk back into floor. The site seemed flawlessly restored. Ivindfor hurriedly checked over Edmund's wounds. Although healed, the dark scars indicated where the injuries had been. And miraculously, Edmund's eyes had returned to their normal state, except for the slight ring of red around the Iris. Edmund could see normally again without the goggles.

"Enough already," Edmund squirmed. "I don't have anything except this cloak on!" he whispered to Ivindfor. "We'll go over things later. Let's just get out of here!"

Ivindfor nodded and let Hazel guide Edmund outside. She peered over her shoulder one last time and glanced at the Mistress of Mirrored Lake. Lazdrazil watched every movement they made and then winked at Hazel. And of all things, Hazel winked back. The only person to catch this exchange was Kalevel, who in dismay, shook his head and rubbed his eyes as if he mistook what he witnessed. After a few moments, he returned to his senses and remembered Gratil standing next to him.

"Ivindfor, we need to take Gratil with us," he stated firmly. "She doesn't want to stay, but she's a little afraid to go."

Ivindfor turned to Lazdrazil with the question in his face, and she replied, "She can go where she pleases. Gratil's a free woman. Not a very wise woman, but a free one."

"Just remember, Laz..." Ivindfor began.

"Oh, I know...," she interjected.

"You get what you give," they said in unison.

With that, Ivindfor walked with the remaining children and Gratil to the doors. They quickly went down the stairs, but Ivindfor turned at the threshold, bowed toward his sister, and a fart came loudly from his butt. Lazdrazil's eyes widened and her face appeared strained at whether to be insulted, or to laugh. Regardless, she raised her arms and with a gust of wind shut the doors right into Ivindfor's face. The echo clapped and disappeared high into the chamber. The last noises The Lady heard were Ivindfor's cries, as he tumbled down the stairs and thudded on the rocky shoreline. Lazdrazil cackled so loudly that the sound shattered a few of her already cracked mirrors.

Elsewhere, a bewildered Bleke watched the ground intently. Then, as the grasses and soil trembled, Beohlor's body returned from the earth below. He gathered himself together shook off the remaining clumps of dirt still sticking in his hair.

"What in the world did you do?" Bleke asked impatiently.

Beohlor situated himself near the campfire they had made earlier and stretched his neck as he gazed up at the starry sky; cracking and settling his joints. "Ivindfor needed me at Laz'. I guess they weren't as safe as I supposed they'd be. Oh, they're all right now. Said they'd be here by morning."

Just then, a bird flew on Beohlor's shoulder and dropped a note into his dirty hand. "Uh-oh," he muttered as he read the letter.

"Uh-oh, what?" inquired Bleke.

"Well, I think Ivindfor and the others will have an easier time getting to Havenshade from here on out."

"Then, why did you say 'uh-oh'?" Bleke questioned again.

"Father is coming. And he knows about everything that's happened with Edmund. From the tone of the letter, he's not very happy with Ivindfor. Said he'd be here in the morning when Ivindfor arrives and he'll travel with us into Havenshade so no more mishaps occur. Well, not much we can do about it tonight. Might as well get some rest, Bleke. Something tells me that we're all going to need it."

Bleke gazed eastward and wished he could have been with Ivindfor and Edmund. The moon gleamed brilliantly back at him, and yet he felt a cold shudder run through him at the sight of it. Bleke was not absolutely sure, but he sensed something untrue in the air that blew toward them. So far, the journey had gone wrong in so many ways, Bleke wondered how he could help make things right. Then, like a spark lit within his mind, the idea came to him.

He gazed at Beohlor, who was just beginning to breathe and rumble the first deep breaths of sleep, when he belted out, "Beohlor! Wake up! I need your help with something."

Beohlor jolted upright and brought along clumps of earth and rock, as if ready for some sort of altercation. "Wha' the?" he shook out himself. "Bleke, I'm exhausted. Can't it wait til' morning?"

"No, Beohlor. I need your help making something by morning. Before Edmund gets here."

With drooped eyes and a heavy, grumbled, sigh, Beohlor reluctantly raised himself, "Well, let's get at it then. Sooner it's done, the sooner I'll get some rest. I tell ya', you all owe me big time for the mess you've gotten me into."

Bleke just laughed, as a sparkle of fire glinted in the reflection of his excited eyes.

What Witched Dreams That Come

> We shutter our eyes when we drift off and sleep,
> so that our dreams and nightmares won't escape.
> Who would think such thin pieces of skin and eye-lashes
> Could restrain the wild workings of our feral souls.
> From, *Dohlemar, Wizard of the Icewash Vales*

Kalevel sat heavily against the hard, back seat of the carriage. His body rocked back and forth in unison with the clomping of the horses' hoofs in front of him. Sleepily, he gazed ahead at the blurred, shaded images of Ivindfor, Driskal, Fulcrum, and Vaespril. Next to him, Edmund and Hazel drifted and shuddered as they also tried to stay awake.

The damp, nipping air felt foreign for lingering long days of summer. Their breath trailed from their lips like spirits wafting into the air. Kalevel sensed something unnatural surrounding them. The very air felt as if it were trying to bond within them. He rubbed his face often and blinked his aching, dry eyes. The repetition of the horse hoofs clapping was hypnotic and the weight of sleep gnawed at him.

"Hazel," he poked at her. "What's going on around us? Seems like the night, the air, everything is closing around on top of us."

"It's her," she lightly yet tiredly replied. "She's here. In the air. Through the moon. Even in the moisture of the dew."

"What is she trying to do to us?"

"Not sure," Hazel gasped. "The elements won't listen to me. I've tried to make it stop. No use."

Kalevel shrugged his right shoulder and woke Edmund. "Come on, keep awake. Ivindfor said that we can't sleep."

"I can't help it," Edmund grumbled. "It's been too long a day. I just want to crawl back in the wagon with the rest of them." Edmund stretched and gazed longingly back at the attached hay filled wagon behind their carriage.

"NO!" Hazel blurted. "Then, she'll have you, too! No matter what, we have to stay awake."

After a few moments of silence, Kalevel trying to think of some way to keep awake asked Hazel, "Why did you wink at Lazdrazil?"

"What?" she innocently questioned.

"As you were leaving, I saw you wink at her. Why did you do that?"

Hazel paused for a moment, then saw Edmund peek around, also curious. With a heavy sigh, she replied: "She whispered something to me. So, I winked back."

Edmund and Kalevel looked at each other and then in unison asked, "What did she say?"

Hazel's mouth and nose wrinkled in hesitation; but sighed saying, "Fine! But you can't tell anyone. Not even Ivindfor." They both surprisingly shrugged and nodded at the same time, and so she continued. "She said, 'Next time Hazel, we may just make the whole sky fall. Next time'."

"And so, you winked at her?" Edmund retorted.

Hazel tilted her head, blushed and said, "I didn't know what else to do!"

They all snickered a little at themselves and felt for a moment lifted and lighter. Then, from out of seemingly nowhere, several bats and owls lowly swooshed silently around them toward Ivindfor. With a few flicks of his wrists, small notes flew into the air and were carried away into the black night sky.

"Who do you suppose he's writing to all the time?" Kalevel wondered aloud.

"More people than we could ever know," Edmund replied.

"I think he's trying too hard," Hazel nonchalantly posed. Both boys looked to her questionably. "Every step along the way has led us into more danger than before," Hazel continued. "I think he's trying too hard to keep us safe. Like he said, there are too many other forces in the world determining how many choices you have in life. Or he said something like that."

"Like the force that's around us here," Edmund reminded them.

They quickly fell back into the sullen dreariness of the night. The quiet was maddening. Not even the crickets chirped. The only sound came from the noisy horses, wheels grinding the earth, moaning wagons, and the shuffling of sleeping children. Once again, Kalevel rubbed his face, even slapped himself to stay awake. Edmund grunted. Hazel rolled her head around. His head bobbed as his chin jammed against his chest. Their breathing became heavier and in tune with the rhythm of the groans of the wagon wheels. They felt themselves drifting into the dreams of the witch.

Then, the screams came.
And the moans.
And the cries.
And a sinister, maniacal laughters.

Kalevel watched as Ivindfor twisted around and snapped, "Just checking to make sure you're all still awake back here."

"We're awake," yawned Edmund.

"Barely," Hazel added.

Kalevel stared ahead, not making a sound. "How are you, Kalevel?" Ivindfor asked pleadingly.

The young scribe did not answer at first. Both Edmund and Hazel shrugged at Ivindfor, as if not really knowing what the problem was. "How am I?" Kalevel finally retorted. "How am I? I guess I'm better than the rest," he turned his head slowly at their leader and with a scowl asked; "What's happening to them? Can't you stop it?"

For the first time, Ivindfor witnessed a flare of discontent and anger from Kalevel. Perhaps it was from the lack of sleep, or constant flourish of events, or maybe both. Every time Ivindfor saw this look of disdain and sound of contempt in any of the children, he felt his muscles tense as if aching to strike them across the face. How dare they ridicule, or even question him? How dare they conceitedly consider themselves entitled to anything? Then, he would wait and remember.

Ivindfor gazed at Kalevel's scowl, but the image was just a blur. Ivindfor washed himself away into the memories of his sister Semmiah. She was desperately arrogant yet confidently absolute. No one understood her, even Ivindfor. Her wicked smile mocked and encouraged him all at the same time. Semmiah taught him many things before she died. One of her greatest lessons was to never let someone else get the better of you. Never let someone pull you into their control. Never give your love to someone, unless you can also let it go.

"I think he's under her spell," Hazel quipped at the boys.

"Hey! You! Ivindfor! Snap out of it!" Kalevel snapped his fingers hard in front of the man's face. Ivindfor blinked slowly and in mid-snap, Kalevel's fingers froze from Ivindfor's power, and the scribe's eyes widened with fear.

"My sister Semmiah was a pain in the ass," Ivindfor grumbled. "But she taught me a great deal before she died. Things I would probably never had learned in a thousand lifetimes. You're lucky she taught me to control my emotions against my actions." He let go of the hold on Kalevel and the boy's fingers snapped. Before the scribe turned in disgust, Ivindfor added, "I cannot stop the spell Lazdrazil is trying to weave. In fact, she's trying to 'bind' them with her. At night, with the moon, I am no match for what power she wields tonight."

"Then, it's over. She'll have them anyway, even if we are away from her Keep," Hazel sadly murmured.

"Not exactly," Ivindfor replied. Just then, an owl swooped low and dropped a note onto Ivindfor's suddenly expected hand. He read the note and tucked it away in his cloak. With a far off stare and sigh Ivindfor continued, "Sorry, a note about my father," he paused and listened to the screams drifting into the night sky. "But, back to your own wonderings. Where were we? Oh yes! Laz is trying to 'bind' the ones she touched *to* her. I believe you three would also fall into her dreams if you slept tonight. The only thing I can do is what I've already done."

Edmund, Hazel and Kalevel scowled in confusion as Ivindfor readily continued. "Do you remember on the beach, when I had all of you pair up and gaze at someone else's card?" Of course, they suddenly remembered and nodded with a sense of recognition. "Well, before morning, we must line you all up, tie you with ropes, and force you all to stare into the cards. This is an old spell Semmiah taught me. A Remembrance Spell. I only hope this trick can break the bonds Lazdrazil is weaving."

"How can remembering a picture on a card break her spell?" Edmund asked.

"Semmiah once said the memories we have of those who have passed on are more powerful than the moments we have with them while living," Ivindfor smirked. "Of course, I argued with her. We always had awfully fiery philosophical debates. Then, she showed me. She performed Remembrances on people to show me how right she was. Memories, past experiences, forgotten moments, family histories and fables are all like spirits within our minds. Sometimes, they drift in like a light breeze. Sometimes, they crash like a hurricane's gale. Either way, they summon us to remember, to react, and to feel just as we did during those earlier intervals."

Kalevel's interest peeked, as he and the other two leaned forward with renewed anticipation. Ivindfor smiled and continued. "When the children wake up with the sun, they may still believe that they are in their dreams. If they can remember who they were before all of this, then maybe they will still have the will to deny her."

Powerful grunts of laughter exploded behind them. With jump, Hazel asked, "Why do they laugh like that? It's not happy laughter; seems rather - cruel."

Ivindfor stretched out his hands. "Lazdrazil is playing a game," he began lifting one hand up, while the other dropped down. "In one moment, the children are being horribly *terrified*. The next they are powerfully *terrifying*. Back and forth. She's giving them a sense of what could horrifically defeat them, or what could violently make them victorious. Either way, they shall have to consider who they are and what is real."

Hazel put her hand to her chin and pierced her lips. The noise of the children made the hair on her arms tingle, as she felt tears well into her eyes. "I don't understand any of this," she spoke as her throat tightened. "Why us? Why now? How are we supposed to bring the rest of the nations together? Especially since, it appears they want us dead? Why did you this to us Ivindfor? Why couldn't we have just been normal?"

Ivindfor felt the sadness and exhaustion float from the breath of her voice. "There are times I have asked those same questions to my father, Beohlor, and myself," Ivindfor softly replied. "There is no easy answer. Some believe in chance, while others believe in reason, and still others believe in destiny. But for me and for us there are only these moments. I am the sorcerer of life. Everything I can control is in the present state. Our spirits are in this form at this time on this world. And for whatever part we play, our legacy lives on in the acts that follow."

They rode for a while silent, yet surrounded with the pain of their friends filling the dark, heavy air. Then, Edmund blurted out at Ivindfor, "That's a load of shit!"

Ivindfor lifted his head in surprise and a little laughter as Edmund continued, "You've planned this for hundreds of years! I may not have been part of it, but everyone else has. You have played our families like peg pieces (multi-colored parts of the popular tabletop game called Pegs) through the years. You've tried to keep one step ahead of everyone else, but now, it's all catching up with you. Isn't it?"

Hazel and Kalevel looked on with wide eyes as Ivindfor replied, "Yes. It is all catching up with me, but it hasn't caught me, or you completely– yet! You are clever, Edmund. But what I said isn't 'shit'. It's true, and so are the ways with which you all will be persuaded."

"What do you mean by that?" Hazel asked as she squinted her eyes and tilted her head.

Ivindfor straitened himself against the rise of the front seat, and began. "Everyone I've ever known (and that's a lot of people) has had to choose a way in which to live their lives. Sometimes, people revisit themselves several times," at this he shook his hands and clarified, "And I don't mean a profession, or trade. What I am trying to say is that people, at some point in their lives, must decide whether they will serve themselves on the persuasion and will of others, or if they will follow their own persuasions and ways."

As the children tried to comprehend Ivindfor's words, he continued. "A wizard I once knew a long time ago, had to make a decision. He could safely serve his master, who had gained and used his power ruthlessly and cruelly against others. This wizard knew if he just obeyed and followed his master's desires, he would be rewarded and well off. But, he also understood the suffering others had endured, and were enduring. This wizard's own soul desperately gnawed at him to fight for those who were needlessly hurting. But, he greatly feared he would die doing so. For death is the fear that ends all fear.

"But, as time passed on, the pain of the others dulled his fears and grew into a hard ache for revenge. He chose to rise against his master and avenge the wrongs they both had committed," Ivindfor took a deep sigh. "In the end, when the battle was over, the two shattered men grasped each other in their last moments of life: the master feeling betrayed, while the wizard feeling free whispered, 'At least I will die knowing what wonder and truth there can be in a man's own heart. Your soul is the empty shell of devious and decrepit desires.' And with the end of the wizard and his master, the sufferings ended for many others.

Ivindfor addressed the children personally now. "My greatest hope is that once we reach Havenshade, all of you will learn your own following. I have learned so much watching all of you grow. And now, my only wish is watch you live, knowing your own soul's following, not in the shadow of my own, or anyone else's approach."

He smiled softly at them all, as he nodded his head in some fancied approval of himself. Then, with a deep breath, Ivindfor looked out into the eastern sky. His eyes widened and mouth dropped. "Oh! Time slipped away from me again! The sun will be rising soon!" Edmund, Hazel, and Kalevel peered back across the screaming laughter behind them, and saw the very first hues of light creep above the eastern mountains. "Well, I hoped to make it to Beohlor and Bleke in time. Oh well, I guess we've got a lot to do on our own!"

Ivindfor hopped off the carriage, ran ahead, and halted the horses, then flagged Atana and Hrowl who were ahead of them. Driskal, Fulcrum, and Vaespril turned back to Edmund, Hazel and Kalevel with tired and confused faces. The children in the rear seat began snickering and pointing ahead, as Ivindfor and Atana wildly flailed their arms in some kind of reckless argument. In the end, Ivindfor won his way, as he usually did. Atana threw heavy coils of rope at Ivindfor, which smacked him in the head. After he regained his footing, the scruffy sorcerer hoisted one coil up to Driskal, then dashed to the rear wagon. He gaspingly announced, "Well, come on! We have to bind everyone up before the tying is complete!"

Hazel tipped her head and with a smile replied, "Don't you mean, 'we need to tie everyone up before the binding is complete'?"

"That's what I sai-," Ivindfor started. "Oh, you know what I meant!"

As Ivindfor turned and stepped toward the wagon, Edmund said with a giggle in his voice, "Ivindfor, I'm not sure this is right. I think I'm having a moment where I should follow my own path."

With smiles of their own, Hazel and Kalevel watched with anticipation as Ivindfor spun, dropped his ropes with a thud, and exclaimed, "Oh for Semmiah's Sake, Edmund, now is *not* the time!" Then, as he saw their smiles, he smartly finished, "But when that time comes, you better take it!"

Ivindfor laughed a quirky, crazy-like laugh and rushed to his work. Edmund and the others giggled at his behavior and went to their work as well. Edmund's smile faded, however, as he grasped at what Ivindfor had really meant. "Could Ivindfor believe that I would leave, or betray him?" Edmund overthought.

"Don't worry," Ivindfor yelled out. "They won't wake up until the sun rises, but they may bite. Or kick. Or hit. Or swear. Don't take it personally!" And with that, Edmund saw Morclyf's foot smack Ivindfor so hard and square in the head; that he fell over backward – twice.

With a half-smile Edmund whispered to himself, "I'll always follow you, Ivindfor. Always."

The Fates of the Families

> If you ask me, that Ivindfor character is a madman.
> Completely off the edge of the map and then some.
> Do I trust him? He doesn't give you the choice.
> From, *Aegil Mallister, Lead Mark of the Alting*

Edmund's mother, Rooth, turned a wooden bowl in her hands with a cloth over and over. Her blurry eyes were caught in the worried thoughts of her son. Intermingled were the visions of her husband, Bryght, who went back to Essil with Waddle several days earlier. Every breath and repetitive spin of the smooth bowl fell with the slow heartbeat knowing something horrible had happened. Rooth tried to be helpful to her mother, sister, and Rayne, the newborn daughter of their family, but a mother's intuition pulled her back into a state of uncontrollable disquiet.

"For Semmiah's Sake," Rooth's mother, Ruda, screeched. "Now, he's sending owls! It's the middle of the day! People will be calling us witches for sure!"

Ever since Rooth had heard of the tragedy at bridge, she wrote daily to Ivindfor in the way he had taught her. She asked several times why it had taken so long for them to get only that far, and if Edmund was safe. Each time, Ivindfor gave the same reply "He's fine. More later." And in response, she shredded the notes, sobbing with every one of his lies. She finally stopped writing altogether. Rooth wandered automatically in a haze knowing full well that Ivindfor was in complete control.

She hated that. Sometimes, she hated Bryght for it too. She began to hate everything and everyone connected to Ivindfor. Then, she would hear herself in her mother's own voice, as Ruda often belittled and cursed the man. But he wasn't a man. Ivindfor was something beyond what a real man was. He wasn't a husband. Wasn't a father (not a real father anyway). H wasn't even trying to hold an office, or position in the world to help people. NO. All he wanted was their children. Her child. And now, she did not know what, or where, or how her son was. She had nothing. She was nothing. She was son-less.

Rooth gazed up and tried to fix her vision on the brown and white owl wobbling and blinking tiredly on the windowsill. Two small, rolled pieces of paper hung bent in its beak. She stood breathless for what seemed an eternity. She looked into the owl's eyes, felt a wave of emotion fill her, and then exhaled, dropping the bowl loudly to the floor.

Ruda hobbled over and snatched the notes out of the owl's beak and shooed it away. Even though Ruda knew she wouldn't be able to read it (Cursed wizard's words, as she called them.), she opened the note and disgruntledly held it out to Rooth. Her hands trembled as she took the piece of paper from her mother. Her eyelids blinked quickly behind her tearing brown eyes. All she could do was hold them. Her own mind had already made up a thousand horrible scenarios for what one small, simple scrap of paper could hold.

"It ain't gonna read itself," Ruda croaked out to her daughter, obviously curious and obviously indelicate of her daughter's condition.

Every little wrinkled of the paper sent a chill through Rooth's spine as she unrolled one of the notes. A single tear dripped onto a feather that was hidden inside, as the letters and words immaculately fashioned in front of her:

> Dear Rooth,
> I promised Edmund I wouldn't write to you until we had arrived in Havenshade, but considering the circumstances, I thought you should know what has happened. (Ivindfor goes on to reiterate the events that have transpired thus far, especially concerning Edmund's transformation.) Although I'm sure you want nothing to do with me anymore, your son needs you. And, so do I. In fact, I ask that you do two things for me. First, visit the Priestess of Semmiah and give her the other note. The feather is for you. If the Priestess refuses to let you leave, thrust the feather into your skin and fly to the Wayfarer's Inn. The innkeeper's wife, Karell, will be able to change you back. From there, two friends of mine will guide you to Havenshade. I'll write more soon. I hope to also hear from you soon. Don't worry. Edmund is doing really, really well. I have not, nor will I ever lie to you, Rooth. Please trust me.
>
> Yours,
> Iv~
>
> P.S. I'm writing Bryght as well. Not sure if he'll forgive me though. Perhaps someday you both will.

As Rooth read the letter, her body had crumbled to the floor. Her mother had shuffled behind her and read along as well as she could before the writing disappeared. Ruda's body shook, not with sadness, but with raging fury. "That...that no good MADMAN!" she shouted and stomped to the window, panting. Rooth's tears dripped on the empty page trembling in her hand. She looked toward her mother and saw specks of dust glimmer and fade in the momentary ray of sun that cascaded into their house each day.

With a tight, dry sound she spoke, "I am going, Ma."

"I'll have none of it!" her mother reeled back.

"My son needs me. I need him," she compassionately whispered.

"He's baitin' you for more trouble than it's worth. You may be a grown woman and mother of your own, but as a mother, as *your* mother, I just can't, can't see any more of this hurt," Ruda paused. "If you leave, you ain't comin' back, are ya, Roothie?"

Rooth's shoulders slouched forward, as if weighed with a heavy burden. The burden of what she felt was the truth. "No. I don't believe I'll ever be coming back. That doesn't mean I won't ever see you again, though."

"Don't bait me into believing *anything*, you – you-," Ruda couldn't finish her sentence without wheezing and crying.

Rooth marched over and held her mother for a long time. Each of them tried to recapture the memories of their lives together, as if holding each other would help them hold on to the memories. At last, they separated and Rooth began packing her things. Ravina sleepily stumbled from her room and asked, "What's all the noise about?"

"Nothin', I'll explain later," Ruda scowled. "Your sis's gotta leave. Now."

Ravina blinked in response, not totally awake and not completely aware of the circumstances. Rooth glided over and hugged her, wishing her and Rayne well. As she passed by Ruda, Rooth grasped her mother's hand, leaned into her ear, and whispered, "Go with Vekt and the other parents. Our world is about to change, and being here may not be the safest place for any of you. I WILL see you again, Ma. Just leave here. As soon as you can."

And with that, she kissed her mother's cheek, hurriedly gaited through the door, and never looked back again.

Later that day, at The Wayfarer's Inn.

Dearest Karell,
As you are well aware, things have gone terribly wrong. Soon, I will attempt to perform Semmiah's Remembrance Spell. I

have only performed it once before, and the results were varied and faded over time. I am sorry for inconvenience of the families I sent to you. I know some of them can be horribly inconsiderate and demanding. However, they will be leaving you immediately. A dear friend of ours, Jarred Jacobi, will be escorting them to Crescent Tier. There, they will board the Vagabond, Captain Vekt's vessel. Where they travel next is better unknown for you. Vekt will tell the families after they set sail where exactly they are going. A word of warning: The Sylfaen's are pursuing use with deadly and deceitful force. I fear that they will deduce everyone who has been involved with me within a week. You and your family are dearest to me, and I urge you to seek refuge in Aeden, or at least Havenshade.

Which reminds me, Karell, there will be a woman, named Rooth (Edmund's mother). She may come to you in the form of a bird (raven, if I recall). She may need help changing back to her proper self. Enclosed is a sample of her hair. Oh, and Jacobi will not be as himself either. He will most likely appear as a tall, thin, blond woman, with the name of Wakesley.

Again, I cannot thank you enough for all that you have done for me. Please, wish your family well. Tell the others they will be leaving. If they give any resistance, then, with Jacobi's help, use any measure necessary to get them out of your home!

Again, take caution and if possible, travel with Rooth to Havenshade. Even with Egylene and her daughter's help, I know I'm in over my head!

Forever Yours,
Ivindfor

P.S. Kalevel is doing masterfully!

As she read Ivindfor's words, Karell's eyes widened and narrowed. "He's going to lose his mind," she thought to herself. The sorcerer had always been a bit off to her, but now, even she could sense there were too many tasks for his mind to handle and control all at once. Karell knew how he thought. Ivindfor always planned ten scenarios for even one decision. The Alchemistress's eyes formed tears a little at the thought of Ivindfor's mind trying to keep ahead of so many different things at once. For each of the

"And through their sufferings,
all people shall recognize the descents arisen."

children, and each member of their families, he could sense and feel exactly the next move they may make. Of course, there was always the probability for an error, or deviation. And so, Ivindfor, in his brilliant madness, tried to figure all possibilities for any given situation, for any given individual, for any given time.

That was one of Ivindfor's curse for having his gifts. He was connected to every living thing and everyone alive, without the will to refuse it. All sorcerers have a curse in exchange for the blessings of their powers. Sometimes, it took everything Ivindfor had, just to filter out all the lives filling the world. Other times, he would let it all rush in, and use that force to make him terribly and horrifically assiduous. Ivindfor's soul, what was left of it, would be tested to its limits very soon.

Karell gazed through the kitchen pass-through and her eyes wandered over the refugees gathering for breakfast. Since they arrived, they argued among themselves about the state they were in, as well as the state of their homelands. Breaver closed the Inn to travelers, which did not come to a shock to any passer-by, considering the turmoil erupting to the south of them. He did offer travelers water, care for their livestock, and sold a few available provisions.

Several times, he groaned that they would be able to make a fortune, if it weren't for Ivindfor's 'friends'. Karell would turn and flash a glare at him. Instantly, he could read her thoughts, "Don't you dare put down Ivindfor! We owe him so many favors that this inconvenience is nothing! You selfish old fool!" Of course, Karell would never say those words aloud, yet Breaver felt them from her eyes, and he was ashamed for it.

Twice, Ivindfor had saved Breaver's life. Once, during a flood of rain nearly washing Breaver and the Inn clear to Pentasentinal. Then, there was the incident when a ramble of outlaws tried not only to rob him, but also tried to rape Karell. Both times, Ivindfor was there to ensure their safety. Ivindfor also helped teach Karell all she knew of the Old Way. The sorcerer always relieved all of their children from fevers and pain. Karell cherished every act of kindness, every blessing, and every gift as if he were their own guardian, their own protector, even in the most peaceful of times. They owed him more than their lives, and Karell would give hers freely if Ivindfor were simply to ask.

As her dark eyes drifted over the crowd of families, she screamed inside her mind, "YOU ALL OWE IVIDFOR MORE THAN YOU REALIZE! YOU ARE ALL NOTHING WITHOUT HIM!"

She motioned for her husband and told him of Ivindfor's news. They held hands and touched their foreheads together for a long, tender moment. "It is not just our little world that's changing, Breev'," Karell whispered. "Every nation of Erst is about to come crashing down on itself. Be brave with me, my love. Be brave for our family and those who have no home."

"I'm only brave 'cause I have and love you," Breaver whispered those words so clear they took Karell sweetly by surprise. Only a very few times did her husband ever speak without his speech impediment: once on their wedding day and again when he spoke each of their children's names for the first time. She knew this was one of those great, yet fearful times of his life. Yet from fear, one may be persuaded to see their own strengths, and prevail.

Karell slipped from her husband's hands and entered the barroom. There, she clasped onto Breaver's forearm tightly. They both took a deep breath and stepped in unison toward the refugees busily eating and talking away their breakfast. As they both spoke in turns, trying to gather everyone's attention, the once animated faces became sober, with widened, sometimes tearful eyes. Many held their heads with their hands, while others tried with pride to not show any emotion at all. Yet, they all knew as Karell said, "The Sylfaen's are bent on keeping their control, keeping their way of life, and keeping an eye on all of us. They would imprison or kill us all if they knew who we were. Ivindfor knows it will only be a matter of time before they found out about us. Whether you approve, or disapprove of Ivindfor's ways, the fact is that he's trying to save all of our lives! And it may not look like it, but the man's also trying to save our world from falling even further apart. So, that's it. Gather your things. We need to be ready."

As Karell finished her last words, the securely bolted doors of the Wayfarer's Inn surprisingly opened and a woman quickly glided in, who, in turn, just as quickly bolted the doors behind her.

The woman was fair, and thin; average in height; blond with pale, almost pinkish eyes; a sharp nose with skinny, pale lips. She wore a revealingly tight outfit of black leather slacks and bustier from which a billowing shirt flowed ethereally.

"Hello, Karell," the woman's voice sweetly sung, as if by songbirds. "Ivindfor said I would come. I am Jacobi. I am here. I am humbly at your service." As she bowed, every man's jaw was dropped (even a few of the ladies) and Karell laughed knowing what Jacobi truly looked like.

"You old fool," she cackled. "You always did want to be something you're not!"

Then, Jacobi's real, scratchy, old voice came out through her beautiful lips, "Karell, koot ta schlee ya!" And further still, everyone's mouth was open, but their eyes squinted, very confused. "Kee've kot vorkt ta do! Ya! Vet's gue!"

Karell laughed hilariously as she gave the disguised old man a huge hug and settled him in at the bar. Breaver, with a twinkle in his eye, ushered every confused guest to gather their things and prepare for the journey ahead. The Innkeeper glanced once more at his wife before heading upstairs, and as he caught her glance he mouthed, "I love you," and she replied with a sultry and slow wink, making him blush every step upward. Yet, sadly, Breaver also knew these were the last steps he would take on those stairs for a very long time, maybe ever.

A small bat zigged and zagged through the shadowy trees in the Icewash Vales. The poor creature had flown hard through the night and was exhausted. Yet, its mission could not be halted, even by the rising sun. This creature of the night was racing toward the Dorman wizard known as Dohlemar. What words this bat carried would affect the lives of many people in the times to come. For the words were a request, a summons, and an order. All of which would change Dohlemar's life, forever.

The short, bald, yet beautifully bearded Dorman wizard stood on a small mound, so that all of the newly arrived families from Pentasentinal could see him clearly. He led them in a series of stretches and poses he performed every morning and each night.

The newcomers thought Dohlemar was a little strange, yet the friendliest, most sincere man they had ever met. His simple, wide smile could relieve any depression, or ill emotion. His long, golden, wavy beard, shimmered in even the grayest of days. But his eyes! His pale azure eyes glistened with a dark, endless center. His whole body gushed with a joy that overflowed into all of the other things.

The bat swerved hap hazardously around and through the families' outstretched arms (which quickly turned to swats and screams) until finally resting upside down on the extended arm and forefinger of Dohlemar. "Oh! Hello, friend," the Dorman happily spoke. Almost panting, the bat let the note fall and the wizard swiftly caught it with his other hand. "Such a heavy burden for such a little one. Go now. Find rest in the darkness of my shed, and stay as long as the insects fly, if you wish." The bat chattered back at the old man, then scurried through the air and disappeared through a notch in the shed not far off.

"Looks like news from Ivindfor!" Dohlemar announced to the others. They all gathered closely, with anticipation and worry. "Let's see what the rascal has to say now." And he began to read aloud:

Dear Dohlemar,
DO NOT READ ALOUD, OR LET ANY ONE ELSE SEE THIS NOTE! (At this, Dohlemar peered over the paper, shrugged as if too late anyway, and continued.) *The journey has been difficult and we narrowly escaped Lazdrazil. The children will hopefully "remember" themselves by morning, yet I'm not sure what the long-term effects may be. I am certain that the Sylfaen's will try to stop us before we reach Havenshade. My father is coming and that may either help or change our situation entirely. Also, I am sending the parents of the Valdic and Stout states to you. They will be traveling with Captain Vekt, through the Specter's Reaches, and then up the Icewash Rivers. Jacobi may be with them, or he may already be with me. When the time comes, I may call on you as well. The choice is not with me, old friend, the Sylfaen's will stop at nothing to hold on to what power they have. The problem is, I don't have any desire to take it away. And they, with all their insight, cannot see past their own fears. Thank you again for taking care of those*

from Pentasentinal. All will be well, once we arrive at Havenshade. I never thought the journey would be this way. The world is changing faster than it can adapt. As such, chaos and fear are prevailing. Be strong. Pray for us. I'll send word soon.

Your Master, Your Friend

Ivindfor.

Dohlemar peeked over the slightly shaking parchment and witnessed what appeared to be half-fearful, half-riotous faces peering burningly back at him. Dohlemar, who considered himself only a student of the Old Way, now became a leader: A leader to the people before him, and to those who would be arriving. All at once, the weight of responsibility filled his chest and pulled on his shoulders. He heavily sat on the ground, cross-legged, and let the morning dew saturate his clothes, as his fingers gently washed themselves in dampness of the grass. In a deep breath, the Dorman wizard drew in every ounce of air for strength as the families drew closer; not with animosity, but inquiries.

"Before the onslaught of questions, or perhaps insults, let may say these few words. And please, sit," Dohlemar motioned, trying with all his might to summon a smile. With great hesitation, the ensemble of families sat with some discomfort on the soggy grass. Glances among each other indicated that their attention would not last long. So, Dohlemar prepared himself and his words with clarity and invocation.

"Secrecy," the Dorman wizard boomed forth, "is the resort of desperation, yet also protection. Now, you may wonder why Ivindfor did not wish you to know the contents of his letter, but let me reassure you – it's too late for any of that now. We are here. Your children are with him. They will be safe. I know of the remembrance spell he speaks of. The future, for all its uncertainties, can muddle the mind with fear. Fear of what may be. Fear of what may not be. Do not dwell on that. I will write to Ivindfor. He will write to me. I will not cloak you in the shadows of secrecy. But for now, you are safest here; just as those following will be. They will have a hard journey. They will need your compassion and cooperation. That is all. Let your minds speak and ask."

Although still worried, the families were alarmingly calmed by the wizard's words. As if, in the vaguest of terms, he had given them all their answers. The first one to speak was Rovarre, Slyte's father. A wealthy Sylfaen doctor to the royalty from Pentasentinal. "We have all known Ivindfor longer than we can remember. But these are our children! How are supposed to sit by while he whisks them away from us. How are we supposed to allow them to venture into harm's way! They could get killed out there. They nearly already have!"

Another parent, Marq, the father of Pahl, spoke before Dohlemar could even utter a response. "Whether or not we've lived in denial, or just hoped this time wouldn't come, deeply inside, we've all known these days would come. Ivindfor kept us informed all these years. If this is a surprise to anyone, then I think it's your own fault for not seeing it!"

"Do not make the love we feel for our children our own fault!" The words rolled on their "r's" as Fulcrum's mother, Palas, lifted her fist in the air.

"W-w-well," stammered Marq at the sudden outburst.

Dohlemar felt the swelling of emotion and quickly stood to subside the crowd from becoming uncontrollable. The wizard held his arms out in a V, which caught a few sparkles of sunlight now seeping through the trees. The leaves rustled above, as the cool, wind calmly swept through, and dripped small drops of water from the damp leaves above. The drops pelted the people like a sudden shower. They wiped and cringed as the brisk cold drops fell into their hair, down their necks and backs. "Come back!" Dohlemar cried. "Flee from your fears, and feel what is present. What is now!"

"Quit trying to make things alright!" Yelled Mahraen, Vaespril's mother. "We have a right to our children! We raised them. He shouldn't just get to have them!" Water dropped on her soft yellowish skin, and mingled with the tears from her eyes.

"Ah! But are your children strictly yours?" The wizard sung back. "Ivindfor has given much of his spirit for the sake of these children. Do you not think that he has just as much to lose, than any of you? If you doubt your children, then you doubt yourselves. For they are the result of all that you are, were, and made them to be. Ivindfor wished that. He wanted them to know their lineage, their history, their people, their customs. Otherwise, he would have taken them away at birth. Do not let your own self-seeking hopes disrupt the whole idea of what Ivindfor wishes for your children."

Dohlemar's eyes flared and his body filled with a glowing that spread and swept over and into those that sat motionless. "The self," he began, "is not only the consumption of one's own epiphanies, or enlightenments. Self is the understanding and acceptance of another, different, and even closed self." He paused for moment for the words to wash with the warmth, then continued, "Wish what you will, feel what you will, but those will not change what is happening now. There are too many forces at work for any of us decide what is truly right, or wrong. For now, what we do know is more families are on their way. They will need us. We should prepare ourselves. I've heard they can be a bit difficult, but then again, so are you!"

As the wizard finished, the faces of the crowd grew complacent, and a few even smiled, as Dohlemar tried to imitate Ivindfor's light demeanor. Then, they slowly parted ways. Each family was later visited by Dohlemar personally, counseled, and relieved. That was the wizard's calling: Relief. Even in the wildest of tempests. He was more than a balance. Someone would always say: "Dohlemar, if anyone was the living 'Experience of Peace', it would be you." Others, from a different place and time, will name the Dorman wizard as 'The Predator of Peace'. But that story has yet to unfold.

Within three days' worth of travel, The Vagabond washed against the banks of Dohlemar's river home. Rovarre, the first to speak out in protest earlier, had suddenly become a leader of communion for the families. Dohlemar weaved Rovarre's strength from aggression, into peace. The wizard even taught him a few charms which could calm a person into listening, speaking, and reasoning. Rovarre welcomed the newcomers, who in their disheveled states yearned for the solidness of the earth, and the smell of vegetation. He and the other families offered them newly built homes (created mostly by Dohlemar's magic), and let them rest. Among the new families was Vekt, who kept proclaiming how his ship actually 'flew through the air', and how impressed he was at Jacobi's prowess.

Jacobi slunk onto shore. He was still maintaining a woman's appearance, but his own gray eyes had returned. Jacobi vaguely saw Dohlemar as he, with the lithe woman's body, fell down, looking for support. "Ivindvor, uv's meve bik-timk!" The Gnomaen's voice gurgled out.

With a discouraged gaze, Dohlemar whispered back, "Yes. I suppose he owes us all 'big-time'. I've prepared the Penta-families as much as I could," Jacobi leaned closer and Dohlemar whispered. "I'm sorry, old friend, but you will have to rest after our next journey."

At this, Jacobi shifted the form of a woman and swiftly stood shorter than Dohlemar. He had a pink, bald head, white long beard, pointed ears, and a wickedly crooked nose, which suddenly supported a pair of azure colored glasses. The Gnomaen glared at the Dorman with what strength he had and whispered, "What 'journey'?"

Dohlemar cleared his throat, then hesitantly, and softly replied, "We are ordered by our Master, old friend. We are summoned for war!"

Ava's mother Therese sat silently yet anxiously near Dannihlia, the Priestess of Semmiah. The Priestess conversed with two ambassadors from the trembling Valdic and Stout countries. Therese did not hear their words, as her mind drifted to the images, the fears, and the realizations her daughter was somehow the cause of all their unrest. Her chest shuddered, as she avoided any acknowledgement of the ambassador's presence. Therese also feared Dannihlia's response to the accounts and events being relayed. The pressure was overwhelming.

Ava's mother endured their conversations for nearly an hour, before the Valdic woman and Stout man departed the Priestess. Dannihlia rose and strolled through the arboretum, obviously deep in thought. Several servants came to her, but she simply raised her hand and excused them silently. Occasionally,

Therese would dare to lift her eyes and catch a glimpse of where Dannihlia strode. Her head began to dizzy. Her breathing shortened. Her throat clenched so tightly that she could hardly swallow. Then, without her own senses, she shuddered as the Priestess of Semmiah sat directly in front of her.

"You fear me?" The Priestess asked, narrowing her eyebrows.

Therese struggled to find her voice. Finally, she cleared her throat and replied, "I fear my own shame toward you and the rest of world. I will never forgive myself. Nor do I deserve forgiveness." Her tears flowed down into her mouth, then dripped heavily into the fabric of her clothes.

Dannihlia stretched out her arm and gently held Therese's hand, which jumped at the very connection. "Oh, my dearest of followers," she softly began. "I do not blame, nor hold you responsible for any of the catastrophe's happening in this world. Ivindfor has deceived a great many people over the years. You – *and your daughter* – are only victims of his insidious plot to unrest the world. I know where your true loyalties lie, Therese. Your service, your commitment, and your devotion cannot be doubted."

"I-I should have never let her go," Ava's mother muttered in between sobs.

"Ivindfor would have taken her with, or without your protest. You proved yourself enough by being here when she left," Dannihlia grasped her hand tightly and lifted her chin, so that she could she her eyes. "Crescent Tier will never fall into the wraith of that madman, or any of his followers! I promise you, as I promise all of the people who devote themselves to our savior! If anything, his plot will only strengthen the beliefs of our people and ways!"

Therese's lips cracked a quavering smile at the thought of people renewing their stewardship with Semmiah, and all things that made Crescent Tier what it was. The two women sat in communal silence for several minutes before a Page interrupted them with a message, which was openly reported from Ivindfor by a female visitor. The elated spiritual bond with Semmiah was broken with the bothersome sound of Ivindfor's name. The Priestess issued in the woman who supposedly brought his words.

As they raised themselves to this messenger, Rooth emerged into the filtrated sunlight of the Temple's arboretum.

In one hand, Rooth clutched the note Ivindfor had commissioned her to deliver. In the other, she fingered the feather he gave her as an escape. She walked calmly toward them. Her attitude resembled someone ready for relief. In truth, Edmund's mother cared for nothing in that house, other than to see her son.

Edmund's mother kneeled and bowed, as was necessary, before the Priestess. "You have not been in this temple for many years, have you?" Dannihlia presumed.

Rooth raised herself and confidently replied, "I have not been on these shores for many years. And so, yes, I have not been in this Temple. The only reason I am here now is to give you this." She stretched out her hand, unwavering and unemotional.

The Priestess motioned for Therese to take the letter, who with darkly shadowed, disheveled eyes tried to remember who this woman was. The small piece of parchment crinkled slightly as she nervously and cautiously set it on Dannihlia's opened hand. Rooth bowed customarily again as if ready to leave, when the Priestess protested, "I have not released you, Rooth."

Rooth stayed bowed and felt the softness of the feather in her hand. Part of her wanted to use it immediately and fly away from that place. Another part wanted to know what Ivindfor wrote, and how Dannihlia reacted to it. So, she stayed and waited for the right moment.

Ava's mother watched the Priestess intensely, as the woman read the letter silently. The perfectly smooth complexion of Dannihlia's face tensed and stretched as her eyes widened and narrowed with each emerging word. Therese could not tell at first when the woman was finished reading, for the Priestess simply stared into the paper expressionless for several minutes. Then, she shredded the parchment into as pieces. The Priestess never spoke of what the letter contained, and as she stepped toward Rooth she uttered a cracked and rattled statement, "When you see Ivindfor, if I let you see him, tell him: 'The Old Way will finally suffer and die," Dannihlia's robes heaved as her breath quickened with a controlled savagery. "Guards!" She suddenly yelled and several birds in the arboretum flapped, stunned by the noise. Three armed men rushed into the great chamber, yearning for their order. "Take this conspirator to the prison! She has threatened me, our people, our Semmiah!"

Rooth heard the beat of the dove's wings echoing in the chamber and drew a deep breath. As she struck the feather into her left forearm, she whispered toward Therese, "I'll let Ava know you're gone." In a tumultuous, screeching instant Rooth's body formed into a raven. The feather was one from Morclyf's cloak. Rooth's caw echoed with the coo of doves as she furiously flew through a slight window high above them.

The guards stumbled into each other as they attempted to grasp what they had just witnessed. Dannihlia clenched her fists so tightly blood trickled between her fingers and dropped and smeared the purity of her white gown. Then, the Priestess turned slowly to Therese huddled on the floor. With a bloody outstretched hand, she screamed with insanity, "Take *her*, then. And never let her see another soul for the rest of her short, tortured life!"

Tears and snot rolled from Therese as she doubled over and shook violently. The Priestess' face became distorted with a building madness. The guards grabbed the unresponsive mother of Ava and dragged her off into the darkness. The young Dannihlia saw the blood on her hands, and with a maniacal giggle, she lifted the sticky blood soaked hands, and allowed the drops of blood to fall and run down her face. "He won't succeed! He won't expose anything! He will die. But before his own death, I will make sure he witnesses all of his follower's die!"

From high above, in a sunlit windowsill, a snow white dove cocked its head and cooed at the Priestess cackling and losing her sanity. Whatever words Ivindfor wrote, perhaps even a spell unto itself, his letter pushed the Priestess of Semmiah into a maddening obsession which would drive her people into warfare, suffering, and doubt.

Remembrance

Always remember to focus your perspective towards the proper point. If your vision blurs, if you become distracted, or stray even a little, the outcome will be tainted and impure.

From, *the Songs of Semmiah*

The mist surrounding Aelen was the work of his friend, Zaephryl, a white dragoness from the glacial flows far to the north. He nestled comfortably in her shoulder blades, as they glided thousands of feet above Erst, yet hidden in a shroud of vapor making them appear as a whiff of cloud, blowing ceaselessly through the night sky. Protected and unseen in the mist, they traveled toward his sons, Ivindfor and Beohlor, but beneath them, through her mist, a discouraging site was revealed into Zaephryl's all-seeing eyes.

She noticed hundreds of flickering torches and in the torchlight, thousands of people. As she peered nearer, Zaephryl viewed the host of heavily shackled and chained Valds, Stouts, Midaens, and Dormans led by Sylfaen wizards and horsemen on either side. Leading farther ahead was the Sylfaen Sovereign; Aereste. A dozen wizards rode directly behind him, and they were followed by a hundred Sylfaen Lancers. Behind the Lancers, the army comprised of prisoners who had been released with the understanding that if they fought and lived, then they would be free. The units marched toward the Old Stone Bridge near Hildrin's Pass. Zaephryl clearly recognized that Aereste intended to stop Ivindfor from reaching Havenshade, at all cost.

The dragoness desperately wanted to tell what she saw to Aelen, but kept silent in the fear of being discovered, even at their great height. She kept on, climbing a little higher. They would only be useful if they could get to Ivindfor. She would tell them both the fate that waited for them when they met. She shifted her gaze away from the dark slinking assemblage of war, and focused on the destination ahead. Along the length of her spine, Zaephryl could feel the shiver of her old friend.

The denseness of her armored scales could not hinder the power of his tiniest movement, and she thought: "What troubles you have lived with your long life. What troubles you, and yours will soon have to see."

She gave a deep sigh, spewing out more mist to conceal them, then heard Aelen whisper, "I know Zaephryl, I can smell and hear their footsteps, even from this height. So begins this war, whether Ivindfor is ready for it, or not." The 'Everlasting' man leaned his body and head onto the softness of Zaephryl's neck. His eyes closed as his mind drifted back hundreds of years ago. He reminisced on the day when Aereste, the young Sylfaen prince of Pentasentinal, walked with him in Aeden for the last time:

"I do not remember this place," Aereste spoke with hard, deep voice. He was an abnormally tall Sylfaen, with long, straight, dark hair. His skin was golden, as were all his kin, and the narrowness of his eyes was so tight, only blackness showed between the eyelids. "My father often reminisces about this valley," Aereste continued. "He's creeping toward death clinging to memories of the past, as if they will save him."

Aelen strolled slowly with Aereste through the dry, hip-high grasses, where the fragments of Stout homesteads in Aeden still lingered. "Your father and I spent many happy days here. The day he left was miserable. Everyone was miserable."

Aereste paused his stride and altered the tone of the conversation, "I am sorry for the loss of Semmiah. I hear Ivindfor is not taking her loss well."

"Thank you for your condolence," Aelen softly replied, somewhat irritated with the subject change. "Her death is ultimately my fault, but Ivindfor...He was too close and present when she was murdered. He blames himself. The poor boy..."

"I have heard rumors that he plans to avenge her death by creating sorcerers to destroy Scythe."

Aelen paused, gazing deeply into Aereste's eyes. Those eyes did not reflect an image, or light, or life – just empty and void. Aereste's accusing tone deeply troubled Aelen, and he proceeded cautiously, "Ivindfor is very confused and very upset. Even Beohlor has disappeared. Where he's gone? I am not certain. But Ivindfor. He is with friends, far away."

"Yes, I know," Aereste replied smugly. "He's on some skiff of land people call Essil. A few people have tried to live there, but they say the winters are too harsh, and the winds are too brutal. Some of which I guess is Lazdrazil's doing."

"In her own self-serving way, what Lazdrazil does, she believes is justified," Aelen replied defensively, yet admonishingly.

"She is the reason for our exodus from Aeden. Now, she flaunts her disdain upon the rest of us without any care at all," Aereste pierced his lips and shook his head. "Ah, I have lost focus!" He shook his head slowly and regained his composure, then continued. "I am thankful you have let me come here, Aelen. I do not blame you for the struggle and quarrels occurring in the world. Choices and decisions have been made by many people. But now. Now that the races are separate and the Old Way is a faded memory, I must confess and implore you to stop Ivindfor from creating these sorcerer children. The lands are settled. Governments, religions, and civility is in place now. Whatever his agenda is, the Sylfaen's will not let him see it through. I will not let him see it through."

Aelen's worn-out face squeezed and wrinkled heavily at Aereste's request. "Ivindfor's desire for revenge will snuff itself out with time. He believes in each individual life, as if it were his own. If he wishes to pass his spirit on and into others, then so be it. His will is his own and I believe, that in time, Ivindfor's desire will be for unity, rather than dissolution."

Aereste quickened his words with disparity, "Ivindfor cannot deliver children of different races into this world with the powers of the Old Way! There is a balance now. There is a New Way. The way of progress, process, and prosperity for each race and class, separately."

"Ah! And in this 'separation' lies your peoples' power," Aelen half-smiled at knowing what Aereste was truly meaning. "There are very few Sylfaen's left that can hear, or speak the language of the world anymore. None of you live forever, as the legends say. So, as the number of your wizards pass on, your people's only source for power has been the partitioning of the other races." Aereste clenched his jaw tightly, insulted at the truth of Aelen's wisdom. Then, the old man continued, "If Ivindfor were to unite the other races and nations through the powers of the Old Way, the Sylfaen's would lose their authority. You and your people would become equal, if not ordinary."

Aereste, losing emotional control, clenched his fist at Aelen, "We will not be lowered into base commonality, old fool! Because of us, the other races were able to survive! After you raised that Fendow witch from the battle field, the whole future became our responsibility. After you gifted power to one of our enemy, none of the others wanted to hear the language anymore. None of them wanted to feel the power our world could offer. They had seen enough treachery to want to forget it altogether! Only the Sylfaen's took on the burden of keeping the Old Way, and using it hidden from society, for societies' sake!" Sweat formed on Aereste's forehead as his whole body shook with rage, "Now, Ivindfor wants to upset all we have accomplished! We deserve our respect, our place, and our position! We are owed at least that, if not more!"

Aelen peacefully, gracefully, and gently took Aereste's angry fist and cupped it with his own. With his own energy and with the spirit of the world, Aelen filtered the earth underneath

Aereste's body into his hand. When Aelen removed his hands from over Aerestes', the Sylfaen prince's fist was nothing more than a clenched piece of red granite. Aereste's eyes narrowed almost shut as he tried to reverse Aelen's magic. In his mind, even Aereste knew that no one, not even his own father, could undo 'Everlasting's' spell.

"A reminder," Aelen rasped. "Remember this day and the hate and fear within your fist. May it serve you better to understand how those things are a waste, like the new found uselessness of your hand. Perhaps, if you understand your opposite self, then your fist full of malice will open for you, as well as others. But for now, you have gained exactly what you have given. Aereste, you may never return to the Valley of Aeden."

Aelen opened his eyes to the astonished face of Aereste floating in Zaephryl's mist. He lifted himself, wiped the dream induced drool from his chin and stretched. He rubbed his eyes and realized they had landed. As the mist and image of Aereste dissolved around Aelen and the dragoness, the first thing the old man saw was the disheveled image of his son, Ivindfor. The most dear and most cursed of all Aelen's conjuring's stood next to Beohlor, his strongest and most steadfast.

The struggle of any bound person emits a heat that can only be likened to as 'primal'. The shuttering of every muscle ached against restraint. The grunting noises emitted within the depths of the throat undulated. And the ropes ripping against one's very own skin to blood, was forefront at the scene of the Remembrance. Except for those who had not been touched by Lazdrazil, the rest of the children writhed with nightmares throughout the night. Now, Ivindfor attempted to undo her malice with an equally dangerous spell he was given from Semmiah.

In a straight line, sitting back to back, the children of the old way were tied together- even those who had not fallen asleep. Of course, they had to be involved, for they had seen the images on another person's card. They were the partner of what they had seen before meeting Lazdrazil. So, the 'sleepless ones' were bound not only in remembrance of who they were before, but also who their partner was.

In the far eastern distance, a soft sullen glow of red silhouetted the Scythian Mountains. Dark, high clouds formed a frame against the upcoming sun. Ivindfor walked up and down the line, paused, and then kneeled in front of Edmund, who with weary eyes and nodding mind tried desperately to keep awake. "Everything is set," Ivindfor whispered to Edmund, as he held his face. "When the sunlight inches over the plains, the others will awaken. At first, they will think they're still in their dreams. But, with their heads and hands bound to focus into their cards - they will remember!" He paused for a moment searching for the appropriate words, then asked Edmund, "After all this is over and even in the years to come, your 'sight' may see those still linked to Lazdrazil. This journey may have caused an interference that I cannot relieve, even with Semmiah's spell."

Edmund nodded and noticed the energy from Ivindfor beginning to flow within him. As the sun finally rose above the distant mountain peaks, the light mingled with the emptiness of night, slowly revealing shapes and forms. Then, a beam of daylight streamed out over them to the west. As the world rotated toward the orb, the sunbeam crawled across the ground toward them. Dew sparkled like a field of diamonds against the struggling fight of night's shadow. Finally, the daylight met the children of the old way, and as its warmth touched their skin, the children's eyes fluttered and fought off the remembrance of Lazdrazil.

Beohlor swung out his massive arm and abruptly halted Bleke from continuing. As Bleke fumbled to stay upright, he muttered, "Hey, what's the big idea?"

"The Remembrance," Beohlor said and motioned forward. The two men watched from a small distance as the children struggled to free themselves of their dreams. "Ah, Bleke. Do you see? He's also performing the Binding."

"Well, I see that their bound with rope, but what do mean 'Binding'," Bleke smartly retorted.

"It's what Lazdrazil attempted to do in her Keep. Except she was trying to Bind them to her. Ivindfor's Binding them to each other, all in the same Remembrance. Very powerful stuff. Dangerous, though."

"What do you mean?" Bleke asked clueless.

"Well, whenever one of them uses their powers, the others will feel it. Not directly, of course, but they'll have a familiarity with who cast a spell. The 'Binding' will always keep them connected in one way, or another. Although, that can provide for some tension, as well. Ivindfor knows these spells work better than me. At least, I hope he does."

After an hour of watching the spell work its course, Beohlor and Bleke strode toward the children. Ivindfor, Atena, and Hrowl were unfastening, washing and giving water to the pale, sweaty, and weary young women and men. Bleke hurried to Edmund, who seemed tired, but not as consumed as many of the others. When he approached, Bleke noticed Edmund could see him, and he sprung alive with excitement.

"I'm so sorry I couldn't be with you in the Keep," Bleke began. "But you look...you look great!"

"I feel pretty good," Edmund replied. "I don't need the glasses any longer, but if I concentrate, I can see the spirits of others. Altogether, though, it was a rough night for all of us."

"I can only imagine," Bleke tossed Edmund's hair, then held him for a long moment. "I made...Well, Beohlor and I made you something." Bleke handed a short staff to Edmund. The sleek, smooth, metallic staff was no more than a walking stick. At first, Edmund frowned at the idea of a seeing stick.

"I know, I know," Bleke interjected. "I understand you have your sight available to you again, and this isn't just an ordinary walking, or seeing stick. Although, you never know, when you might need a thing like this," Bleke tried to focus his words by adding, "This cane has a special feature, just for you. Inside the shaft is a special oil and when you flick the switch, instant flame!"

When Edmund witnessed the blue flame flicker from the top of the staff, his mouth widened into a brilliant smile, "Brilliant!"

"Now, no matter where you are, as long as you have this, you'll have access to fire. Just remember, use it carefully and wisely. The oil is mix of a dragon's saliva and boiled fat. Beohlor's had it for years, I guess. I'm not sure how he got it, but this little bit of oil will probably last a lifetime. Well, a normal person's lifetime. Also, the cane is made from a dragon's tooth. Another mysterious artifact of Beohlor's. He must have dragon friends all over this world. Or maybe dragon enemies...."

Bleke pondered his thoughts as Edmund exclaimed, "Thank you, Bleke! I don't know what to say," Edmund felt honored to be a part of something larger than himself. Edmund truly considered himself a sorcerer now. The idea warmed him with an endearing purpose. Before, there had been panic and dread clinging on to his change. Edmund belonged with the other of the children of the old way. And with his uncle's blessing and gift, he was encouraged to embrace who he now was. They both turned and gazed across the fields, the other children, and the clear blue sky – with the exception of a lingering lonely cloud hovering toward them.

Beohlor and Ivindfor were in a solemn conversation away from the others. As Hrowl and Atena attended to the children, the Stoutess noticed the two sorcerers and remarked, "What are those two pointing at?"

Vaespril and Vigil were nearest her and squinted into the sky. "There's a small cloud moving toward us," Vigil said.

"I don't think it's a cloud, Vigil," Vaespril added.

"Then, what is it?" Vigil retorted back.

"Not sure..." Vaespril shrugged. "But, it's not just a cloud."

"It's him," Hazel's voice answered, as she glided around them.

"Him. Who?" Both Vaespril and Vigil chimed.

"Aelen. He's come," Hazel said monotonously and entranced.

Vaespril, Vigil, and Atena gazed at each other for a moment, then in the direction of the cloud as it crept closer. No one said another word. They just watched. The sun grew higher now, and that one rogue cloud seemed to sparkle in the day's brilliance. Before the others had a chance to notice it, the small vapor settled silently on the ground nearby. They were awed at how the mist rolled within itself. Then, they were completely overwhelmed, as Zaephryl and Aelen appeared luminously through the disappearing haze, glistening like white and silver ghosts from their reminiscent dreams.

Kyndril guided her mount closely to Aereste and gestured into the sky, "The cloud of mist is a dragon, my lord."

Without looking upward and rubbing his covered right hand, the Sylfaen Sovereign replied, "Yes, I've known for quite some time. The beast is actually a white dragoness, Zaephryl if memory serves, and Aelen the Everlasting is her rider. Thank you, Kyndril." The enchantress fell back into line, embarrassed for herself while awing Aereste's abilities. "Going to your sons, are you Aelen?" the Sylfaen Sovereign thought to himself. "You are a small matter in all of this. But I would enjoy seeing your face as I end Ivindfor and the fledglings following him." A small smirk cracked on his thin aging lips, and as he trotted toward Burrow's Bridge, Aereste fascinated about the events which he eagerly anticipated unfolding.

The Crux

At some time in your life, you'll acknowledge your calling. You'll be forced against the wall with acceptance, and believe with every ounce of your being. The choices and answers will be effortless because they will be made from the very core of your being.
From, *The Lectures of Ivindfor at Havenshade*

    Between the dangerous splendor of Zaephryl and the masterful countenance of Aelen, the children's eyes were busily shifting from one to the other. Zaephryl gingerly nestled into the tall grasses, grasping and chewing on what she could reach from her long neck. Aelen was slightly farther off with Beohlor and Ivindfor. They were deeply involved in what seemed a grave conversation. Most of the airborn's were huddled together. They tried with all their might to hear what the three men were saying, but received nothing back except whistling breezes blowing in their eardrums. Several times, one, or more would rub and pound on their ears as if water was clogged inside.

"It's not polite to eavesdrop," Bleke smirked, as he passed by.

"We can't hear anything anyway," Slyte sneered back. "All we get is air howling in our ears all the way down into our throats!"

"Serves you right to try and overhear one of Aelen's conversations," Bleke began sniggering now. "You're all lucky he's partial to you. Otherwise, he might just pop your eardrums and deafen you for sport."

"He'd never!" Slyte snapped back.

"Oh, my dear girl, he has! I've seen it. And let me tell you, there's nothing more pathetic than a wizard who cannot hear the wind anymore."

"You can't blame us, though," Yhan said. "Don't you want to know what's going on? Or, maybe you do and you're just holding out on us. Eh, Bleke?"

"No, Yhan. I don't know what's going on in their conversations. All I know is that I'm very tired. Ivindfor will tell us, but only when he's ready. For now, I'm going to catch up on some sleep. By the miserable look on their faces, I'm guessing we'll all need our rest."

As Bleke returned toward Edmund, the airborn children gazed at Ivindfor, whose solemn face appeared fixed, yet his eyes were concentrated on something much farther, much bigger. They saw him wave to Gratil, Atena, and Hrowl. After speaking with them each for a moment, they departed and busied themselves with other affairs. They did not seem upset by what he said, and so the children agreed they held none of Ivindfor's burdens either. "What could be wrong now?" They asked each other over and again and in so many ways that they finally just gave up.

As Bleke moved closer to Edmund, he viewed Morclyf plopping down beside his nephew, too. Hazel had joined Edmund earlier and tried in their tiredness to make sense of all the recent events. Unfortunately, their mumbled musings offered nothing more than silly guesswork, and assumptions. With the addition of Morclyf, the direction of attention leaned toward him.

Morclyf's pale skin verged to a shade of sickening gray. "You don't look so good," Hazel remarked concernedly.

Morclyf raised his weary eyes and sarcastically retorted, "Well, if you hadn't noticed, I didn't sleep very well last night!"

"You're right. Sorry, but we didn't sleep at all," Hazel smartly retorted. As they all smiled, their exhaustion turned to uncontrolled giggling. Tears filled their eyes and for moment they felt good.

"What kind of mess did Ivindfor get us into?" Morclyf asked.

Edmund soberly adjusted himself, rubbed his eyes, and strained for an answer. "I think if it were up to Ivindfor, we would have been at Havenshade a long time ago. No, I don't think this is his mess. Not entirely, anyway. I'm sure he had his own ideas about how this should have been. By the look of things now, this is nowhere near what he planned."

"Well, at any rate, our gathering is knee deep in his misery," Morclyf answered, somewhat slurring his words.

"Are you sure you're alright?" Hazel asked. "You really don't look good at all."

"LISTEN!" Morclyf suddenly exploded. He heaved and panted at the remark. "You have no idea what I went through last night, alright. ALRIGHT!" He paused to regain moisture in his graveled throat. Then, somewhat calmer, he dazedly continued. "H-hazel, I - I don't remember the images as much as I do the feelings. I hope I never remember all the images. All I know is that horrible things happened to me, and I did terrible things to others. I know I may not be the kindest guy, but I never want to feel so helpless, or make others feel tortured." Morclyf grasped Edmund's and Hazel's hands, which made them jump in surprise. "I'm terrified to fall asleep again! I'm scared she's inside there somewhere! I just want to go back home. I want to go back before all this happened to us."

Edmund was became instantly anxious at the onset of Morclyf's impassioned remarks. If anyone could, he thought, Morclyf would have surly come out of Lazdrazil's the best. No one seemed darker and more dreadful than Morclyf, except maybe Driskal. But now, right in front of him, the young man who helped save his life was begging to go home. Edmund asked himself,

"What do I do?" Then, he remembered his time spent at The Wayfarer's Inn.

Morclyf's soul fluttered and beat against a rhythm that wasn't entirely his own. Edmund held out his other hand, and waited for Morclyf to grasp it. Their hands were cold, but Morclyf's felt dead; he did not, or possibly could not, tighten around Edmund's. For as odd as it seemed for two men to hold hands, their souls connected and became still. With all of his will, Edmund focused on making Morclyf feel safe. After several minutes, Edmund heard a faint "Thank you", followed by the solid squeeze from Morclyf's hands.

"Here, drink this," Atena's voice interrupted their episode.

Feeling half awake, they replied in unison, "What is it?"

Atena rolled her eyes, as if asked one too many times, "Just something Ivindfor wants you to drink. It'll help with the dreams, an' stuff."

The three of them looked at her baggy, dark eyes. Atena somewhat waivered as she blinked hard against the heaviness of her eyes. She set three small cups down and wandered away from the gapping trio. They were her last stop, and not within fifteen feet of leaving them, she stopped abruptly, swayed, and then crumpled to the ground in an exhausted slumber.

Hazel sniffed the drink and sneezed right into Morclyf. "HAZEL!" He shouted as he wiped her snot off his face.

"Sorry," she replied. "It's a mixture of herbs that I'm not familiar with. But there is a bit of pepper, for taste, I suppose."

"Well, she did say drink it, not sniff it," Edmund snickered.

"I'm not sipping one drop of this stuff. I told you. I don't want to fall asleep!" Morclyf whined.

"Oh, come on. We'll be right here with you. Besides, how long do really think you'll be able to stay awake for anyway," Hazel remarked. "As for me, bottom's up!" With a quick swig, Hazel emptied her cup and softly sighed as she gently floated to the ground asleep. Edmund went next, but less gingerly thudded dead asleep and already snored. Morclyf's hand shook, as his heart thudded with fear.

"You don't know what it was like," Morclyf whispered to his unconscious companions. "Ah, filth foul," he ruffed to himself, then leaned closely over Edmund and whispered, "I hope you were worth it."

Then, in a quick motion, Morclyf swallowed the mixture. Swiftly, his eyes blurred. Morclyf gazed around at the other sleeping children, then caught a glimpse of Ivindfor, who happened to be watching him. Morclyf raised his unstable and shaking arm, and made a foul gesture with his hand toward Ivindfor. Without knowing Ivindfor's reaction, Morclyf drifted backward to the ground, while a snarled, defiant grin pursed his lips in satisfaction.

Kallevel awoke with the warm sun washing over his body and the tall grasses peacefully swaying like ocean waves around him. He wondered how long he had slept. The last thing he recalled was helping Gratil with a mixture of some sort. His head was clear and his body felt relaxed and renewed. He lay there enjoying the solace of the moment, when directly above him a large rock sped directly over his body and thudded closely next to his head.

Kalevel sprung up to his knees and found the others in a heated battle among themselves. Unsure of the circumstances, he watched with a paralyzed fear and confusion. "They are only training, my dear scribe," a pleasantly calm voice said. Kalevel turned and saw Aelen sitting behind him. "I was wondering when you would wake. I took the privilege of writing a few notes for you. You've missed out on some important arguments."

Kalevel was almost too shy to speak to the great man, but finally he said, "What's happened. What's going on?"

"Aereste, the Sovereign of Pentasentinal, has come with thousands of men," Aelen said with a solemn face. He calmly added, "They wait for us near Hildrin's Pass. They wish to kill us all."

Kalevel's mouth gapped open. The images of an army waiting to destroy them left him wordless. Aelen returned with a small, reassuring smile, "Ivindfor has inspired the children to fight against the Sovereign, and he has called on some friends for help. Aereste has given us two days to present ourselves before hunting us down. Of course, he already knows where we are, but to Aereste the mere measure of Ivindfor coming to him makes the Sovereign believe he is still in control."

"How did all this happen?" Kalevel said as he shook his head. "Why does this have to happen?" Kalevel lifted his eyes in a desperate plea. Aelen's pale eyes stared long into the boy's face. He tried to count how many faces had asked him that question over the eons. He tried to remember how many different ways he had answered before. Each battle, each war, each life taken was spent for the willingness of power, revenge, greed, resources, beliefs, and basest hatreds. The details may have other names or circumstances, but, in the end, the results were the same. "Please tell me, Aelen. Please."

The old man shuttered himself from speaking his thoughts. Instead, he scribbled them onto a page in Kalevel's journal and changed the subject. "Ivindfor has sent Hrowl and Atena to guide your family to Havenshade," he said with a smile. "Think of them. Think of seeing them again. Not all of this nonsense and waste. This battle has been inevitable. Aereste's entitlement has forced him to lash into a fury and even die before yielding to the loss of power. Ivindfor has known this, yet believes in his children and his purpose."

Kalevel lounged on the balmy ground trying to comprehend Aelen's words as they applied to him. Without satisfaction, Kalevel asked, "Does Ivindfor want me to fight?"

"Oh, no, my dear boy," Aelen said with a boom. "You far too important! You will be near the battle, but hidden and protected. You will be the author of our fates. The words you write will be more glorious than the deeds we do that day!"

With a reassured mind, Kalevel asked, "How did Ivindfor convince everyone to fight?"

Aelen leaned back at Kalevel's eagerness, "Easily enough. He plainly explained if they did not fight that Aereste would relentlessly hunt them down. So, their choice was to flee and eventually face Aereste alone, or fight together since the odds are better."

"Do you think we'll win?" Kalevel snapped back as he cocked his squinted face.

Aelen paused and projected his thoughts for several long minutes. Kalevel sat impatiently, wondering if Aelen were truly seeing into the future, or merely calculating the odds. Finally, with a sustaining sigh, Aelen smacked, wetted his lips, and simply shrugged. "The outcome is beyond my sight, dear scribe. Victory will be told by those who succeed. For those who fall, their stories will end. Although, perhaps you shall carry on the truth of our battles," Aelen slipped a raven's feather from his sleeve, whispered to it, and handed it Kalevel. "Here. It's from Morclyf's cloak. A funny, useful thing after all!"

Kalevel gently held the feather in his open hand, then asked, "Thank you. I think. But why did you.."

"When the time comes, you'll need to make a choice," Aelen interrupted. "If you stick that feather into your skin, you'll become a raven. It won't be pleasant, mind you, but you'll be in the best disguise to witness the battle." After a thoughtful pause the old man slowly and methodically continued. "Or, you can simply fly away. Use could the feather and fly back to your mother, who incidentally can change you back," Aelen said with a wink. "Or, I suppose, you could sit right here, and do nothing at all."

Kalevel's face furrowed into a tight ball of frustration, as he stared down at the black feather. Aelen reached out and lifted the boys' face with his smooth, long hand. "I hope you will come and witness us. You may have seen some of what Ivindfor and Beohlor can do, but when they face Aereste, there will be magic woven and created that has not been seen in hundreds of years. Personally, I am afraid to see Ivindfor and Beohlor's wraith again."

"If I turn into a raven, then I won't be me. Will I?" Kalevel questioned, not particularly listening to what Aelen had just said.

"Oh, you'll still have your own state of mind, for a while at least. The longer you stay the bird, the longer you become it."

"How long would I have?"

"That depends on the mind of the person shifted. Those with strong wills and minds can remain shifted for days, while others may only last for a few hours," Aelen smiled and reassured the boy by patting his knee, "I think you'll be just fine. We need you, dear scribe. We need all your senses, all your words, and all thoughts. For you will write all our stories for world to recall."

As Aelen finished, he handed the pieces of parchment to Kalevel and left him somewhat flabbergasted in the clement grasses. The clamor of the children of the old way training for war surrounded Kalevel, yet he focused on a phrase that Aelen had written.

Aelen wrote: "The perspective from one's principals are interleaved into the sacredness of one's own soul. When we give ourselves to others; when we influence ourselves in others; when we refuse ourselves from others, we interact greatly with the mechanism and movement of life. We can live and die by what persuades and discourages us most. The choices and responsibilities are ours."

Kalevel was not sure what philosophy Aelen was trying to convey, but he was struck at the power at which the words captivated him. Later, in the passing years, Kalevel would reflect on Aelen's words and unconditionally understand what the old man meant, and how appropriate the phrases applied to his own situation.

The day before the battle, Kalevel watched something peculiar rising distantly from the south. He rubbed his eyes several times hoping to correct his vision. Yet, the mystery was still there. From Kalevel's view, an area of the swards seemed alive with shadowy actions, as if a swarm of insects were approaching. With a racing heart, his first thought was they were under attack. Then, Kalevel witnessed Ivindfor lifting and waving his arm excitedly. Two shorter men, Kalevel assumed to be Dorman, came into sight through the haze. Ivindfor shook both of their hands and saluted toward the strange, moving mass around them.

"That's Dohlemar and Jacobi," announced Terrese, who thudded onto the ground, surprising Kalevel with a jolt.

Regaining his breath Kalevel asked, "What's that hovering around them?"

Terrese squinted, "They're called Drago-Sprites, I believe. Their one of the Meta-Caste races, and they live in the Icewash Vale. I guess they came to help."

"What is a Drago-Sprite?"

Terrese squinted her nose and replied, "From what I've heard, they're miniature people with iridescent dragonfly wings. They use shadow and light to keep themselves camouflaged."

"I can't believe all this really happening," Kalevel said as the Drago-Sprites landed and collectively shed their disguises. They were petite, and very short (approximately two feet tall) women and men with dragonfly wings. Their eyes, noses, and ears were narrow. Kalevel noticed that everything about them seemed narrow; from the hair on their head, to the skinniness of their arms, legs, fingers, and toes. They wore leather arm guards, leather breastplate, leather skirt, and shining metal helmets for armor. They all wielded long handled, thinly double-edged swords and fragile looking bows. Kalevel estimated that there were at least seven hundred Drago-Sprites settled before him.

Terrese punched Kalevel in the shoulder and said, "Well, believe it, Kal'. This world keeps on getting queerer by the day, don't it? Oh, by the way, Ivindfor wants to see you. We're getting ready to head out."

Kalevel walked along with Terrese as she galloped past Ivindfor and returned to some of the others. The entire group had changed since they had first met. A bond had formed between them all. The children were able to release their gifts and capabilities freely, while talking, learning, and sharing aspects of their talents. For the first time, they did not feel as if they had to conceal some dark, ugly secret. They felt beautiful, genuine, and normal. Kalevel wondered how exactly he fit in with Ivindfor's following, yet he felt an extraordinary pride being a witness to the events unfolding before him.

"So, I hear my father spoke to you?" Ivindfor asked, already knowing the reply. "Have you decided what you'll do?"

Kalevel fingered the feather and replied, "I'll be keeping one 'raven' eye on you, that's for sure. Wherever you are, most of the action will be," then Kalevel paused, somberly looking outward like Aelen. "Your father said that nothing like this has been seen for hundreds of years. So, I'd be a fool not to have the best seat in the house, right?"

Ivindfor grinned with his signature smart, style, then seriously included, "What you will witness, Kalevel, may very well haunt you every night for the rest of your life. Observe with caution. If we should fail and fall, then quickly seek out your mother. She should be close to, if not at Havenshade. I've made sure the forest knows you and allows you to enter." Ivindfor rested his hand on the boys shoulder and whispered, "May those who live through these days be remembered by your words, while those who die carry on with the meaning of your words."

A burden suddenly filled Kalevel's heart and stomach with a revolting nervousness. He realized the full weight and responsibility of his duty. Aelen had hinted at it, and right then, Ivindfor cemented Kalevel's purpose and directive. Ivindfor slapped him on the back and strutted off, barking at everyone to get into the wagons, while proclaiming to get some food, water, and rest. Solemnly, Kalevel followed. For the first time, the scribe felt like he was a part of something so much larger than himself, yet Kalevel sensed his own 'normal' insignificances and inabilities, as well. "Whatever happens," he thought to himself. "At least I will have played my part, no matter how large, or small. I am just a scribe, after all."

Standpoints

I never planned on being a killer. But, then again, I never planned on getting beaten, or having someone try to kill me. In the end, it all depends on how strong you are, and how badly you want to survive.
From, *Driskal, in an interview with Kalevel*

The sound of thick, heavy chains rattled and clinked relentlessly around the brooding Vald, as he sat motionless on the firm clay. Thrais ran his thick fingers through the dusty soil trying to ignore the groans and mumblings of the other prisoners near him. His matted black hair, beard, and deeply brown skin was flecked with different shades of grit. The journey from Pentasentinal to Hildrin's Pass comprised of a continuous uplift of soil from their shuffling feet. The rains had been scarce for months and the ground powdered beneath their feet. Sweat and body odor filled Thrais' nostrils as the air hung with a heavy stillness. 'Feels like rain', the Vald thought to himself.

None of the prisoners from Pentasentinal knew why they were released from their cells and marched from the city in the dead of night. Speculations and rumors ran rampant throughout the entire trip. A few were optimistic and gloated about the possibility of gaining freedom. Others considered they were being shipped to work in a hard labor camp, or mine. Most of the prisoners prepared for their execution. Thrais fell into the last frame of thought. As he drew in the dirt, the Vald did not wonder about the future. Rather, Thrais eyed the 'extradite' tattoo on his forearm recalling life before his incarceration, and despondency that surrounded him.

In his memories, Thrais returned to the massive Silverwood Trees and Valdic logging camps he once called home. Early every morning, he awoke before everyone else so that he could enjoy a few moments of tranquility before the clamor of saws, axes, and felling trees thundered around him. The dewy air was thick and tasted like pine needles and bark. A few birds and rodents sung and scurried through the pale green needles and branches high above him. For some, the lack of openness and sky offered Closter phobia, but Thrais felt snugged by the overwhelming closeness of the forest. This was his home, his sanctuary, his tradition.

Then, the letter arrived. His family had left the Valdic Nation four years prior to pursue a life within the walls of Pentasentinal. The letter indicated an illness sweeping through the Valdic wards and a quarantine placed over them. They desperately wanted to leave, but they needed money and a sponsor outside the city. With a heavy, resistant heart, Thrais left the forests, herded through the Towers and was tattooed, then made his way to the great central city. While traveling alone, Thrais had only journeyed half way when he was ambushed and sold into the underground slave trade within the worst sections of Pentasentinal.

He never reunited with his family. He never knew of their fate. Thrais was indentured into hard labor within the Dorman foundries. For years he struggled against endless days, cracks and stings of a whip, and little food, or sleep. His heart grew as black as the ash and soot around him. The day arrived of his sale to a different master, and on that day, Thrais took his opportunity to escape. Once loose in the city, the Vald scurried to find food, shelter, and safety. He resorted to theft, assault, and even murder to survive. Thrais had become an animal within the confines of the city. Eventually, the Sylfaen Guard entrapped and imprisoned him for his crimes.

As he continued to draw in the soil, Thrais felt the winds rise a little and the smell of the pine trees across the Inte Aeden wafted into his nostrils. The smell of the forest caused the Vald's eyes to roll gently back into his head, as the remembrance of peaceful days enveloped him. So many years had passed since he had smelled anything familiar of home. The clinking and clattering of chains around him dissolved as he recalled the swooshing sound of the winds as they cascaded through the Silverwood Trees. At that moment, Thrais desired the sentence of death, believing that to be their purpose there. He could not think of a better place, moment, or time to be released from life.

'To your feet, you lowly pieces of scum!' Vilgir, one of Aereste's Sylfaen wizards bellowed. 'It's time you paid for your crimes!'

As thousands of men and women shuffled from the ground, the clanking of chains and shackles filled the air. Thrais slowly shifted, rising to his feet in anticipation. The Vald fondly gazed at the drawing of a Silverwood Tree he had made in the dirt. A small grin formed beneath his bristly beard, and he knew, in one way or another, he would be home soon.

As Beohlor, Dohlemar, Jacobi, Bleke, and Aelen drilled the children how to use their powers aggressively and passively in combat, Ivindfor approached Driskal separately. The young sorcerer from Pentasentinal, who Ivindfor found living in the city's sewer system, knew the sensation of ending another person's life with the forces of Old Way. In fact, Driskal had adapted the dark and torturous use of 'Blood-letting'. The skill a waterborn sorcerer has to manipulate another person's blood is deathly dangerous for the victim, as well as, the attacker. Rendering another creature to suffer and die from Blood-letting required a mind and capability most waterborn sorcerers refused, or could not accept. Driskal was the exception.

His thin, slicked-back black hair held tight to his head and accentuated the paleness of his bony face. Driskal's frame was extremely thin, but every ounce he carried was muscle. Regardless of how arid the weather, he perpetually looked wet, as if he had just stepped out a bath, river, or lake. His dull blue eyes shined brightly against the dark circles of his continually tired eyes. Driskal appeared much older than seventeen, and handsomeness was replaced with hardships. As he shuffled along with Ivindfor, Driskal's eyes gazed off across the fields, unfocused and distant.

"I want you to teach the others," Ivindfor firmly stated. After a few moments without a response from Driskal, Ivindfor continued. "They may refuse to use it, but at least they'll have the option, when the time comes."

Driskal paused, still looking out into the distance, opened his mouth to speak, lingered with the air on his lips, then replied in a graveled voice, "Blood-letting is the easy part, Iv'. You know that. Living with doing it, that's the difficult part. You know that, too."

Ivindfor stared into the young man's eyes and saw how numb they were. Not only had Driskal murdered his father through Blood-letting, he had survived the sewers by honing his skill on rodents and even other people trying to steal, stalk, and hurt him. Ivindfor did not know how many people Driskal had killed, but he was certain the young man had stopped counting. The sorcerer's cold, blank stare attested to that. An unnerving chill ran through Ivindfor, as he responded, "You've led a hard life, Dris', and have had to deal with more than most will in their entire lives. But, you're the only one who has seen someone die by using the Old Way. You're the only one who has faced a fight to the death. You're one the best people to show them how to survive."

Driskal continued to look at Ivindfor with his dead-panned stare as if he had mentally gone somewhere else. But, in his own diminished fashion, he replied, "I suppose. How far do you want me to take it?"

Ivindfor grimaced at knowing what Driskal meant. "To the breaking point."

"Alright," was his only response. Ivindfor appreciated Driskal's no-nonsense behavior, especially toward Blood-letting.

The young sorcerer was practical, methodical, and practiced his skills with the precision of a surgeon. Except his talents were tortured and killed, rather than heal and save. He turned away from Ivindfor without permission and shuffled toward the other waterborn sorcerers who were practicing with Bleke. Another chill swept through Ivindfor as he felt the burden of Driskal's task wash over him. As the sorcerer of life, he detested the use of the Old Way to harm others, especially through Blood-letting, but Ivindfor acknowledged their powers needed to be weapons, as well. Driskal's arsenal would traumatize them all.

Fulcrum huddled and chortled behind a one foot thick wall of stone he had lifted from the ground. Wind rushed over and around him as Hazel focused her energy toward him. She continually concentrated and manipulated the air trying to break his defense, but only small chips of stone flecked away. Jacobi sat leisurely aside watching the witch struggle, then whispered a message that landed softly in her ear. Hazel's eyebrows furrowed, then relaxed as a wicked grin washed across her face. She altered her stance and movements from a thrusting motion against Fulcrum's solid shield, and willed the wind toward her.

Instantly, Hazel felt the air pressure swirl around the Dorman sorcerer behind his rock wall. With circular flicks of her wrists and arms, the air responded and circulated around the unsuspecting Fulcrum. Suddenly, he perceived himself at risk and tried to counter Hazel's new strategy. He shifted his focus and began raising another wall behind him, but it was too late. With a forceful pull and lifting motion, Hazel used the air to lift Fulcrum up and over his protective cover and allowed him to fall hard onto the ground. Gasping, the Dorman struggled to his feet but was disoriented by having the air knocked out of him. Hazel took advantage of his situation, spun in a full circle with outstretched arms, and shoved him against his own defense. Fulcrum's head jarred against the solid stone so hard his teeth rattled and his eyes rolled into his head, unconsciously.

"Ha, ha!" clapped and laughed Jacobi. "Very goot, vy dear!"

"Thanks for the advice," she whispered and winked at Jacobi smiling so wide all his teeth showed and the wrinkles deepened around his eyes. He simply winked back and chuckled even harder.

Dohlemar ran his thick, short fingers through his golden gnarly beard as he reflected on his next course of instruction. His pupil was Edmund, and Dohlemar carefully considered how to train the enchanted young man on how to use his new talents. The Dorman wizard understood why Ivindfor chose him to train Edmund. The degree of control and caution required to shift the energy of fire was more difficult than the other elements. Dohlemar intended to instruct Edmund on how to focus his mind and spirit in order to focus the unpredictable and indiscriminate energy a flame produces. Also, Edmund needed to understand how to restrain the desire to feed off this spirit's desire to consume everything.

"You've been given a gift, and a curse Edmund," Dohlemar began. "The world chose and changed you. This hasn't happened since the world changed Aelen. So, you're in good company. Never forget that!" Dohlemar tried to begin things somewhat lightheartedly. "Since then, either Aelen or another has made us who we are. However, when the lightning struck and burned you, the world made you its child of fire."

Edmund interrupted Dohlemar's speech by adding, "I was made because Ivindfor was too afraid to do it himself. He broke a deal he had made with the world, and I am the settlement. I just don't understand why Iv' was so scared to create sorcerers of fire..."

Dohlemar was at first taken aback with Edmund's rash interjections, but also appreciated Edmund's blunt candor. "Yes, Edmund, you were made because of Ivindfor's lies and failures. Why didn't he create sorcerers of fire? Because, dear boy, the fire within you wants to devour everything. The more your spirit channels with your element, the more you will both want. The release and consumption of your power is unlike anything you will ever feel. I know you used it to help Bleke, but you only awakened your new spirit. From now on, you will need to make sure your desires do not overcome you. As we practice, you will see."

Edmund squinted at Dohlemar with his questioning, damaged eyes and could see his spirit recoil away several times. Dohlemar was one of the most loving and nurturing men Edmund had met, although he could sense a fear from being near and working with Edmund.

The two wandered for a while until they were out of sight of the others. Dohlemar led Edmund near an isolated area that contained a small natural spring creek. The water murmured in the gully where they prepared to unleash Edmund's power. Dohlemar rose rock walls of different thicknesses, whispered to water in the creek, and licked his finger, as if gaging the winds direction. He rolled up his sleeves, jumped across the other side of the creek from Edmund, and said: "It's now, or never boy...spark your torch!"

Before Edmund could reply, he saw the wizard step and dance while swaying his arms in rhythmic motions. Suddenly, Edmund was slammed in between his shoulders with pieces of rock. The force was enough to jolt him forward, and as he turned backward a jagged one caught him against his temple, knocking him flat to the ground.

"Get up and fight, boy!" Dohlemar uncharacteristically screamed.

Edmund shook of the pain in his head and back, and with a scowl of anger clicked his cane which caused the small blue flame to appear. Instantly, Edmund tingled and felt awakened be the sight of it dancing there. Another rock crashed on his ankle, breaking his trance. Hastily, the young sorcerer swiped the flame off of the top of the cane, and held it in his hand. Immediately, the little flame grew and completely surrounded Edmund's hand. He swirled around dodging one stone, and then as another approached Edmund increased and released some of the scorching flame toward the stone. As soon as the flames surrounded the oncoming stone, Edmund experienced that he could increase the flames intensity and melt down the stone instantly. There was no thought or process, just will. His will. At once, Edmund understood how his and the others' energies were linked with the elements of the world, and how they could be manipulated.

While in thought, Dohlemar smiled knowing that Edmund understood and realized the meaning of the Old Way. The Doman inhaled and swirled the air at Edmund in an attempt to take his breath away. The young man turned in anticipation and threw open a wall of blue fire that Dohlemar hurriedly stepped back from. The older wizard regained his composure and responded with a rush of water from the creek, which diminished and dispelled Edmund's flames. As Edmund came into focus, Dohlemar witnessed his chest heaving, but his head and face were cool and controlled. Edmund smiled and joyfully cried out, "What's next, old man!"

Driskal sauntered with other waterborn and Bleke with the task of teaching them how to Blood-let. Ivindfor had prepared Bleke earlier and knew Driskal's purpose. Bleke motioned for everyone to gather closer and remarked, "It's not a secret anymore that Driskal has killed using the Old Way. He developed the waterborn skill of 'Blood-letting', which basically means you all have the power to manipulate a person's blood." Bleke paused for a moment, allowing the words to sink in and be comprehended. Driskal stood motionless as everyone's eyes drifted over him. Driskal showed no reaction, or emotion. Then, Bleke continued. "Driskal will show you how it's done, but I know that most of you will never use it, unless absolutely necessary. You will all practice on me, after hearing and seeing Driskal out."

Bleke stepped back a few feet and gave Driskal their attention. "Blood-letting isn't hard to do," he started nonchalantly. "A person's body is full of the stuff, so focus on it swirling and pumping inside of them. Narrow your concentration and pluck at it, like this..." Then, from Orpholys' round cheek, spurts of her blood shot out and ran down along her face.

"Ah!" she screamed as being poked with needles that had exposed the blood. She immediately raised her hand to the pain, and Driskal withdrew blood from her hand, the same way. This caused her to yell louder and angrier. "Stop it!"

Bleke stepped forward and laid his hand on Driskal's shoulder and firmly said, "I said you were to practice on me!"

Driskal looked at Bleke with unfeeling eyes and shrugged his shoulders as his only acknowledgement. The other waterborn sorcerers gawked at Orpholys as she wiped and smeared the blood off of her. Bleke stepped close and inspected Orpholys' small wounds and returned next to Driskal.

"Those were very small pricks, like a needle," Bleke began. "Driskal will show you what can happen when you focus and pull from a larger swath on the body."

Driskal tilted his head slightly, and asked Bleke monotonously, "Are you sure you're ready?"

"Just get on with it, Dris'," Bleke replied, gritting his teeth.

Driskal took a stronger stance in front of Bleke and within a few seconds pulled his hand back with a quick jerk. Bleke reacted and his torso pulled outward. Instantaneously, a two inch pool of blood soaked into his shirt, as if Bleke had been stabbed. Bleke groaned and grasped at the pain Driskal had inflicted. Driskal pulled again, this time focusing on his left thigh. Again, Bleke responded and moaned. Then, Driskal went wild with several blows in succession, making Bleke's body spasm harshly and scream from the pain. Bleke crumbled to the ground.

Ava was the first to rush to Bleke's defense. She knelt near him and tried to sense the pulsing flow of blood within Driskal. Realizing her intentions, Driskal acted first by drawing a swipe across her forearm. A soft grunt and swear word issued from her clenched jaw, as she refocused her attentions. Then, she heard and became aware of the rhythm inside of the young sorcerer. Ava understood what Driskal had meant by aiming at a certain point and pulling the blood. She was inside of him. Before she, or Driskal, knew what was happening, Ava pulled at him and blood spewed from the left side of Driskal's neck. He flinched at the quarter inch stain letting the blood trail and stain his skin.

Ava gasped at how easily the act was. She was frightened at how accurate her spell was cast. Once she was inside, she had no problem controlling the area she wanted. Ava also knew she could have just as easily captured a larger area and could have done a great deal of harm. The blood dried on Driskal's neck, and for the first time they saw him smirk a little. Bleke sat upright and took in the boy's expression, along with everyone else's. As he gently put his hand on Ava's shoulder, she shuddered and jumped away from him, almost hysterically.

"That's one of the worst sensations I've ever..." Ava's voiced trailed off as she smacked her tongue against the roof of her mouth. "I can taste his blood..."

"One of the after effects," added Driskal. "Once you're inside them, they're inside you..."

Hythrae, Pahl, and Orpholys looked at him with startled expressions, then shifted their attention on the bloodied Bleke. "Ivindfor wants you all to try it at least," he said plainly. "I'm your target. Let's get this over with..."

Driskal crouched nearby, watching the others Blood-let Bleke. He was fascinated at the other waterborn's reaction and resistance to the invocation. 'Just wait until someone's trying to kill them,' he thought. 'Then they won't be so afraid and stubborn to use it. Will they?' As those thoughts trailed from Driskal's mind, Ivindfor whistled so loudly it echoed against the open air. With his arms waving and signaling, Ivindfor beckoned them all to gather near him.

"Regardless if we're completely prepared, or not, we need to move out," Ivindfor began. "The Drago-Sprite scouts have returned with Aereste's location. Their army is settled across the Inte Aeden and they are blocking Hildrin's Pass. Most of them are prisoners, who Aereste considers allowable casualties. There is smaller number of regular Sylfaen soldiers and at least a dozen of Aereste's wizards," Ivindfor paused allowing the message to settle. "You might ask what this means for us? It means the odds are horribly against us. It means we will have to injure and kill a lot of people. It means Aereste has given us no other choice. Once the battle begins, you must fight for your life with every fiber of your being. You must fight for and with each other as we've shown you. Our only advantage is that the prisoners have never seen the Old Way used openly. Especially in battle. We can use their fear and disbelief in our favor. I believe in you all."

As Ivindfor finished, the host of Drago-Sprites lifted from the tall grasses behind him and flew in formation over the children of the old way. The buzzing and hum of their wings beat against their skin, as the air swirled from the collective flutters. Ivindfor's hair wildly tossed in the breeze, as he smiled musingly at the incredible gathering of support from his friends and allies. 'We may not have your numbers, Aereste,' Ivindfor thought. 'But our strength is true, our hearts are loyal.'

Smoke and Mirrors

Beware of any deceptive act or misguided remark imparted upon you. Even the slightest, manipulative untruth can lead you astray from your intended path.
From, *the Songs of Semmiah*

    They had traveled through the night and settled within the small woods called Needle's Rest. The Resting House, a small inn, was nestled in the pine trees near the Inte Aeden, and was rarely occupied anymore. The owner, Larse Fenyl, was an elderly man, and enjoyed the quiet. Travelers and hunters would occasionally stay a night, but commerce and business were absent. The Resting House was the last vestige for anyone who dared to travel through Hildrin's Pass. For the most part, people avoided the area altogether. There simply was nothing of profitable interest there.
    The clear, moonlit night was nearly over when they reached Needle's Rest. They relaxed and slept a little. The army of Drago-Sprites nestled silently into the swishing pine trees, while

Ivindfor's friends, brother, and father sat closely in whispered conversations. Hazel, Ava, Morclyf and Edmund huddled by a small fire Edmund had easily sparked. Morclyf poked around in the damp soil, while Hazel and Ava tried to overhear the elders in their conversation.

"They're not letting anything out," Ava proclaimed with pout.

"No, they're just not letting us in," corrected Hazel.

"Who cares," Morclyf snidely retorted. "Not like we have a choice about what's happening. We're all going to end up dead, imprisoned, or, or, whatever." He had a hard time accepting the fact that his fate was no longer in his hands. His scowl and frown lines had worsened since their time with Lazdrazil. The dreams, torments, and realizations concerning the upcoming battle disturbed Morclyf greatly. Perhaps, the feelings of friendship, of giving, and caring had pierced through his cold heart. Perhaps, for the first time in his life, Morclyf did not want to lose anyone close to him. Perhaps he was tired of being around people altogether. These were some of the frustrations in the scowl and attitude that he couldn't hide.

"Ivindfor's not going to risk our lives in battle," Edmund stated, as he stared into the fire, then shifted his gaze and finished. "At least, not all of ours."

"What do you mean?" Hazel and Ava said in unison.

"This is all a diversion, a trick. Everyone but the elders and I will face Aereste. Aelen and the dragon will attempt to get the rest of you to Havenshade."

"Then, why have we been training? Why the army?" Ava asked. "Why scare us out of our wits?"

Edmund just sat with an empty expression. Hazel moved closer and slid her hand into Edmund's. Unstartled, unmoved, Edmund focused on the flames dancing in the dirt. "He's not sending us away, is he?" Hazel pleaded. "We've been through so much together...."

Morclyf interrupted sharply, knowingly, "Don't you see, Edmund wasn't supposed to be this way. Not like us, at any rate. I've heard that Aereste has the power of fire, and Edmund's got the best shot at stopping him. And, well, if he doesn't - Ivindfor won't have to worry about Edmund interfering with his plans anymore."

"MORCLYF!" Ava shouted. "How dare you say a thing like that!"

Hazel gazed at Edmund's unchanged face and realized Morclyf was stating the truth. "He's not that cruel. He wouldn't sacrifice you for the sake of us!"

"He was willing to sacrifice all of you for me, once. I think Ivindfor finally realized what was truly important," Edmund rubbed his thumb on Hazel's hand and looked toward her. "All of you are more important than I am. I can't beat Aereste. Ivindfor knows it. He tries to make us all feel stronger, better about ourselves, but the truth is, I wasn't part of the plan."

They sat in silence for what seemed forever. Heaviness, frustration, and finally anger wove into Hazel's heart. "We won't let him," she said defiantly. "The four of us started out together, and we'll finish this and get to Havenshade together." Her namesake eyes glared with excitement at Ava and Morclyf, beckoning them to agree with her.

"I didn't help save your life for nothing," Morclyf sputtered and flicked at the dirt.

Ava, feeling as if she should just fade away, breathed heavily rolling back her eyes. "I've been ashamed of myself for so long, and I don't want to hide anymore. If anything, you've all shown me how to finally be myself. I suppose I could die with that. I'm in."

Edmund's lips rose into a half-smile. "So, what's your plan, Hazel?"

What transpired between the four of those seventeen year olds would change the course of history, and of so many people.

The dawn broke the nights grasp with a brilliance of reds and oranges. Jacobi turned to Dohlemar and whispered, "A vad vomen, Vopevully not ver vus!"

"It's just the sun, just another day," Dohlemar tried to soften the mood. "Besides, Iv's got everything settled. All we need is to do our part."

Jacobi looked at Dohlemar with the same hope that the Dorman wizard espoused. "Vit's time to do vy vork!" Jacobi exclaimed and rolled up his short sleeves.

"Not without me," Bleke announced as he rolled up his sleeves also. "Just remember, every good illusion needs its shadow."

"Vi vas vaiting vor vou," Jacobi smiled. "Vet's get going, ven. Vit von't be believavle vitout vou!"

While the wizards were talking, Ivindfor assembled the children into a straight line. Hazel, Edmund, Ava, and Morclyf had purposely spaced themselves away from each other. The other children appeared apprehensive and nervous about the forthcoming battle. The sun barely pierced the connecting pine trees, yet allowed enough light for Ivindfor to see their fear.

"Don't worry. You will not fight this day," the sorcerer said with a half-smile. "I never truly intended you to go battle. I just needed your spirits to believe that you were. My friends will perform an illusion, biding us some time. Once they mimic you, your doppelganger will perform whatever feats, magic, or fear that you normally would. In the meantime, Aelen will take you with Zaephryn to Havenshade. All that matters is that you survive. Yet," Ivindfor paused and motioned for Edmund to step toward him. "Edmund will be staying behind. All that matters is that the rest of you make it to Havenshade. We will meet you after all this nonsense is over."

By the time Ivindfor had finished his speech, Edmund was held underneath the sorcerer's arm. Hazel, Ava, and Morclyf stared at Edmund with a blazing intent, and then Hazel winked with a sly coyness that would have melted any boy's heart. Edmund felt her spirit rise and reach out to him. The four of them had their plan. This was beyond the control of Ivindfor, or any of the other elders, even Aelen. These were their moments, their chances to take their own risks and live by their own choices.

The children displayed expressions of dismay, but also relief. Bleke and Jacobi took their positions in front of the fifteen teenagers, and the two men held on to each other's hand, then raised out their other arm. Bleke knelt to compensate for Jacobi's size difference, gazed at the children and spoke intently, "Everyone, try to be absolutely still. You will feel a strange pulling sensation, but it won't hurt. The whole thing will be over before you know it."

The two wizards closed their eyes. Some of the children pinched their own eyes shut, while others stared directly at the wizards. Bleke and Jacobi trembled a little, stretched out their arms toward the children even further, and then very slowly with clenched fists, swung them back to their chests. As the wizard's arms moved, the children felt a tremor from within, and a pulling sensation as if someone were gently nudging them forward. A few gasps were heard, and the scene began to shimmer with vibrating movements.

A mixture of shadow and light bounced and swirled around the children. Colors, hews, and texture mingled and took the shape of each young sorcerer. Within a few minutes, the spell was complete. Standing in front of the children were their identical twin, as seemingly solid and whole as themselves. None of them could believe their eyes. The illusions were so real that they even had the same shadows, voices, and personalities. With heavy sighs, Bleke and Jacobi smiled at each other and the work they created together.

Ivindfor hurriedly tried to corral the illusions from the real children. But, in the confusion and weirdness of seeing themselves in front of each other, Hazel, Ava, and Morclyf switched and circled with their mimic. As they danced with their illusion, the three convinced their counter that they should go to Aelen. Finally, Ivindfor, with a frustrated scowl, herded the children where he knew they ought to be. Dohlemar rounded the mimics toward the trees, and for as much as anyone could guess, everyone was in their proper place.

Edmund witnessed the spell and noticed how just a thread of all their souls went into the illusion. 'A small price, I suppose,' Edmund thought. In the mingling of spirits, he focused on Hazel, Ava, and Morclyf. He searched and followed them to the trees with his peculiar vision. Their spirits swirled with anxiety, and Edmund knew they were probably slyly winking and smirking with their success. Ivindfor approached Edmund and guided him with the mimicked children. The first part of Hazel's plan had worked, giving them the confidence the rest would fall into place.

Ivindfor led the copied children and his fellow wizards through the forest, and he was happily surprised at how life like, and animated they were. 'Very impressive,' Ivindfor thought to himself. Then, as he crunched through the pine needles, his mind and soul reached out to the children and his breath paused as he felt the living spirits of Ava, Hazel, and Morclyf. Without exposing them, he pivoted his head and saw them with Edmund. He stared at them long enough to catch all of their eyes, and simply, winked.

With widened eyes, the four immediately knew that Ivindfor discovered their deceit. Yet, he just turned and plodded on.

Ivindfor had too many other thoughts and feelings to contend with. He knew that trying to send the other three from Edmund at this point would only be distracting and confusing for the mimicked ones. And that could cost Edmund's life, or for that matter, all of their lives. His friends had decided to stand by him, and Ivindfor respected their decision. The time had come to face the forces of Pentasentinal and Aereste. There would be no turning back.

As Ivindfor and the rest of the counterfeit children disappeared through the shadows Needles Rest, Aelen guided the authentic children of the old way toward the white dragoness Zaephryn, who waited outside the tree line. 'Please hold for moment children,' Aelen paused. They all immediately obeyed his request, awestruck that he would even speak to them. 'Ivindfor may have a few tricks up his sleeve, but so do I,' the great sorcerer added. Aelen closed his eyes and crossed both arms to his chest. The children noticed his lips move, but could not discern any words, or whispers. Then, the old man extended his arms slowly outward. As his arms moved, Aelen vibrated and a mirror image of himself appeared directly on the opposite side, looking back. Just as what had happened earlier with the children, except Aelen performed his magic by himself and within a few short moments.

Both Aelen's smiled back at each other with a pleasant satisfaction. The illusionary man quietly maneuvered with the children, while the authentic Aelen spoke, 'My friend will accompany you to Havenshade. I apologize, but I should be with my boys and friends. You're in capable hands, and be as silent as church mice. Even when you're in the sky! You airborn's know how even a whisper can travel!' Aelen paused for a moment, looking over all of their young faces, with tears suddenly building and running down his cheeks. 'It has been a long time since I saw so many young sorcerers together. It pleases this old man's eyes to know that the Old Way lives with you. I hope to see you all very soon, my dear sons and daughters of Ivindfor.'

Aelen gave one more glance to each of the children of the old way, and then at his mirror image. He nodded to himself and the mimic turned and strode away, motioning and calling out to the children to follow him. Each of them turned, leaving behind the old man, Ivindfor, and the battle ahead. The last child to turn and leave was Pahl and his dog Snarffle. In fact, they approached Aelen instead of leaving with the others.

Without warning, Snarffle nipped and bit into Pahl's ankle, quickly lapping the dripping blood. Pahl flinched and yelped, but otherwise stood still. After a few moments, Snarffle twitched, contorted, and rose into the image of the actual Pahl. After gaining his composure, the young sorcerer shoved a piece of his dog's hair down the mimics' throat and the fake Pahl became Snarffle, once again.

'I suppose it's time I quit pretending to be something I'm not', Pahl uttered, clearing his dry voice. 'I never realized...'

Aelen broke Pahl off from his sentence and stated, 'You are more important than you could ever imagine, my dear boy. Never forget, or hide from that. Promise?'

'Promise,' Pahl answered with tears welling up and streaming down his eyes.

'Now, go on. The others will be waiting,' Aelen smiled, turning the boy in the other's direction.

Aelen watched as they disappeared from view. The Everlasting stood for a several more minutes alone in the peaceful forest, silently communing with everything around him. Then, one by one, the tips of the pine trees trembled with an easterly wind, which built and resonated to the forest floor. Aelen's white hair and robes swirled a little with the wind's motion, and the old man looked upward, whispering 'Well, this will certainly make things interesting!'

A Flame is Snuffed Out

Every battle is like an ancient, corroded two sided coin. On one side there are the victorious, and on the other side there are the defeated. Yet, the scars of the casualties and pallid dead can never be untarnished and undone.
From, *Philosophies and Resolutions by Aelexus of Pentasentinal*

   Aereste awoke to a piercing raven's caw that mockingly cackled at him from across the Inte Aeden. Somewhere in the trees, the bird's resounding voice announced and roused the light of day, as if a trumpeter were calling soldiers to their station. The Sylfaen Sovereign rose stiffly from the dew strewn ground. His personal guard attempted to help him, but the prideful man waved them away with his solid, stone hand. His body was unaccustomed to the rigors of anything uncomfortable. He had been far removed from the plights of any commoner, or lowly servant. Aereste epitomized the stigmas and standards of the aristocratic hierarchy with which he owned. No one was going to dare take that away, least of all Ivindfor.

"My lord," Kyndril, the Sylfaen witch, shyly spoke, "Loelleth, Phyllip, Vilgir, Maephrol and the others are in position, just as you ordered. The prisoners are ready to be armed and in position as well. They are somewhat aware of our abilities now, and they understand that these are same capabilities as their adversaries. Considering our forces, do you believe Ivindfor will come?"

The Sovereign's thin, dark lips curled into a wicked grin. "My dear girl, he's already here!" He snapped the fingers of his right hand, and his Chief Guard, Grys, regally brought Aereste his most prized possession: The Talisman of the Sun. No one else had been informed this item had left Pentasentinal, not even Aereste's wizards and witches. The awe of what they would witness would become legend.

Beohlor created The Talisman of the Sun after the death of Semmiah. He delved deep into the world, finding the internal fires burning within. Those flames were pure remnants and gifts of the Sun, trapped (or possibly protected) in the dark center of world. Beohlor never spoke of how he survived or how he crafted the Talisman, but its marvel had never been equaled. The Talisman's design was as simply bold, like Beohlor.

With the cores' fires, he forged a perfectly balanced steel rod which twisted to a point at the bottom end, where a brilliant diamond was set, glimmering even in pitch blackness. Beohlor forged segments of the interweaving rod with precious and polished metals. The sheer weight and heaviness was misleading, as most men would have had difficulty raising the crippling item. Only Aereste found its weight untroublesome. And as beautiful as the rod was, the true power of the Talisman of the Sun rested in the cap atop the rod.

Beohlor harvested the hardest metals and fused them together in the shape of a four sided lantern. Each solid side contained a rune whose meaning was only known to Beohlor. Inside the enclosed lantern, burned the cores' molten fire. The bearer of the Talisman could unleash its elemental power by commanding the sides to lower, therefore exposing the orange and yellow flames within. While shuttered, the Talisman could also be wielded as a deadly and destructively crushing mace during physical combat. Other than Beohlor and Aereste, there were only a few rumors about who brandished the great device.

Grys carefully slid the rod into Aereste's stoned hand. The Sovereign had his hand properly fitted and drilled for the rod after his 'incident' with Aelen. Grys wrapped several leather straps around his Sovereign's solid hand and fastened them securely. After moving his wrist, elbow, and arm back and forth, Aereste nodded with acceptance to his Chief Guard's work. Kyndril knelt as Aereste turned to her. Most of soldiers and the prisoners had obediently done the same. Aereste appeared taller, larger than life, now that he had the Talisman of the Sun in his grasp. The terrible awe of him made them avert their eyes and shake with dread.

"Those of you we have released WILL fight this day," Aereste shouted authoritatively and his voice boomed and echoed back against Hildrin's Pass' high, vertical walls. "You have seen a few of the powers of the Old Way, and now you know the rumors are real. You are witnesses to the true powers ruling this world! You were once thieves, murderers, or worse. Now, you will be soldiers for your Sovereign!"

As Aereste finished, he strode forcefully along to a filthy Vald inmate, who defiantly stood motionless. The Sylfaen Sovereign hesitated before him, noticed the tree drawn into the ground, and smiled mockingly at the man. Without asking his name, Aereste shouted across to the thousands on their knees before him. "Rise, be refitted, and reclaim your honor!"

Aereste slightly opened and tilted the Talisman of the Sun to Thrais' shackles and chains. The Talisman bonded against the connections as if magnetized. Then, a yellow, then luminous white light seeped through the Talisman, out-shining the dull morning glow. Aereste closed his eyes and focused on the prisoners' bonded together. Beginning with the Vald, his chains shifted, molded, and stretched into a weapon and pieces of armor. Then, one after another, the prisoner's chains shifted to spears and swords, armor and helmets, axes, and maces. The rattle of chains had been replaced with battering weapons of death.

"May your weapons and armor serve you in battle as I have blessed you with them!" Aereste boomed and his army, awestruck and feeling his authority roared with enthusiasm.

Kyndril gazed at the miracle of magic performed before her. The sun's rays had fallen against the soaring, narrow cliffs of Hildrin's Pass. The flat, small plain they had made camp began to fill with a light mist from steaming Inte Aeden. The wind uncharacteristically blew from the east, when generally a chilled wind rushed out from the tight canyon to the west. She felt the presence of something. No, rather, she felt some one. Then, through the heavier shifting veils of fog, Kyndril saw him, in the span, on the cobblestone bridge. Aereste had been right all along, Ivindfor had arrived.

With a half-closed throat, the Sylfaen witch gurgled to Aereste, "M-my King, Ivindfor is on the bridge!"

Aereste narrowed his already slivered eyes, shifted his gaze to Kyndril and then he smirked hard against his chiseled cheekbones. Without a word, he revolved towards the sorcerer. A shadow of a man was barely visible, standing like a ghost that could vanish in the blink of an eye. A silence hushed over the dewy field. A waiting of moves, of commands, of action. None of the other wizards and witches truly knew the extent of Ivindfor's powers. They had only heard rumors, and knew he was a direct son of Aelen, the Everlasting. And what if his father was with him? What chance would they stand, even with Aereste and the Talisman of the Sun?

As the Talisman of the Sun closed, Aereste walked evenly and calmly toward Ivindfor. These were the moments of remembering and of reckoning. To Aereste, no other man would stand in his way of retaining the systems, the economies, and the religions of the people of this world. The two men shared the same power, the same gift, but their ways of how it should be used were completely different, adversarial.

Those were the initial steps of their inevitable end.

"Thank you, Laz'," Ivindfor thought as he stood alone on the slippery cobblestone bridge. The mist was Lazdrazil's work, and she was swiftly on her way. Ivindfor could feel her in the water and on the wind. He could feel her through the east air as it pushed against his back and flapped his clothes. Ivindfor knew her purpose was not solely to assist him, and yet he also needed any help she could offer. The pine trees whispered behind him, and the water rippled underneath the bridge. As if in anticipation of the battle, all of the birds (excepting the lone raven) and animals had scurried off hours before. The silence wrapped around Ivindfor, calming him. In the swirling mist, Ivindfor's mind returned to earlier moments that night and morning with the children, with his friends, and with his brother and father.

    The damp air clung on to Aereste and Ivindfor as they faced each other with civility on the cobblestone bridge. Ivindfor did not look directly into the Sylfaen Sovereign's eyes, only dreamily stared downward with a small smile that wrinkled his own twinkling eyes. He appeared completely unaffected by Aereste's arrogance. Ivindfor's insubordination infuriated the Sovereign of Pentasentinal. The Talisman of the Sun twitched as Aereste refused to speak first. To acknowledge Ivindfor would insult his pride and position, but Ivindfor's aloof silence aggravated his very core.

    Finally, tired of waiting, Aereste cleared his throat roughly, bit his lips and was about to speak when Ivindfor raised his eyes and said, "You should learn to enjoy certain moments, Aereste. Life may be long for us, but that does not mean we should take it for granted."

    "You insolent....," Aereste sneered. "How dare you pass this off as a casual meeting? Don't you realize your own doom, and those children that you love so dearly? I am not here to be cordial. I am here to destroy you and your worthless followers!"

    Ivindfor's sarcastic smile swiftly faded and his eyes became fixed on Aereste's. "In all the years we have known each other, regardless of our feelings, we have always respected The Old Way. You've changed, Aereste. You use your gifts against the very laws of nature that have empowered you. You blindly manipulate everything around you, only to protect a title? Why is any of this so important to you?"

    Aereste's nostrils flared, "How dare you pretend to know what is important to me! I am not going to debate our viewpoints anymore. What you intend on completing with these children will not happen. I will not let it. Give them over to me now, or I will use all of my power to make them suffer horribly."

Ivindfor gazed downward again. The hatred and darkness within Aereste showed through his contorted facial expressions, strained voice, and violent agitation. 'What has possessed him to act like this?' Ivindfor wondered. Even in their worst arguments, Ivindfor and Aereste had always been able to reconcile, but this was not the Sovereign he knew. This was a madman clinging on to desperate shards of power. Then, as if he had an epiphany, Ivindfor understood everything. Aereste was dying.

Ivindfor glanced upward and witnessed Aereste pacing and grunting obscenities about Ivindfor's children. As Aereste was mumbling, Ivindfor felt her very close by. Lazdrazil was about to appear, and change the course of both Aereste's and Ivindfor's plans. "Um, Aereste, you should probably know something. Aereste...." Ivindfor tried to gain the Sylfaen's attention.

Before Ivindfor could finish a flurry of white feathers fell like leaves from a tree around them. In the next instant, Lazdrazil materialized from the fog from seemingly nothing. The sorceress wore a highly polished, silver breastplate, arm guards, a tightly woven shimmering chainmail skirt, shin guards, and was wrapped in a deep scarlet cloak. Lazdrazil decorated herself for battle, while also wearing the Talisman of the Moon. It hung heavily on her bare chest. The only weapon she carried was a beautifully crafted cutlass with an ornate silvery cup and ivory hilt.

She stood sideways by the two men on the bridge, smiling and coyly shifting her eyes on both of them. "You can close your mouth now, Aereste." Lazdrazil stated sarcastically, which also made Ivindfor breath a short laugh at Aereste's expense. "I do hope I'm not intruding on anything important," she snidely remarked, as she shifted her eyes on Ivindfor.

"Well, it would only be expected," Ivindfor teased. "The only question is whose side you'll choose..."

Aereste stood paralyzed at the thought of Lazdrazil being there. She had been the only nemesis in his power over Pentasentinal. Her droughts, downpours, and winds had wreaked havoc on his city, and he had been virtually powerless to stop her.

In retaliation, he would bait her apprentices and slaves to the city, and then kill them. All this had been done through the hands of others, and from a distance. Now, The Lady was there, and he had the very clear inclination that she would side with Ivindfor.

"I'll choose my own side every time, as you already know, dear brother," Lazdrazil lilted. "But today, I would love nothing more than to get rid of this annoyance once and for all." She tilted her head and glared at Aereste. "Besides, if I can't have your brats, then I'm sure not going to let him have them!"

The Sylfaen sorcerer glared back at the sorceress, his eyes burning, "So, then, it all comes to this," he breathed deeply and morosely continued. "We are able to control so many things with the aid of the world's spirit and the spirits that live within us. You just couldn't leave well enough alone. Could you Ivindfor? And you, Lazdrazil. I've had enough of you, too! Prepare yourselves."

As Aereste walked away, Ivindfor commented, "If this is our last day, good bye old friend."

"Good bye, my love," Lazdrazil added softly, yet coldly. Then, she turned to her brother asking, "So, Iv', I hope you have some ingenious ideas for our little situation here?"

"Our fate is in four young hands," Ivindfor shrugged. "But, I trust them more than I do myself."

Four shadows approached Ivindfor and Lazdrazil in the gray mist. The sorceress realized what her brother meant as she saw Edmund, Ava, Morclyf, and Hazel. With her head held high, she simply said, "We meet again, yearlings. I understand that our fate is your hands. Unfortunately, we don't have the time for pleasantries. Aereste is ready to make the first move."

"Beohlor and the others are set and ready for my signal," Ivindfor said, then pointed a stern finger at the children, continuing. "No matter what, do not worry about the other children in battle. Their illusions will probably not last very long in battle, but they will offer us time. Stay together and use your powers together, like we taught you in the training sessions. So, very quickly children, what shall we do?"

Grinning and listless, Hazel floated toward Ivindfor. He was taken by her calmness, as sparkling water droplets from the fog whimsically circled around her. She leaned into him and whispered her ideas, knowing well that Lazdrazil could hear every word. Hazel stared at the sorceress and as she finished, then winked. Ivindfor gazed ahead processing what the young girl had explained. His mind raced with how many ways the plan could fail. Then, with several, long blinks Ivindfor snapped his fingers, and in its echo, the trees of Needle's Rest awoke.

Aereste swiftly pounded the ground as he returned to his army. As Kyndril watched his shadow approach in the fog, she witnessed the Talisman of the Sun open, shining brilliantly and dispelling the fog directly around the Sovereign. His scowl and pursed lips clearly defined his rage and willingness to wage war. The young redheaded witch of Pentasentinal recoiled a little, knowing the ruthlessness of Aereste's rage.

As Aereste approached, he motioned for Grys to meet him near Kyndril. "Prepare the first wave to cross the bridge," Aereste commanded at them. "I'm sure Ivindfor has some tricks, so be ready for anything. And also," he paused in disgust of having to say her name, "Lazdrazil is here. I want her head by the end of the day!"

Grys and Kyndril eyed each other at the sound of Lazdrazil's name, then nodded to the Sovereign without question or hesitation. Aereste opened the Talisman further, illuminating the area, while also trying to dispel the continual fog rolling around and above them. Aereste continued and passed through his soldiers, as Kyndril led the first wave towards Bauldwin's Bridge. Nearly a third of the whole army shuffled in unison, and most of those were shrouded in the menacing mists.

Kyndril proudly rode her steed in front of the unseasoned soldiers. Two dozen Sylfaen Lancers also rode with her, watching, riding, and tightening the lines. Small beads of sweat developed on the witch's forehead, as she tried to remain focused and unwavering. She could feel and hear Lazdrazil's voice in every particle of moisture that surrounded them. As a raven cawed in the distance, Kyndril felt increasingly more uncomfortable leading such a large division of the army blindly through the fog. She could feel something else. A different voice of sorcerery softly interwove with Lazdrazil's. Kyndril was not familiar with its sound, or feel. But then, before she could react, the attack occurred.

Through the mists, a soft swooshing sound of a thousand broken pine branch arrows sailed into the shuffling army. At first, there were only the initial sounds of a few thuds and whimpers as some of the soldiers were being impaled by the tree's first bullets. Then, as the rest collectively rained down, the clatter and horror eerily resounded and became lost in the thick murkiness. Kyndril turned to witness her soldiers clutching bent and twisted branches protruding out of their bodies. As she began to twist the air and misdirect the oncoming arrows, Kyndril shuddered at the four branches that pierced her shoulders and back, then protruded through her breasts and abdomen. She fearfully looked down at the bark encrusted branches soaking in her blood.

As more arrows fell from the mist, she heard more screams and commotion follow. Kyndril attempted to heal herself, but the arrows had a magic she could not speak through. Her body collapsed off of the horse, who had remained steady and unharmed, and Kyndril fell solidly onto the ground. Blood spat and drooled out of her mouth, her eyes bulged, and her fingers curled into the earth, as she gasped for her final breaths of life. Kyndril's last sight was of her white and brown horse calmly breathing and standing above her, as arrows and screams swarmed the gray air.

Aereste listened to the cries and yelps coming from the gray steams, then observed several of his Lancers and the make-shift soldiers retreating toward the rest of the army. He opened the heavy Talisman, and with a swathing gesture unleased waves of yellowish-orange flames. The surge of flames and heat enveloped the wounded and terrified soldiers retreating. Their cries and moans joined with those suffering from Ivindfor's opening attack. No one would retreat from their post, as Aereste demonstrated by sacrificing his own soldiers.

The Talisman opened fully as the Sovereign lifted it higher, unaffected by the flames intensity or heat. Immediately, the haze burned away, as Aereste and the rest of his army beheld Ivindfor and the children of the old way stepping through the collapsed corpses from the first wave.

Fear is too loose a word for what Aereste's soldiers were feeling. At the sight of all the dead soldiers before them, they recoiled and huddled together. None of the prisoner-soldiers had ever seen, or experienced the powers of the Old Way. None of them knew how to fight something ethereal, and unknown. Most of them knew how to basely murder, yet their minds could not manage, nor believe that a person could command and kill with the elements of the world. And so, the army huddled and awaited their orders, or fates.

As Ivindfor's children fanned out into groups, a small 'Tremor' shook beneath Aereste and the rest of his army's feet. The Sovereign quickly spun around, just in time to see a plume of dust and rock rise skyward from against the high, eroded walls of Hildrin's Pass. Several dozen soldiers at the rear of the battalion soared listlessly into the air and fell helplessly to their deaths. As the dust settled, Beohlor emerged with two Trolls, named Gnarl and Gnash. The two gray skinned behemoths donned heavily plated armor, helmets, and great war hammers; along with dark blue-lensed goggles, which protected them from the sunlight.

"Beohlor," Aereste gurgled through his gritted teeth. He witnessed the wizards he had stationed at the rear prepare defenses and assist the Sylfaen Lancers in maintaining order among the troops. Aereste realized that he needed to protect his flanks immediately, otherwise his wizards and troops would be completely overwhelmed. He dispatched two Lancers with messages and commands and pivoted around toward Ivindfor and the children. They stood there waiting, as if daring Aereste to advance.

As his wizards organized defensive walls and pits on either side of the army, Aereste cautiously ordered his troops to move forward. As they approached Ivindfor, he quickened his own pace and the others followed. Aereste began throwing fireballs from the Talisman, but his attacks were thwarted by a combination of earth, air, and water defenses the children used. Then, as they nearly reached the children, Ivindfor switched into a defensive stance and swiped his arms across Aereste's first line of men. All at once the soldiers halted, turned and attacked their own ranks. Aereste found himself halted by Ivindfor's spell, but resisted turning on his own soldiers. Then, the children began an aggressive onslaught of air and earth attacks.

Even as they fought with each other, even as rocks were hurled, as the ground swelled and shut, as the air was gusted and pulled from the soldier's lungs, they managed to finally break through and reach the children. As Ivindfor and the elders had predicted and taught them, the mimicked children of the old way responded to the attack as if they were the authentic ones. At first, they fled in small groups, but continually kept their defenses and attacks going. Ivindfor kept commanding soldiers to turn on each other, then violently made individuals turn on themselves, while keeping a close eye on Edmund, Morclyf, Hazel, and Ava. Ivindfor understood that the illusions would soon fail, and he needed Lazdrazil and the others to act quickly.

As if reading his thoughts, Ivindfor sighted Lazdrazil appear atop one of the flanking defensive walls. She stood there fearlessly smug, as she jeered at the crowd beneath her. With a flick of her wrist, a flight of Drago-Sprites emerged over the walls and descended on the soldiers. From across the battle field the other half of the Drago-Sprite army appeared, as well. As some of them dropped from formation for hand to hand combat, they materialized and horrified the soldiers who could not believe their eyes. Those who flew above used their combined camouflage to offer timely and precisely aimed shots with their small bows and arrows. Confusion and fear caused the soldiers to turn and swat recklessly, and the wizards tried to dispel their formations and aerial attacks with wind.

Lazdrazil softly glided onto the battle ground as she swirled small tornadoes of air all around her. The intense forces air spun and lifted soldiers as if they were leaves being lifted and flung haphazardly. The Pentasentinal wizards worked together and applied as much pressure as they could against The Lady. They switched tactics by using earth and water techniques in succession, and although she remained poised and calm, Lazdrazil felt the stress of their attacks. As she defended herself, she noticed soldiers beginning to close in on her. Although armed with a sword, Lazdrazil (along with all magic users) knew that close, hand to hand combat was a sorcerer's greatest weakness, and she needed to counter their attacks quickly.

On the other side of the field, Bleke, Dohlemar, and Jacobi had broken through several of the Pentasentinal defenses and were assisting the Drago-Sprites with their offensive by countering the Sylfaen wizard's spells. As they were gaining ground and pushing forward, a division of Drago-Sprites flew off to the other side of the field toward Lazdrazil. Stunned, the three wizards immediately felt the swell turn and they swiftly switched to defensive tactics, as the remaining Drago-Sprite allies struggled and fell against the oncoming surge of soldiers. "I knew we couldn't trust that witch!" Bleke shouted as he furiously tried to save and protect his remaining troops.

Aereste watched as his soldiers closed in around the children of the old way. He sensed success and victory was close at hand. The Sovereign wanted to witness Ivindfor's face as the first children fell, and maneuvered closer to the sorcerer, while keeping an eye on the closest group of children. Three of them were surrounded: A Dorman boy shifted the earth for shields to help protect two blond haired waterborn mixed Sylfaen and a wounded white haired Sylfaen, but his power was weak. The soldiers finally broke through, stabbing, thrusting, and beating the young sorcerers to their deaths. As Aereste shifted his eyes to Ivindfor, there was no change in the sorcerer's face, demeanor, or actions. Angered and disappointed in Ivindfor's reaction, the Sovereign looked back and witnessed the children fade and dissolve away into the dirt.

Aereste froze. His wrath began controlled, at first. Then, with each step he took toward Ivindfor, Aereste's blood boiled and the Talisman opened and burned brighter. The Sylfaen sorcerer was intent on burning Ivindfor to ashes. The Talisman shook in his hands as he raised and readied the weapons energy. Ivindfor had his back to Aereste, but had perceived every step the man had taken toward him. The moments just before Aereste was about to strike down Ivindfor, seemed to move slower than the actions around them. And then, they arose to Ivindfor's side.

With horrific precision, a mob of dead soldiers scurried in front of Aereste as he issued a massive wave of heat and flames over them. At the same moment, a gust of wind knocked and carried Ivindfor out of harm's way. Immediately after, a dome of earth covered Ivindfor to protect him from oncoming soldiers. As the dead soldiers burned and collapsed before the stunned Aereste, he saw Hazel, Morclyf, Ava, and Edmund standing before him. Instantly, he discerned that these were not illusionary, but actual members of Ivindfor's following. And perfectly placed was his only mistake, the fire-made Edmund. 'At least I'll have these whelps', Aereste thought and affirmed to himself. 'I'll start with him'.

Edmund stared into Aerestes' dark eyes and felt the fire in his own begin to glow. The Sovereign's intent was incredibly clear, and Edmund grabbed Morclyf and pushed him into Ava and Hazel, yelling "Get them out of here, and protect them! It's going to get too hot for any of you to help me!"

Morclyf scowled back, but understood what Edmund meant. The girls resisted Morclyf as he shifted the earth and moved them away from the battle that was about to transpire. Instantly, however, they were encircled by soldiers and fighting for their own lives. Hazel continually tried to inch her way back to Edmund, but could not also leave Morclyf and Ava to fight by themselves. So, she fought and watched Edmund from a distance with tears streaming down her dirtied, pale face.

"That's a sweet sentiment, but I'll finish them off, after I'm done with you, boy!" Aereste snarled at Edmund, who answered with a click of his cane and snatched up the blue flame into his hand. Aereste smiled and opened the Talisman of the Sun completely in response, exposing the blinding yellow-orange core within. Aereste exclaimed to Edmund, "It will be my pleasure to finish you, firebrat!"

"My name is Edmund!"

Simultaneously, each sorcerer propelled their flames. Aereste's yellow-orange blaze shot like and arrow toward the younger sorcerer. Edmund extended his flames forward into a square blue wall. As Aereste's fire contacted Edmunds, each sorcerer endured the potency of their magic. The yellow flames traveled up Edmund's blue shield and recoiled on itself. Edmund and Aereste burned inside from one another's attack. The pressure and temperature swelled as they continued to thrust and yield. Edmund strained to hold his ground, digging in his heels and pushing forward as hard as possible. Aereste determinately and patiently drove the power of himself and the Talisman against Edmund's will.

The firestorm swirled higher and larger as Aereste slowly crept closer to Edmund. Sweat rolled down each of their faces, their bodies trembled from the tension and pain of using the old way, and they felt as if they would burst from the inside out. Edmund began to slip and he understood that he could not hold on much longer. Even though the blue flames from the dragon's breath were strong, they were no match for Aereste and the Talisman of the Sun. As the final moments began, Edmund knelt down, raising his dragon tooth cane and using both hands and all his will to create a small shield of protection. Aereste loomed over Edmund, pouring more and more fire over Edmund's nearly depleted wall. The Sovereign could taste his victory and Edmund's death across his lips. The Sylfaen filled himself with power and prepared himself to lash out the final blows.

Hazel glowered through the bodies of soldiers surrounding Edmund and Aereste. The battle around them had stopped as people witnessed the brilliancy and direness of their contest. She saw Edmund's body smoking and smoldering from inside and out, as the outer yellow flames singed his clothes, hair, and skin. Her body became numb at the sight of him dying in front of her. Again. Hazel stopped fighting and stood enervated, prepared for her own death, too. With what energy they had left, Morclyf and Ava protected Hazel, but also felt the end nearing for them, as well. Hazel reached out her bruised, and bloody arms, parted her dry, quivering lips, and began to whisper Edmund's name...

"ENOUGH!"

The booming voice reverberated and vibrated across everyone and everything on the battle field. Drago-Sprites lost themselves and spun out of control in mid-air. Soldiers attacking and killing the mimicked children stumbled, and heads turned to see who belonged to such a powerful sound. Then, everything paused. Every person, movement, and action was paralyzed in a frozen moment of time, as if turned to stone statues. Everything that is, except for him.

"It will be my pleasure to finish you, firebrat!"
"My name is Edmund!"

Aelen, the Everlasting, strolled through the crowds of soldiers, wizards, and the dead. Hovering independently alongside him, an hourglass spun continually, and rhythmically. The sands within shifting back and forth with every rotation. The old man meandered through the unmoving people as if leisurely walking through a pastoral field, of forest. When he approached Aereste and Edmund, he took a glance and passed around their situation. Aelen walked over to where Ivindfor lay shrouded in the earthen mound Morclyf had protected him with. He crouched beside the little mound and with the simple touch of his index finger, the dirt crumbled and scurried away, exposing Ivindfor huddled with his knees tightly pressed to his chest.

Ivindfor blinked and stretched as if waking from a long nap. He breathed in deeply as he slowly stood in front of Aelen. His eyes focused on the Talisman of Time, swirling and spinning in front of him, then on everyone else frozen around them. "Look what you've done, Ivindfor," Aelen softly spoke. "Is this what you really wanted? Hasn't this world had enough war and death? What would Semmiah say?"

Ivindfor shot the old father a glare that could cut glass. "I'm doing this because of what they did to Semmiah!" Ivindfor began spitting some of his words in anger. "Maybe if you would have been a better father she wouldn't have ended up nailed, burning on a tree! Don't you judge my actions, old man! You sat behind your great gates in Aeden and let it all happen! You let her die, and You let this hap..."

Aelen had raised his hand to Ivindfor's mouth and silenced him as he had done the rest of the people in the battle. The old man turned toward Aereste and Edmund. Moving determinately, he headed directly into the path of their suspended flames. As Aelen approached, his left arm lifted and casually brushed the flames away, as if he were dusting cobwebs out of the way. The flames vanished and receded around him. He paused in front of Edmund for moment, then pivoted gently, facing Aereste.

With his left hand on Aereste's left, Aelen the Everlasting unwound the leather straps and pulled the Talisman of the Sun from the Sovereign's grasp. Aelen closed the stone walls within the lamp head and sealed the immobilized core fire, and rested the great artifact carefully onto the ground. Then, with both his hands wrapped around Aerestes' hardened and earthen hand, Aelen stared into the Sovereign's menacing dark eyes and spoke, "I had hoped you would have learned to quell your temper and offer mercy to people, my dear boy. You're as bad as Ivindfor. If not worse..." Aelen paused, looking down at the Sylfaen's arm. "Perhaps instead of taking your hand, I should have taken your powers."

A small raven cawed as it landed on the rod of the Talisman of the Sun. Aelen looked down and smiled a little, then somberly closed his eyes, preparing the magic that would release Aereste's powers back to the world. The crow titled his head for a better view, as from around Aelen's hands the rock shifted into the Sylfaen's hand and forearm. Aelen also healed the damage from the hole drilled to fit the Talisman. Even as Edmund crouched completely still, he was the only one who could see Aereste's other spirit leave his body and disperse into the nothingness. Then, Aelen released the Sovereign from his immobile state.

Aereste sucked in a great long breath of air, then exhaled whispering, "What have you done to me?"

"Something I should have done a long time ago" Aelen softly answered.

"I've done nothing but try to protect our way of life, and now you've left me powerless?"

Aelen lifted the struggling man's face and looked into his eyes. "Aereste, the Old Way was never meant to be used your way. Controlling the people, fighting with Lazdrazil, and manipulating other nations' fortunes with the Old Way goes against its very nature. Ivindfor's intentions, whether wholly acceptable or not, still provide for a unified world through the Old Way. Not segregated by it."

Aereste felt empty and cold. However, sweat poured from his forehead and face as he trembled violently. The Sylfaen wanted nothing more than to strike Aelen down and strangle him to death. Instead, the once great Sylfaen Sovereign and Master of the Talisman of the Sun, slunk away and scurried from the battle field. His cowardice followed him like a shadow, and Aereste forever wished that Aelen had killed him that day.

Aelen watched Aereste disappear, then lifted the heavy Talisman of the Sun in both arms as the raven wobbly kept perched. "Hello, friend. I hope you can help me end all this nonsense?"

The raven cawed and fluttered its shimmering wings. "Aelen whispered and blew against the feathers under the stately bird. "Now fly, and awake everyone from of all this harm."

The raven flapped hard and lifted from the Talisman. As the bird flew lowly around the battle field, the mimicked children, the Drago-Sprites, wizards, and finally soldiers all began to very slowly reanimate. The Talisman of Time began to turn slower and slower, until finally stopping, shrinking, and sliding easily into Aelen's pocket. Within minutes, those who were in danger had moved out of harm's way, while the spells and weapons causing harm slowly fell away. The field was filled with the dazed and awestruck remnants of Aerestes' determinations, yet they were filled by another magic that the Old Way offered – peace.

Havenshade

Regardless how ornate or ordinary, we all need a threshold of our very own. Something sacred we can step through and be welcomed by, feel comfort from and have fulfillment with. A place we can call home.
Author Unknown

In the days following the battle at Hildrin's Pass, Ivindfor said very little and kept to himself. No one celebrated or accepted their victory as a success. They merely survived. The dark scars and bodies on the earth from the battle were cleared and buried by Beohlor, Dohlemar, and Morclyf. Patiently and honorably, each body was given a short, but respectful ceremony before slowly opening and allowing the bodies sift beneath the earth. Most of the surviving prisoner-soldiers stealthily left the field, and disappeared somewhere else in the world. A few of them remained. One in particular was the Vald known as Thrais.

He and a few others aided the enormous twin Trolls, Gnarl and Gnash with moving and aligning the bodies for the wizards and sorcerers. Their work coated their clothes and skin with the blood and dirt from the dead. The heaviness of the limp corpses made their work cumbersome, as they shuffled with body after body. The quietness made the task even more somber and morbid. During one of their breaks, Ivindfor visited Thrais and during one of his uncommon conversations, gently spoke with the Vald.

"I am glad you stayed with us, Thrais. All of this must be very overwhelming."

The Vald raised a wet towel from a large bucket and rinsed the dust and blood off of this arms. Thrais thought for a few moments, then asked, "Have you ever seen the Silverwood Trees of our forests, Ivindfor?"

"Yes. I planted the first saplings many, many years ago. I know every tree's name and their mother's," Ivindfor smiled a little in remembrance.

Thrais scowled a little as he wondered how old Ivindfor was, but then continued, "I'm not sure I can return home to my trees. I heard the bridge is down and the countries are a mess, almost at war with each other now. I'm not sure where I'll go, or what I'll do."

Ivindfor scratched his beard with extended, dirty fingernails and replied, "I suppose you could come with us to Havenshade, Thrais. I'm not sure what the others will think, but I know a man with a good heart when I see him."

Thrais shook his head in disbelief and said in return, "I couldn't hurt anyone in the battle. In fact, I was hoping someone would just end it all for me."

"I know. But you're here with us, now. Please. Thrais. Come with us. There is more than enough room. Even for a Vald!"

Thrais cracked a smile for the first time in years. He looked down at Ivindfor who was smirking back at him. Ivindfor patted the Vald on his thigh and finished by declaring, "It's settled! You'll walk with us through the Pass and help us at Havenshade." Thrais nodded, not speaking a word, only showing a humbled appreciation on his face.

Lazdrazil leaned with her hip against the cobblestone bridge, as she listened to the winds blowing through the trees above her and the water bubbling beneath her. Her eyelids were closed and her head was titled a little to the right. Surprisingly, she had not washed or rinsed the blood, filth, and stench of the battle off of her. Her polished silver breast plate was heavily dented along her rib cage and in a few small spots in the back. A layer of her chainmail skirt had torn and shredded away. And her hair was snarled with sweat and grime. Occasionally, The Lady's right hand trembled as she rested it on the bridges' wall.

"Hello, Hazel," Lazdrazil whispered.

Hazel halted, as if she should be surprised, but calmly asked, "Are you alright?"

The Lady raised one side of her lips in a sinister sneer, "Oh, my dear girl. Never ask someone that question...They'll think you care." She opened her eyelids exposing bloodshot, tearful eyes.

"Believe what you want, Lazdrazil," Hazel firmly stated. "But, I do care. So, what's wrong?"

Lazdrazil peered at the young woman for having spoken her name so casually, then replied, "I have not been in a battle like this for a very long time, child. Things like this remind me of the day I died in the Great Battle, and when Aelen brought me alive with the Old Way."

Hazel drew a little closer and asked, "Are you angry he saved you?"

The Mistress of Mirrored Lake gazed at the aquamarine haired girl and cocked her head back in as if ready to strike like a snake. "The old man felt pity for me, and wanted to make an example out of me. He did not 'save' me out of love, mercy, or kindness, Hazel. He made me as his reminder of all the mistakes and horrible things this world has in it. So? Am I angry? No Hazel, I'm not angry. I am self-assured, insensitive, and alone."

Hazel witnessed a cold change occur over Lazdrazil's face, and the young woman retreated a little from The Lady. Then, she asked her, "Are coming with us to Havenshade?"

"No. Ivindfor did not extend an invitation. Nor, will he ever let me into his home. Ever"

Hazel pursed her lips in frustration, then asked, "Why would he keep you out? Especially, after risking yourself for us today?"

Lazdrazil straightened her body from the wall and winced as she approached Hazel, "My dear, dear foolish girl, I didn't come here to aid you, or Ivindfor." She paused, relishing in the confused expression on Hazel's face. "Although the illusions of the other children were not as powerful as the authentic ones, I've learned which of you are his weakest, and which of you are his strongest. Plus, I was given the opportunity to watch some of you die..."

Hazel's mouth opened, aghast and angry at Lazdrazil's tone and flippant casualness concerning their powers and deaths. "You're a horrible..."

"Now watch yourself, Haze-," The Lady interrupted. "I wouldn't want our little chat going sour. I really do enjoy you." Lazdrazil leaned in and examined Hazel closely, as if she were on display. Then, she caressed Hazel's hair and cheek saying, "You're so young and beautiful, Hazel. So naïve and yet so strong. So pure and yet damaged. Loved and yet lonely."

Hazel's eyes welled with tears as her lips quivered at the sound of Lazdrazil's melodic voice. The young woman could hardly breathe, let alone speak. As she was just about to say something, Hazel noticed Lazdrazil's eyes flinch slightly, and then instantly The Lady vanished from in front of her. Hazel stood alone on the bridge listening to the flaps of a dove somewhere in the trees, and a white feather floating down near Hazel's feet.

The girl from the lighthouse drew a little air and lifted the perfectly white feather into the palm of her hand. "You're so horribly wicked, and I hate you. But, you're also so brilliantly wicked that I love you."

A dove's coo echoed from somewhere in the forest depths.

Ava brought Morclyf a bucket of water and some rags as he finished laying one of the last bodies to rest. He was alone, as Beohlor and Dohlemar were off speaking to one another near the entrance of Hildrin's Pass. Morclyf noticed Ava, but did not utter a greeting or glance directly at her. Ava did not care, or worry about whether Morclyf afford any attention to her. She came up to

Morclyf to offer some condolence, some support. Without saying a word, she dredged several towels in the water and washed Morclyf's face and neck. And, he did not fight or refuse her.

After being silent for a long time as she slowly washed away the layers of filth and death from his body, Ava spoke tenderly, "We killed so many people, Morclyf. So many died here. I feel like my body is about to explode with so much death."

Morclyf looked up at Ava with his black, seemingly uncaring eyes, "What happens? When we killed them, what happened to them?"

Ava hesitated. She felt the answer within her, but was reaching for the words and descriptions to satisfy Morclyf's questions. After considering her responses while still cleaning him, she answered, "Just as everyone lives differently, everyone dies differently. For some, their spirits linger alongside their lifeless bodies, unwilling to pass on. For others, they move on peacefully and without hesitation. For a few, the shock of their death leaves them confused and lost. These last few never seem to be able to leave."

Morclyf looked at her sincerity and continued to ask, "Where do they go?"

"I don't know," she quickly whispered back. "They just go."

The two sorcerers from the top levels of Crescent Tier lingered together for a long while. They talked a little about the battle, about home and family, and wondered about Havenshade. "I suppose I need to lay the last one down." Morclyf announced. Before he moved away from Ava, he reached within his shirt and drew out the card Ivindfor had given him. "Remember this odd thing," he sarcastically muttered to Ava. "Seems so long ago when we were home, and Ivindfor handed these out to us." An image of a lone raven began to materialize on the card, swirling and changing into a horse, like the one he rode to The Wayfarer's Inn, then into a black arrow, and then finally into the image of himself with the shadows of the other children being protected behind him.

As Ava gazed at the final image, she rested her hand on his forearm. "What's happened to us?" She whispered waveringly.

"I don't know, Ava," Morclyf responded. "All I know is that we can never go back to who we were, and we'll never be the same after all this."

Morclyf stuffed the card back into his shirt and knelt near the deceased soldier. He found it easier not to look at them after a while. As his hands touched the soil, the vibrations of the earth shifted underneath the lifeless body and slowly swallowed the form wholly. Once Morclyf felt the body was deep enough, he raised his hands off the ground and gently wiped them off on his pants. Without speaking, Morclyf stretched out a hand, which Ava gladly accepted.

From above, a raven circled and cawed.

Morclyf rolled his eyes, smirking, "Ivindfor's forgotten to change Kalevel back!"

Ava added, "Maybe Kalevel doesn't want to be changed..."

Shortly after peace had been restored by Aelen, he disappeared. There were rumors and questions about his departure, but the elders all agreed that he returned to the Valley of Aeden. The most common response indicated that his behavior was just 'Aelen's way'. He showed up when and how he chose. Most of the time, there was no reason, or explanation. Aelen would just surface from thin air, then leave in the same manner. Also, after the dead had been taken care of, Dohlemar and the remaining Drago-Sprites returned to their homes, and Jacobi set out alone to the Forests of Qyn-Fyncial in the far northwest. Ivindfor, Beohlor, and Bleke remained to escort the four children of the old way through Hildrin's Pass and Havenshade.

Beohlor and Ivindfor walked ahead of the others in the narrow, high passageway. The walls were steeply brittle limestone and at different intervals pebbles and rocks would noisily crash down to the valley floor. The sun could not penetrate the high walls, which offered a dry coolness for their walk. The darkness, however, provided an even more claustrophobic feel than needed. Bleke paced with Edmund at the rear of their small group.

"Why isn't Ivindfor speaking to us?" Edmund asked softly.

Bleke looked ahead at Ivindfor receiving a note from a small bird, then replied, "Well, Ivindfor is a sorcerer of life. When there is so much death at once, it affects him in depressing ways. Combined with the guilt of knowing he couldn't have saved you, he probably feels ashamed."

Edmund pondered what Bleke has said for a few moments. "I knew Aereste had won. I was about to die before Aelen stopped everything. I also know Aereste would have killed Ivindfor if we hadn't gotten in the way. Why did Ivindfor do that?"

"I really don't know," Bleke retorted. "I think that's something you should talk to Iv' about after we get to Havenshade. I don't know why Aelen intervened, or what would have happened if he hadn't. I know that we were in a tight spot after Laz' pulled the Drago-Sprites away. I thought for sure we were done for, too."

"So, what happens now?" Edmund queried. As he asked the question, they rounded the last turn in Hildrin's Pass. The view they had was beautiful and horrible at the same time. The Pass opened to a body of dark blue, roaring, tumultuous water. Beyond were dark purple, jagged mountains that rose high into blackish-gray clouds. Lightning rolled continuously and occasionally struck the mountainside, exploding rocks that cascaded into the sea. Everyone except Ivindfor and Beohlor paused at the awesomely frightening sight.

"Whoa," Morclyf uttered pointed as he stood ahead of Bleke and Edmund.

Hazel retreated a little and stood close to Edmund. She took his hand while staring uncontrollably. Steam rolled heavily from their touch. "I've heard of that place..." she started.

"The Fendow Mountains," Bleke finished. "Or the Unnamed Mountains. There is the superstition about saying their name. As if it gives them power, or some nonsense."

Hazel continued, grasping Edmund's hand harder, "I didn't believe the stories could possibly be true, until I saw Lazdrazil drop her guard and expose her true appearance to us at Mirrored Lake. And now, seeing the Unnamed Mountains, I-I just...."

Edmund scowled at Hazel's fear and apprehension. She hadn't been afraid to use Lazdrazil's name, or be afraid of much else as long as he had known her. But right then, she shivered next to him.

"And through their sufferings,
all people shall recognize the descents arisen."

"It's true," Bleke commented on Hazel's remarks and Edmund's scowl. "The Fendow are building machines, and have acquired a few wizards that will help them escape. When? Not even Ivindfor or Beohlor know for certain. I understand that Beohlor has been busy trying to reinforce the mountains, but it's been a difficult task. The seas are even calmer than the last time I saw them. If you can believe that..."

"I remember Ivindfor talking about them and the Syndustrians on Essil," Edmund recalled aloud.

"Oh yes, I forgot about them," Bleke remembered agreeably. "I suppose they'll be coming out their caves at some point, too."

"What happens then," Hazel whispered, as if not really wanting to know the answer.

"We fight," Bleke somberly and mater-of-factually stated.

The remainder of their walk toward Havenshade, whose forests grew over the ruinous city of Sundris was uneventful and uninterrupted. There were a few comments and questions about the old great city, why it lay in ruins, and who lived there. But those older stories will come to light as they appear with the newer ones. Just as this story will be told when it affects the lives of others' journeys, of others' destinies, and of others' experiences.

As they approached the green lush forest and weathered overgrown buildings of Havenshade, flocks of birds filled the air, the trees rustled with anticipation, and out from the underbrush the families of Morclyf, Hazel, Edmund, and Kalevel arose. Kalevel cawed, landing near Ivindfor, and with a quick smile, stroke of his hand, and whisper – Ivindfor changed the boy back to his former self.

In an instant, Kalevel rushed past the others and toward his family and Gratil. Hazel followed with tears streaming down her eyes, yet smiling wider than anyone seen before. Ava hesitated not knowing whether to feel joy, or profound sadness that her mother was not there. Morclyf grasped her hand and guided her alongside him. Edmund watched his friends embrace and be surrounded by their families. The child of fire caught the glimpse of his mother and father, whose eyes overflowed with tears at the sight of their changed son. Without hesitation, Rooth rushed across the grasses to reach her boy. Her embrace almost toppled Edmund as her sobs of joy dripped across his face as she kissed him.

Bleke, Thrais, and Beohlor followed and shook hands, hugged, and celebrated with the families. Slowly, the other children of the old way and their families also arose from the overgrown forest. Soon, the ensemble of people from all races and classes joined together with joyous laughter and relief. Even the plants and creatures of Havenshade flourished with noise and commotion. And there, in the background among the grasses, Ivindfor stood gazing with his simple cocky smile and said, "We're home."

This book would not have been possible without the generous support of these amazing Kickstarter backers:

Scott Leipski
Shannon Urban
Christine D.
Lois Wager
Sherryl Harlow
Michal Benik
Nancy Ternberg
Wally Korngiebel
Sonya Fyans
Kathryn Briggs
R & S Brock
Amber Miller
Melissa Haug
Kevin Menard
Deanna Gierach
Donna Kregel
j-d schall
Chandler Cashman
Kimberly Korioth
William & Barbara Lucas
John and Lori Latham
Joseph Smoot
Jackie Barber
Amy Mitchell
Rukesh Patel
Heather Slaughter
Phyllis Gilmore

Thank you!